Magic Times Three

Lyndon Hardy

Volume 5 of Magic by the Numbers

Bartizan Press
Los Angeles

Version 1
Library of Congress Control Number:2019905570
Print ISBN: 978- 17330950-2-0

Other books by Lyndon Hardy

Master of the Five Magics, 2nd edition
Secret of the Sixth Magic, 2nd edition
Riddle of the Seven Realms, 2nd edition
The Archimage's Fourth Daughter

Visit Lyndon Hardy's website at: http://www.alodar.com/blog

1. Fantasy 2. Magic 3. Adventure 4. New Adult

To my grandsons, Nathan and Ellis

Contents

The Laws of Magic   1

Prologue   3

Part One *What Was*   5

Part Two *What Is*   103

Part Three *What Might Be*   195

Author's Afterword   335

What's next?   337

Glossary   341

Part One *What Was*

1 The Question   7

2 Tantalizing Delight   10

3 A Duel of Wills   14

4 Means to an End   18

5 Where There's Smoke   23

6 Demonsoar   28

7 The Tyrant of Time   34

8 A Maze of Choices   38

9 Fresh Juniper for Sale   42

10 The Fear of God   44

11 Angela's Visitor   48

12 Voices in the Night   50

13 More Places to Look   56

14 United We Stand   60

15 Flame Journey   65

16 The Peril of Traveling Too Far from Home   70

17 A Task for One Who is Faithful   76

18 Paris   78

19 The Imprisoned Queen   83

20 An Impossible Choice   89

21 The Chorus of Succubi   93

22 Outnumbered   98

Part Two *What Is*

1 Plan B   105

2 A Past Life Reborn   107

3 Good Help is Hard to Find   111

4 Friend or Enemy   114

5 Memory Palaces   118

6 A New Opportunity   121

7 Club Exotica   126

8 Renewed Pursuit   130

9 Stakeout   133

10 Briana's New Act   137

11 To Try Again   140

12 The Craft of Seduction   145

13 Drink Dribblers in Action   148

14 To Play for Keeps   153

15 Step by Step   156

16 Double Date   159

17 The Intoxication of Applause   164

18 Devil Trap   166

19 Cards on the Table   169

20 Throwing the Switch   173

21 The Last Handover   176

22 Rising Stakes   180

23 The Vulnerable Underbelly   186

24 Challenge Accepted   190

Part Three *What Might Be*

1 The Search for Help   197

2 Into the Void   202

3 The Lair of a Prince   206

4 Putting Lessons into Practice   209

5 Trantor's Story   213

6 Marshaling Troops   216

7 A Possible Invitation   223

8 The Meeting of Princes   227

9 A Demonstration in Physics   230

10 Possible Aid   235

11 A Desperate Attempt   238

12 Packing for an Expedition   243

13 Into the Unknown   247

14 A Rolling Stone Gathers Momentum   250

15 Renewed Alliances   254

16 Battlelust   259

17 The Fog of War   262

18 The Quickening Pace   267

19 Reluctant Allies   272

20 A Hopeful Outcome   274

21 In the Presence of the Prince   278

22 Demonrealm Astronomy   281

23 A Weapon from Scrap   286

24 Probe Launch   290

25 In the Home of the Enemy   296

26 The Power of Despair   301

27 The Unchanging Past   309

28 The Nadir of the Citadel   311

29 Dominance or Submssion   316

30 Pushback   319

31 Too Many Problems   322

32 Progress   324

33 The Final Reversal   326

34 Separate Paths   330

The Laws of Magic

Thaumaturgy

The Principle of Sympathy — like produces like

The Principle of Contagion — once together, always together

Alchemy

The Doctrine of Signatures — the attributes without mirror the powers within

Magic

○

The Maxim of Persistence — perfection is eternal

Sorcery

◉

The Rule of Three — thrice spoken, once fulfilled

Wizardry

The Law of Ubiquity — flame permeates all

The Law of Dichotomy — dominance or submission

Prologue

ANGELA FELT the familiar tug from the realm of humans. She furled her wings and stepped through the flame into the small library. She breathed deeply, savoring the familiar smell of the burning juniper in the hearth. As always, standing before her was the hunched-over form of the retired history professor, aged by over eighty orbits around the sun.

"Your garb for tonight, demon, is in the bathroom to the right as usual," the old man rasped.

Angela sighed. It was difficult to maintain the pretense that he was the dominant one and she the slave. And it took so much extra effort to get him sufficiently aroused.

"What this time?" she asked.

"Cleopatra, Queen of the Nile."

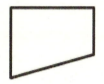

Part One

What Was

1

The Question

FIGARO NEWTON paced back and forth in the small closed office behind the reception area. Three months had passed since his last adventure with Briana, and things were not going well.

He looked in the full-length mirror on the side wall. Gone were the worn and faded clothes of the starving grad student. Now, he sported skin tight pants and a sleeveless vest. He flexed his arm. The three times a week visits to the gym finally were beginning to pay off. He had bleached his raven-black hair to blonde and cut it short. The old glasses taped together across the bridge of the nose were gone, replaced by those worn by real aviators. Only the darting, inquisitive eyes remained of the one everyone called Fig.

He had even noticed a few 'check him out' looks when he was at Waikiki Beach, but they were not what he was after. For him, none of these changes had worked. Briana barely noticed. The relationship was entirely one-sided, he had finally realized. No reciprocity for the way he felt. So today, regardless of the outcome, he would get a resolution.

The door to the reception area swung open. Briana backed in, her arms full with branches of some shrub up to her chin. A sylph of a woman, small boned. Alabaster skin with toned athletic limbs, and best of all, flaming red hair and large green eyes. She smiled at Fig as she skirted around the office desk.

"The door into the warehouse proper," she said. "Fig, can you get it for me?"

"What is this for?" Fig bolted in front of her to grasp the latch.

"A type of juniper," Briana said. "Scaly leaves instead of needles."

"For what?"

"I have decided it's time to dabble a bit. The risk should not be too great."

"Risk?"

Briana's smile widened guiltily. "Nothing major. I will be able to

7

handle them ... I think."

"Handle who? For what? Why? You don't need to continue with this experimenting. Business will pick up soon enough."

Briana scowled. "We are almost out of cash, Fig."

"Yes, but —"

"The last of the credit cards is maxed out," Briana cut him off. "Today is Ursula's last day. We have to lay her off. Occasional exorcisms of old houses don't cover our expenses. No one has phoned back with a stage magician's gig. We have to eat, Fig. It's as simple as that."

Briana's smile faded into a frown. "I don't want to argue about this now. Worrywart, can you help me with the door?"

As he clicked the latch, Fig took a deep breath. It was now or never. "I have to know for sure, Briana," he blurted. "Do you love me?"

Briana laughed. "Of course, I do, Fig. Of course, I do. Back on Murdina, I didn't have *any* brothers."

Like an elevator with snapped cables, Fig's hopes plunged. It had been evident for weeks of course, but now there was no way to continue denying it. He tried to smile back, to recover as best he could. Pushing the door open, he said, "Here, let me help you with the load. As usual, I will assist with whatever you are going to do."

Briana shook her head. "No, Fig. Not this time. I think it best if you stay clear."

With that, she whisked through the door and entered the laboratory at the back of the empty warehouse.

Fig watched her go until she disappeared behind the laboratory door. As she did, he suddenly felt compelled to get some sunlight and fresh air — anything to erase the crushing feeling of rejection starting to build.

"Going out for a while," he mumbled to Ursula sitting at the receptionist desk as he left for the street. Outside, it was hot and muggy even though it was the middle of winter in Hilo. The sun's rays pounded the back of his neck. After only two blocks, he realized merely walking around was not going to help.

Monday, he thought. Today is Monday. Usually, no gym visit until tomorrow. But the place had air conditioning, and he needed to try something else to wash away his feelings. He walked to the gym, and when he entered, waved at the attendant at the front desk.

"No reps today," he said. "Instead, I'm going to work on my personal bests."

After changing, he went into the weight room and slammed one heavy steel disk after another onto the bar. Ten more pounds than he had ever tried before. No matter. If he could not overhead press it, he would try a clean and jerk. He filled his lungs and pushed the bar upwards.

But when it only reached eye level, he faltered. His arms trembled, and then with a crash, the weights fell to the floor. He danced aside as those on the left barely missed his foot. He sighed and bent over to try again.

For the next hour, Fig struggled to lift the bar. He removed some of the weights but still did not succeed. His frustration mounted. Each missed lift resonated with his failures in life. No admission to an accredited university. No Ph.D. in physics. No direction. No money — and no woman.

A mistake to have asked, he decided. So long as nothing was said, he could have continued to dream. Now, his question tasted like ashes in his mouth. Maybe it was time to move on.

Finally exhausted, Fig returned to the warehouse. There was no other place to go. He asked Ursula if Briana had emerged from the lab in the back, and the receptionist shook her head. He grunted and marched into the front office and then through the warehouse to the rear. Briana had placed a sign on the closed laboratory door. 'Do not disturb. I'm busy.'"

Fig banged on the entry anyway.

"Briana, we need to talk," he called out. "'Brother' is not the label I want to have. Even 'friend' would be better than that."

Fig put his ear to the door to listen but heard nothing. He banged again, this time much louder. "Briana."

Silence.

Grimacing, he grasped the handle and flung open the door.

"I don't care if you are busy or not," he said. But then, like being on a runaway motorcycle on a dead-end street, he screeched to a halt.

The large double doors to the kiln gaped open. A few last embers glowed inside. Juniper branches covered the lab workbench. Spice racks filled with reagents and powders hid the walls. Three large storage chests looked the same as they had for ages. But Briana was not there.

Probably in the bathroom, he told himself. For several minutes he waited, but finally could withstand the inaction no longer. He strode to the adjacent facilities and knocked on the door there, too. Again, no reply.

He scanned the voluminous warehouse floor. No obstructions anywhere. No sign of Briana. Apparently, she had vanished.

2

Tantalizing Delight

FIG REENTERED the lab. Nothing had changed. The smoothed rock walls of the massive kiln filled a quarter of the floor. Its twin iron doors, taller than a giant, stood open as before. He took a deep breath. The air smelled fresh, pungent and peppery. Some branches continued to burn. The last embers flickered on the kiln's stone floor.

Juniper, Fig pondered. A variety he had never seen before. And in a fire containing nothing else. Why had she done this?

The answer came immediately. Briana had told him about it. The first law of wizardry. 'Flame permeates all.' Each distinctive type of fire was a conduit through which some sort of demon from another, distinct realm could pass. Pass from their realm into a world of humankind.

And the second law — the realization hit him with the force of a sledgehammer. 'Dominance or submission.' Either control the devil called forth, or else be dominated by it instead. A mental struggle of wills would determine the one superior. Either prove yours to be stronger or else you would be dominated instead. Dominated! A total slave. Forced to do anything your master desires you to do. No chance even to blink an eyelid on your own volition unless as directed.

His thoughts surged. She had attempted too much. Bold, 'damn the torpedoes, full speed ahead', Briana. The woman had skill in the magic crafts, yes. More than anyone else on Earth. But she must have meddled beyond the limit of her abilities. Directing matchmites was one thing, but a mighty djinn …

No other conclusion was possible. Briana had practiced wizardry, and now she was nowhere to be found. Abducted.

Fig remembered when he had first met her. A stranger from another planet thrust into the complexities of modern civilization. The poster child of undocumented aliens. Sleeping on the ground in a park near Hollywood Boulevard. Forced into serving meals at a shady dive in exchange for food. And all the while pursuing an impossible quest. A search to discover if beings from yet somewhere else were practicing magic here on Earth. A hero for the sagas if ever there was one.

Fig shook himself out of his reverie. No time for that now. He looked at the sprigs of juniper remaining on the lab bench. A cold spasm of fear washed through him. No alternative came to mind. As terrifying as the prospect was, he had to act. He had to summon the demon to come back — the one who had had enough power to whisk Briana away. And then, somehow, gain control of the beast — without any clue on how to succeed.

All five of the magical crafts gave him the heebie-jeebies. They were dangerous, every one. Briana sensed his distaste when she tried to teach him the simplest of spells. Yes, perhaps he was smart enough, even if he was only a grad school dropout. No advanced degree. No prospect of getting one. But dabbling in physics carried a high probability of still being around the next day.

Every instinct tugged Fig toward the door. He hyperventilated, each breath a short gasp before gulping another. He felt dizzy and collapsed to the floor. In frustration, he screamed, "This is not going to help. Get control of yourself, man. Briana needs you."

Fig steeled his chest muscles, willing them to stop their spasms. Take slow deep breaths instead, he commanded himself. Become calm, so he could at least think.

It took several minutes, but finally, he returned to almost full control. His pulse still raced but not quite as fast. He had had no opportunity to practice any wizardry himself yet, nothing to build confidence upon. Cold turkey, he had to act as if he were a master. So, he would proceed slowly. Step by step as if it were a science experiment, following what Briana had outlined to him before.

Fig scooped up an armful of juniper branches and thrust them onto the glowing ash in the kiln. Grabbing a bellows hanging nearby, he pumped in blast after blast of air. For a moment, nothing changed, but then, with a whoosh, the new fuel ignited and burned.

One stares into the flame, Briana had explained. Push aside other thoughts. Focus on making contact with the demon. Resist its attempt to explore your innermost secrets, discover your worst fears.

Resist? Resist how? What did that mean? Panic returned, but he bottled it back up and settled cross-legged on the floor. He watched the dance of the revitalized fire. He remembered the hypnotic allure of flame around the campfires of his youth. Had the attraction then been devils trying to enslave him?

After several minutes of intense staring, his peripheral vision blurred. The yellow-orange flame filled everything. There was nothing else to see. No, that was not quite right. Little specks of blackness hurled past him on either side, giving him a sense of forward motion.

Their speed increased. He was on a rocket lifting into space with the acceleration never ending. One speck in the center of his view grew bigger, becoming more than a ragged mote, taking on form. Four limbs. A head. The demon!

Fig slammed shut his eyes, but the image did not go away. His body still sat on a stiff unyielding floor, but his mind, his thoughts continued their plunge. In the blink of an eye, a second image superimposed over the first. A human brain. Pale green hands massaging it like a peasant woman kneading bread. Each squeeze gave him a jolt. He needed the bathroom. No, he did not. His left ear itched. His tongue swelled with thirst. The hands disappeared, replaced by a squirming cluster of newly hatched maggots. They explored relentlessly, probing his mind everywhere.

Fig scrambled to his feet. He could no longer bear what the images were doing to him. Summoning a demon had been a great mistake. He flung his arm over his eyes. He had to escape. If he could find his way to the door ...

He stumbled a step backward. His eyes jerked open. Fig blinked at what he saw. No towering devil stood before him as he had imagined ... and feared. No great beast with a hideous smile of anticipation. No scales as big as platters bristling with tufts of long black hair. No sinews quivering, ready to lash out.

Instead, he gazed at a female about the same height as himself. Yes, definitely female, entirely naked with full breasts and nothing covered below. The face more alluring than any artist's rendering of beauty could be. A petite upturned nose. Come-hither eyes. Red and sensuous lips contrasting with pale green skin. A single small, perfectly placed mole on the left cheek. Two tiny cones budded from the forehead, and what must be the tops of wings appeared over her shoulders. A long sinuous tail coiled behind her feet. Her feet ... they were huge. Far out of proportion to the rest of her body. Long knobby toes spayed with no arches at all.

The demon's smile beckoned Fig forward. An overpowering feeling of desire welled up within him. Perfection! He could think of nothing else. Delicate horns, skin the color of ocean spray. A tail to wrap behind you when you engaged. Why didn't every woman on Earth look this way?

"I am Lilith." The devil cupped her hands under her breasts and thrust them forward. "What you on Earth call a succubus. Kiss me. These will be but a first hint of what delights await when you submit your will to mine."

3

A Duel of Wills

FIG TOOK a step forward toward the demon standing in front of the open kiln doors. He had never felt this aroused at any time before in his life. Blood thundered within him. His pulse quickened. The first sweet embrace was only a few feet away. And after that, indescribable ecstasy.

Submit? Of course. Why not? He had nothing to lose. No agreements. No one to be faithful to. No one to love. No one who loved him back. No Briana.

Briana! As if he had been kicked by a mule in the side of the head, Fig's thoughts jarred and blurred. The way his impulses were leading him was *not* right. Briana was in trouble. No one else to save her. He had to be the one. Be strong enough to resist temptations put in the way.

But the demon quietly stood there smiling, offering herself to him. He unzipped his fly.

Briana. Desperately, part of him clung to the thought. She was the one he truly desired, the one he wanted. Feisty, determined Briana.

Dominance or submission? Yes, that was the key for how to proceed. Perhaps a way to satisfy both of his desires. Control this monster. Force *her* to be the one who surrendered. Demand her to restore Briana from wherever she had been taken. And then, command her to perform the acts she promised … but as a thrall rather than the one who held sway.

"Ah, what do you get if you cross an elephant with a grape?" he blurted.

"A riddle? It doesn't work that way ignorant one," Lilith said. "This is not a mere contest of wits. It is about whose will is the stronger."

Fig grimaced. He knew that. But sometimes, he could not prevent the flippancy he used to cover his stress when confronting strangers. He took a deep breath and pushed aside the impulses bubbling in his head … and in his loins.

"Submit to me, demon," he said as sternly as he could. "You are mine."

14

"Come closer. You cannot touch me from where you stand."

Fig thrust back his shoulders. He steeled himself. "Where is Briana? What have you done with her?"

The tiniest hint of a frown formed on the demon's face. "There is no one else involved in this. The struggle is between only you and me."

"What have you done with her?"

Lilith paused and studied Fig for a moment. He felt icy tentacles of thought probing the inside of his head. "I sense one named Briana gives you focus, an anchor helping you resist your base desires," she said.

The pressure on Fig's resolve increased. He squirmed to keep his hands at his sides. The more primitive parts of his mind shrieked with longing. "What have you done with her?" he managed to gasp.

"I know nothing about the one of whom you speak." Lilith scowled. "But if you submit …" Her smile returned. "If you submit, I will find out wherever on Earth she is."

Fig's thoughts lumbered forward. It was a tempting offer, very tempting, but, no, not enough. Learning Briana's whereabouts was only the first step to bringing her back.

"Insufficient," he said. "Only if first she returns unscathed."

"After that, you will submit?"

Cautious, he heard a voice within him fumble. "I …" He gathered his courage and blurted, "First she comes home, unharmed. Then we will see."

"I have no time for this now," Lilith growled. "We will resume this later." She dropped her hands to her side and retreated toward the large steel doors opening into the kiln.

"Wait! You can't do that. 'Dominance or submission,' right? There can be no other outcome. I command you to tell me what I want to know."

"You beginner wizards. There isn't even a name for you. Such a pain in the tail. It can be much more complicated than that. Yes, if we yanked our thoughts back and forth in one exhausting session, eventually one of us would tire. The law thereby obeyed.

"But, instead," Lilith smiled, baring her fangs. "We can agree to spread the battle out over a period of time. Temporary truces to attend to other things. You don't have to be in such a big hurry."

"I *am* in a hurry. I want Briana returned now!"

Lilith started to reply, but then stopped. Her nostrils flared. She scanned the corners of the lab. "Angela," she said after a moment. "I detect her scent. My sister has been here. Your struggle should be with her, not me."

Another demon? More than one? Fig felt as if he was in quicksand, sinking deeper into a pit from which he would not be able to return. "Why didn't she appear instead of you?" he asked.

"When an experienced wizard stares into the flame, he focuses his thoughts on the one of our kind he wants. A novice like you is like a fisherman with only an empty hook as a lure."

"Then help me get her back." Fig clasped his fist in his other hand. He struggled to regain at least some small sense of control with what was happening.

"Help you? What a novel concept. Don't you understand what we do? The only thing?"

Fig tensed his stomach. He strained all the harder to block out the emotion flooding through him. As he did, the more he thought about Briana, the more the desire for Lilith faded. But the demon was the only link he had to find out what had happened. He had to keep her engaged so he could learn more. Perhaps another tactic than push against shove. Despite his turmoil, an idea popped into his mind.

"I *am* familiar with the legends, the folklore," he tried to say in a condescending way. "I know what a succubus is. But consider this. What you do does not explain why your sister wanted a *female* rather than a man."

"Your folklore? An inconsistent bundle of lies. We do *not* attend to men in their dreams to obtain their semen. Pass it on to what you call our 'male counterparts' so they can implant it into sleeping women. Total nonsense for explaining unwanted pregnancies in your middle ages."

"Why Briana?" Fig persisted.

Lilith studied Fig again in silence, a bit longer this time. "Your will is not a weak one," she finally said. "Perhaps some native talent of which you are unaware.

"But not now." Her eyes danced. "Instead, I will look forward to when we can struggle one against the other another time. It will take some effort to subdue you, but that will be an amusing pleasure."

"You haven't answered my question," Fig persisted. "If you don't know why, aren't you even a little curious yourself?"

Lilith cocked her head to the side. "Well, yes, I guess I am," she said after a moment. "Angela must be up to something … something that probably would interfere with my plans."

"And getting Briana back might provide insight of benefit to you, right?"

"You *are* clever for a novice," Lilith squinted slightly. "I wonder, though, if you are clever enough."

"What do you mean?"

"I will question my sister. In a day, relight the fire, and I will return and tell you what I have learned. In exchange, you will not struggle, and your submission to me will be swift."

An opening, Fig thought. A crack in the door. Maybe he could negotiate this into everything he needed. "I want more than only a few facts. Help me to rescue Briana. When she is *safely* returned, then and only then, I ..." His words stumbled. "I will then succumb to your allure."

Lilith did not immediately answer. She studied the equipment scattered on the lab bench and hefted a weight for the balance scale. She shook her head, then picked up a small Erlienmeyer flask. "Glass," she said. "That will make the transformation easier, and something I can carry."

Clutching the flask to her chest, she reentered the kiln and looked back at Fig. "Agreed," she said. "Relight the flame in twenty-four of your hours. I will return then and finish what you have so foolishly started." She stepped into the fire and, in the blink of an eye, was gone.

4

Means to an End

LILITH'S TRANSITION took only an instant. Returning to her home realm always did. And each time, it looked depressingly the same. In the distance, pinpoints of light shone brightly — the palaces of princes. The brightest was that of Elezar the Golden, the one who dazzles. She had visited only a few times since she had hatched, and the awe in her stem brain had almost completely faded. Only with some effort could she recall the vast expanses of luminescent pathways. The delicate arches. The gilded cupolas. The riot of colorful towers soaring into the ebony blackness.

The lairs of less powerful princes were dimmer but still impressive, nonetheless. They flickered on the edge of visibility; some harbored no danger, others lured the unwary. Too far away to be seen, homes of lesser demons such as herself hid in the darkness. Besides these few exceptions, the realm of demonkind was empty. There was little gravity like that on orbs of the Earth, and the air was thin.

By instinct, Lilith flew toward her tiny lair. Like the slow-moving fans cooling a rajah, powerful wing strokes propelled her forward with effortless ease. While she flew, she pondered the agreement she had made with the human male.

Why had she done that? Finding one hidden person, a hopeless task. Unless Angela were forthcoming, there would be an entire planet to search. Over three billion females, millions and millions of square miles.

And that would take some time. Time she may not well have. Soon, the dribbler females all would be in heat. Their close quarters made almost certain their ovulations were in synch. The males knew this, of course. That is when they returned from the many worlds they inhabited in the humankind realm.

Dribblers. Perfect for the first trial. A proving ground in which to goad them. Small enough demons so the princes and great djinns would not notice. So she could improve what should be done. When it came to the real show of force, not succeeding would be fatal.

Dribblers, rockbubblers, hoseherders, hairjumblers, gremlins, pufferscamps … So many different types, so much like a human zoo. No, that was not right. Each kind of imp, sprite, and djinn was intelligent, able to speak, to think, to plan. But for all, the lot of the females was the same. Ever since she and Angela became twins rather than triplets, she had vowed to change the basic order of things. Change them so the tragedy with her lost sister, Delilah, would not be repeated over and over again.

Triplets. Delilah. The thought of her sister long gone still caused pain after eons had passed. Ripped asunder by a resplendent djinn because she had said "No". Her sibling had so much more life to live before surrendering to the great monotony.

Lilith sighed in the manner of humans. The only solace was that it did give her purpose, meaning for her existence in the hopeless void. Her sister would be avenged by the change she would make happen.

So why had she agreed with the human? The satisfaction of his immediate submission if she did rescue the female would not be all that worthwhile. An easy triumph was nowhere near as satisfying as one that had been hard fought. Had she sensed something special about him? Did she want to see the interaction play out a little longer for a deeper quenching of her desires?

No, not enough time for that. Best to wrap up this side adventure as soon as possible. Focus on what she had more and more come to regard as her true calling.

A feeble glow from an imp imprisoned in a small glass globe came into view. Eventually, Lilith reminded herself, she would have to do something about that, but not now. Like a leaf on a windless day, she gently landed. She sighed, as she always did when she lit, because of what she saw. The sphere containing the imp rested on a simple thin grey slab hanging suspended in the void. Edges faded off into nothingness in every direction. The encircling border rippled in a pleasing pattern, unlike the angles and stark bends of those of the males. But that was all. No steps, no walls, not a cabinet nor a chair. Only a thin featureless slab supporting a single transparent globe.

True, only with great effort could a demon of her size, bring back to the realm clumps of inert matter. But there was the principle of the thing. Why should the princes, the djinns, only the males have lairs of substance? Sturdy floors and walls, the giddy towers and domes. Tables as well as simple shelves. No annoying oscillations underfoot with each step. A reminder of how thin was the slab supporting their tread.

And that was merely a symptom, a minor one of the basic conundrum gnawing at her. The familiar feeling of depression wrapped around her. Why did that always happen when she returned? Why should —

Lilith's thoughts were interrupted by the flutter of more wings. She looked up and saw Angela preparing to touch down.

"Not brooding again, are you?" Angela said as she lit. Like delicate, giant fans, her wings gracefully folded and hid behind her back. "There is no reason to. At the moment, you are not carrying any fertile eggs."

Lilith ignored Angela's words as she usually did. "Playing dress up again? Every time I see you thus, I can't help but resent the waste. A frilly collar. A belt with an attached pouch to your side."

She held out the tiny flask she had brought back from the lab bench in the realm of humankind. "See this? I make a point to return with at least something from every trip I take. I will give this to one of the transmuter devils. He will change it into something that levitates. Material we can add to our slab. Wouldn't you like it so we both could sleep at the same time? Do so without curling up into tiny balls like snoozing rockbubblers? How much better our lair would be if your plumage was also transmuted into more … well, more floor."

"A ruff, not a collar," Angela snapped. "From the time of Elizabeth I. And not a sack. It is called a sweet bag. It is part of my research.

She scowled. "More floor? For what? So the sprites and imps would be impressed when you had them over for tea? Give it up, sister. There is no hope for your plan. When a resplendent djinn comes and tells you to spread your legs, you will say, what, 'I have a headache'? Will he then suddenly change his ways?"

"Of course not, Angela. You always argue the extreme. Everything has more nuance. Asserting ourselves, one by one alone, will only result in being shredded into pieces, I agree. But if we unite, from the tiniest imp to the largest djinn. If we all unite, withholding ourselves, then the males may relent. The humans even have an entertainment describing such a thing."

"The humans? A false analogy. We, the females, are the ones superior to the human men. They are dominated because of their uncontrollable lust."

"And we engage with them so that we get at least some satisfaction in the act ourselves," Lilith smirked.

Angela scowled again as Lilith hoped she would. It gave her perverse satisfaction to upset her sister so. Before Angela responded, she said, "Certainly, no pleasure comes from the oppressive thrusts of the djinns.

They see us as broodmothers and nothing more. Diversions when not engaged in battle or falling prey to the great monotony.

"Don't you see it, Angela? Females have no rights within our realm. Not us, not the sprites or the smallest imps. We have none."

"Thus, it has always been," Angela rebutted. "You will not effect change nor 'liberate' us, as you call it, by talk and gentle actions."

"Yours is a better way? Something the old academic you service has told you?"

"I do not *service* any human male." Angela tilted her head back with indignation. "I dominate him rather than the other way around. But yes, he has taught me useful aspects of mortal nature. Think of it. Unlike our own kind, throughout history, there have been human women who held sway over the men. Salome, Anne of Brittany, Helen of Troy ... Something about them gives them this power — what they wear, their scent, their manner."

"What exactly?"

"I don't know ... yet. But I am going to find out. Apply what works for human females here. If ones of our kind can so easily sway human males, why not the reciprocal? Human females may have the knowledge to control our djinns."

Lilith cocked her head to the side. Their conversations always went this way. In the end, nothing was resolved. She ruminated for a moment on what she had agreed to do. "Find out? Perhaps by, I don't know, maybe abducting a human woman to study her wiles?"

"Don't put on the 'I am superior to you in logical deduction' air, Lilith. Yes, I have spirited away a human female. Nothing for you to be concerned about."

"And she will reveal to you what it takes for us to manipulate the djinns in *our* realm?"

"No, not her. Of course not. She is nothing special as far as I can tell. A 'target of opportunity' as human warriors say."

"Then why?"

"Her red hair. Pale skin. Useful. It will help me get the one I want."

"And after you have delved this great secret, then what?"

"Why, Elezar, the Prince, of course. The way for us to get power is not by parading around with placards on the edges of princes' lairs. It is by seduction ... the same way it is done on Earth. Seduction of those with power. Rule through them to get everything we want. I only need to understand better the details of how it is done."

"A prince will not deny the lusts of the djinns over which he has sway. Even if you were to succeed, for the rest of us, our status would have little change. Drop this pursuit, Angela. It will lead to no good."

"The same I would say about your efforts to recruit other females. The smaller ones might say 'yes' when you stared at them. But when you were gone, they conveniently would forget and revert to customary ways. The word of a demon is worth nothing. You know that. Besides, even if you somehow did get all the females to agree to a stand, the unrest will focus Elezar to where I do not wish his thoughts to go."

Lilith sighed. As usual, her sister was a devil in the mud. Unmoving. Unyielding. Following one idiotic scheme after another. But this one might be troublesome. Interfere with what must be done.

Trying to remain focused, she asked, "So where exactly have you secreted this human? Nowhere in our realm, surely. The air is too thin for her to survive for long here."

"Of course not." Angela bristled. "But where? I'd rather not say."

"Come on. Tell me. What difference does it make?"

"You can't leave it alone can you?" Angela exploded. "Sure, it is fine for you to pursue the noble betterment of our lot. You, the example, the one with the high standards for others to emulate. But they pay a price, don't they? They must fall in line behind you and jump in unison each time you say to do so. How will it end? Would I end up having to call you *Princess* Lilith?"

"Princess? You are one to talk. Befuddle the reason of a prince so you can wrap him entirely inside your wings. Obey every beck and call. 'Another cushion, dear? The sleeping bench not firm enough? Of course. Let me dispatch a djinn to retrieve what you need from the realm of the fey.' No matter the effort needed. No matter the cost. So long as Angela, the succubus, is satisfied, then everything ends well."

"You disgust me," Angela spat. She unfurled her wings and soared off into the void.

Lilith let the emotion drain away. She had been successful in finding out what she wanted. Now to fulfill her part of the bargain with the naïve human, have a little pleasure, and then get back to what was important.

5

Where There's Smoke

FIG FIDGETED in front of the open doors of the kiln, watching his phone countdown. The demon had said to light the fire again in twenty-four hours. He did not want to mess up, even for a second. The slow passage of time had been torture. He had no idea at all about what Briana had to face. He could only wait.

At least, no numbing awe over what had happened yesterday engulfed him. Somehow he had taken interacting with a devil in stride. This is a new experience to be sure, but not an overloading shock.

His phone alarmed, and he lit the fresh batch of juniper branches. In an instant, Lilith reappeared.

Fig blinked. "Don't I have to summon you again?"

"Typical rookie mistake." Lilith stepped from the kiln onto the laboratory floor. "Only wizards who dominate can compel those they control to appear at will. Otherwise, we come and go as we please. More effort without the tug, of course, but it can be done."

"Never mind. Have you found Briana?"

"What I said when we met last was correct. Angela indeed is the one who abducted your female. She told me so herself."

Lilith bared her fangs slightly. "So, now that is settled, let's get on with it. I have other things to attend to. You said you would submit when I returned."

"That's not the bargain," Fig's voice hardened. "Briana has to be returned safely first."

"Look, after we have done our little dance, I will let you deal with Angela. I will even set you up."

"No! First, you have to help."

Lilith tilted her head to the side, still smiling. "Remember how you felt when we first met?"

Fig's longing returned, but he called on anger to push the thoughts

23

aside. Briana. Focus. Keep to the task at hand.

"Will is an aspect of character," he surprised himself with where his thoughts led him. "And part of character is honor. Following through on what has been agreed to. How could you hope to dominate a wizard if your character is sullied by reneging on a deal?"

"I am only trying to save us a little time … Look. The woman is gone. She could be anywhere."

Fig scowled. His anger grew. But instinctively, he knew he should not allow himself to get out of control. He had to use his strengths — bring the analytical part of his mind to bear. "Could Angela carry her anywhere … flying through the air?"

"Yes, our arms are strong. Our wings even stronger. Your kind is easy to tote. Some of our thralls even request it as part of the thrill."

"When you are done with someone, you return to your realm, right?"

"Of course. After the event is over, there is little to keep us here."

"How do you get back?"

"Through flame. It is a two-way channel."

"And if the flame is no longer burning?"

"Then through another fire of the same type. Which one to use does not matter." Lilith again cocked her head to the side. "I feel the engine of your ideas, beginner. Impressive. But where are you going with these thoughts?"

"You met your sister back in your realm, right?"

"Yes, so?"

"With a captive somewhere, wouldn't she always have a juniper fire burning nearby? For traveling back and forth as she wished."

Fig saw Lilith's eyes widen slightly in surprise. He felt a hint of pleasure. Training for physics might be good for more than only puzzling about particles no one could see.

"So," he drawled. "The search is not over large areas, but only around the few fires burning the correct fuel." His voice became harsh. "I … I command you to undertake the search."

"You do not understand. Spiky-leaved Juniper is common over most of southern Europe and into Asia as well."

"But burning in fires?"

"Still hundreds, maybe thousands of them. Your folklore has it keeping away disease. As recently as your World War Two, the French used it in their hospitals when they ran out of antibiotics."

"Hundreds or thousands. So be it. Use your wings. I will burn more

24

juniper every day at this time. Return when you have found where Briana is captive. We have an agreement you must honor."

Lilith sighed. She did not speak for a long while. Finally, she said, "Why is it always this way with the males who actually are interesting?" She thought for a moment. "Yes, we will proceed, as you say. Because … Because it is a manner of honor, and in that, I must be beyond reproach. I will be back shortly."

FIG PACED nervously in front of the newly lit fire. Three full days had passed, and Lilith had not returned. The supply of the special type of juniper was dwindling. Southern Europe? Asia? Where had Briana been able to get any of the stuff anyway?

More importantly, had the demon merely blown him off? Was there any sense of honor in their realm? What did he know of the inner workings of their minds? Did they even use the same abstract concepts common here on Earth?

As he pondered, a blast of air pushed out of the kiln. Lilith strode forth once again.

"Where is she?" Fig blurted. "It took you long enough. But never mind. The important thing is that she is found. How is she confined? With your help, can I rescue her?"

Lilith waved her hand for Fig to stop, her face grim. "Even with your insight, there were too many places to look. For each fire, I had to wait until the dead of night to approach. Not arouse those of your kind who might be sleeping nearby. Then wait a few moments for my senses to adjust, to detect Angela's particular scent in the air.

"And the locations are not laid out in a precise grid," the succubus rushed on. "Instead, they are strewn about like seeds cast by a child. I tried to keep track of those I had already visited and those yet to check. But after several hundred, I could no longer remember which were which. I began wasting time visiting the same fires over and over again."

Fig did not know what to say. His feelings were mixed. Glad Lilith had returned, but she did so without success.

"Go back and try again," he managed at last. "Be more careful this time. Use a pattern like starting from the far west and always continuing to the nearest in the east."

"I did think of that, human," Lilith snapped. "I am more than merely external allure. But at altitude, I could see that the next in logical progression might be hundreds of miles from the last. Another, a tiny bit more to the east, only miles apart. There would be too much wasted motion traveling back and forth, north and south."

"There must be a way," Fig clinched his teeth and started to pace. "Let me think a minute."

Lilith did not answer. A hint of amusement lit up her face. "What good does the walking back and forth do?" she asked.

Fig held up his hand for silence. After several minutes, he reached into a pocket and offered Lilith his cell phone.

"Here, use this," he said. "Go to a high altitude and hover over the fires as you did before, but do not swoop down to investigate. Don't spend time trying to detect your sister's scent. Instead, use the GPS app in the phone to record your position and move on to the next. Staying up high will help you remember better where you have been and where to go next."

"How will that help?"

"I will feed the locations into what is called a traveling salesman algorithm. It's a classic math problem to determine an efficient path with which to visit each location. And guarantee each one is examined only once."

"But most of the time is taken up by the sensing."

Fig smiled. Despite the circumstances, he felt proud of himself. "For rapid sensing and detection, you can use an artificial nose."

"A what?"

"Let me get a sample of what you exude. Probably close enough to trigger on your sister too. Get a reading in a fraction of the time you have to take to filter out the interfering odors."

"I cannot manage all your gadgetry, human," Lilith scowled. "It is enough for me to concentrate on maintaining stealth. Watching out for low flying aircraft."

"Yeah, I guess you do need a navigator," Fig agreed after a moment. His brow furrowed as he thought some more.

Lilith watched Fig resume his pacing. After several minutes, she spoke again. "Just as Angela bore your female away," she said at last, "I can carry you in the same way. Clasp you to my bosom, and you can direct me for the direction to fly next."

Fig blinked. He was startled. What was he being asked to do? He could whip the software and equipment together in a day. But flying through the air at night only held by the arms of a being from another realm? Was this merely a ploy to study his mind some more, make him easier to subdue?

He shook his head. "I am not going to travel through the flame with you."

"Then get to Europe by yourself … Portugal, I believe you call it. Outside of Lisbon. Summon me from there."

Fig hesitated. What else was there to do? Briana in trouble. Each day not found made things worse. The basic parameters were unchanged. He was the one, the only one who could save the day.

"All right," he replied. "We will do this together. Start in Portugal. But when we are flying together, I think it will be better if you get some clothes on first."

6

Demonsoar

FIG PAID the cabbie with the last of his euros. The airfare to Lisbon had been expensive. He had to sell most of the lab equipment to the Hawaii Community College to pay for it. The trip had taken more than twenty-four hours. He had jetlag and needed sleep but could not afford it. He needed food also, energy to press onward.

The cab disappeared down the dirt road outside of the capital. Fields surrounded him. Surprising how rapidly the scenery changed from the big city. A small, run-down house lay in the distance, a discarded food wrapper on rolling waves of green.

Pushing himself forward, he trod to the weathered door of the abode and knocked. A little boy answered, clothes dirty and torn, face smeared with the remains of a meal. Fig smiled and pulled the old Polaroid camera out of one the pockets of his cargo pants. He snapped a picture. The boy startled at the flash but did not run away.

After the irritating wait for development, Fig extracted the print and offered it to the child. The boy saw his image, laughed, and rushed back inside to show what he had found. Soon, three adults crowded around the doorway. Arms folded across their chests, they frowned at the stranger who had interrupted their meal.

Fig alternated pointing at the camera and pantomiming eating with an invisible fork. After three repeats, frowns morphed into smiles of comprehension. He was ushered in. At least, simple barter would keep his stomach filled. That is if he had purchased enough film packs from the pawn shop to last for the entire search.

AT DUSK, in a nearby clearing, Fig removed the juniper branches from his backpack. He started a fire and stared into it, not sure exactly what to do. Somehow he had to focus his thoughts on Lilith, not cast about for any sexy bombshell who happened along.

Fig envisioned Lilith in his thoughts, and immediately his body responded. Not that, he told himself. Too general an image. Many of the succubi probably looked very much the same. What about her was unique and different?

He ran his thoughts over her body, finding it more and more difficult to concentrate the longer he dwelt on her form. Her face in particular, so ravishing, so inviting … even the mole. The tiny blemish on her left cheek was exquisite.

Fig focused on the blemish and continued to stare into the flame. Almost immediately, the succubus stepped from it. "Well done, beginner," Lilith said. "You are learning at an impressive rate."

Fig said nothing. He pulled an abaya and a hijab from his pack and offered it to the demon.

Lilith inspected the cloak at arm's length. "Unnecessary," she sniffed. "A man can tell nothing if this is worn."

"That's the idea," Fig said. "I have made a slit in the back for your wings. Put it on along with this hood and let's get going."

FIG ADJUSTED his goggles. Lilith unfurled her wings, and with one powerful stroke, she lifted him from the ground. A tiny cloud of dust swirled from where they had stood. The succubus' arms clasped about him, and his face nestled between her breasts. But he could not see where they were going. Rising higher and higher etched a frightening image in his mind … slipping from the demon's grasp and falling to his death.

Lilith said nothing. Her wings beat in a steady reassuring cadence. Gradually, like a passenger on his first plane flight, Fig felt some of the tension dissolve … to be replaced by the distracting presence of the demon nestling his cheeks even though they were garbed. He squirmed, trying to look toward the ground. But he could not estimate their altitude nor the direction in which they were moving. More importantly, he could not read his phone or manipulate the artificial nose.

"No good," Fig shouted over the rustle of the wind. "I can't operate anything."

The pair landed and experimented. Better for him to face forward. They even decided to use two belts to fasten his legs to hers at the ankles. No dangling in the air and increasing the drag the succubus had to overcome.

Then, it became perfect. Exactly as Fig had imagined as a child, the wind whistled in his ears. The landscape sped below him. He was engulfed in a deep black sky. Marks of civilization glowed in the moonlight like colonies of glowworms.

Most of the upwelling had nothing to do with burning juniper, of course. And some of those fires would be inside, hidden from view. But Lilith could sense them nevertheless. With unwavering decision, she flew like an arrow to wherever they should check next. In only two days, she had collected the data needed to construct a near-optimal route of discovery.

Lilith did not struggle under the load. Like the thrust of an engine's pistons, stroke after stroke of her wings propelled them forward. They skimmed over the ground, moving at hundreds of miles an hour. Somehow, the demon manipulated the airflow around them. Only a gentle breeze caressed Fig's face.

And the dives to get closer when they neared the next target, how wonderful they felt. Like a hawk who had spotted prey, Lilith folded her wings and plunged earthward. Then, with a gut-wrenching swoop, she rotated to hover vertically a few feet from the ground — above an open fire with no one nearby awake. Lilith feathered Fig to hover above the blaze. In a mere second, he took the reading, and they were off to the next.

Over seventeen hundred fires they had to visit. The foolish hope of hitting the jackpot on the first stop soon evaporated. Fig settled into the routine. Like a factory robot programmed to perform a series of tasks, he repeated the steps. Turn on the nose. Start the intake fan. Suck in the hot air and, after a moment, take the measurement. If not a positive result, turn the nose back off. Click the button on the phone to get the direction to the next site.

FOUR HUNDRED and ninety visits later, and no luck yet. Dawn already hinted in the east. Despite the improvements, the search would still take

30

days. By now, Fig was quite used to the flying, but his emotions were going up and down like a yo-yo champion's toy. Before each stop, he just knew it would be the one, and his expectations soared. After the negative result, he plunged deeper into despair. Time was so precious. Who knew what horrors Briana must be experiencing? He had to find her soon.

As they touched the ground for the next possibility, it appeared to be difficult. The moon had not yet set, and they were vulnerable in its light. He might pass for an early morning riser, but Lilith would be much harder to explain.

"The blaze is in the apartment building, on the fifth floor." Lilith took cover by a tree and blended in with the trunk. "You will have to go inside alone."

"Let's hope the entrance is unlocked." Fig nodded and put the cell phone away.

He tapped each of his cargo pants pockets for the reassurance his other gear was still there: the nose, the camera, battery pack, mirrors, the tongs and all the rest. He was not worried about getting in, only the extra time doing so required. One of his hobbies as an undergrad had been learning how to pick locks, but it had been years since he had any practice.

Fig approached the door and gave it a tentative pull. To his delight, it swung open easily, and he entered. An elevator stood nearby, but using it in the middle of the night with its groans and rattles ... not a good idea.

He climbed four flights of stairs illuminated by exterior windows on each floor. A heavy fire door opened onto a narrow hall. Fig breathed deeply. "Out of shape," he muttered to himself. "So, out of shape. After this is over, I gotta add more cardio."

Up and down the hallway every door was shut, five on either side. Tiptoeing along the corridor, he stopped at the first. He put the probe at the baseboard and dialed the setting for 'juniper' rather than 'essence of a succubus.' The success light did not blink. But maybe weather stripping prevented getting a sample from within.

Fig growled in frustration. This was going to take too long. There were too many door openings to check. The many targets already eliminated with ease had been because of luck. What to do now?

Fig scanned the passageway one more time. Perhaps something to give him ... A fire extinguisher hung near the other end of the hall. And next to it must also be an alarm. Without another thought, he strode down the corridor and gave the red handle a jerk. Retracing his steps, he banged on each of the doors.

"Feuer! Incendie!" Fig shouted, not knowing if either word would be understood in whatever country he was in. Two of the doors opened. He pantomimed everyone inside to exit and pointed them to the stairs. As they complied, more sleepers came out. They hesitated a moment and then followed those who preceded.

In a couple of minutes, nine of the apartments had been evacuated. Fig switched on the probe and stepped inside the doorway of each one. Seven had no fires lit, and the two that did smelled of cedar, not juniper.

Only one apartment was left to check. He put his ear to the door and banged again, this time with more force. *"Fuego! Fuego!"*

The entrance suddenly opened. Two odors mixed and wafted into the air. Peppery juniper and another that stung the eyes — vinegar, strong acidic vinegar. A fact from Chemistry 201 popped into his head. One smell an attempt to disguise the other. Pure heroin being diluted for sale.

A tall man with a scruffy three-day growth of beard rose and scrambled to the doorway. He waved a revolver, motioning Fig to go away. Fig nodded and took a step back. But he still needed to check the room's fireplace for Angela's scent.

Pulling a fake smile onto his face, Fig initiated the measurement sequence with the nose. It would only take a second. The thug squinted at the device with its twinkling status and process lights and scowled. He yelled something Fig did not understand and pointed the gun at his head.

Now would be the time for some of Briana's magic crafts, Fig's thoughts raced. But he only had forced himself to learn a few simple spells. The thug did not seem to care about that. He pushed the gun into Fig's face and growled a second time.

"Sorry, sorry, big mistake, leaving now." Fig rattled off the words. He held his breath, stepped back into the center of the hall, and walked away. Out of the corner of his eye, he saw the thug lower the gun. The artificial nose beeped: another non-detection.

Adrenalin coursed through him, his emotions a tangled confusion. On one hand, he was still alive. On the other, Angela had not been here, another hope dashed. The frustration boiled over. Somehow it had to come out. Unable to stop himself, Fig whirled back to face the thug and gave him the finger.

The reaction was immediate. The blast and its echoes ricocheted down the hallway, but the shot missed. Fig turned and fled toward the stairs. Stupid, stupid, stupid. Two more shots, one within inches of his ear.

Fig reached the end of the hall. Down the stairway shaft, the half-way landing to the fourth floor beckoned. With a single jump, he leaped the full distance and crashed onto it. His ankle twisted on impact, the rush of adrenaline masking most of the pain. He hobbled a single step and grimaced. His legs were not doing what they should. Pounding footsteps grew closer.

Suddenly, the large window shattered. Lilith crashed through to the inside, her arms crossed over her face.

"Let's get out of here," Fig yelled. He caught his breath as she lifted him through the opening and soared into the sky. His ankle throbbed with returning feeling.

"Why did you save me?" he asked through gritted teeth. "Why?"

"When this is all done, we are to struggle, remember? I want to keep you whole until then. All things that must happen eventually will."

Lilith shrugged. "Who knows? Perhaps the Tyrant of Time controls the future as well as the past."

The Tyrant of Time

THE TYRANT of Time glanced at the empty throne beside her own, a twin bolted arm flush with the arm. The other occupant was not present. He never was. The two chairs sat near the center of a large circular room; it was like the largest slice of a giant grapefruit, the centermost level of the sphere.

Her stomach rumbled. For the millionth time, she decided she should cut back on the snacks. The soup bubbling in the recycling vats had better uses.

She studied her reflection in the polished plate of gold leaf standing nearby. Very long ago, before the realm became overrun with demons of other kinds, she looked very much like a goblin. Short of stature. Tiny eyes atop a bulbous nose. A mouth stretching from ear to ear. The hunched back sprouted no wings.

But after eons and eons of seclusion, her body had grown in ways she could not control. The left side of her face was slack. Drool dripped from the sag in the corner of the lip. The eye struggled to remain open, but was a vacant portal showing the emptiness within. Her arm, withered from lack of use, hung lifeless at the side. The scalp was entirely bald to the midpoint of her peaked head.

As the Tyrant studied her reflection, her left side grew even more repulsive. The loveliness on the right all the more a thing of beauty. With her good right hand, she placed her palm perpendicular to her nose, blotting out the gruesome part of the view on the left.

The Tyrant smiled at the image of her vibrant black hair rising a mere gnat-length from where the baldness ceased. Perfectly coifed and free of tangles, it matched the color of her glowing right eye — the one alert and dancing from side to side like a kestrel looking for prey.

She touched her ear. The mirror did not lie. The one on the other side of her head was twice as large and flapped as she moved about. Tufts of hair filled the lobes. Lice living there made the eyes of her minions turn away.

Because succubi could travel through time, only they witnessed her handiwork and gave her a name — demonifying the phenomena they observed. 'The Tyrant of Time.' She liked that and began to refer to herself that way. Besides that, little else of this place remained in the lore of the demon realm outside. And even those tales had been reduced into broodmother prattle — like the tale of the toenail fairy.

One of the Tyrant's minions ascended from a spiral staircase in the very center of the level. On hands and knees, it approached its ruler. "Another succubus has traveled back in time. A young one leaving her broodsisters for the first time and eager to explore the realm of humankind. I suspect she will attempt to make a change."

The Tyrant frowned. She was annoyed. "Then, stop her," she commanded. "Wasn't your training clear?"

"I understand my liege," the minion said. "But this *is* important. She is visiting the orb called 'Earth.' She has gone to the Battle of Chancellorsville in 1863."

The Tyrant jerked to attention. Her heart pounded. "Earth," she growled. "There are thousands of orbs with sentient beings in the realm of humankind. But only a few are populated as savagely as the one called Earth. What is the situation? How long did you delay before coming to tell me?"

"General Stonewall Jackson is wounded there and subsequently dies. Some say that if he had been alive for Gettysburg, the South would have been victorious at the battle. Then, as a result of that, triumphed in the Civil War. But on the other thumb, when he dies might make no difference. I don't know what to do."

"Do you recall the first law of time management?" she snapped. "To the vats with you now. You deserve — " With an effort, she slammed her mouth shut. Her emotions sometimes were too powerful — a failing that she had a hard time controlling. But then, better to give them at least some life than to be like him with his somber moods, always under the tight control of intellect.

"Yes, my liege. 'When in doubt, do not let the change take place.'" The minion rattled off. "But the succubus intends to distract the Confederate soldier who mistakenly shot Jackson. She has brought a swirling dervish to raise a funnel of obscuring dust. I do not know how to stop that distraction from happening."

"Incompetents," the Tyrant growled. Her back stiffened. She must always be firm, unyielding. Make the fear so palpable that no one dare

35

think of deviating from the rules. Fear was an emotion well worth understanding. "Take me to your station. I will show you what to do."

The Tyrant rose regally from her throne and grabbed a key hanging from the armrest. Descending to where her minion still knelt, she kicked it in its side and smiled when she heard the snap of a rib. "Come on. Get up. You can still function. Tell me your name. This event shall be added to your entry in my Doomsday book."

"Crawling Scum," gasped the minion as it struggled to stand. It was small, shorter than the Tyrant. All four limbs were smooth and rubbery as were his face and head. Except for the pale blue coloring, it could pass as an Earthling's doll.

The pair walked to the spiral staircase. The Tyrant looked up the shaft for an instant, then turned her eyes away with disgust. Most of the top half of the sphere was filled with minions and machines. But it was wasted space, all of it. Only the volume downward was of any practical use. Every level served a purpose, even the mass in the bottom polar-cap provided gravity for the entire sphere.

They spiraled down a level. A tight cylindrical wall enclosed the stairwell from ceiling to floor. In one side stood a door, featureless except for its protruding knob. They entered onto another cylindrical slice of the confining sphere.

The Tyrant scanned the level. Everything appeared to be in order. Thousands of viewing globes were arranged in a large circle around half of the periphery. In front of each sat a minion like Crawling Scum, intent upon its task, tracking the movements of one of the succubi who had not yet surrendered to the great monotony.

The Tyrant smiled. The minions here were superior as well. Not as simple as those in the zenith hemisphere above. Instead, burnt into the innermost fiber of their being was an unwavering of purpose — keep the record of time the same as it is recorded. All significant events were to remain the same. No matter what the challenge, that was the rationale for their very existence.

The Tyrant craned her neck, looked behind herself, and grunted with satisfaction. Everything was exactly the same as when she last visited. A wall stretched from one side of the level all the way across to the other. It was featureless except for two more doors in its middle standing next to one another.

"Which station is yours?" the Tyrant asked.

Crawling Scum led the Tyrant to its empty observation chair at the periphery. The minion at the station to the left frantically wheeled his chair back and forth. It watched first its own screen and then Crawling Scum's abandoned one.

"What took you so long?" the frantic minion asked. "Your succubus has lured the shooter into a little copse of willows. He is not going to take his shot."

The Tyrant shouldered the minion aside and sat in front of the globe. "Watch," she said. "Watch and learn."

First, she concentrated on the succubus. Telekinesis, the humans called it. Didn't Crawling Scum realize that it could move animate matter as well as stones? The Tyrant induced a twitch in the demon's left calf. She stumbled as she stepped forward toward the soldier and fell to the ground. The trooper blinked. Good. He was coming out of the alluring spell.

Next, a quick survey of the battlefield revealed an abundance of choices. She selected the jacket and hat of a fallen major. Those should be senior enough. She flew them into the copse, and, behind one of the willows, arranged them so they looked to the fighter as if an officer approached.

The soldier's eyes widened as he saw the motion. Scrambling back to pick up his rifle, he fired towards Jackson's small troop. The general went down.

When he did, the Tyrant felt a rush of apprehension. 1865? That was more than one hundred and fifty Earth years ago. One hundred and fifty! Suppose the action had not been taken soon enough? Despite the readjustment, suppose something of significance had been allowed to change.

"Back in your chair," she commanded the minion. "Scan the present and compare."

"I HAVE looked at dozens of places," Crawling Scum said sometime later. "At all the nodes of power. Everything is the same."

The Tyrant felt her apprehension melt away. Nothing had changed. It would have been a shame. She was so very close. She cupped her good ear and strained to listen. Yes, there it was — a low frequency grind and then a sharp click. The countdown continued towards the end. The end of the future as well as freezing the past.

8

A Maze of Choices

EXCEPT FOR the one standing before the Tyrant, the rest of the minions on the level kept their heads down, concentrating on their tasks. The Tyrant studied Crawling Scum with her good eye. Should this one continue? she thought. It was unclear. Best to test.

"Let's learn how nimble your thinking is," the Tyrant said. "With age, memory is the first to go."

Crawling Scum's face froze in fear. "Not the vats," it said. "I did the best I could. Only disturbed you to be absolutely sure."

"One returns to the vats only if it fails to navigate the maze. The number of doors to remember is but a smidgen compared to the requirements of a station such as yours. Come, we don't want your neighbor to be burdened with covering for you too long."

Crawling Scum did not speak. Its shoulders slumped. Resigned, it followed the Tyrant back to the central wall. "Your choice," the Tyrant pointed to the two doors flanking the entrance to the stairwell.

The minion remained silent, head down.

"Very well, then. I choose the left." The Tyrant pulled open the door, and the pair entered a small alcove containing three more interior doors. Each displayed a simple glyph distinguishing one from another.

"Choose," the Tyrant said.

The minion did not move.

"The one on the left, then," the Tyrant said. "Note the glyph carefully when we pass."

Crawling Scum nodded, opened the door, and the pair walked through. They entered the second alcove about the same size as the first, but with only two exit doors this time, one directly ahead and another on the right. Each was marked with a unique glyph as were the ones before. Crawling Scum made no attempt to choose again.

The Tyrant took charge. In rapid succession, she raced through the maze, opening doors in what seemed to have no pattern. The minion tagged behind. After a dozen choices, the pair reemerged through the second of the two doors in the bisecting wall.

"Now, it is your turn to navigate by yourself, Crawling Scum," the Tyrant said. "Prove to me that you still are sufficiently sharp and do not need to be reconstituted."

"You started with the other door," Crawling Scum said. "I remember that."

"No, you must begin with the one from which we just emerged. Travel back through the maze and exit from where we began. Remember where we have been. Reverse your course. It will be easy."

"There were so many choices along the way."

The minion hesitated, but the Tyrant did not. She opened the rightmost door and shoved Crawling Scum through the entryway. "Now traverse quickly, I feel a change coming on, and there is something more I desire to look in on before returning to my throne."

Crawling Scum centered itself in the alcove, and the Tyrant followed. The minion shrugged and opened one of the choices leading farther into the maze. The revealed cubicle appeared almost the same as all the rest, one blank wall, two more shut doors. The only difference was the glyphs they displayed.

"This time, you made the choice," the Tyrant growled. She kicked Crawling Scum in the back, sending it stumbling forward. As the minion stumbled forward, the floor of the alcove hinged to one side. Crawling Scum screamed out as it plunged into the level below.

The Tyrant came to the edge of the flooring and leaned over to watch. Crawling Scum flailed, but nothing impeded its fall. Unerringly, it splashed into a vat from which a searing acid vapor rose in the air. Crawling Scum floundered to stay afloat but soon submerged. In a single heartbeat, parts of its flesh flaked off and rose to the top of the caustic brew. If it had only kept calm, unemotional, then perhaps it could have survived. After all, the maze was a test of serenity under stress, not one of memory and intellect.

The Tyrant swirled her cape around herself in a grand fashion. From Crawling Scum's essence, a new minion would be crafted, one better than before. One even more dedicated to keeping all the significant events of time in the realm of the hominoids always as first they occurred.

But before she could savor the feeling for long, the sense of change intensified. She put her foot onto the first upward stair step, but then stopped. There would be enough time, she reasoned. This little adventure with Crawling Scum had not taken all that long.

She began to descend instead. Two levels farther down, she entered the bottommost of the sphere. It was cylindrical like the others, but with the highest ceiling, and the circle of the floor the smallest of all. Only the nadir cap providing the gravity for the sphere was lower. The Tyrant looked about. The volume did not matter. What was important stood halfway between the central stairwell and the sloping walls — the giant ratchet mechanism.

The lower end of the ratchet ended in a toothed claw that scraped against the floor. The upper end pivoted on an axle running across the level's volume. On the floor, along a circular trace lay a series of rectangular logs arrayed in a circle. They looked like the ties for a train with the rails stripped away.

As the Tyrant watched, the floor of the level rotated around an invisible central axis centered in the stairwell. And as it did, when one of the ties reached the stationary ratchet, the claw climbed up its side. Then, as the floor continued to rotate, it dragged across the top and fell back to the floor.

In some ways, the mechanism resembled the escapement of a human clock. Each rise and fall of the ratchet represented one tick. But the resemblance was only superficial. In a clock, the ratchet released a wheel so that the hands of the clock could turn. Here the mechanism worked in reverse. It was the rotation of the level floor with its circle of impediments moving the ratchet up and then back down rather than the other way around.

Whenever that happened, a click resounded from a counter mounted on the level's ceiling. The Tyrant looked up at it and grinned. Originally, there had been almost one hundred counter wheels arranged in a long row spanning the top of the volume. Now only one still showed symbols. All the rest were blank.

The Tyrant's smile broadened. She admired her handiwork. It had been accomplished so long ago she no longer remembered exactly how she had achieved it. Time in the realm of humankind was a river. It flowed relentlessly forward pulling everything with it. The affairs of men and the lives of animals and plants. The transfers of energy occurring everywhere in the realm.

And she had harnessed it. Directed its flow to this very level. Used it to power the uniform rotation of the floor. The ratcheted counter recorded with its clicks how long she had been doing this. How long she had kept the past unchanging.

Now only the last gear wheel remained to reset to zero. And when it did, *she* would be the winner. He still had thousands of demons to contend with before they were all gone.

The Tyrant's satisfaction was cut short when another minion scurried down the staircase and interrupted her reverie. "The succubus named Angela," it said. "She is a wily one, and we cannot figure out why she is doing what she is."

Fresh Juniper for Sale

ANGELA FLEXED her wings. They felt uncomfortable underneath the long dress she wore, but at least they were hidden. The cowl hid most of her face as well. She looked like an old, hunched-over widow, nothing more.

The palace stood majestically before her, offset from the slow-moving river behind. Angela pushed back when other peddlers jostled her cart. There was little space between the bank and the edifice itself. She needed to be in position when the attendant came forth.

The stone, mottled and irregular, showed its age like the skin of a dowager princess who never married. It had been many years since the edifice had rivaled the abode of the king. The entrance door sat deep between parallel wings on either side of an access path. At the very front stood cylindrical towers capped by tall, blue conical roofs. Each supported a weather vane at the very top.

"Juniper," she cried out in French. "Burn it for its scent. It covers the stench."

The wicker entrance door opened. Several young women, attendants to prisoners inside, strode out. They dressed not so differently from Angela herself. Brighter colors and simple white scarfs over the heads instead of hoods. But the fabrics were coarse, faded, and well-worn.

"Juniper, you say." One of the women approached. "My lady will be pleased." She reached to test the freshness of the branches but then halted when she caught Angela's gaze.

"Are you ill?" she asked. "Your skin is a sickly green."

"There is no risk, my dear," Angela smoothed the concern beginning to bubble in the wench's mind. "Go ahead and examine my wares."

The attendant hesitated.

"Most of these vagabonds are different each day." Angela waved her arm in a wide arc. "You can never be sure from one to the next if they will return. But if you buy from me, I will be here faithfully every morning. And my branches always fresh, too." She broke off a sprig.

"Here, smell and you will see."

The woman accepted the offer and inhaled. Her nose twisted to the side. "Most unusual," she said.

"Yes, from the south, not one of the common varieties one finds around here." Angela motioned to one of the other peddler's crowding near. "And far more effective than the cloying scents others hawk."

The woman continued to hesitate.

"And only two *deniers* for six branches."

"Two for six!" The attendant nodded with decision. "I will take some." She reached into a small purse and extracted the coins.

Angela accepted the money and tipped her head. "Pick which you like best."

The woman did so and hurried back into the palace.

Angela watched her go. She looked around the buyers and sellers who still bartered over the goods for sale. One stood apart from the rest. A little tray hung at her waist, supported by a dirty strap looping around her neck. On the jutting table stood a dozen small dirty vials, each filled with liquids transparent as water.

"To entice the older swain," the weathered crone said to Angela. "A dab behind each of your ears is all you need. Even we can still long for the embrace of a strong arm."

Angela studied the woman. Could it be as simple as that? Smell a more powerful allure than a pleasing sight? On an impulse, she decided to give it a try.

"Two *deniers* is all I have," she said before she could change her mind.

The woman smiled, pleased with the transaction.

Angela felt pleased as well. She pulled the cork out of the little bottle and sniffed. She wrinkled her nose, mystified and then shrugged. It was something to experiment when the proper moment came. She glanced back at the ancient palace and grinned with satisfaction. Yes, the first step of her plan was complete.

10

The Fear of God

ANGELA STEPPED out of the ancient prison's firepit and hesitated. She heard only breathing and no voices. Except for the juniper fire, the room was almost entirely dark. Only a single candle flickered, all that was allowed. She waited a moment for her eyes to adjust. Dimly, she made out the two side-by-side beds along the far wall. Not very distant, since the room was so very small. On one of the pillows, she recognized the brown locks of the woman to whom she had sold the juniper. Then the other must be —

Her thoughts faltered. The tresses of the other woman were pale. White mixed with the red. What the humans called 'strawberry blonde,' but even that color would be more vibrant than what she saw.

Angela breathed deeply and coiled her fingers into rigid fists at her sides. She calmed herself. It did not matter that much. History recorded that a small white cap was worn on the upcoming crucial day. In the excitement of the moment, no one would notice. And the guards would be easy to confuse. Human men: the train of their thoughts ran on a single pair of rails.

She resumed her survey: a writing desk, two chairs, and a smaller table, a three-drawer chest, all plain and unadorned. More importantly, the screen. A barrier for privacy in name only, barely four feet high, it partitioned the room into two.

She detected a soft snore emanating from behind. The guard on the second shift took his duties lightly. Angela craned her neck upward. The bottom part of the window had been boarded shut. From the angle where she stood, she could not tell if the other guard was peering in. Fortunate that the juniper fire would be out of his sight if he were. But first things first. Take care of the guard on the inside tomorrow. Then, when he was under control and had the duty outside, dominate his partner as well. When that was done, she will have completed step two.

AFTER THE two guards had been dominated, Angela returned again to the prison. The scene was the same as it had been on her last visit. Light from a single, feeble candle. Cold, damp and sweating walls. A half-bordered up window.

She looked at the nearer of the dreamers, reassuring herself that her plan would work. A powerful and important figure, she thought. The recordings of history were emphatic. But to look at her, one did not guess she caused such an impact. Surely, with such skill, she must have secrets that would control male demons as well as human men.

Angela adjusted the wire halo that kept slipping down over her brow. She smoothed the white choir robe stolen from Notre Dame. Dominating the two sentries had been easy. Even if she obtained no personal satisfaction herself from doing so. And in the end, even the pleasures she had given them would fade into forgotten memories.

But a woman was another matter altogether. The one named Briana, the one from the future, and hidden away elsewhere — she had put up quite the fight resisting abduction. It made no sense to engage in another protracted battle in the dingy confines here. Too bad the attendant was not a nun.

On tiptoe, Angela approached the farther of the two beds. There slept the one who, forever after, would be identified as the final stewardess. "Rosalie," she whispered. "Wake up and attend unto me."

The young woman's eyes snapped open, but she caught herself before she screamed.

"Who … what are you?" Rosalie managed to whisper.

Angela shook her head. These humans were so slow. She spread out her arms. "Look at me. Is it not obvious? I am an angel sent by your Lord."

Rosalie sat up abruptly. "An angel? I don't see your wings."

Angela scowled. She slowly turned to the side.

"Those are puny, transparent, with thick blue veins. Shouldn't they be huge with white feathers?"

"Never mind that," Angela snapped. "Do you want to save your lady or not?"

"Save my lady! But of course."

"Then listen carefully and do as I say. Through the grace of your Lord, her salvation has been assured ... assured provided you obey."

Rosalie crossed herself. "What is it you want me to do?"

"Behave as if nothing has happened. Everything is proceeding exactly as planned. Nothing is strange."

"I do not understand."

"There are three tasks you must perform." She reached into the bag hung at her side and retrieved a small vial. "On the last evening, add this to your lady's dinner. It will cause her to sleep soundly through the night. She will not call out in her dreams as often happens."

"How will this save my lady?"

"All will become clear at the proper time. Listen. The second task is for you to give me the white dress and cap."

"But they are to be for —"

"Don't interrupt. Get them for me — now."

Rosalie hesitated. "Do you think I sought this task willingly?" she said after a moment. "Confined as much as the prisoner. Eat the same scraps of food. Endure the same suffocating cold. I will be the one blamed when the garb is found missing." She took a deep breath. "Angel of God or not. What's in it for me?"

Angela sighed. It was good she had prepared for this. Even white robes and mysterious appearances were not enough. She reached into her purse and withdrew a smaller sack that jingled. "All golden *Louis d'Ors*. You will be able to live for a year with what the Lord provides you."

Rosalie took the offered bag and inspected its contents. She bit one of the coins to be sure. "Very well," she said. "Her nightgown will serve instead." She hustled to the chest, retrieved the garments and presented them to the demon.

With the hint of a smile, the servant girl fingered the contents of the bag. "*Merci,*"she said.

"I am not done," Angela said. "After all this is finished. Years from now, you will relate the events that will happen here."

"Ah, more gold can be obtained for this task after all."

Angela scowled and readjusted the halo again. If this urchin is what she had to deal with, was the costuming even needed? So quick to change her mind. Could she be trusted over the years?

"Listen to me," the succubus said. "The third task is that you relate the events exactly as everyone expects, not what actually transpires."

Rosalie jingled the coins. "And why should I do that?"

Angela sighed again. "You are little credit for your church, but never mind. For each remaining year of your life, a similar gift to the one you now hold will come."

"You will reappear yearly, on the anniversary of today? Find me no matter where I am?"

"Not me, but smaller cherubs." Angela thought quickly. "You might see them as gargoyles but the gold will be as pure." She put as much command as she could into her voice. "Provided you always relate the events of this time, as I command you, exactly as everyone expects."

Rosalie took a deep breath. "Another sack now and a double amount each year in the future. The prices of almost everything keep going up."

Angela retrieved a second bag filled like the first. There was not a third. The attendant must be convinced and convinced now. Otherwise, they will be bargaining all night. A flicker of frustration boiled in her stomach. She bent forward until her horns pressed into Rosalie's forehead. "Twice a year. Agreed. I will see to it that it is done. But if you do not comply, you will feel the full wrath of your God and be damned to an eternity in Hell. Do you understand?"

"Yes, yes, sainted one," Rosalie gulped. "Forgive me. In the dimness, I was unaware that God's messengers have ... such beautiful protuberances. You truly are holy. I will do as you say. Speak of nothing out of the ordinary."

She reached out and snatched the sack from Angela's hand. "For my own salvation ... and the salvation of my lady," she added after a moment.

Angela nodded. "That is more like it. Know that I will visit you one final time." She grinned with satisfaction. Everything was going according to plan. She would have her first captive entirely out of the time stream soon.

11

Angela's Visitor

ANGELA PACED along the narrow and flat slab of tissue-thin rock — the lair she shared with her sister. As always, it hung suspended by unseen forces in a vast, almost overwhelming blackness. Flickering lights in the distance appeared rooted in place.

It was good her sibling was not there. They would soon be at each other's throats if they were present at the same time. It was all so depressing when it happened. She stopped her pacing for a moment with the thought. Unusual that Lilith had not appeared in a long time as measured by the clocks of the humans. What exactly was she up to?

Angela shrugged. She would learn of it soon enough. For now, a moment's rest. A chance to savor how things would be once Elezar obeyed her every whim. She could arrive unannounced in the lair of his subject djinns when they were rutting. Parade in front of them with nonchalance. Watch the frustration of desire on their faces and the twitch of muscles they dare not use. Merely to touch her would mean certain death. But then how sweet it would be if one were to attempt it.

In the end, it all came down to power. The power over others, forcing them to do as one wished. She must have that. Indeed, would have in the end. Nothing else mattered.

The succubus' thoughts halted. The thin slab of matter buckled and oscillated under the sudden increase in weight. It was a lightning djinn, his chest bulging with deep definition and lust burning in his eyes.

"A moment," Angela said, reaching into her purse and pulling out the small vial of perfume she had purchased. Many human females dabbed it on various places of their bodies. How much, she did not know. But if a little bit was effective …

No time to be subtle. She poured about one-half of the contents over one ear and emptied the bottle over the other. She strode toward the demon and mimicked the smile of a human female.

"Perhaps, we can chat a moment, first," she said as she used both her hands to waft the human scent toward him. When she neared, she asked, "Isn't there something about me — "

The djinn growled, shoved aside Angela's arms and thrust her to the slab. He forced himself between her legs. In a few brief moments, it was over, and he flew away without looking back.

Angela struggled to sit. She tried to ignore the bruising and pain of tender membranes. There was no solace in the fact that she had learned something. If odor was what human females used to control the males around them, it did not work on demonkind. Until she had mastery over the prince, it always would be this way, the way it had been for eon upon eon.

She felt small, violated, and unimportant. She curled into a ball, knees drawn up, arms folded about her chest. It was always this way, every time it happened. And as they always did, her conscious thoughts spiraled her deeper into viscous gloom.

Once, she had broached the question with her sister. How did she handle the situation when it occurred with her? But there was no satisfaction in the answers. No admission that this, too, was her experience again and again. Nothing that helped to rebuild self-worth, no comfort for each other. Lilith was a dreamer, spouting slogans, mere platitudes about how all the succubi had to unite. Together they would avenge Delilah's death and the mistreatment of others.

Angela closed her eyes. Sleep was the only option that would help. Sleep away the time until she had something definite she had to do — return to the French prison for the very last time. Much better than wasting time on one of her sister's hopeless crusades.

12

Voices in the Night

TURKMENISTAN. THE Karakum desert. In the distance, Fig saw the *Derweze*—the 'Door to Hell,' the Turkmen called it. A natural gas deposit still burning so many years after it had been lit.

Lilith and Fig touched down on a small hillock a few hundred yards north of the sound of pounding drums. Turkmenistan was a remote part of the world. Rural Turkmenistan, even more so. There were primitive, nomadic tribes who still lived there, practicing animistic religions as they had for perhaps thousands of years.

The ground all around was flat and unfeatured—no buildings, only occasional rock outcroppings far into the distance. The hillock on which he and Lilith stood was large by comparison, the remains of a dome thrust upward eons ago. The north side of the monolith stood unweathered; the south flaked away into rubble piling up at its base.

In the distance, a dozen or so men clustered around a single campfire. All wore large, bushy sheepskin hats, telpeks. At their very center, next to a well-muscled drummer stooped a shaman dancing around the blaze. He was burning juniper, no doubt about it. But there was no way to sneak up close enough to get the final reading verifying Briana was here.

Fig could not believe it. What were the odds? It had taken them a few days, but now only a single target remained—the very last one! He had calibrated the artificial nose time and time again as the search continued. More and more often as the number of remaining choices dwindled. But no matter. His excitement bubbled. Briana was nearby. She had to be.

Looking about, Fig could not imagine where Briana had been hidden. He would not only have to verify Angela had visited, but also track the demon to wherever she had built a lair.

"The warriors all seem intent on the shaman," Fig said. "If we hovered directly over the fire and slowly descend, I can get close enough for a reading."

Lilith did not reply. She slipped behind Fig, stooped and affixed his legs to hers. Fig kept his mouth clamped shut. He had figured out that when she touched his ankle, his little gasps irritated her. He could barely hobble, but seeing a doctor would have to come later.

Grasping Fig firmly, Lilith soared back into the sky. The dust swirled. After a moment, she hovered far above the roaring fire. Almost as if she were the operator of an elevator, they descended, stopping every ten feet or so.

"Is this close enough?" Lilith asked when they were the height of thirty men above the blaze.

"I don't know for sure." Fig wiggled in Lilith's grip to get a better view. "The closer we get, the better—"

Suddenly, the shaman cried out and pointed skyward. Lilith spun around to see what had startled the medicine man, and Fig groaned at what he saw. The moon. They had forgotten about the moon. The outline of what must look like a beast with bat-like wings silhouetted against the glare. The men surrounding the fire sprang to their feet shouting. A spear hurled upward and then two more.

"Later. We can come back later," Fig yelled, but too late. A shaft tore through one of Lilith's wings. The demon cried out in pain. Like taut tissue paper nicked by scissors, the appendage tore. The pair plummeted toward the ground.

Lilith grunted, trying to maintain altitude, but she could no longer keep control. Like an escaped toy balloon, the pair flitted in the air. More spears soared around them, and Fig grew dizzy from the jerky motion. One instant, he was head up and the next looking downward at the ground streaking by.

The motion was not entirely random, he realized when the earth came back into view a few more times. Besides fighting for height, Lilith also moved away from the fire, from the tribesmen as best she could. Down below, the Turkmen raced after in pursuit.

Fig strained to look at the damaged wing. The tear had reached the trailing edge. But except for an ooze of green ichor along the flapping sides, no more damage was apparent. And there up ahead, the outcropping, a place to hide and decide what to do next.

Lilith's breath grew more ragged. She flew lower. Despite the pulls and tugs generated by the erratic motion, she still managed to hang on to him—although now, he felt the tremor of her arm muscles pressed to their limits of strength.

The outcrop grew closer. They were descending. The ground rushed up. Too fast, too fast. With a last shudder, Lilith flung Fig away from herself. He flipped upside down, feet still bound to her legs. He bent his back and clawed his way upward, reaching the bows on the fetters. He pulled on the first and his leg swung free. A fresh stab of pain coursed through him. All his weight now tugged on his injured ankle.

Fig looked downward, his face only inches above the ground. Gasping, he freed his fettered leg and dropped the remaining distance. Rolling into a ball as best he could, he placed his hands about his head. His back hit the earth, knocking his breath away. Rolling forward, he somersaulted three or four times, then slowed and crashed to a stop. His head hit a rock, and with a flash of white light, consciousness vanished.

FIG WIGGLED his head, dazed. He had been out long enough for the moon to set. It was pitch black—except to the far left. Lilith must have veered in that direction after he freed himself. Torchlight. In the midst of half a dozen of the tribesmen, there was another form, smaller and different. Hands bound in front, and wings fettered behind, Lilith had been captured.

Fig staggered to his feet, reaching for a sword that was not there— never was there. This was Earth, not another place or time. He was in no condition to fight. Besides, all Lilith needed to escape was to get near enough to a flame. Even one of the torches might do.

No, that was not right. Not any fire. It had to be the special type of juniper, nothing else. Okay then, the large blaze where they had first arrived. It burned the correct fuel. If Lilith could get closer, she could vanish from …

Incorrect again. The succubus was his *own* way out of here, too. It was a long way to walk from Turkmenistan to Hilo, Hawaii. Lilith had to be rescued.

Fig took a first cautious step and then another. Pain shot up his leg. He was able to walk but only barely. Even the slow-moving guards around Lilith moved faster.

Think it through, he told himself. Focus. Even on two good legs, charging into the shaman's circle would be suicide.

A distraction, then. Something to draw the natives from the fire. If only the shaman were left, he could be handled. Yes, lure the others, but not to where he waited. He needed not only a distraction but one that also misdirected.

Shielding his cell phone light with his hand, he looked about. Looming a short distance farther north stood the hillock on which they had first landed. The southern face reminded him of the shell of an outdoor theater—a concave indentation focusing the sound of an orchestra toward the audience.

The structure gave him an idea. His fingers bounced over the icons on the phone. After what had happened in Spain, he had made sure he was better prepared before each target. He brought up the English to Turkmen dictionary and composed a message.

"*men Äpet döw. sen ujypsyz towshan.*—I, mighty demon. You, insignificant rabbit."

Incorrect grammar, his accent horrible, but it would have to do.

FIG HUDDLED in the shadow of the largest nearby rock he could find. He had finished his message and put it in a loop. He set the timer and propped up his phone in the rubble to face what he hoped would work as a directional antenna.

He scanned the camp. The juniper in the central fire had been cleared. Cedar burned in its place, and nearby, Lilith slumped, tied to a log with wheels at its base. The shaman and his followers were not taking any chances. They planned to burn her to death.

Fig pushed on the dial illuminator on his watch. Only a minute or so to spare. He had barely managed to circle the camp to the south in time. He watched the seconds tick away until the narrowcast.

His voice, of course, was faint when it reached the tribesmen, only a whisper, but the shaman heard it. He put a hand behind his ear and called for quiet. The babble around the campfire halted.

Fig hoped the natives would think they heard another demon. One coming to rescue its mate. The shaman listened for a moment. Then he pointed in the direction of the eerie voice and shouted commands. At first, no one else responded. Then, the repeated insults and taunts to manhood became too much. As Fig had hoped, the tribesmen gathered up their spears. They trotted off in the direction of the sound. After a minute, only the medicine man remained, and Fig could …

Damn! The drummer had stayed behind as well. The muscles in his arms pulsed like the waves on a stormy sea when he pounded against the drumhead. A long ceremonial dagger hung from a jeweled belt.

But there was nothing else to do. This was a mental game, not a physical one. Rising from his hiding place, Fig walked forward slowly. He changed a few of the words. *"Men ozge dow* — I, another demon," as he approached.

The shaman and the drummer stood transfixed. With a flourish, Fig removed the Polaroid from his cargo pants and snapped a picture of each of the pair. The popping of the flash made them back off a step in surprise.

The drummer frowned and withdrew his dagger. Fig pointed to the camera with his free hand and indicated with an upraised palm for the native to stop. For a minute, no one moved. Then with a flourish, he pulled the photo out and showed it to the shaman.

The medicine man's eyes widened as he saw his image take shape on the exposed film. Fig glowered in what he hoped looked devilish and indicated he was going to toss the picture into the fire.

"Eÿelemek ruh — Capture soul," Fig said. *"Yu olmek* — You die."

The shaman bolted immediately. Fig pointed to the drummer. The taller native hesitated for a moment and then ran off as well.

Fig hurried to where Lilith stood captive and freed her from her bonds. He inhaled satisfaction for what he had accomplished, but then halted in midbreath. He had not thought all the way through what to do next. He was lame, and so was the succubus. The respite was too short. Soon, the other natives would return when they did not discover any more demons and …

Lilith twisted Fig around and secured him in her grip.

"Wait," he said. "If you cannot fly—"

"One wing is good enough to provide us with some push. Raise your knees to your chest and grasp them tightly. I can skim rapidly along the ground. They will not be able to keep up. My wing will take a short while to heal completely. I rapidly repair."

Lilith flapped her good wing. It threw Fig off balance to the side, but the demon managed not to stumble.

"We have been together for many of your days," she said. "I told you my name on my very first visit. Now, I would like to know yours."

"Figar … Wait a minute. You're not starting the 'dominance or submission' game, are you? Can't we at least wait until we are somewhere safe?"

"It is not for that." Lilith frowned.

"Then for what?"

"I … I want to thank you for saving my life. I hatched over six thousands of your years ago, but no being has ever done this for me before."

"Is that true?" Fig asked. "You tell me this on your honor?"

"I am not sure what that means, but, yes, my words are spoken truly."

"Okay, I guess," Fig said. The adrenaline had run its course. He felt too tired to ponder the matter any deeper. "My name is Figaro Newton. You can call me Fig."

"Then, I thank you, Fig."

Fig's thoughts brightened. He had been successful after all. They would be able to return to Hilo unscathed. He basked in the feeling for a moment. But then, like a bird brought down from a hunter's blind, his feelings fell back to where they were before. Going to Hilo was not the goal.

"We can't leave. I have to find where Briana has been hidden."

"She is not here. I had enough time to test for Angela's smell while they debated on the best way to have me killed."

"But this is the last possibility. The very last." Fig felt the frustration he had managed to suppress for the last week escape to poison his thoughts. "We will have to start again from the very first. Somehow, for one of the targets, I have made a mistake."

"No mistake. You do careful work, Fig. I have watched you."

"But we have searched everywhere!" Fig shouted out. He could keep his voice quiet no longer. Briana. He was failing her when she needed him the most.

"Yes, we have, indeed. We *have* searched everywhere, but not *everywhen*."

"Everywhen? What do you mean?"

"We succubi can travel into the past," Lilith said. "If Angela has not hidden your Briana here in the present, then she must have done so somewhere else in time."

55

13

More Places to Look

AFTER THE better part of an hour, Lilith stopped running. The surroundings were very much the same as they had been around the campfire. A flat plane in every direction. Occasional outcrops scattered about like blemishes on smooth skin. She released Fig, and he looked back the way they had come. No Turkmen in sight. They were not being pursued.

"My wing will only take a few hours to heal." Lilith flapped it back and forth. "There is nothing else for us to do here." She cocked her head to the side. "So, do you want to start the struggle between us here, or first, I fly you home?"

"We have not found Briana yet." Fig protested.

"Yes. We have established that, here in the present, Briana is nowhere on Earth. The conclusion is inescapable. My sister has taken her into the past."

Fig goggled. He had seen a demon from another realm. Even flown with one, half way around the world with one. As hard as it was to be believed, Lilith's existence could not be denied. But what she was telling him now …

"But how?"

"We sense not only the fires burning now but also those having flamed before."

"You are talking in riddles."

"I also see the fires from a month ago that already have flickered out. And not only recent ones. I see those for the entire year gone past as well. Two years, ten, a hundred. Even farther and farther back. The more ancient, of course, the dimmer they appear to me. Until the most remote fade to nothingness at the beginning of time. But, like every one of my kind, I detect them all, even so."

"So, you step into a fire here and emerge through one in the past?"

"Not quite. We go from the first flame back to our realm. Then select another flame in the past into which to emerge. The greater the jump, the more the effort required, but yes, that is what I can do."

Fig considered for only a moment. The burden on his shoulders lightened. "Let's get going. Where, I mean when should we search first?"

"No, Fig. Such a task is impossible. There is no point even to start. We have no idea to when Briana was taken. The past is too vast. Too many choices. We are done."

"We have agreed," Fig thundered. "Briana returns home first. I did not save you from death so you could merely walk away."

"I repaid that debt when I carried you across a desert."

Fig thought furiously. It could not end this way. It just couldn't. He had to push as hard as he dared. "Angela is the key," he said. "She had admitted to you she was Briana's abductor. Engage her again. Learn the location of her hiding place. This time, when as well as where."

Lilith did not immediately answer. "Fig, you are most bold. I give you that. But I have no time left to spare for your quest. The search so far has consumed more than I first imagined. There are other things back in my realm to which I must attend."

Fig scowled. "Yes, yes. I suppose we all have our To Do lists. Why not demons as well? But is anything on yours so very important that you toss aside an agreement made in good faith?" He rushed on before Lilith could reply. "I warned you before about the impact of breaking your word. It damages your feeling of self-worth. Remember? So let's go ahead and battle right now. Right here, as you suggest."

Lilith opened her mouth to rebut but then shut it again. She hesitated. "I did not envision it to be like this."

"We are judged by our deeds, not our words." Fig's voice rang with steel. He might be able to pull this off. He set his jaw, and, unblinking, stared into the succubus' eyes.

Lilith flexed her wing and grimaced. "All right, I agree. Now is not the time for our duel. I am tired, and first I must heal."

"And then?"

"After I am whole, I will take you home. Then, return to my realm. Seek out my sister a second time." Lilith pointed a finger at Fig and waved it back and forth. "But understand that I may learn nothing more. And if not, then, indeed, your quest will be over. Entirely over. And my feeling of self-worth, as you call it, will be perfectly fine."

FIG STOOD in front of the locked doors of the Hilo nursery and looked from side to side to verify no one was watching. The journey home from halfway around the world took some time, even for a demon. What he had returned to was little better than Turkmenistan. Maxed out credit cards and no cash left at all. Somehow he had gotten through the day on what was left of the box of cornflakes in the warehouse pantry. There had been no milk, but he had managed to get it all down. At least, his ankle was getting better.

He thrust the lockpick into the keyway. Inserted the torque wrench into the space remaining below. Despite himself, he smiled a bit. How many movies and TV shows had the hero or heroine thrust a single tool into the vertical slit and wiggled it a bit. Then, almost as if by magic, the lock opened. Almost as if by magic. Yeah, right, Fig thought. It had nothing to do with magic at all.

He concentrated as he raised the tumblers one by one. A grunt of satisfaction marked each successful positioning to its correct height. Finally, when the fifth and last was placed, the keyway turned.

Fig pushed the door open, poked his head in and listened. Silence. No dog trotted forward to challenge his entrance.

He strode through the interior and onto the vast, open garden in back. Largest in Hilo, the website had bragged. 'Come here for exotic plants.' This probably was where Briana had found her juniper, the special kind only succubi used. He hoped so. Without light, Fig could see only dim row after row of shrubs stretching into the darkness. This was going to take some time unless …

He recalled the memory of his first encounter with Lilith, drawing her forth from the flame. That wizardry came out okay, didn't it? And thaumaturgy—far less risky than dealing with the realm of demons. He did not like exercising any of the five crafts, but events were compelling him forward. Reaching into a pocket, he removed the incantation Briana had given him as 'homework' some time ago.

'Once together, always together—the Principle of Contagion,' she had explained. The rag rubbed against an undesired wart maintained the connection. And after the cloth was buried and rotted away, so also would the wart disappear. 'Like produces like.'

Fig withdrew from another pocket the juniper sprig he had brought with him. He waved it back and forth, listening for an answering sound. Space was a premium everywhere and especially in a nursery like this with a huge inventory. The juniper shrubs were crammed so close together. Their branches intermingled and touching one another.

Silence.

Of course, he thought. He hadn't spoken the incantation yet. Without that, nothing happens. Stumbling over the words of a language entirely foreign on Earth, Fig managed to get to the end. He waved the sprig and listened.

There, off to the left. Soft, like the rustle of silk petticoats, and very faint. But a sound even so. Fig walked toward it, continuing to wave the sprig, each step drawing him closer. Five minutes later, he had located the correct row. The scribbled sign at the end stated 'Junipers.' He clicked on his phone light, deciding it was worth the risk. His presence illuminated only for a little while longer, each step quicker than the last.

Fig reached the end of the row and realized he had overshot. He reversed himself and with more care continued the search. Finally, he stood midway down the length and verified that the sound was fainter a few steps to either side. The shrubs before him were junipers all right, but not of the variety he sought. Holding his phone in one hand, Fig pushed aside the branches in front and peered deeper into the foliage.

There, in the back, behind the others. A tiny potted juniper with scaly leaves. Too small itself, but no matter. He would harvest more branches from cousins nearby. Fig swung his light back and forth to illuminate neighboring plants.

His shoulders slumped. There were no more scaly leaved junipers. Only the one tiny planting, he held in his hand. Briana must have purchased all the rest. Maybe smaller nurseries might have more. But starting another search rose up in his mind like an unclimbable mountain barring his way.

He had measured how much fuel remained in the lab before he had started. That result had only added to his concerns.

"One or two more trips are all that is left," he said aloud to himself. "Lilith had better find out exactly how to direct where they should go."

14

United We Stand

LILITH SCOWLED with frustration. As usual, like a great cloak, the darkness of the demon realm hung heavily upon her. The tracking of a single human female could wait a few hours more on Earth, even days, she told herself. The time of rutting for the dribbler males was now. If she did not act, she would have to wait for an entire great cycle for them to return.

She looked at the line of female dribblers standing in a ragged row on the edge of the broodnest. They were small as Earthly flies. Bony arms hung from caved in torsos. Thin fingers with needle-like nails stabbed the air. Grotesque bumps covered out of proportion heads. Vibrating wings created annoying whines.

The total area of the lair was tiny. More than a score could be placed on the featureless surface of Lilith and Angela's own. But they were much more sculptured and decorated. Almost as elaborate as the palaces of the princes who fought one another over who ruled the realm. Splashes of color everywhere with no pattern or logic. Shallow pits in which the eggs were laid. Small staircases, three steps high leading to gentle slides nearby. Trinkets from other worlds scattered about for the newly hatched to explore.

Lilith strained to remain focused, but it was hard to do. Two challenges at once were difficult to manage. She should not have taken on the second. Getting all the males to agree to some measure of equality was more important. But it beat the alternative of having none. Having none was the first step down the road to the great monotony.

"Remain in the formation," Lilith said, for the dozenth time. She wished she had some sort of noisemaker to draw everyone's attention. Of all the smaller imps, everyone knew the dribblers have the dimmest wits. After all, was there any real point to hanging out in the hearths of dimly lit human bars? Darting forth to pierce the side of a shot glass before a drunkard brought it to his lips? Funny the first time it happened. But nothing worthy of the attention of demonkind. On Earth, one even could buy a 'dribble glass' that worked as well. No help from buzzing imps needed.

Experimenting with the dribblers was a necessary step, Lilith told herself. Locking arms and staring down djinns without some dry runs was a folly. First, see how tiny males behaved when faced with a united front. First, dribblers, then gremlins, rockbubblers and the rest.

Finally, when the kinks were smoothed, a mass protest at the gates of the lairs of the princes. Respect, courtship, a say in decision making. The customs of the realm of humankind no longer regarded as quaint. Instead, they would be integrated into the very fabric of all demonkind. And finally, dare she think it, not at first, of course, but total equality with the males. A fitting final tribute to her sister, Delilah, who was no longer here.

Like a drill sergeant, Lilith surveyed the preparations one last time. The dribbler males were due any moment. Another advantage of trying them first was the herd instinct. Following the lead of the boldest, no matter how foolish it might first seem.

"Here they come, girls," one of the dribbler females called out. "Garish face paint like always. I wonder which I should respond to." The little demon paused and looked at Lilith. "Oops! That's not part of it, right? We are supposed to deny them, not get them more aroused."

"As I have explained from the start." Lilith sighed. "No, that is *not* correct. The males set the schedule of their appearances. You have no say about it at all."

"But look at the nesting pits. There are so many empty ones there this time. More of us standing here in this silly line than the number of males who will come. In the end, some of us will have to wait until the next fertility cycle."

Before Lilith could reply, the swarm of male dribblers swooped down onto the broodnest. "What is going on here?" the first to alight said.

"Why is a succubus hovering around?" the second's brow crinkled in thought for a moment. "Disgusting!" he spat out. "Are you here to *watch?*"

"Here, big boy" one of the females cried out. "Let's get this over with."

"Roundheels," the male leader replied. "Ah, well, it is that time again, and you will do as good as any other."

"Tulipbulb, don't call me that!" Roundheels said. The whine of her wings rose a full octave. "My name is 'Wispy Willow.' You know better. It is the name given to me by my mother. Not the slang chosen by others

61

like you."

"And I'm not a frigging flower, either," Tulipbulb thumped his tiny chest. "Impwart! Why do we have to go through this every time? We come. We do our thing, and we leave. Honestly, if you had not called out, I would not be able to tell you from any other."

"This time is different," Lilith interrupted. "Tell them, Wispy Willow."

Wispy Willow puffed out her chest. "Well," she said. "The other girls and I have been thinking about things and ..." She glanced up at Lilith. The succubus nodded and smiled back with encouragement.

"Yeah, thinking about things, and we have decided we do not get any respect. I mean you guys fly in here expecting to get to it right away. No small talk, no 'How was your day?'" She looked at Lilith again and took a deep breath before continuing.

"What are you talking about?" Tulipbulb said. "You enjoy it too, don't you?"

"Yes, but ..." Wispy Willow threw up her hands. "I can't explain it. You do it ... with the big words."

Lilith stared at Tulipbulb. "It is quite simple. Starting now, you don't do anything with the females without their consent. And you can't pick and choose. See them lined up here. They are united in this."

"Shove off, lady," Tulipbulb said. "This is dribbler business. None of your concern."

"I am not leaving." Lilith unfurled her wings and looked as menacing as she could. "I stand with all the females throughout the realm, regardless of what our kind happens to be."

Tulipbulb looked at the succubus' stern face and shrugged. "Okay, then," he said. "The guys and I will come back some other time after you are gone."

"No, wait," Wispy Willow said. "That will be too long."

"Which is it?" Tulipbulb said. "Look, Round ... Wispy Willow, I mean ..."

"Yes, Tulip ... Wait, what name do you like to use, anyway?"

"I am 'Galactic Overlord,'" Tulipbulb said. His scowl morphed into a smile.

Wispy Willow tittered and battered her eyes as best she could. But the warts on her lids kept getting in the way. She sat down on the slab and patted a spot beside her. "Come sit a while. I want to hear more."

"Okay, you'll do," Tulipbulb said as he lit.

The other female dribblers saw what was happening, and the line dissolved. They spread out along the broodnest length and indicated spots beside them. A babble of voices competed for attention. "Your name. Tell me your true name." In a flash, the males swarmed to accept the invitations.

"No, wait," Lilith cried out. Like a referee calling a play dead, she waved her extended arms palms down across her chest "We want more than that. We have to be strong."

The small imps, male and female both, ignored her. The trial was over.

Was she wrong about this? Lilith wondered. Were the dribbler males actually that bad? Perhaps not. They did not behave as did the great djinns. Had she and her sisters attempted such a protest, their flesh and ichor would become a fine haze polluting the vastness of the realm.

So now what? Return to her lair and think about what to try next? No, there was the beginner wizard. That obligation still to be filled. A distraction at best. Her time could be much better spent on how to improve her tactics here.

And yet. And yet, distraction was not quite the right description. Fig, more so than any other human with which she had dealt, focused on his end goal unwavering. Something she could emulate here in her own realm. And, too, there was the thrill of the chase. Against all odds, might this Briana actually be found? And she had to admit. Fig was … interesting.

WHEN LILITH approached her lair, Angela was there. She reclined in sleep. Not good. Rousing her some two thousand years ago remained a vivid memory: snarling bared teeth, claws coiled forward ready to fight, daring her to engage.

Lilith flew closer to examine the slumbering form. Angela lay on her side, still wearing the ruff around her neck and the little bag on her uppermost hip. Why did her sister carry those things about her all the time? Each transfer of inert matter through the flame took effort — the more the mass, the more the strain.

Lilith hovered closer to get a better look. The ruff looked quite ordinary, crimped rather than pleated. But even so, only a wide collar undulating up and down around her neck. The purse, if that what it was, sported embroidered flowers, a simple clasp, and …

Lilith looked closer. The top layer of material did not lie flat. It bulged slightly. Something inside. She studied Angela's breathing. Her sister was in a deep sleep, dreaming who knew what.

With her hand as steady as she could hold it, she placed her palm lightly onto the bag. Angela stirred, threatening to turn to the side.

Lilith withdrew her arm and waited. After a moment, her sister settled again, but now most of the purse was hidden under her bulk.

She watched a few moments more and then decided. There was no other way about it. Although most of the purse was covered, the clasp still was barely visible. Using her fingers like scissors, Lilith grasped the loop surrounding the fastener and gently pulled. Enough of it came free that she could tug it over the button it had surrounded. Then, the flap itself was flipped. And finally, a small notebook dragged free, a cautious fraction at a time.

A 'whiteberry.' Lilith had heard of such things in the realm of humankind before but had never seen such a thing.

Lilith riffled the pages. Most of them were blank. Writing was only on the very first. She scanned it and saw a list of names, places, and dates. The very topmost had a check mark next to it.

She smiled in triumph. The name meant nothing to her, but the rest looked important. A where *and* a when. 'Paris. Fall. 1793.'

Fig was a smart enough lad. He would understand the significance of what the entry meant in the affairs of humans.

15

Flame Journey

FIG PACED back and forth in the deserted laboratory. He twirled a curl of his bleached hair that reached almost to his shoulders. Lilith stood in front of him while he pondered what she had found out.

"A list of times and places with the first item checked and nothing else?" he asked.

Lilith nodded.

Fig lifted his chin from his chest. "I have been thinking. What you claim is a clear violation of the laws of physics. How can it possibly be true?"

"The laws of physics." Lilith put her hands on her hips like an orator before a large crowd. "The sacred human laws of physics. What is it they say about the existence of a realm of demons and beings like myself?"

Fig stopped pacing and frowned. He was silent for a long while. "Okay, I guess I must accept the possibility," he finally said. "If I accept one set of fantastic anomalies, I cannot merely deny another out of hand." He eyed Lilith curiously. "So you can travel through time. Go to any when you want."

"Only to the past and back, not the future," Lilith replied. "And to each segment only once. We cannot return for a second visit to any time when we have already been."

"That doesn't make any sense at all. Are these restraints something to do with this so-called Tyrant of Time?"

"No, he has nothing to do with it." Lilith shrugged.

"Other demons can do this, too?"

"Nope, it is merely part of being a succubus. No other type can."

Fig resumed his pacing, but this time only for one small circle around the room.

"Okay, let's do it," he said.

Lilith cocked her head to the side. "Well, I must admit, I have never done anything quite like this before. Carrying another being on a journey through time. The past cannot be reached merely by flying through the air. Instead, there are two legs. First from here to my realm, then from there to another juniper fire at the final destination. The air is too thin for puny beings such as yourself where I have my home. But if you take a deep enough breath and hold it, you might be able to stand being there for a short while."

"Hold my breath?" A sudden twinge of doubt engulfed Fig. It was as if he were sinking into quicksand. First, summon a demon — repeatedly. Then fly about with one for several days. And now, visit another realm and another time …

But like a bowling ball rolling down a gutter, the progression of logic always ended up in the same slot. He had to continue until Briana was home.

"Okay," he said. "Let me run a quick calibration check on the artificial nose, and we can be ready to go."

Lilith frowned. "Too much inert matter. Your electronics. The phone. Who knows whatever else you have stashed in your pants of many pockets. I cannot carry all that through the fire."

"But the total for everything is much less than what I weigh by myself. How can the rest — "

"Inert matter is the problem. You are a thinking being. One who is alive. Your resistance is tiny; that of other things is large."

Fig frowned. "I don't like this. Without instruments …"

Lilith did not reply. He thought a moment and decided. "Okay," he said. "But at the very least, I should go to the library, Check out a book on French history. Understand the times."

"Well, one book. But if you want to take along the hijab, abaya, and bungee cords, you will have to leave behind your clothes."

"My clothes?"

"Yes, best if you are naked." Lilith grinned. "And facing me rather than looking where we are going."

Fig stepped back, the beginning of a blush coloring his cheeks. He pondered for a moment. "How about if I only strip to my skivvies … and face outward?"

"I can manage," Lilith sighed. "But it will take more of my energy reserves."

"Agreed," Fig said. Now that he had decided, it was time to get on with it. "I will come back from the library shortly."

66

WHEN FIG returned with a book, he shed most of his clothes and rolled up Lilith's garments into a tidy ball. Soon, with the demon's strong grip holding him to her chest, he watched wide-eyed as the pair stepped into the fire.

At first, Fig felt an intense upward rush of blistering heat. He cried out in anticipation of certain pain. But as swiftly as the feeling had overwhelmed him, it vanished. Instead, he felt as if he were falling down an elevator shaft, his speed increasing with each beat of his heart. He saw nothing of color, only blacks, whites, and greys filling the space around him, indistinct streaks speeding by, each one more rapid than the last.

His stomach lurched, and he slammed his eyes shut, trying to blank out everything he saw. The speed terrified him. Something must have gone wrong. Lilith was out of control. They were going to crash headlong into some barrier, shattering them both into pulp.

His other senses went haywire as well. Cacophonous shrieks blasted his ears. They rose higher and higher in pitch, and then rapidly faded to muddy inaudibility. He smelled and tasted bitter fruits he could not spit out of his mouth. An itch between his shoulder blades pulsed where he could not reach.

But when he could bear it no longer, the rush of heat returned. Lilith stepped out of another fire.

Fig collapsed to his knees. Before they left, he had consumed the last of the corn flakes and a can of pickled beets. He retched in heaving spasms until he could expel nothing more. His arms gave way, and his face slammed onto packed dirt.

"I got as close to Paris as I was able," Lilith said, standing over him. "Too little time to investigate all the possibilities when we were in my realm. It took most of my concentration to get the year right."

It was only minutes after dawn. They stood in the shadows of a narrow alley. Fig staggered to his feet and wiped the remains of his breakfast from his chin. He gasped for breath and tasted its difference as he inhaled, salt air and a fishy smell.

Fig looked about. The alley opened onto a wide boulevard. A little distance to the right stood dozens of small stalls constructed haphazardly from rotting wood and discarded planks. Noisy vendors shouted from each, touting their wares at busy buyers. Merchants bargained for the best deals from the catch of the day.

And despite the haggling, to Fig's ears, the scene was quiet. There were no rushing cars, horns, and rumbling busses. So busy with the trading, no one noticed the pair of them at all.

Behind them were the calm waters of a long, narrow harbor. It extended more than a mile before surrendering to more violent waves of the open sea. Anchored along both sides of the port were small boats. Farther away, larger and larger ships. In the distance, Fig saw the tall masts of frigates rocking in the gentle pulse of an incoming tide. From the tallest, national flags flapped vigorously in the breeze. Mostly, the French tricolor and a few of the Dutch. One ship, with eighteen cannons poking through its gun ports, flew the Union Jack.

A memory from when Fig was younger bubbled into focus. A frigate with thirty-six guns and British. The number the *Lydia* had carried in the stories he had read. He squinted at the flag, and it did not look quite right: something odd about it. He thought for a moment and remembered. The diagonal red stripes were not added until 1801. Lilith had done it! The undeniable truth slammed into him. He had been transported into the past.

As he looked about again, his sense of wonder retreated before a growing concern. One lurking in his subconscious until it could no longer be ignored. He was in the past and would be moving about. Interacting with others, breathing the air. Disturbing the very ground on which he trod.

What would that do to the future — his own present? Would one of the horror stories come true? The butterfly effect. The insect crushed under the time traveler's boot. From a simple action, other changes multiplied and grew. The future changed in a way no one could predict.

"How careful do we have to be?" Fig asked. "So the future is not changed."

"For what we want to do, there should be no problem," Lilith said. "Briana does not belong here. Neither do you."

Fig took a deep breath. Lilith did not seem bothered. Surely, she would have given him instruction on how to act if there were a possible problem. Somehow, his — and Briana's — presences here would have no effect.

His thoughts snapped back to the problem at hand. "Lilith, you will pass without too much notice wearing the gear we have brought. I need something like …" He pointed at a workman in shabby but clean clothes shuffling from the market and back up the boulevard. A road marker stood nearby proclaimed '*Le Canebière.*'

Lilith nodded and donned the hijab and hood. Fig pulled the large garment over her wings and tugged the opening closed with two bungee cords. Peeking out onto the thoroughfare, he watched the workman turn into the next alleyway.

Fig rose to pursue, but before he had taken a single step, a restraining hand tugged on his shoulder. "Now what?" he asked.

"I will take care of it," Lilith said and stepped out to follow the man into the alley.

Fig waited for no more than five minutes. When Lilith returned, she carried a shirt and pair of trousers over her arm.

"He said there were a few coppers in one of his pockets. Enough for you to get a meal."

"How did you manag …" His voice trailed off. "Oh, of course. That is what you do."

"Yes. And I am quite good at it. When this silliness is over, you are going to find out how good I am."

16

The Peril of Traveling Too Far from Home

LIKE A row of sleeping babies in a nursery, the line of ships at rest in the long, narrow harbor rose and fell with the waves. Fig studied the buildings lining the *Canebière*. Most were two or three stories with façades of stone. But intermingled with the rest were single level structures made of wood. Even from a distance, he could hear loud voices shouting to be heard over one another.

"A tavern," he said. He pulled the coins out of his pocket and patted his stomach. "The next thing to do is to see if I can keep the local fare down. You can stay here in the alley. I will not be long."

Without waiting for an answer, Fig jogged to the tavern and entered. A quarter hour later, he returned, clutching his midsection. In the alley, he again emptied his stomach. "Too rich, too foreign, to rotten" he gasped.

"Then what is there to do?" Lilith asked.

"We need coins of gold, not copper." Fig straightened, breathing deeply. "I saw some other food being served in the tavern I can stomach. Fish from this morning's catch, simply prepared. What looked like a well-to-do merchant had one served to him. He dressed much more finely than any of the others …"

Fig broke off and pointed. "There he is, coming out of the place and heading uphill. Do what you do with him … and then empty the sack at his waist."

"I am not a glutton," Lilith said. "Once in a while is often enough. I do not relish this becoming our standard mode of operation."

"Won't be. I promise. Come on. Let's follow him and see where he goes."

A SHORT while later, Fig and Lilith crouched around the corner from a dwelling on a side street. The merchant, if that was what he was, directed the efforts of several men. They sweated in the morning sun even though the air carried the briskness of fall.

Snow harvested from the Alps melted in a nearby shed. Two laborers shoveled what remained onto the bed of a two-wheeled cart. Rough-hewn side-planks kept the icy crystals from spilling out onto the ground. Three more men appeared, hunched over by large sacks of freshly caught fish.

One by one, they emptied their loads onto the snow. The last halibut flapped for air as it landed on top of the rest of the cargo. A canvas was pulled tight over the entire load. The vender strode to the cart, pushed down on the covering and measured its height from the ground. He scowled and yelled his disappointment at the workers. One of them showed both palms and shrugged his shoulders. The others stood silent. Finally, the merchant reached into his purse, paid and dismissed each of the laborers. He kicked open the door into his house.

Fig crept to a window and peered through a crack in drawn curtains. He saw a room with a small table, chairs, a couch and little else. The tradesman entered through an opening in the far wall, sat down on one of the chairs and bellowed. A boy in his teens scurried in from the hall to take his coat and unlace his boots.

When the servant finished, the merchant yelled something more. He banged the boy to the ground. Something the lad had done, or the way he had done it had not been carried out in an approved fashion. Crawling on his knees, the boy vanished back through the hall.

The vender called out a second time, and an older woman appeared, standing in the hall arch. The man motioned with his hand, demanding the lad's return. The woman shook her head, speaking in French. Other than repeated *Monsieur Dubois, si vous veuillez*. Fig did not understand what was said.

Dubois roared even louder, insistent his command be obeyed. Fig saw the woman try to smile, but that was not enough. The merchant rose and pulled her into the room. He grabbed her roughly by her shoulders, shaking her head back and forth. Fig heard a loud crack. The woman's eyes widened for an instant in surprise and then rolled back up into her head. Like a sack of flour, her arms slumped to her sides.

"No!" The servant boy rushed back in. Without looking, Dubois flung the lad to the floor with one hand. He slapped the face of the trapped woman with the other. She did not respond. He slapped her again. And then two times more.

71

Outrage boiled up within Fig. None of his business, but the man was a brute. He should not be doing this. Without thinking, Fig raced around to the open door and burst into the house. He was in what must be the kitchen. There hanging on pegs on the wall were several cooking knives. He grabbed one and entered the other room.

Fig motioned with the blade for Dubois to move away from the woman and boy. He had not been very successful with any of Briana's training before. But perhaps the merchant did not have any fighting skill either.

The tradesman recovered from his shock. He dropped the woman to the ground. A grin like that of a wolf with cornered prey spread from ear to ear. He drew away from the table, pulled a dagger from his belt and sliced it through the air.

Okay, maybe a trained opponent, after all, Fig thought. Now what? He tried to don a confident face, but that only served to deepen Dubois' smile. The merchant feinted to the left, and Fig twisted his body away from the thrust. Almost as an afterthought, he extended his blade.

The merchant pressed forward, and after a few feints more, Fig stood with his back to the wall. His heel banged into its unyielding base. He lost his footing and tumbled to the ground. In a flash, he was looking up at Dubois towering over him. The vender stooped, taunting with his dagger in front of Fig, ready to thrust it home.

Fig shut his eyes, trying to deny what was going to happen. But then he heard a dull thud, and the weight of the tradesman crashed down on top of him. Fig's eyes blinked open. The dagger lay on the ground, a mere inch from his arm. And standing next to it, the serving boy clutching a large skillet with both of his hands.

Fig pushed Dubois aside and scrambled to his feet. "Thank you! Thank you!" he spouted.

"You are welcome, *Monsieur*. You have saved my mother, and I had to repay."

"You speak English!"

"*Oui, Monsieur*. Sometimes my master sells to the British ships docking here for supplies. He needs me to translate during the bargaining. I am named Theo, and am quite fluent with your language."

"And your mother?"

" Yes, my *Mama*." Theo handed Fig the skillet and ran to his mother's side. "*Mama, Mama…*"

The rest of the words, Fig could not follow, but the intent was clear enough. After several minutes, Theo broke into tears as he cradled his mother's face in his hands. He looked back at Fig, not hiding any of his grief. "She is gone. The shock was too much. It was going to happen sooner or later. I knew that. Her heart was so frail. The master was always so very rough."

Fig staggered. Theo's mother was dead! The rush of adrenaline evaporated like morning fog. The nausea thundered back. This was not playtime. Was he the one responsible for what had happened?

"Why did you put up with it?" He looked at Theo and grasped at the first thought that came to him, trying to make sense of it all.

"My mother did so only because of me. We have nowhere else to go." Theo looked down at Dubois and shuddered. "Now it will be me alone who has to answer to his every — "

"I don't think you will have to worry about this one," Lilith interrupted.

Fig spun around to see that in the confusion the demon had entered the room.

"In my experience, sometimes with the older ones, the strain is too much for the heart." She shrugged. "And it stops."

Fig's knees buckled. Not one death, but two. He was not a mere tourist lightly treading the past. His footprints were like those of a giant trampling wherever he stepped.

Theo's eyes widened. "You have wings! Who … what are you?" The boy shied away from Lilith and pressed his back to the wall. He shut his eyes and crossed himself, even as tears continued to flow like undammed rivers from his eyes.

"She is with me," Fig said. "From … from far away. Don't concern yourself about her. Everything is going to be …" He looked at Theo's mother. "Well, at least, now you are free."

"But what have I done?" Fig looked at Lilith and frowned. "Certainly, the past has been changed."

"I doubt it," Lilith disagreed. "Nothing that happened here would ever be recorded in history. The big events will remain the same."

"Free?" Theo interrupted. "No, don't you see? The horse for the cart will be delivered within the hour. It is becoming as bad as Paris here. I will be charged with the crimes. Last week I became sixteen. An adult. My life will be lost."

"Where is *here*?" Lilith asked.

Theo's eyes darted back and forth from Lilith and the body of the merchant. His face tightened with the strain of what to do.

"Marseille," the boy finally said.

"We came here only to get some gold so I could eat," Fig protested. "There was no intent to — "

"And that will be easy to accomplish." Lilith kicked at Dubois' body. "We know where we are now. A flight of a few hours will get us to where we want to be."

Fig's thoughts spun back to what was important. He nodded to himself. Of course, garner enough coin for a few meals in the time ahead. He could be off, soaring through the sky, back on the trail of why he had come. Any time wasted is a mistake.

He studied Theo's anguish for a moment. Like a distant mountain being covered by afternoon haze, his steadfastness softened. What would happen to the lad? "You say you have nowhere else to go. Maybe another city?"

"I have never met her, but *Mama* says I have an aunt in Paris. If anything were to happen to her, I was to try to go there … although that was a plan not thought out in detail. It is more than a fortnight by foot, and there are dangers along the way. I would not survive such a trip by myself."

Without pondering, a new thought flashed into Fig's mind. "Come with us," he said.

Theo eyed Lilith and shuddered. "I have no other choice," he said. "But I will stay as far as possible from her."

Fig pushed aside the curtains and studied the cart of fish waiting outside. He turned his attention back to Lilith. "Remember how you were able to carry me away from the pursuit in Turkmenistan?" he asked.

"I cannot carry two of you on foot," Lilith scowled.

"But you could pull the cart," Fig rebutted. "We dump most of the fish, and Theo and I climb aboard." He walked back into the kitchen and surveyed the cooking ware hung on the walls. "We could even manage to carry a few things that might prove handy. Some pots and pans, recipes, spices, pen and ink. … Oh, yes, the merchant's gold. He must have it hidden here. Theo, do you know where?"

Lilith bared her fangs. "A loaded cart pulled by a demon will cause too much attention."

"Even if the two of us flew, we would have to wait for nightfall anyway," Fig said. "And there's nothing we can do in Paris until daybreak. Yes, on foot it will take the entire night for the travel, but the result is the same. When it is dark, no one will be about.

"Go to the stables," he told Theo. Tell them to come tomorrow, not today."

A ray of hope swept onto Theo's features. "Yes, I will say the catch was bad today."

"Your quickness of thought sometimes is not appealing," Lilith grumbled. She cocked her head to the side and considered for a few moments. "Very well," she said at last. "Tonight I will become your beast of burden. But it will be for only this one time."

"Great!" Fig said. He had convinced himself as well. "Not *all* of the halibut needs to go to waste. Theo, when you return, can you use one to prepare a breakfast for me?"

"Every moment we tarry, the trail to Angela and your Briana grows a moment colder," Lilith said.

"Yes, yes, we must find Angela." Fig clutched his stomach. "But when that happens I will be of little use unless I first have had something to eat."

17

A Task for One Who is Faithful

IT WAS not quite dawn. Angela emerged from the flame, again wearing the white robe and halo. She carried Briana's inert form in her arms. The two women slept nearby, and the guard slumbered behind the screen. They looked the same as when she last saw them.

Angela lowered Briana to the floor and studied her one final time. The white dress was too short, but it would do. She had hacked the hair so that only a few curls peeked out from the borders of the cap. The slumber she had imposed was deep.

The succubus circled the bed to the other side and pulled back the covers. There, the occupant's gown and bedding were stained with blood, but that was to be expected. With a heave of one arm, Angela brought the woman to her feet. With her free hand, she tried smoothing back the covers over the stain. Rosalie stirred with the noise. The demon stopped pulling at the bedding and pointed to where Briana lay like a rag doll forgotten by a child.

Rosalie looked first at her lady's sagging form and then stood up to see what Angela indicated. Her eyes widened with understanding. As Angela pulled Rosalie's lady clear, the attendant finished smoothing the covers. She circled the bed and pulled up Briana to lie on top of them.

"There is one final thing," Angela whispered. "When you write of these events, there shall be no mention of the interventions of the Lord in the night."

"But the gown looks too short, the shorn hair."

"State that you, yourself, dressed and coifed in the morning. No one will ever know what really happened."

"But —"

"Remember the annual gifts of gold. Remember what will happen to you if you do not obey."

Rosalie nodded as Angela dragged her cargo back toward the flame. She carried the woman easily, but could not prevent her feet from tangling with the hem of the night dress. The woman opened her eyes and looked back at her bed, perplexed.

"Rosalie," she whispered, "Some assistance. Help the Lord fulfill his divine plan."

The attendant nodded and pulled the gown up to the knees. The woman closed her eyes and drifted off. Like a three-legged dog, the trio stumbled their way to the fire. As she stepped into the last flickers of flame, Angela exhaled with satisfaction. Secure the one she carried within a circle of skulls, and the preparation would be done. All that remained was to watch the spectacle unfold.

18

Paris

LILITH SUDDENLY stopped and stepped out of the jerry-rigged harness. The two-wheeled cart flipped backward. Fig and Theo tumbled to the ground. Angry thoughts flashed through Fig's mind, but he bit his tongue and said nothing.

They had made good time. Still several hours until daybreak, and they had reached the outskirts of Paris. Only sporadic candlelight illuminated the street they were on. Despite that, Fig was anxious to continue the search immediately.

"How many juniper fires do you sense?" Fig asked.

"Several hundred," Lilith replied. "Without the artificial nose, it will take more than one night to do a thorough search."

Fig pondered. He placed one fist under his chin. What was the best way to go about things? How could they be the most efficient?

"When the sun rises, we will need another meal," Theo said. "What does the demon from Hell eat?" He shuddered. "Not blood or human sacrifice, I hope."

Fig couldn't help shaking his head. He marveled at the boy's resilience. His mother killed. Journeying to an unfamiliar place in the company of what he considered a monster. Driven by desperation, having to find an unknown relative in an unfamiliar city … or else.

"Not blood or human sacrifice, I hope," Theo repeated.

Fig still did not answer. He had to focus on why they were here. What would make one fire stand out from all of the rest? What subset should they investigate first?

"Lilith, if you had to pick out the one blaze that was the most unusual, what would it be?"

"A juniper fire is a juniper fire," Lilith said. "You humans light them all over the … Well, there is *one* that seems out of place."

"Where?"

Puzzlement colored Lilith's words. "It is underground."

Fig reached into his waistband for the book he had convinced Lilith to bring into the past. Theo lit a match so he could better see the text. "Underground," he muttered as he flipped the pages.

"The catacombs!" he cried after only a moment. "Paris is honeycombed with them. Abandoned stone quarries converted into a huge ossuary. A perfect place to hide. What about it, Lilith? Is that a logical place for Angela to choose?"

"I am not my sister's keeper," Lilith groused. "I seldom can fathom the workings of her mind."

"I'll take that as a yes," Fig said. "Come on. According to the map in the book, there is an entrance at what was called the *Barrière d'Enfe — The Gateway to Hell.*"

"That was back in Turkmenistan and in the present," Lilith growled. She raised her palm in the manner of a traffic policeman. "A moment. There is a reason why I stopped."

"Yes?"

"I realize that an aura of invincibility is important to maintain. But …"

"But what?"

"Think of it, human. For several days almost nonstop, I have carried you over the globe at great speeds. On foot, I saved us from the pursuit of the Turkmen. And now, I have lugged not one but two of you on an old, creaky cart nearly the entire length of France."

Fig frowned, puzzled. Lilith was complaining? She had never done so before.

"It is almost as if we have already tested our wills against one another," Lilith said. "And you were the victor. That has never been my intent."

Fig stiffened. He had been awake during the entire bone-shaking journey in the night, but he could not let that show. This was not the time to struggle with a demon. Briana was yet to be saved. "Why then have you agreed to all I have asked of you?"

"We do have an agreement to postpone our struggle to later … and I must confess that this pursuit has an intoxicating element to it. Somehow without you overtly trying, I have become enamored by your determination."

"So, I do dominate you?"

"No! Never that! In the end, I will be the one who is the winner. It is

79

only that …"

"What?"

"The things we do that seem so effortless to you come at a cost. I am weary. I need to return to my realm and refresh."

Fig blinked. He had never considered such a thing. Could demons get tired? He asked. "How long will this take? You need food just as I do?"

"Two of your hours at most. No longer than that it to capture some of the smaller imps and make myself a meal. I will be back before dawn."

"Or we can listen for the whinny of horses," Theo said. "If Paris is anything like Marseille, there will be livery stables near all the main roads. Transport for hire."

"Horses?"

"Riding in a cart will be much easier than relying on our feet. I can manage the steeds. I have done this so many times back in Marseille."

FIG AND Theo peered at the steps receding downward into the darkness of the catacombs. The candles they held did not illuminate where they ended. Their tumbril, now outfitted with a team of two stood tethered nearby. Theo had been right. Even with the time it took to find a stable and harness up, they still made better time than they would have on foot.

"More than a hundred steps to get down there," Fig said. He looked at Theo and considered. "Perhaps it would be better if I got you to your aunt first. You said she lives on one of the streets we passed?"

"Yes, *Rue Daguerre*. But it is still not light. I would rather stay with you and deal with my aunt's surprise after daybreak."

Fig frowned. He did not like the answer. The boy was a responsibility on his shoulders, and he rather be rid of it as soon as he could. But Briana was the most important, he finally decided. All his actions should be directed toward saving her first. "Okay then. Here we go," he finally said.

They descended the stairs. With each step the air grew damper, as wet and cold as a colossal cave. At the bottom, a rough gravel-strewn floor in a narrow passageway beckoned them forward. Their footsteps crunched on the pebbles. Soon, a larger tunnel loomed leading away on both sides.

Fig picked one of the choices at random. He regretted they did not have any breadcrumbs to mark their trail. But since they did not, he shrugged, and they raced onward. Their cupped hands barely kept their candle flames from blowing out as they ran. A side passage opened on the left. Fig extended his taper to illuminate its interior. Theo gasped. A few steps from where they stood the walls opened onto an alcove.

Directly in front, the rear wall was covered floor to ceiling with thousands of bones and hundreds of skulls. At the very bottom, four rows of femurs were placed end forward. The looked like stacked fire logs from impossibly white trees. Somehow, they formed an eerie but almost level shelf.

On the ledge, a single row of skulls stood temple to temple. They stared with vacant eye sockets and open mouths, shouting unheard ghostly chants. More skulls peeked out between their brethren in the first line, and above them were another half-dozen rows of femurs. Then another row of skulls and a dozen more of the bones. At the very top of the vault stood skulls facing the other way, only the crown of their heads showing.

The pair hastened to another alcove farther along the tunnel. It looked very much the same — skulls and more skulls, bones and more bones. After the original graveyards of Paris had been filled, six million graves were exhumed to make more room. The remains were redeposited here in the catacombs as macabre arrays in hundreds of alcoves.

"Let's backtrack before we get lost," Fig whispered. Speaking aloud seemed too inappropriate in a place like this. "It looks like it will take forever to search everywhere down here."

"But you said we would meet at the flame." Theo found his voice. "The devil gives me shivers, but down here, I would rather have her with us than apart."

Fig looked one more time into the alcove in which they were standing. "There must be a way," he muttered.

FIG STUDIED Theo standing rigidly beside him. The boy was visibly disturbed. He had not spoken another word after the two of them had begun the gruesome task — extracting a hundred skulls from the alcove wall without causing a cascade of bones. But now, that job was over. On to the next.

Alchemy. Executing any formula in the craft always carried risk. The outcome was never certain. By chance, powerful disruptive forces could be unleashed rather than what was anticipated. Fig did not like performing any of the crafts, but of them all, alchemy was the worst.

He pointed at Theo's knapsack. Wordlessly, the boy handed him the three halibut inside. Using one of the kitchen knives, Fig sliced the first open and smiled. A female. He was in luck. He cut out the egg sack, clasped it tightly in his fist and squeezed. The eggs and sac fluid oozed out between his fingers into one of the upturned skulls.

"Such a sticky mess." Theo frowned. "Something we usually throw away."

"Yes, sticky," Fig said. "The basis for making something even stickier still. 'The Doctrine of Signatures — The attributes without mirror the powers within.'" He surveyed his handiwork for a moment after all the skulls were prepared. "Now the mustard powder. Sprinkle it over the slime as I write the formula for the activation.

"Briana told me about this when she had taught me the basics of alchemy," he explained. "An easy enough formula to try for a beginner. Likely to succeed almost all the time."

After Fig had finished writing the arcane symbols, he stirred the powder and egg-sack fluid together. With a spoon, he ladled a small amount into each of the other upturned skulls and smeared it around.

Then, he gutted both the remaining fish, dicing their flesh into many small cubes. Finally, he placed each one next to an adjacent skull.

"Why are you doing all this?" Theo asked. His voice was tense. He fidgeted from foot to foot.

"Watch."

It took only a few minutes for the pair to see the first. A mangy rat scurried into their alcove from an adjacent one. It did not back off from the treat as Fig stooped nearby. While the rodent was busy eating, Fig scooped up the nearby skull and thrust it down onto the little beast.

Immediately, the rat tried to exit the enclosure, but the goo stuck fast to its fur. Fig tapped twice on the top of the cranium, and the rodent scurried away, propelling the skull surrounding it.

"He will return to his lair," Fig said. "All of them will — each to his own territory. At least I hope so. If we are lucky enough, we will get most of the catacombs explored." Without pause, he imprisoned the next rat and those coming after. Soon, a hundred skulls were slithering through the tunnels of the ancient quarry.

"I still don't understand," Theo said.

"Rather than only one search party — ourselves, all the ensnared rats are doing the work. And none of them has to worry about getting lost."

"But even if they find the fire you seek, we will be no wiser about where it is."

"I think we will. Patience. You will see."

AN HOUR passed, and then half of another. Fig tried to remain calm and still, but the urge to pace grew stronger and stronger with each passing moment. He kept glancing at his wrist to look at a watch that was not there. Theo appeared more composed, perhaps because his personal nightmare could soon be over.

Suddenly, the halls of the catacombs echoed a terrified scream. Even Briana would be scared by the sudden appearance of a skittering skull.

"Quickly," Fig said. "We will follow the sound. It will lead us to where we need to go."

The pair rose and entered the transverse tunnel. Another scream. This one from the right. There was little doubt about it. Fig began running. At last, he was going to save her, the one he loved.

Theo plunged after. At a cross tunnel, they halted for a moment, awaiting another scream. It came a moment later, to the left and down the side passage.

Three more screams, and Fig's lungs burned from the frigid air as he pulled to a sudden halt. In one of the alcoves. Success! There she stood — in a nightgown of all things. Surrounded by a ring of skulls at her feet. Her flaming red hair …

Wait. Something was not right. The hair color was pale, not deep. And the face … This was not Briana but someone else!

The woman spoke French. Fig did not comprehend any of it. He barely noticed Lilith entering the alcove out of the corner of his eye. Of course, the juniper flame guided her.

"What is she saying?" Fig demanded. "I do not understand a word … or anything else. Where is Briana?"

Belatedly, Theo began translating.

"I fell asleep guarded by men." She pointed at the skulls. "I wake up here trapped as surely. Save me. I am Marie Antoinette, the Queen of France."

19

The Imprisoned Queen

LILITH APPRAISED the Queen. Pale, anemically pale. Shallow cheeks. Bags under the eyes. White mixing with light reddish hair. Was this what Angela wanted? How did the one the Fig sought for so fervently fit into this? With a question on her face, Lilith studied Fig. She cocked her head to the side, wondering what he would say.

"The note in Angela's little book. 'Paris, Fall 1793,' right?"

"Yes, it did. There were names too, but I didn't think they were important."

Fig exhaled a theatrical sigh. He opened his mouth to say something, but then stopped. Instead, he reached into Theo's knapsack and pulled out the reference book. "Marie Antoinette," He mumbled as he riffled the pages. In a few moments, he found the appropriate section and read its contents.

"What month is it? What day is today?" he asked after a moment.

Lilith shrugged, but Theo answered immediately. "October. Today is the sixteenth."

Fig dropped the book. He was wide-eyed with shock. "The guillotine." He choked out the words. "Today is to be the day, the day she is to be …"

He eyed the Queen. "How did you get here? There is no mention in the book about the catacombs."

Theo translated the interchange. "I thought it was a dream. Another substituted for me in my bed. I don't understand how it was done."

Lilith saw Fig's eyes widened. "Angela has put Briana in the Queen's place," he said. "So, she would be the one to … But why? Why would your sister do this?"

The demon shrugged. She had no idea.

"No matter," Fig scowled. "We can figure that out later."

He raced to the succubus and sunk to his knees. Like a whirlwind, he

84

ripped the pages from the book and scanned them on both sides. When he finished each one, he tossed it away and finally gripped one last. "The *Conciergerie*! They held Marie Antoinette at the *Conciergerie*."

He looked up at Lilith with pleading eyes. "I submit to you. I will do *anything* you command. But first, sense the location of the juniper fire in the prison. Take me there now. I must rescue Briana."

"Find the fire!" Fig rushed on. "It must be close. Dawn was approaching when we descended into these tunnels. We have dawdled far too long already on this quest. We have to rescue her before it is too late."

Lilith stooped and lifted Fig to his feet. She sighed. "I am not sure we will succeed."

Fig grimaced. "Our agreement! Remember?"

He shut his eyes for a moment, then reopened them with an angry squint. Immediately, Lilith felt the tumult of Fig's thoughts. A presence in her head other than her own. Rapids crashed over rocks that had endured for over six thousand years. Fig struggling against her innermost feeling of self — probing, clawing, and ripping at the very essence of what she was.

Lilith pushed back, but the flood of Fig's emotions continued to rush forth. They were strong, threatening. She had never experienced such a challenge before. Could it be that this beginner, one with virtually no training in wizardry ...

A deep corner of her mind rallied with reassurance. Fig had no experience, no skill, no finesse. The energy of his attack would not be maintainable. Retreat slowly. Let his thrusts dissipate against the bartizans and towers of her outermost keep.

Another thought surfaced through the maelstrom. This was not what she wanted, what she had savored in anticipation more than once. Her victory over Fig was to be ... well, a pleasant interlude. The taming of a playful kitten as opposed to snuffing out the free will of a rogue beast.

"No, Fig. Not now," she managed to say. He was stubborn, like a hatchling. He would have to learn for himself. "This is not the time. I can help you more with my faculties intact."

Fig hesitated. The pressure in Lilith's mind slowed and after a moment, stopped. His presence retreated. "You are right," he panted. "I need your powers to be as mighty as they can. Take me to the prison. I will do the rest."

"You have a plan?"

Fig was quiet for a moment. His panting slowed to normal breathing.

"The simplest is best. You carry me as you have before. Together, we step out of the flame. There are confusion and alarm, sure. But you are a demon. All eyes will be focused on you. I scoop up Briana and pass her to you. You vanish with her and take her back to here. After that, a second trip to get me."

"The guards will resist. You will be outnumbered. How do you propose you will survive while I am busy being a taxi?"

"That is far as I have gotten." Anger flamed in Fig's words.

Lilith considered. "Very well," she said at last. "Let us see what will happen."

DAWN HAD not yet broken when Fig and Lilith emerged from the flame in the *Conciergerie*. A single candle between two beds provided the only other light. The woman sleeping farther away, Fig did not recognize. The one nearer, he certainly did. Briana, slumbering like a baby with no cares in the world. Behind a screen off to the side came the snores of what must be a guard. There were no voices. No one was awake.

Briana! At last, he had found her. Halfway around the world and over two hundred years in the past. He stood transfixed, letting the emotion wash over him, a joy filling his soul. Fig disengaged from Lilith's arms. He took a first cautious step. No creaky floors to worry about either. Cold stone, satisfyingly firm.

Five long strides at the most, and he would be at Briana's side. How was he going to do this? Wake her first with a gentle stroke on the cheek and his other hand ready to cover her mouth? Or perhaps hoist her up and over his shoulder?

Two more steps and he had yet to make up his mind. He raised his foot for another and immediately heard a loud clang. He looked down. He had kicked a chamber pot, a few feet from the bedside. In his haste, he must not have seen it in the darkness.

Fig waited a full minute, unmoving as a monument, but no more noises came from the direction of the barrier. He glanced down to make sure where the chamber pot had rolled and shifted himself to the side. He judged his distance to the sleeping form and crept forward one more step.

Again he clanked into the container. This time it rolled to the wall and wobbled noisily from side to side. The guard behind the screen stirred and pushed off of his rifle to rise. Fig hunkered down next to the bedside, hoping he would be invisible in the shadow cast by the candle.

The guard peered over the screen for a few seconds but finally settled back down. In less than a minute, he was snoring again.

Fig could have sworn the new position of the chamber pot did not lie on his path. Was the tension of the moment distorting his vision? He took a deep breath. Calm yourself, he commanded. This was important. The most important thing he had to do in his life.

Cautiously, he rose to his feet and returned his attention to Briana. She had rolled to the far side of the bed, her arms draping over it, into the gap between the other. Now, he would have to climb onto the mattress on his knees merely to reach the sleeping woman. And if he did put his arms under her, then what?

Suddenly, strong arms engulfed him and lifted him from his feet. It was Lilith. He struggled for a moment but knew it was useless. She was too powerful. In an instant, the pair vanished from the prison and reappeared in the catacombs.

"WHY DID you do that?" Fig shouted as he was released and fell to the stone floor.

"The flame was down to its last flicker," Lilith said as calmly as she could.

"But If I had gotten to the bed, I could — "

"The chamber pot would have moved again," Lilith said. "I suspected something like this would happen. I just didn't know what. For your safety, we had to leave when we did.

Fig grabbed his head in his hands and shook it. He did not understand.

"The Tyrant of Time." Lilith shrugged. "There is no way the one in captivity could escape her execution. History has already been written."

Fig's frustration boiled over. He made two fists and shouted. "You told me that Briana and I would not have any impact on the future because we are not from this time."

Lilith held up her hand, fingers spread before Fig said more. "Time is like … a muscle, a muscle stretched taut. Composed of many fibers, everyone's lifelines, streaming along together. Yes, a few strands can be pulled away temporarily, but inevitably they snap back into place."

"The butterfly effect." Fig persisted.

"You do not understand," Lilith said. "Time acts to keep the collective memory of it the same — but not every microscopic and insignificant happening. One butterfly makes no difference. How could it? But the big events, the ones that do cause history to be recorded, remain cast in stone no matter what."

"What, who moved the chamber pots? Another kind of demon? How is that done?" Fig frowned in disbelief.

"Who? How? No one knows. Eons ago when we succubi first discovered we could travel in time, we learned that the past could not be changed. We demonified the evidence we saw into a female being. Thinking life was responsible for ensuring there are no significant changes."

"She? How do you know this being is female?"

"We don't, Fig. Succubi are female, so it was the natural thing to do. Look, just as you humans have a myth that the God named Zeus is the one who causes lightning, we have a myth about what causes the immutability of the past. In my realm, our broodmothers spin tales for the hatchlings about the Tyrant of Time. And, after eons and eons, we have found no evidence to the contrary."

"But Briana. She is not the Queen of France."

"Evidently, as far as history is concerned she will serve. A woman with red hair lost her life on the sixteenth of October, 1793. That is what matters."

Like a pile driver, Fig hammered on. "What about the queen? Appearing after her 'death' will cause — "

Fig stopped. In a rush. It became clear, all too clear. "All along, Angela's target was Marie Antoinette, not Briana! Briana dies in the Queen's place, and history is unchanged. As long as your sister keeps the real queen hidden, her existence contradicts nothing. She has a thrall to do with whatever she wants."

Fig sank to the ground, his energy spent. "I will figure out a way," he managed to croak.

An Impossible Choice

FIG'S HEAD pounded. He could not figure out any way around it, and he squinted from the pain. He looked at the Queen, still huddled within the circle of skulls. She returned his stare with pleading eyes. Saving Briana could not be a simple matter, an exciting deed performed with aplomb by a dashing hero. Instead, he would have to reverse Angela's swap. Send the woman in front of him to her death as originally intended.

The impact of what that meant slammed into him like an avalanche. Put Marie Antoinette back in the *Conciergerie*? He would be complicit. A murderer. An enabler of her death.

One woman would die. That could not be changed. The facts of history had been set in stone. But which of the two? Somehow, out of nowhere, a choice had appeared, and the decision had fallen into his hands. He was the one to decide.

Of course, he wanted to save Briana. That had been the reason, the only reason, for the dash back into the past. And without Angela's meddling, the Queen would be the one beheaded anyway. Somehow he had to perform another swap and save the love of his life.

But that thought brought no peace. If he switched the Queen back, blood would be on his hands, guilty as much as any other who wanted her to die. Yes, some said Marie Antoinette was a bitch. Others, a mere pawn in a complex game of politics. But no matter. A life was at stake here, one he could save — or not.

Fig paced from one end of the alcove to the other mulling over the possibilities. Theo and Lilith watched, saying nothing. Time ticked away.

How many circuits he made, Fig could not recall. But as painful as it was, he finally accepted that he did not have the luxury of thinking anymore. He took a deep breath and decided. He did not feel at all good about himself, or with his choice, but he had to move forward.

He was not like the heroes of his youth, he realized. No Percy Blakeney of *The Scarlet Pimpernel*, no Rupert Rasendyll of *The Prisoner of Zenda*. They would find a way to save both women, but he was less than they. He could not.

Fig stopped pacing. He nodded to convince himself. He would focus on rescuing Briana. The Queen must die. He would make that come about. Saving monarchs was a task for more resourceful heroes than he.

Even if he could bring himself to sacrifice the Queen — how? So much had been written about the guillotine event. Anything he thought of probably would have pitfalls like the moving chamber pot.

He considered. Anything? Or perhaps *almost* anything? What did the history book say?

In a frenzy, he scooped up the pages scattered about the cold stone floor. Where could he intervene? And somehow without any mention in history. He scanned the pages over and over, but nothing became apparent. He needed a diversion, he decided. Something simple and commonplace, not noteworthy enough to be recorded.

He choked on where his thoughts were leading. He had to get the Queen to trust him, to do exactly as he said. There was no record of a queen struggling to escape. The words for Theo to translate came out painfully, one at a time.

"Tell the Queen I am an English nobleman," Fig told the lad. "My comrades and I are here to help her. Coming here is merely the first step of the plan. She must follow exactly what I tell her to do."

Theo relayed the message. Marie Antoinette gazed up at Fig, puzzled. A hint of hope appeared on her face. Fig's heart ached. He could hardly bear what he was doing.

"She asked your name, monsieur," Theo translated. "How should she address her savior? Is the Carnation Plot ready to unfold at last?"

"Tell her I am … the Scarlet Pimpernel," he forced out at last. "That we must hurry. Every minute counts."

Without waiting for a reply, Fig stepped into the circle of skulls. He put his arm around the Queen and led her out of the confinement terrifying her.

"Oh thank you, monsieur," Theo translated. "If you can do that, then, of course, I trust your power."

Marie Antoinette tightened her grip around Fig's waist. Like a new-born puppy, she gazed at him with wide eyes. "Dare I hope?" she asked. "It has taken me so long to prepare myself, to accept what is to be."

She choked over sudden tears. "And now at almost the very last minute, my emotions start to churn again. Of course, I want to live, to breathe the clear air of spring. To laugh and sing."

She paused a moment. Her lips churned as she composed what she would say next. "Do not deceive me, monsieur Pimpernel. Such a cruel jest no one deserves no matter how heinous their sin. On your honor, tell me. Will I truly be saved?"

Fig exhaled deeply. The Queen was desperate. Of course, he had gained her trust. If only ... No, no time for more planning, no regrets about what he was going to do. He did not answer. He could not. Instead, he plunged into relating the details of his plan.

"Theo, climb back to the surface. Get a white dress and cap for the Queen. Use as much of the gold as you need. Return here and get her dressed. Shear her hair until it fits under the widow cap. Explain to her you are preparing her disguise. We don't want her to be recognized like she was on the flight to Varennes. While you are doing that, I will find somewhere a wooden bench which can seat two."

"Lilith," Fig commanded, "Go to Notre Dame. Do your thing. Get a priest to surrender his cassock. Preferably, my size. And also a man's suit. From where I don't know. Something Theo can wear. Bring the garments back here."

"To what purpose are — " Lilith began.

"Now! Just do it! There is no time to explain."

The demon cocked her head and frowned. "Is this an attempt to dom — "

"When that is done, go to the *Quay de Hotel d'ville*. You will see gendarmes escorting a tumbril with the *Conciergerie* as its destination. That is what the history book says. It is still early. Hopefully, no one else will be about. I don't know how many men, maybe a dozen or so. Divert them as you usually do and then — "

Lilith frowned. To Fig, her eyes seemed to smolder.

"Our agreement still stands," he said before the succubus could speak again. "Briana is not yet rescued."

Lilith remained silent for several moments, then finally spoke.

"Very well. I will continue. But even so, there are limits. I have told you before I do not care to use my skill as a mere tool as part of your grand designs. A dozen men? One after another? No, that is too much. I refuse."

Fig's thoughts raced. He tensed his hands into fists. "Then, return to your realm. Recruit more of your kind. Have them keep every one of the troops occupied and as far away from the prison as they can."

"Is that all?" Lilith asked.

"No, there is more." Her tone had been sarcastic, but Fig did not notice. "Also bring back some whirling dervishes when you return from your realm. Look for the tumbril we brought from Marseille. Theo and I will be coming down the *Rue de Lobau*. It will intersect the *Quay de Hotel d'ville* at the bank of the Seine."

"Whatever you have in mind sounds very elaborate. Is any of this going to work?"

"I don't know. I don't know. But I'm trying to match recorded history as best I can. A twist of the past that does not run afoul of this so-called Tyrant of Time. He glanced quickly at Marie Antoinette still looking at him, awaiting his answer. He sighed. "And ... I can't think of anything else to try."

The Chorus of Succubi

THEO, GARBED as a non-descript attendant, guided the cart down the *Rue de Lobau*. Behind him, Fig sat on the bench facing backward. He twitched uncomfortably in the coarse cassock. It was a size too small, but if he held very still when the time came, it would do. He looked skyward but saw only the somber grey of morning. Feeble sunlight struggled to pierce the gloom.

When they reached the dead end at the *Quay de Hotel d'ville*, Fig scanned the east. In the distance, another tumbril listed to one side. Two unhitched horses stood placidly nearby. The accompanying gendarmes were otherwise occupied as he had hoped.

Theo turned the cart onto the quay and then to the right. The *Boulevard du Palais* fronting the *Conciergerie* on the other side of the river was a few blocks west.

At the crucial moment, no one would be raising their eyes to the sky, Fig thought. They would track the tumbril slowly covering the remaining distance to the quay. After picking up the expected passenger, their eyes would follow the entourage turning to the left and out of sight. So far, so good.

"Wheel us about here," Fig called to Theo over his shoulder as they reached the *Boulevard du Palais*. "Line us up ready to cross back over the Seine without delay."

As Theo maneuvered the tumbril, the central doors of the *Conciergerie* opened. A small troop of gendarmes marched out, carrying their muskets across their chests. Fig strained to see who stood behind, but his view was blocked. He filled his lungs with fresh air. Everything depended on what happened in the next few minutes.

The troop marched closer down the boulevard, and Fig stood up to see over their heads. There, behind them strode Stanton, the Executioner of Paris, and next in line —

Yes, it was Briana! His guess had been correct. With her crimson locks chopped off, it took a moment, but it was her. And he had been right. Somehow Angela had managed to substitute Briana in place of the Queen.

Another group formed the rear. Fig gawked in disbelief. Briana appeared dazed, not even aware of her surroundings. She was behaving like a silent marcher in the middle of a parade. Her hands did not show, bound behind her. What was everyone worried about? What could one small woman do?

Fig snapped back to focus on what needed to happen next. "A gendarme will climb into the cart in a bit," he called to Theo again. "After you hand him the reins, climb over the barrier between us and stand in the rear. Be quick about it. Stanton will follow and take your seat. For anything you have to say to me after, come forward and whisper in my ear. The noise of the crowd will prevent being overheard."

Fig could not continue speaking. So far there had been no hitches. He chanced a glance skyward, and a small part of the tension dissolved. High overhead, Lilith hovered. And around her a constellation of whirling dervishes ready to descend. Nothing had prevented her from being there. He raised one arm, palm up. Not yet. Wait a moment more.

The procession from the *Conciergerie* reached the cart. Stanton mounted next to the driver. Two of the gendarmes assisted Briana up onto the tumbril bed and placed her next to where Fig sat. She showed no sign of recognition, no distress.

Stanton twisted and said something to Fig. He did not understand, but Theo immediately came forward and whispered. "The rope. He wants the free end of the rope binding the woman. He says he is the one responsible, the one in charge."

Fig passed the rope into Stanton's grasp. While he did, the gendarmes who had surrounded Briana reformed fore and aft of the tumbril. When they finished, the crack of a whip jolted the horses into motion. The travel to the *Place de la Révolution* had begun.

Now for the most critical part — a disturbance. Fig waved skyward. In response, the dervishes whirled. Each of their bodies caught the air around them and spun it in spinning vortices. Their features dissolved into a fuzzy blur. While all eyes were still on the tumbril, the dervishes descended earthward.

The dirt and dust of the road around the cart billowed up into the struggling cyclones. For an instant, there were individual small funnels filled with debris. But they soon converged into one large impenetrable cloud. Stanton, the gendarmes, everyone could not see anything in front of them.

There was a shout of alarm about what was happening. A chorus of coughs added to the din. In the confusion, Lilith lit in front of Fig. "Now what?" she asked.

"Back to the catacombs. Bring the queen. Angela has switched her with Briana. This is the only way. I must switch her back."

Lilith sped away like a raptor that had spotted fresh prey. In the span of a few heartbeats, she returned into the confusion, bearing Marie Antoinette in her arms.

"Once I have the Queen settled beside me," Fig whispered to Lilith in the swirling dust. "Whisk Briana back to safety. Have the dervishes disperse." He pulled a knife from a pocket and sliced the rope near Briana's wrists. "I will handle it from there ... I hope."

Lilith snatched Briana from the tumbril. The coughs turned to curses and the sound of sharp slaps of arms against sleeves and chests. A commander's call for attention cut short the babble about had happened. Tales about similar experiences of dust devils in the past died on the gendarme's lips.

After the switch was completed, Marie Antoinette recognized Fig sitting beside her. She cried out to him in panicked French.

"What is happening," Theo translated. "She wants to know — "

"Tell her it is part of the plan." Again the words came so hard to say. "She has to trust me. No matter what I do."

Fig's heart pounded. What had he become? But there was no time to think about that now.

He reached into another pocket and retrieved a short coil of rope. Grabbing the Queen's hands, he bound them behind her and knotted the end to the fetter leading to Stanton's grip. As he did, the little windstorm stopped. Like raindrops, a gentle shower of the last of whirling dirt returned to the earth.

Fig held his breath. What would happen now? The history book only had said a disturbance had occurred, but an unspecified one. But he did not have time to ponder long. The Queen struggled to rise. She stared at Fig, shouting louder with each breath.

Stanton answered gruffly from where he sat. "We have provided a priest. Make your final confession to him," Theo parroted.

"You told me I was to trust you," Theo crept forward and whispered. "What is your plan?"

Fig's tongue froze in his throat. He mumbled, "Tell her, 'It will be over in at most an hour. She will be at rest.'"

He winced at Antoinette's glare when the words sunk in. "Along with the rest, you have betrayed me," Theo translated. "Took from me what little time I had left to prepare."

Fig's chest hurt. He could hardly breathe. "Use the time to compose yourself to end everything with dignity. You are a queen deserving to be remembered for her conduct on her last day."

Antoinette continued staring at Fig as they crossed the Seine. But finally, her attention turned inward. Fig felt compelled to place his arm around her, but she shouldered him aside. Slumping her head onto her chest, she ignored him for the rest of her final journey.

Fig let out the breath he had been holding. All would go well now. The switch was complete. The Tyrant of Time, if there were such a being, would prevent anything else out of the ordinary from happening. But there was no satisfaction in it for him. He was the one who had made the choice. To switch the two women at the last moment. To send one to her death rather than another.

ANGELA WATCHED the small procession approach the *Place de la Révolution* and grinned. Everything was going according to plan. The woman she had abducted from the future appeared surprisingly regal. She held her head high as if her name had been announced while entering a grand ball. Perhaps the vixen had better control of her emotions than she had thought.

Soon, it would be over. Marie Antoinette would be hers. No great beauty like the others on her list. No reputation for being a *femme fatale*. But years in the company of men of power. She must be well versed in understanding the nuances of their conversations — how to manipulate them with words. A good choice for the first one to enthrall.

The blade sliced down.

All that remained was the grisly business of showing the crowd the severed head. These humans, Angela thought. They view denizens of other realms with such disfavor. They should amend their barbaric rituals first.

The dripping exhibit was held aloft, and the cap ripped from the unfeeling scalp. "*Vive la Révolution,*" the crowd shouted, at first in sporadic clumps and finally in rousing unison.

Angela startled. No! The hair! It was not the right color. Marie Antoinette's weak red mingled with white. Not the vibrant richness of the one she had so carefully put into the Queen's place.

How could this have happened? Who gained benefit if her plan were impeded and sidetracked?

While the citizens of Paris rejoiced, Angela ducked into an alley. She unfurled her wings and streaked skyward toward the catacombs — where Marie Antoinette had been secured. She would pick up the trail there.

22

Outnumbered

FIG HAD managed the impossible. Briana had been saved. But he did not feel any elation. His mouth tasted bile. He had guided a woman to her death.

Theo brought the horses to a halt at the entrance to the catacombs. He placed a hand on Fig's arm. "I do not understand everything that has happened, who you are, or where you are from. But you did not merely rescue one person." He pointed at himself. "No, you saved two."

Fig studied the young man. How bizarre this must be to him. "Don't tell anyone about any of this," he said.

"I'm not stupid. No one would believe anything I babbled."

Fig sighed. Perhaps in time, the horrible memory of the plunging blade would fade. He reached into one of his pockets and extracted the gold coins that remained. "Here. These and this cart will make it easier for your aunt to accept a nephew appearing by surprise."

Theo nodded as Fig dismounted from the tumbril. "Go to her now," he commanded over his shoulder. Without looking back, he trod down the dark steps into the catacombs.

When he reached the bottom, his spirits lifted a bit. After all this time, finally, he was going to hug Briana! Tell her what he had done. Explain everything about how he had rescued her … No, that was a tale best remain buried.

Loud grunts and the sound of small avalanches emanated from the first cross tunnel. They came from the direction of the alcove with the juniper flame. Fig raced toward the commotion. What now?

In moments, he reached the alcove and gawked at what he saw. Briana was surrounded by skulls and bones piled at her feet. She steadied herself with one arm against the side wall. Her eyes were more alive than they had been at the *Conciergerie*. But her slack face showed she still was not quite present.

In the center of the room, next to the flickering fire, two succubi grappled with one another. One must be Lilith, but which one, Fig could not be sure. The other, Angela then? Ichor dripped from arms and chests. All four hands ended in claws Fig had not even guessed existed. They swiped at each other from a distance and then closed, trying to bite whatever they could reach with their teeth. The remains of a fancy collar and a small purse were strewn to the side along with the tattered remnants of two black robes.

With a clatter, the two demons plunged to the floor and into a tight bundle. They rolled on the ground over the scattered bones. Dirt and dust clung to the open wounds marking where the slashes were particularly deep. Both were out of breath, trying to gain the strength to continue their fight.

"I was right," the one who must be Angela gasped. "It was you. My sister placed her tail in a place it should not be."

"Why are you doing this?" Lilith answered, her breath, shallow and labored.

"Don't you get it? Have you any sense of how difficult a substitution is?"

"Yes, the Tyrant of Time. We all know about that. How useless it is to try altering what has already occurred."

"Alteration was never the goal. What has been done is done. But my substitution. So brilliant, performed close to death. It meant I obtained a female totally free of constraints. As the humans say, enabled to pick her brain for as long as I wanted. Find out the secrets of manipulating the males. It could take as long as necessary … months, years, decades."

"But why?" Lilith managed to release Angela's grasp and stagger back to her feet.

"I have already told you," Angela rose and grabbed Lilith in a tight hug. "So Elezar would do as I asked."

"Elezar has told us to act cautiously in the realm of humankind. Not to interfere in any meaningful way."

"I will change his mind," Angela snarled.

She butted her head into Lilith's chest, and Fig's companion staggered back. She tripped over one of the skulls and slammed to the ground. Angela pounced on her, bent her elbow and pressed her forearm into Lilith's throat.

Lilith flung out her hand and grabbed one of the skulls. With it, she began battering her sister's face. With each blow, Angela faltered. But only for a moment. After a short pause, she persisted with her attack.

Fig glanced at Briana. Her eyes were becoming more alive. Whatever

99

had entranced her was fading away. Angela ignored Briana's awakening and switched tactics. She grabbed a skull and was able to trade Lilith's onslaught blow for blow. A well-aimed one slammed into her sister's chin. Lilith released her weapon, her eyes rolling upward, her arms lax.

Fig winced at the sound of the blow. His companion did not move. Angela laughed and grasped one of the scattered femurs that had broken into two sharp shards. Holding it like a long dagger, she prepared to plunge the weapon into Lilith's chest.

The return to the catacombs after the execution had taken too much time, Fig realized. He should have been here sooner to help. Without thinking, he raced to where Angela stood. He grabbed her tail, trying to tug her away from her inert sister. Angela growled and glanced over her shoulder. She scowled and swished her tail back and forth, but Fig held on. He would not let go.

"No," Briana shouted. Fig saw her eyes were now alert — as if she had been wakened from a long, deep sleep. Whatever Angela had done to her was wearing off. Briana reached down for the other half of the shattered femur. She staggered toward the demon. Angela looked back and forth between the two humans and rose from the ground to defend herself.

Lilith stirred. Free of Angela's weight, she rose to her feet. With faltering steps, she advanced on her sister. Fig let go of Angela's tail. That wasn't accomplishing anything. In imitation of Briana, he grabbed one of the scattered femurs and waved it like a caveman brandishing a club. Angela glanced over her shoulder and retreated from his threat, but only a half-step. To go farther, would mean impalement on Briana's blade. Like a swivel head doll, she looked at each of her adversaries in turn. Anyone of the three would be no match, but the outcome with them all attacking at once far more uncertain.

"Three to one is more than I can handle at the moment," Angela panted. "But know this, sister, I will have my revenge for what you have done. When I gain control over Elezar and the djinns at his command, I will send them to track you down. No matter where you chose to hide, they will find you and tear you limb from limb. Reduce you to mere atoms that even a weaver from our realm will not be able to reuse.

"And both of you." Angela glowered first at Fig and then Briana. "You will be hunted as well. Your futures will be bleak ones, enslaved to powerful djinns who will use you as an amusement while they rest between their battles. Watching sex performed by other kinds is a delicious pastime for them."

Angela turned toward Fig. With a swift feint, she backed him to the side. Through the gap in the encirclement he left open she dashed for the juniper fire. Before anyone could react, she was gone.

Fig dropped the femur and raced to Briana, pulling her into his arms. He kissed her with passion. No more obstacles. Definitely now, she was saved.

But Briana did not return the embrace. More like a statue, she stood stiff and unmoving.

Fig's thoughts tumbled. This was not the way he had imagined it. His quest was not yet done. His relation with Briana was something still to be sorted out. But not now. That must wait for later. Later, when he felt again to be of some worth rather than merely a felon, a murderer, not yet punished for his crime.

He shook his head to clear it. "No matter," he managed to say. He turned at Lilith. "Angela's twist of time has been uncoiled. Return Briana to the present, then ... if you choose...come back for me."

"Angela's threat cannot be ignored," Lilith said. "She is most vengeful."

"It sounded to me like a loser's braggadocio," Fig disagreed. "Thanks to you, Lilith, our adventure is over. I don't think we will hear anything about Angela ever again."

Part Two

What Is

1

Plan B

AS SHE traveled through the flame, Angela's frustration grew. Her plan to pull Marie Antoinette out of the flow of time had been foiled. She would be unable to return to the same era and try again. One visit to a segment of the past was the limit. She was no closer to her goal of learning how to bend male demons to her will.

She strained against the resistance of the flame. Only embers remained of the juniper fire she had targeted. With a last gasp of effort, she popped through and exited the kiln. The Hilo laboratory looked much the same as it did when she had left with Briana days ago — except that most all the equipment had vanished. The workbench was bare.

She did not like returning here. Lilith and the others would soon follow. But her exit from the catacombs was rushed. There was time to consider and select another place.

She did not understand how it worked. The march of time was the same everywhere since the very beginning of ... well, she did not know when. Every moment she spent back in the eighteenth century also clicked off in the present at the same rate. She could not return either earlier or later than when she did. Those rules also were part of how things behaved.

But there was no point in pondering such mysteries again. She never had been able to figure them out. Best to move forward. Come up with a new plan. Get out of here. Determine what she should do now.

Angela drummed her fingers on the lab bench. It had taken so much planning. Getting juniper into the prison cell at the *Conciergerie*. Seducing the guards. Coercing the attendant so recorded history remained the same. Substituting for her target hours before her death. Getting possession of a human female so she could learn all her skills for dealing with males.

She paused with a thought. Why not the *present* rather than the past? Forgo the complications and constraints presented by what has already gone by. She reached for the whiteberry. Of course, it was no longer there. Ripped away by her accursed sister.

Angela frowned with the effort of concentrating. She had spent many hours remembering the list in case of such a contingency. On it, hadn't there been one who was *contemporary*? Cleopatra, Mata Hari, Lucrecia Borgia, Mary, Queen of Scots, Eleanor of Aquitaine …

Yes, there it was. Natasha Gorshok. A worldwide reputation as the consummate female spy. The one who stole American military secrets. Now a television show personality living in Moscow. Unlike Marie Antoinette, a true *femme fatale*. But one in modern times. She should do.

Angela glanced about a second time. The lab was not empty. There on the floor were a few remaining leaves of juniper, not yet placed into the kiln. Those would be enough to return to her realm. Convince a gargoyle who was desperate for a chance to see this world. A quick stop there and then onto Moscow. She added the last of the juniper to the fire and stepped into the renewed flame to be on her way. "Natasha Gorshok," she said aloud. "Let's see if you are as good as everyone says you are."

2

A Past Life Reborn

BACK IN her small office, Natasha Gorshok puzzled. She could not believe that Dmitry had announced she was taking a short leave. On a live broadcast! With her sitting right next to him. What could she say?

After the 'all clear,' Dmitry protested he was as surprised as she was. He showed her the scroll on the teleprompter. Her back tightened. The action reminded her of similar ones by the KGB so many years ago.

Natasha smiled at Alexei sitting across from her. That was all it took. He was so simpleminded. Even another man saying 'hello' to her in the hallway tumbled him into a cauldron of doubt. 'Is she having another affair?' he would think. Or 'Has ours run its course?' He revisited such incidents over and over, pushing him to the edge of despair.

So passive and non-demanding, but everything she could want in bed. Low maintenance. Totally unlike the other brutes hitting on her. She sighed. He was worth it.

"On your way now," she cooed. "Meet you back at our place after the evening broadcast is over."

Alexei rose, smiled back and went to the door. As always, with elaborate clumsiness, he fiddled with the knob. "This time, it *is* stuck," he said. "I guess I will have to stay."

Natasha circled her desk to stand at his side. With a twist and pull, the door opened a crack. She gave him a quick kiss on the cheek. "As always," she said. "Now, please go home and wait. I have things to do."

After Alexei left, Natasha looked at the large clock on the wall across from her. She had a three-hour break until the evening news. There were no pictures on the walls, only a full-length mirror next to the door across from her. She adjusted a single wayward strand in her jet black hair and smiled at her reflection. She knew she was attractive. Big blue eyes and the fair skin of a baby. Over the forty's hump and still no need for

107

pancake makeup.

A single filing cabinet stood like a sentinel guarding a standard desk. Well, almost standard. She had had the feet cut down so the chair the network provided worked with her diminutive frame. The desktop was almost clear. There was no need to worry about someone straining from the guest chair to read the few items resting there.

Attending to the papers could come later. First order of business was to solve the riddle. Who had put the text about her 'short leave' into the teleprompter text?

A FEW minutes later, the door pushed open. Natasha did not have to wait long to find the answer. A somber man in a black trench coat walked in. "Greetings Comrade Natasha," he said. "You can call me Comrade Viktor. We need to talk."

A trench coat, no less, Natasha thought, as memories flashed back. How many of these goons lived as if it still was the nineteen sixties?

The intruder shut the door. He settled his bulk into the guest chair slowly — showing his weight was under control. "I have news of your next assignment," he said.

Shock raced through Natasha. Involuntarily, she grasped the edge of the desk. *Next* assignment? All that was behind her, so long ago. "You must be mistaken. I have already served you, and served you well."

"You were caught," Viktor growled. "An embarrassment. To get you back we had to agree to a personnel exchange."

"It was my handler who bungled, not me. I have debriefed this more than a dozen times."

"Even so, a new opportunity presents itself. A wonderful one. The SVR has decided you are perfect for the job."

Natasha set her face into a grim mask. This was the new Russia. She no longer could be pushed around like that — heed every instruction of her handler, no matter how sordid. Do things with other men that she never wanted to think about again.

"I refuse!" her words exploded.

Viktor ignored the outburst. "You will take another trip to the west. Do what you have done for us before. Only this time, it will be much more important."

He drew in a deep breath as if he were an orator. "The Americans are so naïve. Their memories so short. They think they won the cold war.

"It is not yet over." He pursed his lips and shook his head. "But it will be soon, a month at most after you have placed the last piece in the puzzle. The US will be brought to its knees. Begging us for help. Begging! Oh, I like the sound of that word so much. They will agree to any terms we demand. The return of Alaska. Total withdrawal from the Pacific. Unconditional surrender. Complete capitulation."

Viktor leaned over the table until his face was inches from Natasha's. Her every instinct was to pull back. But despite the smell of vodka-laden breath, she steeled herself to remain still.

"This is the courtesy call," he said. "You know that. A chance for you to volunteer. It will look better in your record that way."

Natasha did not speak. She did not know what to say.

Viktor rose abruptly. His face twisted into a cruel smile. "Alexei, your boy toy. The name suits him, but he has been looking a little pale recently. Needs a checkup to find out why. When you return to your apartment at the end of the day, you will find him gone. Give you some time to think and weigh your options. Reconsider your hasty decision.

Natasha's heart sank. Alexei, gentle Alexei. She could not let anything happen to him. But return to her former life, one she struggled with daily to forget. What was she to do?

"I look forward to hearing your answer when I return," Viktor said. "Return with your new passport and airline tickets. Pack a suitcase for warmer weather. You fly to SFO a few days from now. Then to Sacramento, California. A short cab drive from there to your final destination, the small town of Folsom."

He reached into one of his coat pockets and pulled out a photo. "Here is what your handler looks like. Memorize and destroy. In the California airport, he will 'brushpass' your instructions to you in the usual manner."

Natasha sucked in her breath. One last thing to try. She circled the desk and placed her back on the door before Victor could open it. When he was in range, she ran a finger down his cheek and looked into his eyes.

"You say my apartment is empty, Comrade. Perhaps we can discuss this assignment more there this evening. After I'm done with the afternoon broadcast."

She smiled in a way she had not used in years, almost surprised how quickly it came back to her. "You seem to be a logical sort. Who knows? You might be rewarded personally if you argue to your superiors that

109

someone younger is better suited for this task."

Victor scowled and shoved Natasha aside. "I will bring your documents tomorrow, Comrade. For you, there is no turning back."

Natasha slumped. "I understand now — the reason for the leave announcement."

"Of course you do. See you tomorrow."

3

Good Help is Hard to Find

ANGELA PULLED her wings as tight against her back as she could. Huddled in the shadow of the tall building's buttress helped keep her out of sight. Not as busy as Red Square. The fewer humans around this suburb was a good thing. Most of the structures were apartment houses — featureless façades peppered with tiny windows like sketches drawn by children. Only a dozen cars braved the unswept street.

The building Angela faced did nothing to protect her from for the windblown snow. She stamped her feet and rubbed her hands together. Could the ichor in her veins freeze? Is that what the humans called frostbite? Why anyone, human or not, chose to live in Moscow was a mystery.

She could not get the anger she held toward her sister out of her mind. Nor her disappointment about not being able to do anything about it. The acid of her frustration burned her stomach and sometimes derailed her thoughts. But three against one in the catacombs had been too many. Lilith's payment would come about as the climax of a more carefully thought out course. A climax from which no aid would come.

Angela felt a tap on her shoulder. Finally, the gargoyle was back. It had taken long enough. "Hold tight," she commanded as she stepped into the feeble glow of a nearby lamppost. "Let's get out of here and into some flame where it is warm."

"This is nothing," the smaller demon on her shoulder answered. "My cousin, Beefcake, has stood on one of the towers of Notre Dame for over two hundred years. He never moves a muscle in the sunshine, rain, or even snow like this."

"Never mind that. What did you find out?"

"Gimme a break," the gargoyle said. "It's not so easy posing as an empty flower pot when someone is looking. Up close work takes skill,

111

and I must say I'm one of the best at it."

Angela ignored the sprite. "Get a tight grip. Here we go."

She unfurled her wings and soared into the sky. It was dusk, and few people were still walking in the square on which the studio facilities abutted. Those who did bundled up head to foot. They kept their eyes on the ground to make sure they did not step into any slush.

Soon, the pair zoomed through a narrow window into a room on the eleventh floor of an apartment building. Run down and neglected since a construction spurt in the nineteen fifties. The landlord was glad for whatever tenants he could get. He did not look too closely at the tall, strangely clad woman in black — one who needed professional advice about her facial acne. It was sufficient that she paid two months in advance.

Angela wasted no time in getting a fire going in the hearth. She spent a quarter of an hour in front of it warming herself on all sides as if she were on a vertical rotisserie. While she did, the gargoyle sat on a threadbare divan thumbing through an old magazine. "Can you read any of this stuff?" he asked. "The letters look so strange."

"What's your name again?" Angela asked. "All of you look alike."

"Yeah, we get a lot of that. But each of us is quite different … although there are some similarities."

"Yes, yes. You all have lizard-like bodies, slender head to match. Short horns arching backward. Large staring eyes. Wings for show only. Good for gliding and nothing else. Coarse, scaly skin. I don't care about th — "

"The humans alter our basic design, of course. But the ones they make do not count. Stone only. No beating hearts inside."

"Your name?"

"Oh, yeah. You can call me Adonis. Everyone else in my lounge does."

"Listen, Adonis. I don't care about your background. Who your broodmother was. Your sire. Exploits of great-uncle whosit. None of that stuff. The deal is you get to see the human world a bit. In exchange, you do what I say … exactly what *I* say. Get it?"

"What you say, no exceptions. Yadda. Yadda. The usual. But just so you know. If it were not for the competition of the human-made synthetics, we *all* would be hanging around in our own gigs. And if our travels together do happen to take us to where a new cathedral is being constructed, I'm bailing. Get a real job guarding a tower all my own. Inferior copies? Who needs one when you can have an original?"

"Enough! What did you learn?"

"She's there all right. Does a show called *Dobry vecher Rossiya* — Good Evening, Russia. Another longer version in the morning. Evidently, very popular. Big soundstage. Lots of equipment. Nothing shabby or old."

"Yes, what little I have learned says she is very popular. Where is her office? How do we get to her?"

"You don't understand how this is done, do you? First, I had to time the door opening to be as it is almost closed, scamper through onto the ceiling. You're lucky I haven't begun my growth spurt yet. Full grown, I would never fit on your shoulder."

"Never mind th — "

Adonis crossed his arms across his chest. "I'm a professional. The full story or nothing."

Angela sighed. Good help was so hard to get. "Go on," she prompted.

"So if I'm spotted on the ceiling, I flip over till only my back shows and hope for the best. Otherwise, I transit across the entryway and exit to the next. At some point, I have to start working the floor. If spotted, drop on my haunches. Cup my hands together and give a fake smile. Sometimes stick my tongue out to the side. The humans like that a lot. Look like a misplaced doorstop. Or maybe a pencil cup. If I'm picked up, the difficult part is remaining still. Be hard as a rock. No giggles."

"So what did you — "

"I'm getting to that. Found her office. Next to a conference room. She kissed a guy waiting for her there. Together they went inside. Then a third human appeared. Not a happy camper. Rigid scowl. Trying for the 'Don't mess with me' look. Tapped his foot impatiently, waiting for the first guy to leave."

"Wonderful. You have to get back there right away. I need to hear what is going on."

"No need. I scampered in when the first guy left. Made myself look like a wasp nest on the ceiling. Heard everything. You're going to like this. Change of venue for Natasha. If you want to pursue her, its 'Sunny California' here we come."

4

Friend or Enemy

BRIANA TOUCHED the cold kiln door in the laboratory to be sure. Yes, she was back home in the present. She waggled her head to clear away the haze. How long had she been under Angela's domination? What had the succubus done to her? Vaguely, she remembered being carried into the flame, not once but twice.

She recognized she was in the little laboratory at the back of the warehouse in Hilo. There was the kiln through which she had just been carried and next to it the workbench …

It had been stripped almost bare. No analytical balance, no centrifuge, nothing. And something else did not feel right either. She reached behind her neck and gasped. Her hair! It had been lopped off. When had that happened? Why?

Briana heard a groan. It was Lilith slumped on the ground. She studied Briana for a moment, then cocked her head to the side. "I am quite curious to learn what makes your swain so attracted to you."

A spasm shot through her from head to toe. "Human females," she gasped. "Usually, you are such amateurs when it comes to controlling your men. What is it you have that could turn the head of a djinn?"

Briana willed herself alert. "What have you done with Fig?" She waved the sharpened femur she still held. "You will not be able to trick me again. This time, I will be the one who dominates."

"Put down your weapon." Lilith waved the threat away. "There is no cause. I have no interest in bending a *female* to my will."

"You were eager enough the first time we met."

"Not me. Angela, my sister."

Briana frowned, reaching into the fog of her memory. "A sister. You *did* mention one such as that. Your evil twin, you said."

"Well, yes *Angela* is the evil twin, even though she calls *me* that," the

114

succubus growled. "If there is a pit of evil anywhere around, Angela is the one deep into it; you can bet. But not me. You can call me Lilith."

Briana concentrated, letting her mind reach out toward the devil she faced. But much more cautiously this time. Not to engage in the mental struggle to see whose will was the stronger, the one to dominate. Instead, only to learn more of what this demon was like. The tales in the sagas did not do justice to how difficult dominance was to achieve.

Yes, the basic impulses of a succubus were there, she realized as the thoughts mingled with hers. The lust building up over time that eventually resulted in a trip to the earth through a beckoning flame. Afterward, satisfaction lasting only until it was time to come again. Those traits were the same. But beyond that, there were differences. The contours of the other mind ...

"I sense you as well," Lilith said. "Can't you tell that I am not the one who imprisoned you in the past?"

Briana nodded slowly. The words rang true. There was no pressure to dominate her will. No, not *her* will but ... Fig! What do you want with Fig? He is my ... my ..."

"Your what? Yes, he adores you. That is very clear. But I detect you do not cherish him in the same way."

Briana pondered for a moment. "No, I guess I don't. I care for him immensely ... but not in the same way. He is intelligent. Forceful at times. But emotionally, he is like ... well, like an obedient puppy. Full of love, given unconditionally. A hopeless romantic. If he could, he would relive *The Prisoner of Zenda* or — "

Lilith interrupted. "Human woman, you do not deserve him. His worth is far greater. He would be wasted on one as unimportant as you."

Briana blinked. She felt threatened. Not for the safety of her free will, but for ... what? Was this Lilith trying to steal Fig away?

"Fig is none of your business," Briana snapped. "Look elsewhere for your next victim. Isn't one man as good for you as the next?"

Lilith shrugged. "Over thousands of years I have sampled many of your male humankind," she said. "Few have been so never at a loss."

Was this Fig the demon was talking about? Her Fig? The thought startled her. "Is it possible Fig has dominated you instead of the other way around?"

"We have not yet had our struggle." Lilith shrugged. "He ... convinced me to join him in rescuing you. Now that has been accomplished. I am quite looking forward to when we grapple ... although there is something else I must take care of first."

"You think *you* will dominate *him*?"

"At first ... I definitely thought so. But since then we have worked together. Saved one another. Even done the impossible and rescued you, I am ... less sure." Lilith's face erupted into a broad smile. More than merely the tips of her fangs showed. "But whatever the outcome when we spar, our union will be most enjoyable."

"Have the two of you already been having — "

"No, not yet. He is not a pretty toy to be played with and then tossed aside. It will be much grander than that."

Briana bristled. Yes, she had been a fool to think she could control a succubus with little preparation and on her first attempt. Forcing a demon to get a message to her father had turned out not to be a good idea. But the prattle about Fig's merits and her worthlessness? Words from what must be a shifty devil. They had no value. Time enough to sort relationships out later.

Lilith suddenly grabbed her side and groaned, interrupting Briana's musing. She watched the demon's eyes start to close because of pain. Her feelings softened. The demon was hurt, wounded in a dozen places while trying to protect her.

"How thoughtless of me." She reached out and steadied the succubus. "I have something here that might help."

Briana began rummaging through the chests remaining under the lab bench. After a few moments, she located what she was looking for and extracted a large mason jar from its box.

"Sweetbalm." She held up the container. "Basic alchemy. I brewed a batch to see if I remembered how to do it after I had been here for a while. Where does it hurt the worst? I have never tried to use it on a demon before. We can find out if it works."

Lilith frowned suspiciously at Briana. "If this is a trick to — "

"Tell me how this feels," Briana interrupted. "It is the least I could do for someone who helped save me."

She opened the jar and scooped out some of the balm in her hand. Before Lilith could protest, she lathered it over the demon's most grievous wounds.

Almost immediately, Lilith opened her eyes wide in surprise. "This stuff is amazing!"

"Good to know," Briana said without emotion. "Let's get it working everywhere it is needed."

She watched fresh light green skin emerge from the demon's bruises, her cuts close and heal.

"Doesn't Fig provide for you?" Lilith asked. "Isn't that the basic pattern everywhere on this orb? The man furnishes the livelihood, the woman, the lair."

Briana's expression clouded with annoyance. "Go ahead and retrieve him," she said. "And then you can be on your way."

5

Memory Palaces

IN THE Paris catacomb, Fig watched the juniper flame, waiting for Lilith's return. Now without distractions and alone, the gloomy alcove filled with skulls was oppressive. The row upon row of gaping eye sockets seemed to watch his every move. He wanted to return to Hilo as soon as he could.

After a few minutes, the succubus reappeared.

"I'm ready." Fig jumped up. "This place is starting to give me the creeps."

"Even healed, I am so too tired from all this travel," Lilith gasped. "A few moments before I attempt a third journey through time."

"There is no reason to stay here. Let's go now."

"I said I need rest," Lilith snapped. "Leave me be. Or do you want to have our contest for dominance now?"

Fig scanned Lilith's body. He did not see any marks. Briana must have tried sweetbalm, and it worked. But he had no idea of the effort required to go through time. It was amazing she had agreed to transport Briana before regaining her strength. A mental struggle now would be to his advantage. He might never have such an opportunity again.

He pondered for a few moments. A battle when she was not fully ready? No, that did not feel right. Throughout it all, he could not have asked for a better partner. A provider of more than a dozen helpers from another realm. A beast of burden for the trip from Marseilles. Wearing an abaya, so unlike the way she wished to appear …

"Take your time," he sighed.

He eyed Angela's little book on the floor and picked it up. "I will study this while you recover."

Fig riffled the pages. "Only info on a single page. There are a dozen more entries there."

118

Lilith stuck out her hand. "Give the whiteberry to me. I will memorize its contents."

Fig looked at the tattered remains of Angela's little purse. "I can fashion something like that for you when we return."

"Give the whiteberry to me," Lilith demanded. "I am not going to parade around wearing such silliness as that."

Fig shrugged and handed over the notebook. "Okay. Anything to get you going."

An hour passed while Lilith mouthed the dates and locations on the list over and over. Impatient and irritated, Fig paced in a small circle, but he dared not speak again until Lilith was finished.

Finally, the succubus flung the notebook across the alcove into a clatter of skulls. "Names, times, and places. Twelve is too many. Only the wisest of demons could retain so much." She shuddered. "Memories. The broodmothers taught us to refrain from such stressing activities. If we did, they said, our faces would freeze into smiles."

"Maybe you will not need the book," Fig was surprised at his words. He arched his back and stretched. It felt good to take himself out of a mental stupor. "You can keep the list in a 'memory palace.' I can teach you how it is done. Use some familiar physical place that you can visualize. A standard mnemonic trick. A list this short would be a snap."

"I don't understand."

"Okay, here's an example." Fig retrieved the notebook. "Imagine the women on Angela's list are somewhere within the warehouse in Hilo. In my head, I'm going to visit them one by one. To start, I'm standing at the exterior doorway.

He pantomimed waves with his hands." I envision Cleopatra there waiting to go through the front door with me … because the street in front flows with traffic like the Nile at Alexandria. I open the door to the lobby. I see Mata Hari standing on the receptionist's desk, ready to perform her dance … because the desk is like a stage at the Follies Bergere. I nod to her and move to the door leading into the warehouse proper …"

In a matter of moments, Fig finished the exercise and handed the little notebook back to Lilith. He then recited the information in order without a falter.

"It's easy," he explained. "All I have to do is visualize walking through the warehouse again. All the women on the list will be where I placed them. The dates take a little more effort, but that's the basic idea."

"Name and place will be enough," Lilith said. "I can use the name to refine the dates each of the named women died. The internal net can give us those. You can teach me the details of your method when we return."

As if it were infected with a rare disease, she flung the notebook into the skulls a second time. She cocked her head and studied Fig. "There's always more about you, human, that I continue to learn. When I have dominated you, your captivity will be most delicious."

6

A New Opportunity

AFTER LILITH vanished back to eighteenth-century Paris, Briana was alone in the present. She took a deep breath, and her thoughts decluttered. She looked once more around the bare little room she and Fig called the lab. "I remember now," she said aloud. "We are out of cash. We can't pay the rent."

Things were not working out the way she had planned, not the way she wanted at all. Bad enough being marooned on an alien planet far away from home. When she stared up at the stars at night, her heart ached. Around one of them revolved an orb filled with the five crafts: thaumaturgy, alchemy, sorcery, wizardry, and magic itself. But she did not know which twinkling light was her home.

The portal that brought her here was magic, but it no longer worked. And the grand idea of 'Earth's guardian' was turning out to be flawed. A grand mirror, cracked beyond repair.

Yes, the Earth was primitive in the ways of the crafts. Someone with evil intent could take control of everything in a heartbeat. But since the defeat of the exiles, she had learned of no such attacks. The only uses of the five crafts were simple ones performed by Fig and herself.

There was no money in having such a role. No employee number with Homeland Security. No biweekly paycheck for keeping her eye on things. And if that were so, then what? Use her skills for trickery herself?

No, not the daughter of the Archimage, she told herself sternly. Victories achieved without honor were hollow shells. They soon crumbled under the scrutiny of others. Her father would be shamed if she stooped to using magical skills for dishonest gain. But that resolve did nothing to relieve the heartache plaguing her more and more. More than anything else, she wanted to find a way to return home.

"Hello! Is anybody there?" A voice echoed through the emptiness of the warehouse.

Briana blinked. It sounded like it came from the visitor's lobby. Maybe whoever it was would lighten her mood. She hastened to the front of the building, looking down in disgust at what she was wearing. A shapeless white dress. Perfect. The ideal attire to present to someone who might be bringing a job.

CLIFFORD SEAWALL scanned the young woman who came out into the warehouse lobby. He dropped the satchel he had been carrying to the ground. His mouth gaped in surprise.

Besides the two of them, the room was empty. No receptionist. A simple desk and shut doors in the rear. It felt like the grand tomb waiting for the death of the king.

"Your name is Briana, right?" he said as she approached him. "Fig's girl?"

"Yes, my name is Briana, but I'm *not* Fig's *girl*."

"Well, he certainly is a good salesman. Said you had a magic act that would have the audience on their feet." He stuck out his hand. "My name is Cliff."

"Magic?" Briana eyed Cliff with suspicion. "What exactly do you mean by that?"

"You know. Stage magic. Saw the woman in half. Move the ball from under one cup to another. What is it exactly that you do? Doesn't have to be much, merely an opener to warm up the crowd. Zantos is the main draw."

Briana did not immediately reply. "How much does this pay?" she finally asked.

Cliff smoothed down the back of his coal black hair. He knew he appeared much younger than he actually was. A broad face and gold-rimmed glasses. Fashionable two-day stubble. A ready smile. Jeans and a plain white shirt.

"Two hundred bucks and any tips you get mingling with the crowd after. I know, I know, it is not much, but I'm desperate. And frankly, from the looks of things, you might be, too."

"Two hund ... How long an act?"

"Fifteen minutes, tops. One show a night." He reached into his satchel. "I have a contract right here."

"But you haven't seen me do anything yet."

"Look, I'll be honest with you. The owners of the club are not exactly Boy Scout troop leaders. When they tell you to do something, you had better do it."

"So if I showed up dressed like this and did a little mumbo-jumbo, you would be off the hook?"

"Well, dress a little bit better. A simple, what do you call it, an A-line would do ... if it were cut low enough in front."

Briana's stomach growled. Cliff saw her wrap her arms about her torso, trying to cover up the noise.

"The place has an open buffet," he said. "All you can eat. No questions."

"Ice cream?"

"Sure. The standard three flavors. Is that good enough?"

"Where do I sign?" Briana held out her hand for a pen. "When Fig gets back ... from his errand, I'm sure the two of us can whip up something. A few little imps dancing around. That sort of thing."

"Imps. Yeah, great. Whatever." He handed the contract to Briana. "The address of the club is on the back of your copy. You're on at ten tonight. Don't be late or both of us will be in a lot of trouble."

BRIANA COULD hardly think straight. Cliff had been gone for an hour. She pressed her arms even tighter about her waist, but it did not help. She was so hungry! She had not been given anything after she had been whisked away.

Signing a document more than a page long had been troubling. Who knew what she had agreed to? What had Fig always said? 'The devil is in the details.' Optimistic Fig. 'Don't worry. It will work out. If not today, tomorrow a break would come their way.' It was great to be so upbeat. But after a while, a little change in attitude would be welcome.

More like Cliff's. Not pushy like other guys, always leering and turning everything said into a *double entendre*. And not so in your face like Fig, always mooning over her. Cliff seemed like a guy merely doing his job. She was a woman; he was a man. No big deal. That was kind of nice.

The door leading into the warehouse opened. Fig and Lilith came into the lobby.

"Easier than expected," Lilith explained as they entered. "I thought there would be only embers by now, but instead there was much more flame."

Fig spotted Briana. He spread his arms wide and rushed to her, enclosing her in his arms. "You are safe. I'm so glad."

Briana accepted his embrace. A flicker of desire rose for an instant but then faded away. She thought for a moment about what Lilith had told her. Illuminating about Fig but not ... convincing. Shouldn't there be something more? Something visceral that made her heart throb. She felt confused.

"Not now, Fig." She withdrew from him, smiling to soften his disappointment. "Something more important. We have a gig! A magic act, exactly like you said. One of the angles we were pursuing. Two hundred dollars is not much, I realize. But at least we can restock the pantry."

"Where? When?"

Like an old shirt, Fig seemed to shed what must be his feelings, Briana thought. He had a new problem to solve. It felt good that he was there for her, even if ...

"Tonight at 10 PM." She managed to pull her thoughts into line. "At a place called the Club Exotica. Not much time. I already have an idea, though. You'll have to visit a nursery to get the shrubs I need for the summoning. Something for a will-o-the-wisp or a tooth exchanger."

"The Club Exotica. I've heard of it. On the street, it does not have a good rep."

"Who cares? I get control of a few imps and have them do little tricks, loops and spirals, and such. It will be perfect. Performing real magic but with no one here on Earth the wiser."

"I don't think so." Fig frowned and wagged his head. "The place seats a couple hundred. We need something much more grand."

He studied Lilith for a moment, rubbing his chin. "I recognize you have done everything I have asked. Briana is safely returned ... But, well, we have been through a lot together, and it looks like I need a favor."

"A favor. What is a favor?" Lilith asked. "There is only a single remaining thing to be decided between us."

"When you do something for … friendship's sake. Not a barter. Nothing expected in return. You just do it, because — "

"I must start my search. Find Angela and neutralize what she intends to do. Otherwise, I will never be able to rest." Lilith glowered at Fig. "We have postponed this long enough. Let us duel now to see which of us has the greater inner strength and get that out of the way."

"How about this?" Fig rushed to reply. "Rather than a favor, consider it a *quid pro quo* exchange." He pointed at his head. "I take your list of names to the library. Research them on the internet. If I'm lucky, figure out where Angela has gone first. Or even find a pattern that dictates the entire order."

"I do not want to stay here. Finding Angela is what I must do."

"Where Angela will go next is a riddle," Fig insisted. "The payoff for solving should be a tempting reward."

Lilith cocked her head to the side and pondered. "You *are* good with puzzles, Fig," she said.

"Listen, Lilith. There are a dozen names on the list. A dozen. Think of it. The chance of you and Angela visiting the same woman simultaneously at random is very small. Your entire pursuit might be for naught."

Lilith did not immediately answer. Her eyes closed and her brow wrinkled in thought.

Briana watched the demon's concentration take control. Like a statue in a museum, the succubus stood immobile, oblivious of her surroundings.

After almost a full minute, Lilith shuddered and again became alert. She furrowed her brow to emphasize what she was going to say. "Okay, *one* more task. But that's all. Understood? That is *all*. What is it you want me to do?"

"Nothing much."

7

Club Exotica

BRIANA COUGHED when the backstage door to the Club Exotica opened for her. The haze of smoke reminded her of a smoldering volcano. A rack of painted panels stood near a sprawl of colored lights and snaking power cords. Ropes and pulleys hung beside stately rows of curtains standing guard over a featureless back wall.

"I'm the opening act for Zantos." Briana smoothed down her hair. "Cliff said I should report here."

"And we need to talk with the magician before we go on," Fig called over her shoulder. "We don't have much time to prepare."

"Where are your tricks, your apparatuses?" The door guard examined the pair. He frowned at Briana's simple A-line dress. "And what is it you are wearing?"

"Zantos," Briana ignored the question. "We want to speak to Zantos."

The guard shrugged and pointed to a row of dressing room doors lining a side wall. "The third from the left. But he does not like interruptions while he gets ready."

Briana did not waste time with thanks. She and Fig hurried in the indicated direction. She knocked on the door with a ripple of loud thumps.

"I'm not sure about this," Fig said softly to Briana as they waited for a response. "It was the only thing I thought of that might work on such short notice."

"Not to be disturbed," a base voice thundered from behind the door.

"We need to borrow a cabinet," Fig called out. "One you are not using tonight. For a good cause. First time out for a newcomer. Perhaps you remember when you were starting yourself."

Silence for a moment, and then the door opened.

An elderly man, hair white as freshly fallen snow poked his head through the opening. A face wrinkled like that of the leading elephant in a migration herd. His eyes were set deep as if they had been drilled into his head. He looked Briana and Fig up and down and finally smiled.

"I *do* remember." Zantos nodded. "The first time is always the hardest. Which one of you is the performer?"

"I am," Briana answered before Fig could say more. "My ... assistant can tell you what I need."

"A standard disappearance cabinet," Fig burst in. "As tall as you have. I assume the stage has the standard structures."

"Yes, it does," Zantos agreed. "No magician can perform successfully otherwise." He peered at Briana again. "This is not close up work. There can be over a hundred in the audience on a good night. And they are easily displeased."

FIG STOOD in the wings as the curtains parted. Putting on a show when one had knowledge of real magic was easy — no reason to lose one's calm. Even so, he crossed and uncrossed his fingers nervously. There had been no time for a rehearsal.

The audience venue was an array of small tables, some for two, most for four, and in the back stood several longer ones. The haze of smoke hung even more densely than backstage. Briana strode out and bowed. The chatter in the audience continued unabated. No one applauded.

"May I have your attention," Briana spoke into the wireless mike draped around her neck. Her voice boomed, and the mike shrieked with feedback. The babble stopped. Eyes turned to scowl at the interruption.

Briana froze her face into a fake smile. With one of Zantos' wands, she tapped the tall cabinet standing in the center stage. "Many of you have seen magic with cabinets such as these before. Perhaps many times.

"A volunteer enters," she explained. "The door is shut, and after a few moments reopened. The assistant has vanished! The door closes. Another few words and tap of the wand. A final opening, and magically, the volunteer reappears!" She could not help smiling. "Yes, magic, true magic."

The hum of conversation rose again. Briana knew she had to move swiftly before the attention evaporated. "But this cabinet is different.

Vanishing and reappearing is child's play compared to this. Watch and be amazed."

On cue, Fig advanced to the cabinet. Briana pantomimed that he enter. After she shut the door, the stage lighting blinked on and off like struggling neons. When they again were steady, Briana reopened the door with a flourish.

Several in the audience gasped. The cabinet was not empty as expected. Instead, it contained a pale green woman, completely naked — one with wings and even horns on her head. Lilith's appearance was familiar to Briana now. But she remembered her startled reaction when the demon's twin sister first emerged from the juniper flame.

Lilith stepped forward and extended her wings. With one intense burst of strength, soared out over the crowd. Now there were more than mere gasps. Some stood up, knocking their chairs backward. Others reached for napkins being blown about by the sudden rush of air. Like a burbling brook, a cacophony of voices mingled in wonder.

The two women at one of the nearest tables flung it on its side and ducked for cover behind it. In an instant, their escorts joined them as well. Along the left wall, one of the patrons grabbed a half-empty bottle of beer. He threw it at the moving target flying past him on the other side of the room.

The succubus returned to the stage, reentered the cabinet, and the door closed. Briana tapped her wand and said a few more words of gibberish. Fig reemerged and bowed. The audience roared their approval. A few stood, clapping enthusiastically. More and more followed.

"How did you know a trap door would be available to use?" Briana whispered as they returned for a curtain call.

"Most stages do," Fig shrugged. "No real magic at all."

BRIANA PATTED her stomach. She felt better than she had in a long time. The ice cream after a full dinner tasted *so* good. Eating off a card table backstage of the Club Exotica rather than in a fancy restaurant did not matter.

She savored happy things, recalling the feeling she had when she went back on the stage for the second and third bow. All that applause. Everyone so enthusiastic. Something she could get used to. Maybe staying on Earth would not be so bad, after all.

"Thank you, Cliff." She beamed. "A check *and* a meal."

"So we are clear. Take a look at the check," Cliff said.

Briana examined the slip of paper a little more closely. "It's only for one hundred seventy, not two hundred."

"Right. I took out my fifteen percent as your agent."

"My agent?"

"The contract you signed. Remember?"

"I don't under — " Briana began.

"The bosses are as enthusiastic as the rest," Cliff said. "You're the opening act every night except Monday when we are closed. No argument about it. I got it set up. Another contract with them. Flows through me and then to you." He paused. "I thought you would be pleased."

Briana ground her teeth. An agent's bite was irritating if nothing else. Cliff should have explained all the terms before she signed.

The mood was broken. Her daydream skidded to a halt. Lilith, the succubus, was going back to her home realm, probably as soon as she returned to the lab. She had done what Fig had asked — but agreed to do it only once. The sight of a demon soaring over a crowd was never going to be repeated. A full belly and almost a couple hundred bucks was a good thing, but now what?

"Ah, see you tomorrow night," Briana shouted over her shoulder as she headed for the door. "I have to take care of something."

8

Renewed Pursuit

BRIANA BURST into the warehouse lab. She saw Lilith trying to breathe more life into the fire in the kiln. "Wait," she said. "Don't go. I need you."

"And what about Fig?" Lilith asked.

Briana hesitated. She looked about. He was not there.

"He is at the library to do some research for me," Lilith explained. "Part of our agreement. You know that."

Briana stopped speaking. Things had become complicated. She realized a new desire burned within her. Using the crafts for entertainment would not disturb the cultures on the Earth. There would be no harm. There were a zillion things she could do. Like chains suddenly bursting apart, balls within cups within balls ... A sense of liberation swept over her — not only fame but freedom to act as she chose.

But Lilith was part of that. She must remain. And if the demon did so, then what about Fig? Ideally, he would dominate the succubus rather than the other way around. But could he?

Before Briana puzzled her way through the rushing tide of her thoughts, Fig entered the lab.

"I have remembered something," he said. "The clue, Lilith, was your remark when we came back from the catacombs. That the fire should have been down to embers, but it was not. And the few branches left on the bench were no longer there."

"Meaning what?" Lilith asked.

"When Angela left the catacombs, she came *here* rather than go somewhere else in time, instead."

"Why would she do that?"

130

"I'm not sure, but of all the names on Angela's list, there is only one woman who is alive, living here in the present."

Before Lilith could reply, another voice from outside the lab rang out.

"Briana, where are you?"

It was Cliff.

Fig looked at Lilith and then Briana. "He can't come back here," he said.

"I will stop him," Briana agreed. She rushed out, headed for the warehouse lobby.

"Where?" The demon asked when Briana was gone.

"Moscow."

"I will go there now." Lilith stepped toward the flame.

"Our own struggle?" Fig asked. "What about that?"

"I have thought it through. I will not be able to concentrate fully so long as Angela remains free. I must go."

"Wait a moment. Go and do what?" Fig tried to stand in Lilith's way and failed. "Another hand-to-hand fight? You must have a better plan than that. Explain to me why you have to do this."

"Angela thinks she can seduce the mightiest of princes in my realm. Elezar is his name. Get him to satisfy her every whim." Lilith took a deep breath. "Her mind is like a steamroller. Once she has decided on doing something, she continues to push everything in the way flat.

"You heard her in the catacombs," Lilith reminded him. "Declared she would see that I was ripped asunder. I can hold my own against her teeth and claws — but not against the power of several djinns who were following Elezar's commands."

"Then stay. Briana must see she needs you now, and — "

"Fig, there is more involved than that." Lilith wagged her head emphatically. "I have my own ... calling. The power of the princes in my realm is wrong. The battle lust of the males makes things the way they are. And as a consequence, the females like myself: dribblers, gremlins, gargoyles, rockbubblers, hoseherders, hairtanglers ... all the rest — we are nothing more than chattel. We have no purpose other than to provide sex on demand. Bring forth new demons to replace those fallen in battle or eaten for a meal.

"If Angela succeeds in her quest." Lilith waved her arms like an orator. "It is more than I who will face a personal doom. Her capriciousness will make women's servitude even worse. Another spike will be driven into the coffin confining half of demonkind. I must stop

131

her, not only for myself but for all my sisters."

Before Fig could reply, a loud laugh filtered into the lab. He opened the door a crack to hear what was happening.

"Oh, Cliff," Briana said with another laugh. "You're just saying that."

Fig shut the door hard. He slammed his fist against the wall. He could not believe what he heard. Flirting! She was flirting with Cliff. Frustration bubbled within him. He blinked at the intensity of his feelings. The logic was inescapable. He saved her from a gruesome death and got what? Only a simple 'thank you' and a brief hug in return. Yet for someone whose only purpose in life was to take fifteen percent off the top …

He breathed deeply, fighting to regain control. "Moscow," he said at last. "I need a new venue, Lilith. There is little for me here. I'm going with you."

9

Stakeout

FIG RUBBED his hands together, but it did little to help his numbed fingers. Moscow's temperature was a brutal change, not what he expected. The onion-like domes of Saint Basil's were nowhere in sight. No Kremlin. No Red Square. The television studio stood on a street a good mile west of there. It was wide but drab grey like an old flannel blanket left out too long in the sun. Only the studio across the intersection broke the boring line of apartment buildings receding into the distance in both directions. He and Lilith had staked out the place starting shortly after dawn. Now it was dusk, and they had not yet seen any sign of Angela.

The journey halfway around the world had been an impulse. Fig knew that. He should have stayed with Briana — been there for her. But damn it, now he had something else important to do. She was not the entirety of his universe.

And now that he thought about it, there were a few other differences as well. He was a crack of dawn guy, anxious to start the new day. She liked to wake at noon and stay up to all hours of the night surfing the internet. Looking for signs, any clues that aliens were on the Earth. The existence of real magic, not the sleights of hand stage actors performed.

And there was Cliff, the new development. What did she see in the guy? Business, but nothing else, right? No, not right. He recalled her laugh, her tone of voice when he overheard them talking. Had she ever interacted with himself in the same —

"There!" Lilith pointed. "In the alley between the studio and the first apartment building. She must have been waiting for darkness before moving about."

Fig peered into the dusk. Yes, it was Angela lurking in the shadows across the street. Finally, after hours of searching in the cold, they had spotted her. He squinted at the cloaked demon scurrying away. "What is sitting on her shoulder?" he asked.

"A gargoyle. A minor sprite in the hierarchy of my realm. My sister has recruited some help. Hurry, we must follow before she vanishes from sight."

"Wait a moment." Fig put his hand on Lilith's arm. "Now that we have located her, we can be more efficient. One of us tracking while the other takes a quick nap is going to be exhausting. We can't continue this way. Don't you have some helpers, too?"

"Helpers? Well, not as useful as gargoyles," Lilith admitted. "Dribblers and such are the ones I have dealt with most recently."

"Okay, dribblers. What do they do?"

"Not much."

"Can one of them shadow Natasha and report back to us?"

"They are tiny as small insects." Lilith apologized with thrown up hands.

"Are they good enough? Can they do the job?"

"Fig, they are the only ones I can suggest."

"Okay, let's go with it. Get one tracking, now."

"Very well. You stay here and watch. Follow Angela as best you can wherever she goes. I will return with some dribblers to take over the surveillance." She shook her head slowly. "I hope this will work. They have very little brain."

THE DAY had passed from dawn to noon and then to darkness. The night was moonless. Angela looked about. She saw no one in the narrow street where she waited, far from the studio. The shopkeepers who tried to sell the motley collection of goods a decade old had long since gone home. None of the streetlights worked.

No one could see anything in such shadow, Angela told herself for the dozenth time. Yet, she could not help the feeling someone was watching. Had watched her every movement for most of the entire day.

As Angela fumed, Adonis, the gargoyle, appeared in the transom above the doorway at which she stood. The Cyrillic had been hard to read, but the costumes in the display window gave no doubt as to what was rented and sold.

"This is the last female one in your size," Adonis shrugged. "If not that, you are going to have to settle for something like Peter Pan."

Angela unfolded the dress handed to her. "A cartoon character?" she asked.

"Yeah, wicked queen of something. I'm not sure. The Hunchback of Notre Dame is the movie I'm more familiar with. If you don't like — "

"It does have a high collar," Angela appraised the costume again. "Perfect," she decided. "Tomorrow morning, I can change out of this abaya. Bring along the rest of the stuff we have collected."

THE NEXT day, after opening hours, Angela came out of the toilet stall in the GUM department store. Cautiously, she approached the long mirror above the row of sinks. A few of the human women nearby raised their eyebrows, but not alarmingly so. She flexed her back, and the corset binding her wings to her body did not yield. The high collar and long flowing robe of the costume made her profile look more natural. Not perfect, but it would serve.

Now the tricky part. She read the instructions again but was not sure what all the words meant. 'First, apply a light concealer a few shades lighter than your skin tone over the entire area. Then a heavier cream using a makeup sponge or a stippling brush …'

Angela grimaced. For a few minutes, she watched what the women were doing. Her discomfort grew. She realized she should have stolen different applicators along with the foundation cream. She scowled. Eyebrow curlers, mascara, rouge, lipstick, nail polish. Was any of this necessary? Part of the human female's secret formula for seduction?

She painted her face, fumbling with each product, one after another. Gradually, she got the job done. The pale green color of her skin now looked pale beige. The demarcations between the scales no longer visible in normal light.

More curious glances came her way. She adjusted the sign across her chest to display prominently. '*The Snow Queen — Episode Two — Coming soon to a theater near you — Get your free autograph here!*' it read.

For the last touch, Angela donned the wig and studied herself in the mirror. The long bangs in front covered her horns well enough. At last, she was done and gave a sigh of relief. Now, she was ready to meet with Natasha Gorshok and make her pitch. No need to deal with the likes of Marie Antoinette any more.

10

Briana's New Act

BRIANA RETURNED to the lab after searching the entire warehouse. Neither Fig nor Lilith were anywhere. Her head hurt. It felt as if the muscles in her neck were being stretched tight by a mischievous mite. Cliff had been reluctant to leave the reception lobby. From the way he acted, it was apparent he was there for more than only reassurance. But he had acted quite properly. Even a little shy. If not for everything else, next time she might give him some encouragement.

Next time? Encouragement? What was she thinking? No time for that.

Next time was less than twenty-four hours away. "Yes," she had told Cliff. "I will be there tomorrow night."

But Fig and Lilith were gone. She had no act. She had to think.

Call forth and dominate another succubus? No, that was too risky. She had been unable to dominate Angela and probably could not succeed with another. Imps then, ones she could control. Ones not overawed by the environment of the nightclub with hundreds of people, dim lights, some drunken and loud.

"Drink dribblers!" she shouted the answer aloud. "Yes, small and dimwitted. A milieu not different from that of a bar. And summoned, how?

One by one, she pulled open the drawers from the chest of ingredients in the corner of the lab. It was one of the only things of any importance left behind when Fig had sold almost everything else. No wonder. Who would find any value in the materials stocked there? Wisps of grey hair, mushrooms, pebbles of fool's gold, cinnabar. Hundreds of items with no real value or interest.

Tobacco. Yes, tobacco, she remembered. The channel for dribblers into the realm of humans was burning tobacco. Well, yes. Of course. It was abundant in dimly lit bars, perfect for bridges between the realms. She had to get some, but how?

Briana wrinkled her nose. She was not sure about this. Much of human culture she had not yet learned … cigarettes! Yes, that is what they were called. She would have to buy some. She hurried to the office opening to the lobby and grabbed a purse out of a desk drawer. Silly damn thing. Why did women use them in public? What did one carry in them anyway? Pockets were so much better.

She looked inside the purse. Right, the check. To the bank first to convert it into cash. Fig had taught her how to do that. Fig. Did Lilith really take him? Should she instead be thinking about …

No, first focus on the show. That would bring in money, lots of money. Enable her to amass enough so tracking down Fig would be easy.

BRIANA PULLED off the paper binding from the last cigarette in the pack. She added the contents to the pile. It had taken several trials to get things right. Not too much so that a blaze hard to control resulted. Nor too little so that she had to blow constantly to keep it from winking out.

She settled her thoughts and reached out with her mind. The experience of every wizard was different, her father had told her once. Sometimes even different for each type of demon, too. A shudder ran down her back as the memory of Angela rose to the top of her thoughts. Before she could panic, she imagined a large blanket, one able to cover a score of beds. She placed it under her mental representation of the succubus. Then she directed her thoughts to grab each blanket corner into a bundle and soar upward. With the image of the demon trapped, she flung the cloth aside and cleared her mind.

A dribbler was different. She waited for the first light touch. Almost immediately the caress of a soft feather tickled her mind. There was no resistance to her summons. Instead, an eagerness, a desire for the journey, even though it meant being subject to another.

Briana reeled in the dribbler toward her. With a soft pop, it appeared above the smoldering tobacco — a speck.

"Okay, babe, what's the job?" a high-pitched voice shrilled. "Big party tonight? Lots of guests? Need a boost when things start to sag?"

"More orchestrated than that." Briana said.

"Not so loud!" the dribbler put his hands over his ears. "I'm only a few feet away, not halfway to Timbuktu."

"I will need lots of you," Briana said more softly. "Hundreds. Maybe two. Can you convince many more to come?"

"Well, not me personally. But you have come to the right place. I have the ear of our leader." He paused. "Ready for this? I am the first buddy of no less than the Awesome Nabob."

"Bring him here," Briana raised her voice again, but only a trifle.

"Hey, babe. You might be missing your big chance here. The Awesome Nabob is not sitting on a frog wart waiting for the next request to show up. He has a schedule — things to do. But, as I say, I have his ear. I can ask him to adjust priorities."

"Bring him here." Briana stomped her foot. "Time is short, and you guys are so flighty, we will have a lot of rehearsing to do."

11

To Try Again

ANGELA STOOD outside of Natasha's office. She studied her face in her compact mirror and grinned, satisfied. She heard sounds from the other side of the closed door and knocked.

Inside, Natasha looked around one last time. She had filed the papers on her desk. It was entirely clear. She did not want to be doing this, but with Alexei being held captive she had no other choice. Best to perform the job quickly so he would be freed as soon as possible.

"Who is it?" Natasha called out. "I'm busy and have a plane to catch."

Angela's grin broadened, almost to the point of revealing her fangs. The woman sounded frustrated. She would be receptive for what she had to offer. The succubus' grin grew as if produced by an overzealous pumpkin carver. Getting the guard at the door to let her in had been easy. Of course, the costume immediately caught his eye. A few minutes in the men's room with him in exchange for a visitor's pass was a fair trade. The succubus opened the office door and entered without waiting for permission.

"I said I have no time," Natasha snapped. She looked up and blinked at the strangely garbed woman standing there. "The Snow Queen," she read from Angela's placard. "Coming to a theatre near you." She scowled. "Dmitry will be filling in for me. See him to arrange the day you will appear to plug your movie."

"Moscow to San Francisco and then on to Sacramento, California," Angela ignored the command. "There are still three hours until your flight."

Natasha blinked. "How do you know? Are you SVR, too?"

"Not the Foreign Security Service," Angela wiggled her head slightly. She pulled out the compact from one of her pockets, powdered her nose, and lowered her voice to a whisper. "CIA."

The petty interplay of humans reminded her of warring princes back in her realm. She hoped such complications would not interfere with her goal. They sounded dire. Unconditional surrender? Complete capitulation? A month at most after Natasha completed her assignment?

"What?" Natasha said, jarring Angela back to focus on her plan.

"Keep your voice low, Natasha. Your office is not bugged, but you know how thin the walls are."

"This is a test, right?"

Angela shook her head a little more emphatically. She reached up to touch her bangs hiding her horns. Good. They were still in place. "No, not a test. I will meet you in the Sacramento airport. Come up to me after you have received your instructions from your handler. We will go somewhere and talk."

"Why should I?"

"Do you actually think this will be your only assignment? You want to see Alexei again, don't you? That is what the Company can provide."

IT TOOK three flights for Natasha to get to Sacramento. She had had plenty of time to think. Any good agent always had a backup plan. She would push forward with her instructions from Comrade Viktor, certainly. But at the same time, string along with the CIA. Remaining in the US with Alexei was the goal. But who knew which path would lead to her lover's release first.

When Natasha finally arrived in Sacramento, her legs had fallen asleep. She hobbled out of the terminal and walked toward the taxi queue. The brushpass from her SVR handler had been textbook. Detailed instructions now resided safely in her over the shoulder purse. She had also spotted the CIA agent who called herself Angela but had walked past. Too dangerous to make contact so quickly. Didn't the woman even know the basics?

Natasha entered the next cab in the line. "Folsom," she said. "Take me to a bank."

"There's one on Sutter. A historic street," the cabbie said. "Quite scenic. Will that do?"

"Perfect."

As the taxi entered the airport traffic, Natasha leaned to the right in the back seat. She watched the curb through the side view mirror and nodded with satisfaction. Angela *had* caught another taxi and was following.

Folsom, she thought. She had to admit she was curious. Why did the SVR have any interest in a place like that? Perhaps she was to contact someone in the state prison?

Natasha opened her purse. Her first instructions were in a separate envelope from the rest, and she started to read. Simple enough. Put the rest in a safety deposit box to go over later in private. Had to do that. Leaving incriminating information around in a hotel room would be risky. But she knew enough now to hook this Angela with a nibble. Negotiate to get Alexei out of Russia before handing over the rest. She slumped. Jet lag. First, get some sleep.

NATASHA EXITED the bank and looked about. The cabbie had been right. The other side of Sutter Street did look historic. A row of small two-story buildings butted against one another. Each painted in a different bright color. Most had balconies of brilliant white. The second story rooflines were all different. Some straight with a row of windows, others peaked by central triangles or curlicues.

Angela, of course, was easy to spot. She stood in the center of a crowd pressing around her. Some held autograph books while others shouted questions about *The Snow Queen*. Her English signage was working even better than the one in Russian had.

Natasha shouldered herself to stand close enough to her CIA contact that she could be seen. She caught Angela's eye and then entered the small café two doors down the street.

"A coffee. Black, no sugar," Natasha told the clerk with a satisfied smile. It had been a while but her English came back perfectly. She could tell there was no trace of an accent.

It took another five minutes before Angela appeared. The succubus closed the café door forcefully so no more curiosity seekers would follow.

"So, what is the mission?" the costumed woman said as she sat down at Natasha's table.

"The *Independent System Operator* offices are here," Natasha answered.

"What job is that?"

"Control of the electric grid."

Natasha watched Angela's eyes open wide, her mouth curving into a small 'o.' The spy held back her laugh. This had to be her contact's first assignment. "You know. Power distribution. That sort of thing."

"Not important," Angela shrugged. "What is it you are to do?"

"Vector in on one of the employees, an engineer. Get him to do a few things for me."

Natasha waited. She imagined the gears turning in Angela's head as she pondered.

"Yes, the grid," Angela said at last. "The professor has told me about it. Cause a disruption like the one in the Ukraine some years back. Remotely throw circuit breakers. A rolling blackout —"

"No, not anything that crude. I have read that such an interruption would be a temporary inconvenience at worst. The engineers simply would go to the substations and manually turn the generators back on. Happens frequently when there is a big storm."

"Then what?" Angela frowned, puzzled.

"First, tell me about Alexei. What is the plan? Does he end up here in the US with me? Do we both get asylum?"

Angela's tone hardened. "I need the details. How exactly do you get control of the engineer?"

Natasha frowned. She felt a strange, unfamiliar pressure on her brain.

"Showing is better than telling," Natasha said. "You can watch if you want. Every step along the way."

"Exactly!" Angela said. "That is why you have been chosen."

The pressure faded away. Natasha took a deep breath to clear her head. She was too old to keep doing this. But if it meant getting her lover back …

"What are the details about Alexei?" she asked. "I need to know, or else there is no deal."

"Asylum. Both of you. The US. Sure, sure," Angela said. "Whatever you want."

"That came too fast." Natasha frowned. "Do you have the authority to make the deal? How do I know you are not stringing me along?"

"Natasha, the same can be said of you."

The pair both lapsed into silence for a while, until finally, the spy spoke again.

"Okay, let's start the process to get control of the engineer. Do the first few steps. Get to know each other a little better as we go."

"Yes," Angela agreed. "Instruct me with your methods. That is what I want most of all."

12

The Craft of Seduction

IT WAS dusk a day later. Natasha and Angela had parked in the visitor lot of the California Independent System Operator. Employees were filing out of the building, some going directly home and others to downtown Folsom.

"There, that one," Natasha pointed out through the windshield. She glanced at Angela. It felt strange to have herself driving, and her CIA contact the one in the passenger seat.

"Why him?" Angela asked. "He looks much the same as the rest."

"A loner. Not chatting with anyone else. An engineer rather than a paper pusher. Receding hairline. Somewhat older than the rest."

Natasha lowered the binoculars she had bought with the credit card the SVR had provided. "And no ring. It's much harder when they are married."

"So, you go up to him and introduce yourself?"

"No, too obvious. Let's hope he stops off somewhere before going home."

NATASHA GLANCED at Angela and sighed. Her CIA contact sat at the corner table in the coffee shop signing autographs. The operative had wanted to stay glued to her side, but a wing woman was not part of the play here. The place was almost full. Natasha scanned the room as if she were looking for an empty spot.

She butted into the edge of the table where her target was sitting and yelped. As she did, she dumped the contents of the glass of ice tea she

145

was carrying against her chest. Instinctively, the man sprang to his feet as she flailed to regain her balance.

Safe in his grip, he guided her to sit down. Natasha watched his eyes as he glanced at her thin blouse. The ice in the drink had done its job.

"I'm so sorry," she said. "I should look where I'm going. Did I get you wet, too?"

"Ah, no. No. I'm fine," the man stammered. "Here, have a seat."

Natasha slid into the booth. She said nothing, letting an awkward silence build while she studied the man facing her. Bushy eyebrows above large glasses. Stubble already showing after a sloppy job of shaving in the morning. Overall, he was pleasant enough looking. She had had to stomach much worse.

"My name is Robert," the target blurted.

Natasha's smile blossomed like an opening flower. Only twelve seconds. It never failed. The target had to be the one speaking first. The initiator. The aggressor. The thought of being set up would never get a foothold in his mind.

"Natasha." She dipped her head slightly as she extended her hand for him to shake. "Thank you for saving me from a nasty fall."

Startled for a moment, Robert recovered and offered his own. His hand felt like a dead fish as they clasped. Natasha caught herself from shaking her head. Men. What was it with men when they shook with a woman? Her bones would not break any more than would a man's. He blinked as she applied pressure with her grip. As strong as anyone's, so she had been told — a tag for him to remember her by whenever they met again.

"I, ah, come here every day after work to unwind a bit," Robert said. "But I don't recall seeing you before."

Natasha shrugged. "Newly arrived. Me and my son. Had to get somewhere new to start over. Messy divorce."

"Oh, I'm … I'm sorry."

"What is it you do?" Natasha ignored the remark. She leaned forward and opened her eyes wide. It took a little practice to get the dose of belladonna correct, but she had had much training. In the middle ages, women did it all the time — dilating their pupils. For some reason, that made men think they were interested in them.

Natasha glanced over at Angela. Between autographs, the agent was furiously taking notes. But, surely, the CIA used these minor bits of spycraft as well as the SVR. She turned her attention back to Robert and let the conversation struggle on for a few more minutes. Always look him square in the face, she remembered. Show interest in everything he says.

When things had ground to a halt, Natasha stood and walked around the table between them. She touched him on his forearm, letting her hand linger for a few moments more than might be expected.

"Thank you again," she said and left the coffee shop.

As she did, Natasha thought about Alexei, worried about the conditions he was in. The thriller writers made it seem so fast, so easy. This mission will take at least a month, she estimated. Perhaps, several more.

And it was complicated. She was playing at two games, not merely one. Get a firm commitment from the CIA about asylum. Push that as hard as she could. But if that did not work, follow the SVR instructions to their conclusion. One way or another, she would get Alexei back.

13

Drink Dribblers in Action

BRIANA SMOOTHED her costume. She was not comfortable even after a week of wearing it. A jungle of colored spangles. Sleeveless and bare legs. But Cliff had insisted. It was what the audiences wanted to see. Part of the total package. And with the raise he had negotiated because of it, she had paid for her plumage with the income from a single show.

She looked out over the audience through the curtain peephole. The serving girls could barely maneuver between the extra tables and chairs. Zantos stood scowling in the wings behind the closed curtain. He did not like it. His was the opening act now, and he received no curtain calls.

Substituting a swarm of dribblers for a succubus had worked out better than expected. There were only a few grumbles about not seeing the large beast flying overhead again.

The curtains parted. Briana strode to center stage and took a slight bow to the opening applause. With no preamble, she started her act. The first few tricks were standard — colored balls moved from one inverted cup to another, an almost endless supply of scarfs fell from a small wand.

When the last ring became free of the others, she stopped and addressed the audience for the first time. "Stage magic has been around for over a century," she said. "Up close magic hundreds more. But interactive magic is something new. As you will see, after years of study with monks high in the mountains of Tibet, I have mastered their secrets."

Briana tapped a wand on a large porcelain jar Cliff had found in an antique store. "My helpers sleep most of the day so they will have the strength to interact with you now. Can I have the lights dimmed, please?"

The illumination over the audience faded. Still bright enough for one to see across a table after a moment but too dim to tell what actually would happen.

"You sound like a friendly enough crowd," Briana said. "I want everyone at each table to link hands in a circle." She paused. "This is important. If there is a break in the chain, nothing will happen for you.

After a moment, she said, "Let's check. Everyone stretch their clasped hands upwards. I need to see that all are connected. Remember. If you release your grip, the spell will be broken."

Briana watched the audience comply. "You there, in the last row."

"He is my ex-boyfriend," a voice answered. "This double date was a bad idea."

The audience laughed, and Briana smiled. Cliff's idea had been a good one. He found one table to go along with the gag at each performance. And he was clever enough to create a different script each time. The intertwining was not only for amusement. With all the hands coupled, none of the dribblers would experience a mosquito's squishy death.

Briana returned her attention to the large urn. With a flourish, she removed the lid. "Creatures of darkness, go forth. Show everyone you are here."

The audience fell quiet. Word had gotten around. In perfect silence, the buzz of the emerging dribblers was heard. There were hundreds of them — enough that each one had the responsibility for only a single customer.

"Now, my flock, let your subjects know you are here."

The dribblers droned into the audience, but they could not be seen. Too dark for that. The tiny imps communicated with the frequency of their wingbeats, sorting out the individual customers rapidly. Almost in unison, they descended on their targets and pinched them on their cheeks.

"Shrieks of surprise erupted throughout the large room. Several people bolted for the doors. Those in the audience returning to see the act a second time kept their hands clasped. A few of the newcomers instinctively broke their grips and slapped. Briana had warned the dribblers this could happen. And, after the first few fatalities, the tiny imps had learned to disengage and fly out of harm's way.

"Now, now," Briana scolded from the stage. "Behave, or I will have to leave."

After another round of laughter died, Briana continued her patter. "Next, I want each of you to concentrate. Think about who you want to spend the night with after the show is over. Hands still clasped, whisper that name aloud as low as you can, so low no one else can hear."

A distinct slush of words filled the air for a moment and then, silence again.

"Soft, but not quite soft enough. My children have sensitive ears. Inform them, my pets, the lucky recipients of this desire. Give each of them a love bite on their cheeks."

A moment passed. Then, a single person at each table gasped. Each victim's face stung from the stabs of pain from, not one, but three or more tiny, simultaneous nips. A second later, the implication of what had just happened sunk in. The dupe concluded he or she was the focus of *everyone else's* desire. A sea of conversation arose like billowing summer clouds.

After the hubbub quietened, the dribblers dove and pierced every glass with their sharp nails. The last tasks done, they returned to the urn.

"Now release your grips," Briana commanded. "And toast the creatures of the night who have paid you a visit."

The newcomers followed the instruction. Almost instantly, they sprang to their feet. The remains of their cocktails dribbled down their chests. Returning customers, wise to what was going to happen, did not take part. They chuckled at the newcomers' surprise.

Briana bowed and stepped back as the curtain closed.

BRIANA SHUT the dressing room door. "No conversation tonight, Cliff," she called out. "I need some time alone to unwind."

The adrenalin rush had been the same as the very first curtain call a week ago — a fantastic feeling. She wished she felt that way all the time. She sighed, knowing that after a while, the euphoria would fade. Her pulse rate would slow, the tingling slip away.

The highs were astronomical. She feasted on them. But before she started doing the act, her homesickness was something that she could bear, able to push it aside and think of other things. Read, exercise, do those strange human puzzles that crossed words against one another. Now, the contrast with the lows that inevitably followed a performance were becoming excruciating to bear. She could not sit still, push the longing for home out of her mind, concentrate on anything else than watching the minutes tick by. Waiting until when she would again taste the rush of on-stage excitement.

What she needed was an aid to keep her high from totally vanishing.

Something to keep her spirits up when she was not on stage. But not a physical drug. They were too dangerous and habit-forming. Rather, something that would replace melancholy with the mellow.

She wondered. There was one thing she could try — self-enchantment, one of the chants of sorcery. Most of a sorcerer's craft was concerned with the manipulation of others — making them see vivid images and obey nefarious commands.

Most, but not all. Sorcerers routinely enchanted themselves to see what was happening in faraway places or events unfolding in the future. And besides those, Briana recalled, there was another, even more different from the rest. It provided peace to the caster — a feeling of calmness, of well-being, a retreat from a noisy and chaotic world outside.

There were dire warnings about using it, of course. The whispers were that once you started self-enchanting yourself, you would be unable to stop. Briana thrust the thought away. Her will was stronger than that. After all, she was the daughter of an archimage. And the upside was enticing. It couldn't hurt to try it only this once tonight. Force the release of chemicals into your brain. Wrap yourself in calmness rather than crash into despair.

She sat down in the folding chair and closed her eyes. The charm was simple enough. One of the first a tyro learned. "Thrice spoken, once fulfilled," she muttered aloud — the fundamental law of sorcery.

Briana spoke slowly. She knew not to hurry. Each of the three repetitions became harder and harder to enunciate properly. The tiniest slip meant a miscasting and a headache lasting for hours.

The first run through was easy. She sounded like a child singing a nursery rhyme. But when she started the second, her tongue behaved as if it had a mind of its own. It lay thick and sluggish in her mouth as if a dentist had missed his target with his needle of Lydocain. She could hardly get her lips to move.

Grimacing with the effort, she forced out the first word. "Namodrel," echoed off the confining walls. "Persipopol, actonbromel, landrinum," quickly followed. Briana took a quick breath. Not too fast, she told herself. Precision was more important than speed. Like a troop of soldiers at the end of an all-day march, the rest of the second passage lumbered into existence.

Briana felt the pressure of the charm converge on her. Her head ached, a fragile gourde being squeezed by giant hands on every side. Only the final time through remained. But what was the first word again? "Namb ... no, Namob." A flutter of panic rose from her stomach. She

151

tasted bile.

"Nam … o … drel", she managed to shout at last. Now, on to the next. 'Persipopol', she thought. Yes, that was correct. It came to her almost immediately. But at the same time, like a steel trap, her jaws slammed shut. Her lips felt as if they had been sewn together.

Sweat formed on her brow. Zigzag lines filled her vision even though her eyes were closed. Briana took a deep breath and then another. Yes, she *was* the daughter of the Archimage. The most simple of charms would not defeat her. Like springing open a wolf trap with her bare hands, she forced out the second word. Then she steeled herself for the third.

In a semi-conscious daze, she strained her way through to the end of the recital.

BRIANA PULLED herself awake. How long had she been out, she was unable to tell. But, neither did she care. She felt as if she were wrapped in a warm fuzzy blanket. A soft glow of contentment filled her from head to toe. With the reasoning still functioning within her, she knew that eventually, the feeling of peace would fade. She would return to the world as it really was. And when she did, the time to perform would be only minutes away. For now, she had no cares, no worries. Nothing mattered. Not the performances, not the happenings in the world, neither Cliff nor Fig. What would be, would be.

14

To Play for Keeps

FIG MUNCHED on the trail mix. He felt more guilty with each bite. Once the dribblers had reported where Natasha had gone, he and Lilith had followed. Carried along by the succubus' haste to track Angela, he had forgotten that money was still a problem. One meal at Club Exotica a week ago did not last forever. Luckily, an attempt at an ATM with his debit card produced results. Briana had deposited the check from the first performance and then ones for larger amounts thereafter. But he did not like making withdrawals without talking to her about them first.

He stepped out from the cover of the old oak and surveyed the scene. It was pleasant and quiet. The Folsom central city park was close to the library. A few nocturnal calls could be heard from the nearby zoo. No one else was about.

"As soon as Cutiepie reports back with Natasha's current location, I will go there. Angela can't be too far from here."

"Wait. What is your plan?"

"Plan? I need no plan."

"We have been over this before. She almost beat you in Paris. Why would this time be any different?"

"I slipped."

Fig said nothing.

"Well, okay," Lilith conceded. "We are evenly matched. Twins after all."

The demon paused. "But you are here with me. That will tip the balance. I ... we will prevail."

"Prevailing means ..."

"Ending her life, of course. Only then, can I be safe." She cocked her head to the side and thought for a moment. "You are also at risk, Fig.

You and your entire planet. Remember what Angela said in the catacombs. She threatened you and Briana, too."

Fig's stomach lurched with a spasm. The falling guillotine flashed in his mind. He had been part of enough death already. Getting some distance from Briana in order to think was one thing, killing someone else quite another. He had to slow down Lilith's run away locomotive.

"Rather than death, wouldn't confinement in your realm serve as well?"

"That's not possible. All it takes is someone to light a juniper fire here on Earth, and she escapes through the flame."

"Okay, how about a prison? One holding her captive in our realm, not yours."

"Wouldn't that be counter to what your Briana wants to guard against happening? Would all the guards have to be secret wizards? Surely, that fact could not be kept under wraps for long."

Before Fig could say more, something fell onto the picnic table behind him. He turned on the bargain store flashlight he had bought earlier. Now, there was an Ouija board on the tabletop. As he watched, escorted by a dozen or more dribblers, the planchette lowered onto its surface.

The little board suspended on casters darted back and forth rapidly. Fig barely could keep up with what was being written. Dim-witted or not, the dribblers had decided to change their method of communication.

"Is this the way you talk to dribblers when you are home?" Fig asked. "Ouija boards?"

"I can't explain it." Lilith shrugged. "In our realm, all types interact by voice with one another. Here in yours, speech frequencies are a function of size."

"Small bodies mean small larynxes," Fig mused. "And that means the wavelengths generated are small as …"

"Let's focus on the job at hand," Lilith cut him off. She clenched her fists. "You can regale me with your background in physics after this is over."

Fig shrugged and did not try to finish his explanation. Lilith was tensing up. He could recognize the signs. As he and the succubus watched, imps reported the latest they had learned.

'Found Natasha lair. Angela is there, too. In a large building. More humans in other rooms. She does not know any of them. None the same tribe as hers. Go figure.'

"Good work, Cutiepie." Excitement bubbled in Lilith's words. "Write out the address." She turned to Fig. "Are you ready?"

Fig quickly thought of what might be the drag brake. "You want my help, right?"

"As always, your logic is sound. Of course, it makes sense to have the edge."

"Then first, let's learn some more. Slow down a bit. Not reveal our presence yet."

"Why?"

"Discover a weakness of your sister. Some characteristic that can be exploited. Perhaps, your encounter can be a *coup* rather than a bloody fight."

"I am surprised, Fig. I did not suspect you would become suddenly timid."

"Besides Angela's threat, there is another, Lilith. What is *Natasha* up to? She is not in the US as a tourist. She must mean harm as well."

15

Step by Step

"THIS IS much better." Angela listened to the speaker wired into the bathroom. "I will hear everything you are going to say. Are you going to get him to have sex with you right away?"

"No," Natasha wrinkled her forehead. "No, no, ugh!" She sat on the apartment living room couch and spoke loudly so she could be heard through the shut door. "There is no reason to set up a honeypot." She frowned, irritated at the buzz of a mosquito she could not quite see.

"Honeypot?" Angela asked.

"A honeypot is when you record the target having sex with you and threaten exposure unless he does what you want. But the grid control company doesn't care about Robert's private life. He has no security clearance with access to classified information. Didn't your basic training cover things like that?"

"I'm not clear on everything that has happened with your meetings in the café. How did you get Robert to agree to come to your apartment?" Angela's tone hinted a growing frustration.

"It has to be done gradually. Having the target not think you are a prostitute is important."

"How did you get — "

"We have been over this before." Natasha scowled with irritation. "Take notes or something."

"Do you want to see Alex — "

Natasha sighed. "You must have put a tail on my handler whenever he shows up at the airport. Haven't I done enough?"

"We haven't been able to identify him yet. The airport is a crowded place. Our goal is to follow him to find out who he is working for, to roll up the entire ring. Alexei won't be free until we accomplish that."

16

Double Date

NATASHA OPENED her eyes as wide as she could. The bar room was dark, impossibly dark. Even the belladonna did not help. Those who frequented here must want it that way. She glanced at Angela sitting ramrod straight beside her, eager for the action to begin. Only the soaring collar hiding the top of her wings remained of the original costume. Bangs from the wig still covered her horn buds. The floor-length skirt and simple blouse would be good enough to pass.

There was something about Angela that had been suspicious from the start. Something off in the way she acted. Like no other woman she ever knew. And then the answer. It had been so unexpected, a total shock. The US CIA had made contact with, what, another 'realm?' Was Angela even with the Company? She boggled at the memory. Mind-blowing. Impossible to believe. But there was no denying what she had seen in her apartment after Robert had left. Bat-like wings, coarsely veined and almost transparent. With a few effortless strokes, the succubus had levitated from the floor and hovered. Completely naked except for a small purse hanging at her waist.

Natasha noticed Angela had caught her glance at the purse. "A second one," the demon said. "The first was lost … some time ago."

What was the bag's purpose? Immediately, Natasha had wanted to know, but of course, she received no clear answer. Only a few mumbles of indirection. About being able to swoop down and snatch Alexei from wherever he was captive. Reunite them both and get them asylum here in the US.

And if there were such things as demons, anything was possible. Her training had taught her to take advantage of the unexpected, no matter how bizarre. Actually, now her hopes were even a little higher. There might be some truth to Angela's boast that her lover's rescue would not be much of a challenge.

159

This was the most important step in her operation. Nothing should be left to chance. Getting access to one of the control computers and, as far as Viktor would be concerned, she would be home free.

"Why both of us?" Angela's whisper broke through Natasha's reverie.

"You understand your part?" Natasha asked. "No reluctance?"

"I have explained what I am very good at," Angela sniffed. "For me, the seduction of a human man is easy. It is males of my own kind I want to learn techniques that will work."

"Well, I don't know what makes your kind tick. But, here in my world, meeting the target's male acquaintances is an absolutely necessary step. With Robert's offer to involve his boss, I took advantage of the opportunity."

"So *I'm* what makes it possible for Dave to meet you?"

"Exactly. Male egos are big, but they are so like a child's balloon. For a man, if friends say he is dating a dog, the balloon pops. The relationship is over. But if they say he has a 'keeper,' the balloon expands. The target feels better about himself. He will want to see you more and more. Do whatever it takes to keep you around. … Mission accomplished."

Natasha stopped talking. She could make out Robert and Dave dimly through the low hanging cloud of cigarette smoke. She waved to get their attention, and the two men approached. As they neared, she slid from the booth and maneuvered Dave to take her place beside Angela. She and Robert sat in the facing chairs.

"So this is the cutie you lined up for me?" Dave scooted up against Angela. The demon did not flinch. But with lips closed to conceal her long canines, she smiled at the face suddenly so close to hers.

"I'm Dave," Robert's manager said.

"Angela," the succubus replied.

"Natasha has asked me for a small favor," Robert said immediately. "Naturally, I told her I would have to clear it with you first."

With a dramatic show of reluctance, Dave turned his attention away from Angela. He studied Natasha for a moment and then nodded to Robert. "Not bad, Bobby. Not bad at all."

Perfect. Absolutely perfect, Natasha thought.

Dave immediately looked back at Angela. He tried to slide his arm around her but could not navigate around the high collar. He scowled for a moment and then slid his hand under the table in front of the demon.

The two females glanced at one another, nodding their understanding. The full-length skirt would prove to be another frustrating obstacle.

"What is it you guys do?" Natasha smiled directly at Dave. "Robert has told me some of it, but it would be great to hear your take … as the boss."

"Our task is to keep the supply of power matched to the demand," Dave launched into a spiel. "If we don't, we will have a brown or blackout, or even worse, damaged TVs and appliances."

"Does the power add together … like putting more batteries in a row?" Natasha asked.

"Something like that. Power is generated as alternating current, not direct. So not only do the physical connections have to be made, but every source must be in synch at sixty cycles per second. Otherwise, a power plant becomes a sink rather than a source. We use — "

"Ah, Dave. Natasha's favor?" Robert interrupted.

"Yes, a small favor," Natasha seized the opening. "All this sounds absolutely fascinating. And I would like for Robert to get me a screenshot of a generator control screen … for my son's science fair project."

"Security. Security," Dave said. "The press, the internet. They make such a big deal of it." He raised an eyebrow at Robert. "Remember when that outside firm came in to do an audit? Of course, we wanted to get them out of our hair as soon as we could. Air gap? 'What air gap?' we asked them."

"Air gap?" Angela asked as she withdrew Dave's hand with one of her own, gloved to the elbow, and placed it back on the table top.

Dave blinked. At least, Natasha thought he did. It was hard to tell in the dim light.

"Yeah. Air gap," Dave nodded. "It means the hardware control network is disconnected from those managed by IT. No electrical contact at all to business, admin, the internet, all that stuff. No way for malware to get to the control computers."

"And they didn't find a path here at Folsom." Robert beamed.

"Yeah," Dave leaned forward, hungry for some of the credit. "Claimed they always had found at least one in every facility they had tested so far. Simple things like a master rebooter or some such."

Dave puffed out his chest and spoke directly to Angela. "And you know what I did when I heard that? Took the so-and-sos over to a console; Robert's in fact. The one for the generators and showed them the screen. 'See that?' I said. A jumble of boxes and lines with acronym

161

labels and nothing else. 'Okay, wise guys, suppose you could get in and see this. How would you know what to do next?'"

"The displays *are* cryptic," Robert jumped in. "Have to go through a lot of training to understand what to do."

"That's why Jimmy wants the screenshot." Natasha poured excitement into her voice. "The whole point of his presentation is to prove exactly what you said."

"So, okay Natasha, what's your pitch?" Dave asked.

"A minute of activity." Natasha tried to sound as off-hand as she could. "Nothing more. Transfer a screenshot of the control panel onto a flash drive, and Jimmy will take it from there."

Natasha watched Dave's expression carefully. He scratched his chin. No smile. Not good. Maybe she had come on too strong, too suspicious.

"Computer stuff? Not a camera?" Dave asked. He pondered a moment. "Nah, I don't know about doing that."

Natasha steeled herself to show only a tiny bit of her disappointment. 'No big deal,' she hoped her shrug said. Then, she signaled Angela with a small nod. On to Plan B.

"*My* pitch is that it is getting stuffy in here," Angela said. "I can hardly see through the cloud of smoke."

"Won't be any brighter outside," Dave said. "The whole town shuts down by eleven. This is the only dive staying open until two."

"Outside? I wouldn't mind that," Angela squeezed Dave's hand.

"In the back?" Dave said. "More privacy there."

Natasha relaxed as she watched Angela nod agreement.

TWENTY MINUTES later, Angela and Dave returned.

"Natasha's friend is quite persuasive, Robert," Dave said. "I do want to see her again." He shook his head, "But no dice on the flash drive. 'Stick it in. Take it out'… That's for people, not computers." He smiled at Angela. "Enjoyed the evening, babe. You say you're staying with Natasha, right? I'll get the number from Robert."

A LITTLE later, Natasha slammed the apartment door. "What happened, miss hot stuff? I thought you said human males were easy. Get Dave under your 'domination,' whatever that is. Force him to tell Robert that using a flash drive was okay."

"No, I didn't dominate him," Angela said. "Didn't even try."

"What! Why not?"

"I wanted to practice with what you have been teaching me. 'Look him in the eye. Act interested. Ask what he really loves …'"

"So, despite appearances, you are more bluff than bite." Natasha exhaled slowly and let her disappointment evaporate. "Okay, never mind about seducing Dave. Robert will have to be the one."

"Won't it be obvious that something is not quite right?" Angela asked. "When he looks at the files listed in the top level directory on the flash drive. He will see there is more than only a single .bat file. The code for the malware will show up, too."

"Yes, I'm going to have to gamble a bit. Without Dave's permission, Robert will want to act as rapidly as he can. And only the .bat file will appear. All the others will be hidden. Robert could undo that, but I bet he won't want to spend the time exploring the drive."

Natasha's tone hardened. "Let's be clear here. After I have convinced Robert to act, that's the end of it. I make a final report to my SVR handler, and I'm done. This time, don't drop the ball trailing him. But successful or not, you get Alexei out of wherever he is to safety. That is our bargain."

She took a deep breath. "And if you do not, there is going to be a lot of publicity about this. Maybe even about a strange creature working for the CIA."

17

The Intoxication of Applause

HALF AN ocean away, Briana paced a tiny circle in her dressing room. It was sparsely furnished. A table with three drawers in front of a mirror bordered with lights. A portable clothes rack and hamper. One guest chair and nothing else.

The last performance of the evening was over. The word-of-mouth for her show had continued to grow. Sold out for two weeks in advance.

But the excitement of the applause had begun to ebb. That was no longer what she looked forward to each day.

Without knocking, Cliff burst into the room. "The reps from Austin loved it!" he exclaimed.

Briana stopped pacing but did not immediately respond.

"Well, don't you get it?" Cliff rushed on. "Contract already signed. The mainland! We are on our way. Sustain the draw in Austin and then on to Vegas. Time for a celebration."

He moved forward to embrace Briana in a hug, but she took a step back.

"That's … good news, Cliff. But not now. No more excitement. I want to be alone for a while."

Cliff's face clouded with disappointment. "You always say that." He stood frozen for a moment, then shrugged and left as quickly as he had come.

Like the fragrance of a fall blossom beginning to fade, the adrenalin rush from the show had provided less of a jolt each time Briana performed. It had become much more routine, no longer needed to force her thoughts away from her plight. Yes, nothing basic had changed. She was still marooned with no chance to return home. But the enforced calm was artificial. Perhaps, she no longer needed its manipulation of her thoughts.

164

The dangers of addiction spoken of by the master sorcerers were for their tyros. Not for someone who had knowledge of all five of the crafts like herself. She had the strength to stop anytime she wanted, and she would prove it tonight. She would just ...

Just do what? Yes, Cliff continued his cautious courting. But probably another year or more before anything significant happened. Hours and hours of nothing but small talk became boring after a while. The hints she dropped bounced off him as if he were made of rubber.

Fig was the only one she knew well. Someone she was comfortable with. And he had been gone for weeks now. The credit card bills had indicated he was in California. Was he ever to return? She sighed. Taking him so much for granted might have been a mistake. *Why* would he return?

So that left ...

She frowned with where her thoughts were taking her. Well, one more night couldn't hurt. Tonight. Yes, *tonight* — the very last time. In a few minutes, it would not matter if Fig were here or not.

18

Devil Trap

THE ONE-ROOM apartment contained no major furniture. A crumpled sleeping bag lay next to a hotplate supporting a beaker full of water for instant coffee. Two plates, utensils, cereal boxes, and TV dinners sat near a small microwave oven. A large thin sheet of copper leaned against a wall next to a coil of fencing wire. Fig pounded the last nail into the rough wooden frame he had assembled. Lilith fidgeted nearby.

"How much longer is this going to take?" the demon asked. "We've camped in this town long enough. The dribblers hiding in Natasha's lair have nothing new to report. After some pleading, Robert has agreed to use the flash drive at his facility. Angela hovers nearby, getting more and more anxious. She is increasingly frustrated that Natasha is teaching her very little more."

"Almost done," Fig shooed Lilith away from looking over his shoulder.

"Angela's interest in Natasha will soon be over," Lilith said. Frustration coated her words. "I don't know if she will rescue Alexei as she says or not. But in either case, my sister will be on to another *femme fetale* somewhere in the past. And we have no idea which one."

"There is still the matter of thwarting whatever the malware on the flash drive is supposed to do."

"I don't care about human incompetence. Electric power control is no concern of mine."

"It matters to *me*." Fig attached a hinge to one of the doors he had made. "It can't be as simple as merely causing a short-term outage."

Lilith simmered for a moment, then calmed. "Okay, tell me what happens next."

"We need to trap Angela here on Earth, right? Back in your realm will not work."

166

"*Trap* her? A so-called *devil trap*? Surely, you are not planning on using those diagrams from the Middle Ages. King Solomon's heptagram. Arcane scribbles on parchment, and all the rest. Supposedly, if a demon stepped onto one, he would not be able to escape. Those things don't work. Pure fantasy. Human folk myths. We joke about such things all the time in my realm."

She pursed her lips with disapproval. "You humans pollute your heritage with so much useless clutter. It is no wonder the true crafts of magic have never been discovered."

"No, not mystical arcana," Fig wagged his head. "I'm thinking of using a Faraday cage."

"What's that?"

"It's what one calls a box made with metal mesh on every side. Used to block electronic signals generated outside from penetrating. For physics experiments and such."

Fig hesitated for a moment, unable to suppress a smile. "Actually, we don't need one for squelching signals. It's merely the pretentious name used for a wire cage. I have come up with a third application and ordered the rolls of chicken coop wire over the internet."

"Third application. What's the second?"

"Why, cooping chickens, of course."

"Let me guess," Lilith scowled. "The third is the devil trap, right?"

"Yes. The power grid is what gave me the idea." Fig rushed on before Lilith said more. "We build a mesh cage big enough to hold Angela, but with only five sides. Nothing for the floor."

"On the bare earth then?"

"Almost right. The cage will rest on a perimeter of insulation to shield it from the ground. The copper plate will reside inside, not touching the cage or its insulation anywhere. The plate will be grounded, but not the cage."

"That's *all* it takes for a devil trap?"

"Almost. I'll show you the rest later."

Lilith frowned and examined Fig's handiwork a little more carefully. "I don't understand," she said. "Why does it need two doors rather than one? Why on opposite sides?"

"One for entrance; the other for exit. And when I was internet surfing, besides the wire, insulators, and the plate, I also found a book we can use — *How to Catch a Man*, by a famous movie actress. Evidentially, it is a classic."

Fig put down his tools and admired his construction for a moment. His enthusiasm faded a bit when he then looked at Lilith. "Buck up. We will get Angela isolated from Natasha soon. And for that, you will play the most important part."

19

Cards on the Table

NATASHA PEERED down from the visitor's gallery to the operations floor of the control center. If she stood on tiptoe and leaned out as far as she could, she was able to see Robert as he sat at his console. A crowd of about twenty other people hemmed her in. If something went completely wrong, she would not be able to escape.

Silly thoughts. She was a tourist listening to a talk, nothing more. She smiled at Robert and gave him a discreet wave. He did not look up. He seemed nervous and stiff. Behind her, Dave droned on with his spiel.

"I heard the independent grids in the country are connected," the visitor next to Natasha said. "Can we get power here in California from another one?"

"Yes, we can," Dave replied. "Except that between grids, power is transferred as DC." Dave did not miss a beat and plowed on.

Natasha tuned him out and returned her attention to Robert. She saw him stand up and glance back and forth at the controllers at the other consoles. The layout of the floor impressed her, as much as what she had seen on TV of NASA Houston. A panorama of a dozen large screen displays covered the far wall. A half-dozen or so men sat at half-circle workstations, each with its own array of monitors and keyboards.

A floor supervisor approached Robert, and he quickly sat back down. His movement was jerky, Natasha thought, and sure to arouse suspicion. But nothing happened. The two men chatted for a while, and the supervisor moved on.

For several minutes, Robert sat like a statue, unmoving and staring straight ahead. Finally, he took a deep breath and fumbled the flash drive out of his pocket. He tried to insert it in the console USB port, but it would not go in. With increasing panic, he twisted it over and tried again. No luck with the second try.

Robert sat back down. He seemed to be hyperventilating. Natasha held her breath. She reviewed her contingencies. If Robert could not perform his task, then the most important thing to do first was to retrieve the flash drive. She frowned where the logic was taking her. Then, pick a new pigeon and start the process all over again.

Robert looked up at the gallery and spotted Natasha. He stood up, stuck out both hands, and, with a shrug, rotated his palms upward. She widened her smile as much as she could and blew him a kiss.

Robert sat back down and took a deep breath. He grimaced and tried to insert the flash drive again. This time it entered the port smoothly. It must have been his nerves the first time, Natasha thought. She scanned Dave and the crowd around him. No one else noticed what Robert did.

Robert twisted his head left and right like a nervous chicken. A minute passed and then another. Finally, he blinked. A message appeared on his console screen. The .bat file he had clicked had worked perfectly. A screenshot of his generator status had been transferred to the flash drive and the malware throughout the control network. He jerked the little drive out of the port and stuffed it in his pocket. Bending head down onto his tabletop, he sighed not once but three times. The job was over.

BACK IN her apartment, Natasha donned her sternest face and stared at Angela. She pulled the thumb drive out of her purse and waved it in front of the demon.

"Robert gave it back to me at lunch. We are done with him. Nothing more he has to do. No more steps in the protocol needed. And once I pass this on to my handler, I'm finished as well. The mission is over. Your guys have one last chance to identify my contact in the airport crowd, and that is all."

"I have been thinking," Angela said. "Robert did not do anything he thought was grossly illegal. Suppose you had to have him cross the line. What then, the honeypot and blackmail?"

"No, more of the same," Natasha shrugged. "Many small steps leading the target further and further astray. No sex until absolutely necessary, the very last enticement.

"That's important," she emphasized. "After you have coupled with a man the first time, almost all your leverage vanishes. The allure will be diminished. The tantalizing mystery solved. His interest will turn to another. It is not the lust of the target you want to inflame. Instead, he has to fall in love with you."

"Ah, I understand," Angela said. "For humans, sex is the very *last* step rather than the first. Bizarre. But it is beginning to make some sense. Teach me. Show me the rest of the steps."

"Our agreement, Angela." Natasha waved the flash drive again. "Alexei's return and the asylum."

"Alexei's return?" Angela hesitated a moment. "No problem, but, well, maybe 'asylum' was a bad choice of words."

Natasha scowled. Her forehead wrinkled, even though she had always fought not to have that happen. The way Angela acted was becoming too suspicious. Hope had kept her from accepting the obvious. She had tried to signal whomever watched every time she and the handler met. But always the tipoff was not recognized by Angela's cohorts, whoever they were. This succubus was more interested in technique than results.

"You're not CIA after all, are you?" Natasha gave voice to doubts lingering from the very start. "No government connections. You *can't* provide asylum, can you?"

"I do not need a human bureaucracy," Angela sniffed. "Come on in, Adonis. Explain how it will work."

The apartment door cracked open. At first, Natasha thought no one was there. She glanced down and saw what looked like some sort of lizard creeping into the room. It was a large one, the size of a Gila monster.

No, not a lizard, she decided as it rose to standing and came up to her. Lizards did not walk upright or have such hideous faces. For a moment, she felt again the numbing shock of when Angela had revealed her true form.

Natasha pushed away the paralysis. She relaxed her stare. If there can be one kind of demon, then why not others? This was important. Go with the flow. Alexei's life was at stake.

"Adonis is a gargoyle," Angela said. "He was the one who stalked you in Moscow for me. He would be very handy for your line of work."

"Please, let me explain," Adonis moved in front of Angela and stood as tall as he could. "Not asylum, but something more like … witness protection instead."

"Protection from the SVR? Those guys are ruthless to those who defect. They will find a way to get the government records no matter where they are stored. Once a defector is found, they are murdered a short time later."

"What you will receive is much, much better." Adonis fanned out six documents. "Three each for both you and Alexei. Birth certificates, social security numbers, and driver's licenses."

"How did you get Alexei's picture?" Natasha could not stop herself from asking.

"I told you the rescue would be easy," Angela bared her fangs smugly.

Natasha thought for a few moments, then her expression soured. "Forged documents never hold up against sophisticated examinations. Ask any counterfeiter when he is not in jail."

"Birth certificates will be originals," Adonis rebutted. "It's one of the things my kind does while waiting to grow big enough to place ourselves on cornices. Drop into a small county vital statistics department late at night. Use original paper, enter exactly the needed information on a computer terminal. Press 'Print.' Presto, one completely original birth certificate. And if there is time, make and store the file copies, too. As easy as getting lucky when a female is in heat."

"The other two." Natasha put her hands on her hips. She was not convinced.

"Driver's licenses are easy. So are the Social Security IT facilities. Sneak in at night and use the equipment. Presto two and presto three."

"So, you will get everything you need, provided you teach me more." Angela grabbed the documents from Adonis and shoved them into her purse.

Natasha pondered. Who was the bigger liar here? Angela or the SVR handler? Both? Neither? She shrugged. There would be no change in her plans. She would continue to play along with both sides to the end.

"Okay," she said. "I will make an appointment for the final meeting with my handler to pass over the flash drive. While I'm gone, rescue Alexei and bring him here …"

Natasha studied the sparseness of the apartment. "No, Angela, wait. The shock will be too great for him if he does not see me here. It will look like trading one prison for another. Wait until I get back. Don't go off on any adventures. *After* I return, perform the rescue. You bring back Alexei and give me the documents. Then we are done."

20

Throwing the Switch

FIG EXAMINED his handiwork for the last time. This will work, he told himself. Sure, it would. Once Angela takes the bait, she will be captured. Dusk was fading into night, but the moon provided enough light. He was able to see his way around the power substation. High fences surrounded it on all four sides but they were not designed to keep out a demon who could fly. Most of the area was filled with high voltage electrical equipment. A small brick service building stood to one side.

Fig's footsteps crunched on the gravel as he performed a preliminary survey. The air crackled around the thick, looping cables swinging from high towers. Like a column of soldiers, the steel structures marched into the distance. Smaller wire hawsers swung down from them onto squat, fat transformers reducing the high voltage to that of everyday use. The hum of sixty cycle power saturated the air like the buzz from millions of bees. Yes, a power substation. The perfect place.

No light came from the windows of the service building. It was unoccupied, and, as Fig had suspected, contained the tools and supplies he needed. He kicked at the place where he had disturbed the soil leading from the structure to one of the transformers. In the dim light, someone would have to be deliberately looking to spot his additional cable buried there.

"All set," he whispered to Lilith. "You know what to do, right?"

"You have repeated the plan to me more than a dozen times," Lilith rumbled. "Yes, I know what to do." Without another word, she soared into the sky.

LILITH FLEW back to the Folsom town center. She checked that no one was about on the street and then hovered outside the windows of Natasha's apartment. The lights were on and the curtains open. She saw her sister sitting on a couch talking to the gargoyle. Lilith grinned a bit as she watched Angela squirm, trying to get into a comfortable position. Human couches were not made for beings with wings.

Human couches. Human customs. Yes, just the thing. Lilith tapped on the glass, and Angela looked up. The hovering succubus stuck out her tongue. She put her thumbs in her ears, wiggling her fingers back and forth. Had her sister been visiting Earth enough to understand? Angela's face distorted with rage. She leapt up and sprang across the room. Evidently, she did.

Lilith feathered back from the wall as her sister crashed through the glass. She took the first strong stroke with her wings and flew toward the substation. Glancing over her shoulder, she slowed a tiny bit. The goal was for Angela to be close behind.

The pair streaked across the sky, one behind the other. They were shadows in front of the moon only for an instant. Lilith stretched out her wings, banked to one side, and circled over the substation site. In a smooth arc, she dove for the Faraday cage. It stood clear of the central building with its two doors open and beckoning.

Lilith flew through the first door and, without landing, immediately out the second. She heard her sister's pursuit, still close behind. As she had practiced, she grabbed the frame of the second door as she flew past it, and flung it shut with a satisfying clang. Angela's mouth opened with surprise by the action. She crashed into the wire mesh, and, in a tumble of arms and legs, fell to the ground.

As Lilith circled back to the first entrance, Angela picked herself up. Then, for the barest of a moment, she stopped. There on the floor lay a book with the intriguing title *How to Catch a Man*. She stooped, picked it up, and tried to stuff it into her sweet bag, but it was too big.

The tiny delay was all Lilith needed. She slammed the door shut and indicated a thumbs up to Fig watching from the building. He threw the switch he had installed onto the wall, almost ripping out the rigged up connections.

Angela regained focus and attacked the entrance, trying to smash it open. But as she did, she was jolted to the ground. She rose and tried once more, this time more cautiously. Again she fell, stunned, her eyes watering and twitching from side to side. She attempted to stand but could not, the muscles in all her limbs in spasm. Crawling to the exit, she extended a single finger toward the wire mesh and touched. Her arm snapped back, unable to withstand the pain.

The succubus tested all four walls and even the ceiling, but the results were the same. She could not remain in contact with any of them. As she circled on her hands and knees to look for something to grab hold of, one of her wingtips grazed a wall on the side. She roared in frustration and curled into a tight ball on the sheet of copper.

Lilith grinned with admiration. She had to marvel at what Fig had accomplished. The high tension lines held the potential of hundreds of kilovolts. The cable he had attached and buried ran from one of them to the Faraday cage. When he threw the switch, the voltage of the cage soared into the hundreds as well. And with Angela standing on the copper plate, her body was the conduit to ground. The succubus could sit or stand on the metal sheet with no problem. But touching any of the walls completed the circuit. She would experience agonizing pain. Fig had built a devil trap, indeed.

Fig came out of the supply building. Being careful not to touch the cage at any point, he threw tarps over it. "This is only temporary, of course," he said. "But unless there is a problem, substations are not manned. That will give us time to build another trap. In a remote place, where power lines cross mountains somewhere."

"I will start looking now," Lilith said.

"No," Fig drew his lips into a thin line. "We stick to the plan. For now, your sister is not going to be able to slink off into the past. Instead, get your dribblers to report where Natasha has gone. We are going to get to the bottom of it all. Everything."

21

The Last Handover

NATASHA SAT down at the designated table in the 'pre-security' Starbucks in Terminal A at Sacramento International. From time to time, she glanced at her watch until it read precisely 10:42 AM. When the moment came, she slipped the flash drive out of her purse, shoved it into a napkin dispenser about a dozen layers deep, and exited.

Her handler, Yefim, arrived ten minutes later and entered. She stood at the entrance, watching him for his signal. After a few moments, he raised his head from his laptop, smiled like a Cheshire cat, and welcomed her over.

"Well done, comrade Natasha," he said in a low voice. "I have examined the flash drive and see the screenshot is there."

"Why is the picture of any importance?" Natasha asked as she sat down across from him.

Yefim carried the wrinkles of an older man, not quite mature enough to be Natasha's father, but close enough. White hair in need of a trim, bushy eyebrows, crinkly eyes like a garden gnome. A dull brown sports coat and solid color tie. He swiveled the laptop so she could see.

"Because it proves you did as instructed," he said. "The drive was inserted in the controller's computer, the one with this very display on the screen. No other way could that image now be found on the drive. Folsom was the last. Now, the malware will have been installed on every one of the US power grids. All that remains is for the timer signal to start."

"I thought an air-gap separated grid controls from any other computers at a site."

"We had an agent on the survey team, the contractor testing all the control systems. He learned of an undocumented way 'across' the gap in almost every case." Like an actor, he paused for effect. "Almost every case. All except one, Folsom. The California Operator Center. Because of your good work, that system is infected, too, and our plan can proceed."

"So, I have done my job," Natasha said with steel in her voice. "I have fulfilled my part of our bargain. Now, it is your turn. Release Alexei."

"Well, there is a slight problem." Yefim shifted in his chair. He looked in Natasha's direction but averted his eyes from her face. "Another situation has come up. You will be perfect for it."

Natasha clenched her teeth to prevent from immediately replying. It was as bad as she had feared. Now, only a single option left. It was up to Angela to get Alexei back. And, by damn, this time she was going to make sure there were no more excuses. She stood up feigning awkwardness and then pitched forward across the table, grabbing hold of her handler's coat.

"Sorry, Uncle Yefim," she said in a loud voice. "For some reason, I'm very clumsy today."

Yefim tried to fend Natasha off, but she kept her grip. "Oops, here I go," she cried, sagging to the ground and pulling Yefim down with her. It hurt, but it was worth it. Even the most junior CIA agent watching could not fail to notice who her handler was now.

Several other patrons rushed to help the pair up. When order was restored, she shooed them off with her thanks, and they melted away.

"Why the dramatics?" Yefim asked with a soft growl as he brushed himself off.

Natasha tugged her clothes back into order. "I'm not going on another assignment for you or anyone else."

Yefim's eyes squinted into tight slits. He studied Natasha for a moment. "You've been turned, haven't you?"

"Very well, then," he snapped shut the laptop and motioned to another table deeper within the café. Two large, burly men immediately rose and walked toward where Natasha stood.

"You are going to have more to worry about than your boy-toy's skin, Natasha — your own."

FIG AND Lilith entered the terminal. Thanks to the dribblers, Natasha had been easy to follow. They entered the café as one of the thugs deftly lifted Natasha from her feet. He smothered her into his chest. Crew cut and thick jowled like a bulldog, he had a face incapable of a smile.

The second wrapped his arms around the first in a group hug, with Natasha sandwiched between. Like overweight ballet dancers, the pair shuffled her out of the café.

"You handle those two," Fig called out to Lilith. He pointed at Yefim. "That guy must be her handler. *I'll* go after him. He is the one more likely to know what is going on."

Yefim blinked at Fig's words. He sprang from the table, surprisingly agile for a man his age. Fig reached out as he passed, but was only able to snag a button from the handler's coat sleeve. Walking rapidly, the older man followed the other Russians out of the coffeehouse.

By this time, most of the customers were on their feet, eyes wide with astonishment. More people involved would only get in the way, Fig thought. He had to do something to divert them.

"Okay, cut," he called out. "It's a wrap." He scanned the room to make sure he had everyone's attention. "Thanks, everyone for making the scene seem so realistic. Don't look for the cameras and sound booms. They were hidden to maintain realism. But if you stick around until noon, you can snag some free tickets to see the premiere."

An excited buzz and laughter exploded from the patrons. Fig raced out the café doors and saw Yefim leaving the terminal and board a shuttle bus. As the doors closed, Fig ran to a taxi waiting nearby and jumped into the backseat.

"Follow that bus!" he called to the cabbie.

"The rent-a-car shuttle? Why?"

"Just do it. You'll get a big tip."

The bus and taxicab pursuit arrived at the car lot almost simultaneously. As Fig emptied his wallet to the cabbie, he saw Natasha's handler toss some paperwork into an 'Instant Checkout' box. The agent ran to a car, climbed in, and headed toward the airport exit.

As Yefim sped past him, Fig read the car's license plate. He watched the Russian agent merge onto the airport circuit-way and vanish out of sight. Fig scowled. The bastard was getting away. Almost as an afterthought, he opened his clenched fist. It still contained the handler's coat button.

'Once together, always together.' Like a returning boomerang, memories of the Hilo nursery came flooding back. He recited the incantation that reconnected the button with the coat. Yes, that would work. But he needed transportation, too. And Lilith was nowhere to be seen.

Of course! Fig slapped his forehead. He hurried toward the rental office.

FIG CREPT onto the freeway as slowly as he dared. Already, three cars queued behind him, one crowding his bumper, disenchanted with his rate of speed. Out of the corner of his eye, he watched the coat button sitting in the driver side cup holder. It had moved off of dead center towards the left.

Sacramento, not Redding. The transition choice on the left. He looked again at the button. Yes, the incantation must have worked. Aided by thaumaturgy, the little fashion accessory would try to reunite with the rest of the coat.

Fig merged onto Interstate Five and remained in the slow lane. The button began creeping toward the front of the cup holder. He ignored the angry honks coming from behind. It would take a while, but eventually he would get to where he wanted.

Sometime later, he pulled to a halt on a quiet side street south of downtown Sacramento. Separate cookie-cutter houses lined up like children's blocks. The button crept toward the curb. He had tracked the handler to his lair. If Lilith was as successful with Natasha, the mystery might start to unravel.

22

Rising Stakes

NATASHA STUDIED the almost bare apartment. A staging area for …
what? Pine boards and chicken coop wire scattered in an unkempt mess.
Paper plates and plastic cups littered the floor. One rumpled sleeping bag
next to a chest of tools.

And it had happened so suddenly. Angela appeared out of nowhere to
save her at the airport. Pushed aside the brutes forcing her into the back
seat of a car. The demon lifting her skyward to come to wherever this
place was.

She frowned. No, that wasn't quite right. The naked being who
squatted beside her insisted she was not Angela, but her sister instead.
They looked exactly the same. Not one demon, but two. The headache
she was getting blossomed. Another type of creature, as
well — gargoyles. Were there even more? Natasha blinked, trying to
recapture reality, but the confusion did not go away.

"You bugged my apartment?" Natasha rubbed her forehead and
plopped back down on the threadbare couch.

"In a manner of speaking, yes," Lilith said.

"Okay. Never mind about those details. Everybody does it all the
time in their own unique way." Old habits kicked in. Natasha tried to get
a grip on herself, appear to be more than a hapless victim. She stared at
Lilith as best she could. "And if you want information from me, you will
have to pay for it."

Lilith tipped her head to the side at the sudden return of Natasha's
composure. "Pay? At what price?" she asked.

"I want Alexei brought to me … brought to me as soon as you can."

"Is that all?"

"There is also the matter of some documents in Angela's purse. I
want those, too."

"Retrieving those will take a little more effort."

"Alexei, then. How soon can you — "

Without a word, Lilith opened a window, stroked her wings, and flew away.

THE TIME on the microwave dinged, and Natasha removed the frozen dinner. She had been almost a whole day alone and unguarded. She could have walked out of the apartment with no one stopping her. But then, why would she? She had no money, no identification. Nowhere to go. Her spirits flagged. This was not the way the glamorous role of a female spy was supposed to be.

A sudden rush of air stirred the room. Lilith flew in through the window. Natasha could not believe what she saw. The demon carried Alexei in her arms!

"Like you humans call it, a pound of cake," Lilith said.

Natasha did not pay attention. She stared at the man sagging to the floor before her. He scratched a gross unkempt beard and flailed flabby arms and legs. Bruises and scars were everywhere. He wore only tatters of underwear, and his eyes revealed a traumatized soul.

"Alexei!" she shrieked. "You are safe."

"Water," Alexei croaked. "Please, even a few drops."

Natasha searched through the litter of paper cups on the floor. She grabbed the cleanest looking one and hurried to the sink.

"I am not sure about human internal workings," Lilith said. "But I believe you must start slowly. Only little bits of drink and food."

"Thank you, Lilith, thank you, thank you," Natasha said as she held the cup to Alexei's parched lips. Demons, gargoyles. Who cares? Alexei was back. Nothing else mattered.

ALEXEI CURLED up in Natasha's lap. She tried to relieve the pressure on her legs as she sat on the floor, but could not.

"Poor baby," she whispered over and over as she stroked his hair. It was still sticky with greasy oil, but Alexei protested when any water touched his head.

Alexei was not the brightest bulb in the lamp store, Natasha had to admit. But in her stressful world of live television, his simple needs had been a welcome respite. No reason to overthink things. Simple, unsophisticated meals and then to the bedroom with the four-poster bed. Glorious sex, as much as she wanted. A boy toy, others said. They were merely jealous of the life she led.

The door burst open, and a short man with blond locks curling to his shoulders walked in. This must be Fig, Natasha thought, the one Lilith rattled on about. He should be paying more attention to keeping his bleaching up to date. The roots were showing.

"Once I left the freeway, there were so many choices," Fig shook his head as if he could not believe his words. "Took forever for the button to sense all the turns. I never went faster than twenty miles an hour."

He stopped and looked at Natasha and Alexei. "Great work, Lilith. You rescued both of them. And since I have found out the address of the handler's safe house, you can go to him and do your thing. We can fill in the missing pieces for what is going on."

"I have already told you I do not like being put in that mode whenever there is a hurdle," Lilith scowled. "And I have handled such a task already twice today."

"Then why did you rescue Alexei?" Fig asked.

"Because ... because there was a difference. I sensed Natasha's need was one of the heart, not of the brain."

Fig marveled. "I swear, Lilith. You are getting more and more human every day."

Lilith did not reply.

After a moment, Fig said, "Ah, just to remind you of our latest agreement. I captured Angela for you, didn't I?"

"*We* captured Angela," Lilith snapped back.

Natasha squirmed. The last thing she wanted was a squabble among her ... her what? Benefactors? Well, certainly that. But what was their angle? Not CIA, Lilith had said. Another agency? FBI, NSA, DIA ...

"At the airport," she rushed to say, "The handler told me Folsom was the last. All the electric grid control centers in the US contaminated with malware. He might know what the software does, too."

"Give me his location, Fig," Lilith sighed.

NATASHA WATCHED while Lilith and Fig tucked Alexei into the sleeping bag. He was awake, but still not responsive. The demon had not taken long on her journey, returning within a half hour with Yefim in her thrall. Her former handler stared ahead as blankly, a stiff, unmoving statue.

Natasha seized the opportunity. Like a pickpocket on uppers, she went through all of Yefim's pockets, and in an instant, held up the flash drive in triumph.

"Now, we can find out what is on — "

"That may not be necessary," Lilith said. The succubus stared at Yefim. "Tell us everything," she began.

"I was born in St. Petersburg in — "

"Whoa, not everything," Lilith cut Yefim off. "The plot. The plan. Whatever it is you are trying to do in the US."

Beads of sweat formed on Yefim's brow. "Classified. You do not have a need-to-know."

"I am your master," Lilith's voice deepened with command. "Do as I say."

Yefim's body trembled. He slammed his mouth shut and gritted his teeth.

Fig started to say something, but Lilith held up a restraining hand. "Sometimes it takes a while," she said.

After a full minute, Yefim spoke again. "The power grid. So vulnerable. Fifty-four Hertz. Fifty-four."

"I don't get it," Fig said. "Why the power grid? Sure, there have been a lot of alarmists posting on their blogs. A widespread blackout throughout the US is very inconvenient to be sure. But technicians would go to all the substations and turn everything back on manually. Accomplished everywhere within a day. Meanwhile, airports, hospitals, police, fire and the like all run off gasoline-powered generators. There wouldn't even be a gap."

"But the malware would still be running," Natasha said.

"The code in all the facilities would be examined," Fig rebutted. "The malware discovered and expunged. Tighten security and the threat for more disruption completely over."

"I heard the lecture in the Folsom control room," Natasha said.

"Everything is connected together. All running at sixty cycles per second so the inputs could be added and subtracted at will. Somehow that was very important, but Dave, the manager, did not explain why."

"And Yefim said something about fifty-four." Fig rubbed his chin. "That there are *two* numbers must be important somehow." He looked at the laptop. "I wonder if there is a text-book online." He sat down and started to type.

NATASHA MARVELED at how rapidly Fig figured it out. Fifteen minutes at the most.

"The frequency *is* important," Fig said. His voice sounded as if he were lecturing first-year undergrads. "Very important. All the generators are constrained to run at the same rate of rotation. Within a few hundredths of a cycle per second or so. Each controlled by a governor to ensure that happens."

"So?" Lilith asked.

"So, there are big consequences if there is a deviation. A generator out of synch takes energy from the grid rather than adding to it. More current pours into the generator coils than had been designed. Windings get hot and start to melt. It only takes a few minutes until there is permanent damage."

"Surely, that would raise an alarm," Lilith said.

"Normally, yes. But suppose the malware has reset the governors to a lower spin rate. And, at the same time, overrode the measurements to the monitoring and alarm systems. The displays would continue to show sixty Hertz. No hint of a problem. The damage complete before anyone found out about it."

"But there are backups waiting to go online." Natasha frowned. "The lecture I attended talked about those, too."

"Then, one by one, they fail, also," Fig said.

"The emergency generators keep hospitals going," Natasha persisted. She had been in sessions such as this before. Everyone played the devil's advocate before a major campaign.

"Until they ran out of gasoline." Fig disagreed. "Yes, solar power would still be operating, but for the most part, the entire US would be crippled."

"Then comes the ultimatum," Natasha remembered Viktor's boast. "Agree to anything we demand. Unconditional surrender. Complete capitulation."

Before Fig could say more, the apartment lights flickered and went dark. Fig raced to the window to look outside. Folsom was completely black. And probably the rest of the United States as well.

"Angela!" Lilith exclaimed. "Without power for the devil trap, she will escape."

23

The Vulnerable Underbelly

FOR A moment, nothing happened in the darkness. Then Alexei released his grip on Natasha. He pawed around and kept grasping empty air. Finally, he sat up and screamed. "The silence. The blackness. I'm in it again."

Natasha scrambled to her feet. "I'm here, Alexei. You are safe. It's all right." She hugged him tightly, and Alexei stopped talking. He relaxed in her grip and sobbed.

On hands and knees, Fig crawled through the clutter of tools and equipment on the floor. "Ah, here it is," he said. "Use this to keep him quiet."

A sudden beam of light from a flashlight focused on the pair. "We all have to concentrate — starting now."

His words were punctuated by a screech of brakes and the crush of metal on metal. "Traffic lights." Fig nodded. "On batteries, some intersections will blink red for a while, but the rest will be out."

Fig bent down and balanced the flashlight's heel on the floor so that the glow radiated upward in a wide cone. Natasha settled Alexei back to the floor. As her eyes adjusted, she saw Yefim still standing like a statue, unfazed by what had happened. Lilith squatted next to him, her eyes with a glow of their own. Fig placed his hands behind his back and chin down on his chest, deep in thought.

"Food and water." The survival training rushed into Natasha's consciousness. "Those should be our number one priorities. People will start stocking up. In a few days, supplies will run out. There will be riots at the stores." She waved over the clutter on the floor. "We pack this place before everything is gone."

"A temporary measure at best," Fig said. "In the end, all the stores will be depleted. No more gas for trucks to bring food into the cities.

186

Crops rotting in the fields because hand harvesting will not be enough."

"How do you deduce that so quickly?" Natasha asked as she shifted Alexei to a more comfortable position.

"In the news some years ago, there was a big 'what if' described." Fig shrugged. "An electromagnetic pulse from an incoming nuclear bomb wipes out the transformers and transmission lines on the electrical grids. Eventually, more than ninety-five percent of the population dies."

"So, the same scenario applies now, only enacted differently," Natasha said softly. She felt the heaviness of guilt descend. She was responsible, well, at least partially. As Viktor had said, Folsom provided the final piece of the puzzle so the attack could be launched. This was no longer another pointless move in the same dreary game.

Natasha pulled Alexei tighter. No matter. The two of them would survive. After the surrender, Russia surely would provide aid and reconstruction. What was the point of conquest if none of the conquered remained to be exploited? And she and Alexei would have American identities. Proof the same as millions of others ...

"Angela," she said. "I must get the documents from her."

Fig shook his head sadly. "No longer in the trap. When the power went out, she would be confined only in a flimsy box of pine and wire. By brute strength, she would manage to escape."

"Where would she go?"

"We don't know," Lilith replied. The demon slumped, talking barely louder than a mumble "To another time or even back to our realm."

Natasha could not stop sudden tears. Capitulation or recovery; either way spelled doom. If the US surrendered, there would be registration of everyone required. Showing proof of legal status, and she and Alexei had none. And if the US resisted to the end, it would be much the same. Two Russians with no legitimate reason for being here. No reason to share whatever food remained.

She took a deep breath. Pull yourself together, she scolded herself. She had been in tight situations before. And trained to reason her way out of them.

"Figuring out what the malware does will take weeks, if not months," Natasha said. "I'm sure it is written in machine code, no comments, and no header text. In the meantime, whenever a generator comes back online, it will be disabled again."

"We can speed up the repair process!" Fig exclaimed. "We have the flash drive now. We can turn it over to the FBI. At least, our side will know what to look for ... what to delete from each computer controlling the grid."

Natasha perked up. She patted Alexei still cuddled in her lap. "Yes," she said. "Tell them who did this. Who was responsible. This was an act of war."

Fig did not immediately respond. He was quiet for a while. Finally, after several minutes, he spoke again. "I don't think that part of it is a good idea."

"Why not?" Natasha shot back. "Don't you care? Don't you want revenge for what has been done to your country?"

"That's what I worry about," Fig said. "Revenge. Indeed, this *could* be the start of a war."

"Come now," Natasha spat. The frustration of the situation boiled within her. "Saner heads will prevail."

"Either way, it does not buy us much more time. Getting the grid up could take months. What is needed is a way to get it back much sooner … before the food riots start."

He rubbed his chin for a moment, then looked at Lilith. "But maybe there is hope. Besides the dribblers, what other kinds of imp can help?"

"Well," Lilith said. "Although I know very little about them, it sounds like gremlins might be the ones you could use best."

"Okay, gremlins. Are they strong willed like yourself? Does it take concentration and powerful minds to call them forth?"

"I don't know. They are … standoffish. Have airs. Think they have superior intellects to all others. But as a general rule, the smaller the imp, the lesser the power of will."

"Sounds good enough," Fig said. "What kind of material is used for their flame?"

"I don't know that, either."

Fig frowned and started to pace, but only for a moment. "Perhaps you do not, but Briana might. We have to fix things as soon as we can. The grid on the Hawaiian Islands is not connected to the continental US. They may still have power. Lilith, let's fly back there right now."

He hesitated a moment to study Natasha. "What about you? By rights, you should be on your way to prison, but given the circumstances, that is not a high priority at the moment. What are *you* going to do?"

"I have no remorse," Natasha shot back. "I did my job. It is the government functionaries who cause the crises, not the workers who are forced to carry out their plans." She looked around in the dimness and kicked the package of assorted cereals lying near her feet. "Alexei is in no condition to travel, at least, not yet. We will be safe here for a few days. Time enough for me to find a gun shop and be ready to riot with everyone else when the time comes."

24

Challenge Accepted

"WHAT THE hell is happening?" Cliff stormed as he faced Briana in her dressing room. "You were out there for only two minutes. One little gimmick, and that was all. Did you hear the booing as you walked off the stage?"

Briana sat up. The couch was too lumpy for curling up anyway. "I really don't care, Cliff. My happiness is the most important thing."

"If this gets back to Austin, the mainland deal will be off. Don't you get it?"

"I get it." Briana shrugged. "But you know, I have been through a lot. Stress you couldn't even imagine. I deserve a reward for what I have done in the past. A little time off. What's so bad about that?"

Cliff reached down and pulled Briana to her feet. His cheeks glowed a fiery red. "I found you, babe. Before I did, you looked like you were on your way to the streets."

"Maybe we can talk more tomorrow," Briana's head flopped to the side. "After the charm wears off."

Cliff let Briana sag back onto the couch. He pulled the first drawer from the table and dumped its contents on the floor, looking for drugs. As he did, Fig burst in, took one quick look around and rushed to kneel at Briana's side. "Are you all right?" he asked.

"Fig," Briana said, surprised. There was a spark in her voice, but only a tiny one. "I thought you were gone forever."

"Never," Fig said. "It hasn't been that long, really. What? A few weeks at most."

"Lilith?"

"She flew me back from the mainland and then went to the lab." His eyes widened as he studied her. "What's the matter with you?"

"No big deal. Just some self-enchantment." Briana shrugged.

"You warned me about that!" Fig said. "You of all people. How could you do such a thing?"

"Get out," Cliff shouted behind him. "You're not needed here."

Fig turned and stared at Cliff. "And you, buddy, are out of your league. Leave now!"

Before Cliff could react, Fig grabbed him with both arms. He clasped them together behind the other man's back. With a grunt, he lifted Cliff from his feet and duck-walked him through the open door. Cliff broke free, but it was too late. The door slammed in his face. Fig turned the lock.

He returned to Briana's side and took a deep breath. "I hope I remembered what you taught me about this," he said. He took a second breath and steeled his resolve. Taking careful aim, he slapped Briana's cheek.

Briana's eyes widened in anger. Then, almost immediately, she blinked. "Oh, thank you, Fig. I tried to stop. I tried so many times. But the roar from the crowd, the excitement, the adoration pouring forth. It was all too much to handle. Too much of a high. I needed to escape. To calm down. To be quiet.

She touched Fig's arm. "But earlier and earlier each evening the desire to shut everything out overwhelmed me. Since I cannot return home, I wanted to drift away into my own little world. I'm so homesick, Fig. I cannot stand it. Either the excitement of the applause or drunken forgetting. I had no other choice. So, tonight, for the second performance, you must watch me. Make sure I do not speak the charm again."

As her feelings came back, she rubbed her cheek. "Ouch!" She rubbed her cheek a second time. "The masters profess there are no withdrawal symptoms from self-enchantments. But they were not quite right. Maybe next time don't be so hard with your swing."

Then she said softly, "No, disregard that. Next time, do whatever you have to."

"Next time? Aren't you done with the charm?"

Briana puzzled for a moment. "I'm not sure. Tomorrow will be the first test. I think I can do it, but you may have to be my guard and protector for a good while to come."

Fig could not help but smile. "Guard and protector. I like the sound of that."

"Well, perhaps that came out a little stronger than I intend —"

"Don't worry about that," Fig cut her off. "There is a problem to be solved first. A much bigger one than you and me."

He did not wait for a response. For the first time in what seemed like a long while, he felt good about himself. The image of the slashing guillotine blade was still there, but it had faded. Now, it was not only a single life at stake, not unrequited love, but the fate of an entire nation. And right in the middle of it was Figaro Newton, the adventurer who would save the day.

"What is the flame that is the conduit for gremlins?" he asked.

"Electric arcs," Briana said. "Strong enough to ionize the air. The higher the voltage, the better."

"Do you have your purse here?" Fig scanned the dressing room. "Where's your credit card?"

"Middle drawer." Briana pointed. "Did you lose yours?"

"No, still got it. But you should get dressed and get out of here. Do something different. Go to the grocery and stock up. The pantry in the warehouse is bare."

"You'll come with me?"

"No. Another task. I'm going to buy some gear and bring it to the lab."

BRIANA REARRANGED the contents of the warehouse pantry — several times until she was satisfied. Stopping at the ATM and the grocery had been pleasant. Good to have a task to do other than performing stage magic — or doing nothing at all.

With the last package in place, she went to the lab and marveled at its emptiness. Well, no matter. There were enough earnings from Club Exotica to replenish all the missing equipment. Now, all she had to do was await Fig's return.

She slumped to the floor and pondered. Cliff showed an aspect of himself she had never seen before. Maybe his interest in her was only as a cash cow rather than a mate. Although, if that were true, he was a very good actor. So sincere, so caring the times they had been together.

And Fig. He was back. She felt happy about that. His emotions had been like those on a one-string banjo, constant and unwavering ... although his disappearance was a new note even for him. He had changed somehow, and he seemed as if he didn't want to talk about it.

Her act. The owners of Club Exotica were not ones to cross. And the mainland, Austin. The next step, Cliff had said. But was a rocket to stardom something she wanted to ride? What about her original purpose for being here on Earth?

Then, through the dim remains of her stupor, she remembered the rest. A total blackout in the mainland, the chattering radio had said. Performing in Austin definitely was not in the picture for the moment. It had been almost a full day and no estimate yet for when things would be fixed.

The future was murky. So many choices. She found herself not wanting to decide which one to take. It was too soon. Too hard to choose. Too stressful. So, for tonight, it was justified … but certainly, this would be the very last time.

Briana sighed and began the self-enchantment.

THE LAB door opened, and Fig struggled in, carrying a box of equipment. "No," he shouted as he dropped his load. He bent down beside Briana and slapped her cheek as he had done before.

"Not in the middle of the casting!" she shouted angrily. "Now, I will get headaches. The sorcery masters say they are severe."

As she spoke, she immediately saw patterns in the corners of her eyes — irregular lattices of dark lines like the web of a spider on a hallucinatory drug. They flickered in and out of existence, consuming more of her sight with each repetition. Then the pain commenced. A powerful throb at the base of her skull pulsed with every heartbeat. She cradled her brows with both hands and bent forward nearly to the ground.

"Sorry, sorry," Fig said. "But we are going to have to go through this until your will is back to being entirely your own."

Briana's head bobbed in a small rocking motion. She could not speak.

Fig took a deep breath. If power was to be restored soon, the crafts must be employed. He looked again at Briana. She was in no shape to perform any. Getting rid of the aftereffects of an interrupted charm would take hours — hours that could not be wasted.

He was the one who had to act. Angela had been foiled in her attempt to twist the past. To unsnarl the present, he was the one.

Part Three

What Might Be

The Search for Help

FIG LIFTED a portable welding machine onto the lab bench and plugged it in. There was plenty of space. Not time yet to repurchase the original equipment that had been there. But every hour without the power restored increased the chance of anarchy on the mainland. In the warehouse lobby, Lilith waited for him to finish what he was doing.

For a moment, Fig studied Briana sitting quietly on one of the stools. No longer enchanted, but not functional yet. She still needed time to recover. Breaking oneself of addiction, even with no physical side effects couldn't be easy. But if anyone could do it, Briana would be the one. He patted her affectionately once on the arm.

Fig turned his attention back to the new gear and arranged the cables. He donned a helmet, grounded one electrode, and took hold of the other in an asbestos glove. When everything looked in place, he switched on the power. Almost instantly, an arc jumped from one electrode to the other.

Fig opened his mind, reaching out exactly the same as he had for Lilith the first time he had tried to be a wizard. His thoughts felt boxed in. He needed to expand his mental search but was unsure how to do that. It had been easy with Lilith. He has stared into the robust and billowing juniper flames and, bingo, there she was. Frightening, to be sure, but there she was.

He looked at the electric arc and squinted. Even through the dark glass of the helmet, it glowed painfully hot. It was a tiny thing, an inch across at most. How could a demon manage to come into the realm of humankind out of that? How big was a gremlin, anyway?

Nothing happened for several minutes. Fig decided he would have to risk it. He removed his helmet and closed his eyes to the merest slits. Wincing from the brightness, he dared to look into the ionized air of the arc.

Almost immediately, a strange thought glimmered in his mind. "Yeah, whatja want?"

Fig slammed shut his eyes. He could withstand no more. And when he did, the alien presence vanished.

Fig frowned, frustrated. He was stymied. With the helmet on, he was unable to make contact. With it off, he could do so, but only for an instant before searing his retinas. It was a puzzle like that of the monkey with the coin in the jar. He could reach inside and grasp it, but if he did, his hand no longer could be extracted through the opening.

Fig paced about the room. He always seemed to think better when he did that. Okay, the helmet was essential. No way to change that. So, what else could be … His attitude, he realized almost instantly. How a gremlin could squeeze through a tiny arc was its problem, not his.

He imagined himself grabbing the coin and swinging his arm against a wall, smashing the jar. Then he put back on the helmet and stared at the flame.

"Come through the arc and be my thrall." As best he could, he projected the thought.

Instantly, in his head, he heard a reply. "You feel like a smart enough guy. Use your brain. Fix whatever is on the fritz yourself."

"I have a bigger problem than that. Power generators."

"Hmm, generators, huh? Sounds interesting. Okay, I'll give you a visit. If I like the gig, I'll even do it gratis. No need to worry about the dominance or submission stuff."

The electrode in Fig's hand jiggled. There was a pop as the arc sputtered for a moment and then resumed. Next to it hovered what must have been a gremlin, its tiny wings rapidly aflutter. About the size of a guinea pig, its skin was pockmarked and convoluted. Large mischievous eyes hovered over a flat nose in a face that only a mother could love. Small sparks danced between his fingers, tiny ones between his toes.

"Shorting out a generator is easy," the gremlin said. "The rotor windings are so close together. Pierce adjacent holes in the insulation and *voila*, offline in an instant. Oh, my name is Faraday, by the way."

"Faraday as in 'Faraday's law?' Why not Maxwell for 'Maxwell's Equat — "

"Yeah, 'Maxwell's Equations.' I get that a lot. But the name was already taken when I hatched so I had to settle. 'Que será, será.' Anyway, what generator do you want to be knocked offline?"

"It's the reverse," Fig said. "I want to restore generators to operational status — thousands of them. And as fast as possible."

"Galloping ohms! Thousands, you say? That's not the job for a single gremlin. It'll take a bunch of us. Need several for each generator working in parallel. Putting in new insulation. Removing sections where the copper has fused from one winding loop to the next."

"Yes, exactly!" Fig thought for a moment. "So, do we have to go through the 'who's the boss' thing after all?"

"Look, buddy. For me, you might have the chops. But even if you did subjugate me, you get only one gremlin, no more. And as good as you may be, I doubt you, or *any* wizard for that matter can take on a gallop of us."

Fig frowned. He had to convince the demon. This was so damn important. But he had never dominated one, was not confident he could. He would have to convince him with logic, *sell* the concept to him. But how? He felt as if he were trying to trade sand to Bedouins. What could be an inducement, not for a single demon, but for a great number of them? He looked at Briana. Could she provide additional help?

No, she needed more recovery time. Probably not. Turn the problem around, then. Quit the hard sell approach. Instead, first find out what the customer wants. "In your realm," he said, "is there something a lot of you desire?"

"Funny you should ask," Faraday said. "We don't want to talk about it much, but some of the larger devils are not sticking to the rules."

"The rules?"

"Yeah, you know. If somebody is smaller than you, it is okay to eat them. But only if you catch them on the fair and square. 'Thins the herd,' as you say here on Earth."

Faraday shook his head. "Sweeping nets to trap our males while we ponder should be outlawed."

"You need a united front." Fig heard Lilith's voice behind him.

Fig whirled. The succubus was standing in the doorway.

"I was curious," Lilith said, "and decided to see what you were going to do with the new equipment, Fig. And, I am glad I did. Gremlins — the perfect choice."

Things were getting complicated. Fig again glanced at Briana. She still was dull-eyed. Faraday beat his wings furiously and continued hovering above the bench top. And now, Lilith. Three beings from nowhere on Earth. And somehow he had to be in control of things.

"I have been thinking," Lilith said. "And have concluded that to continue tracking down Angela isn't going to be productive. We have no idea of where in the past she might have gone — or even if she's in the past at all. Instead, she might have returned to our realm."

"Then what have you decided to do?" Fig asked.

"Go back to what I had been doing, Fig. Before you summoned me ... getting the social fabric of my realm to change. But I admit I might not have been going about things in the most efficient way. Start with the smaller imps, yes, but making an example with the dribblers turned out to be too hard to do. And, even if that worked, would any other females be convinced enough by the example also to try?"

"We used drink dribblers to help us in Moscow and Folsom," Fig said. "Without them, we could never have figured out what Angela was up to with Natasha."

"Yes, but gremlins have more status. If I can get the males to accomplish something by acting in unison, then convincing their females to do likewise will follow. Step one and then step two."

Fig's thoughts whirled. The help of the gremlins was crucial if the US was to survive. It would be complicated but ... "So, Faraday, if Lilith here can get the bigger devils to stop preying on you unfairly, would you fix the generators here on Earth as a fair exchange?"

Faraday thought for a moment and then shrugged. "Okay, No guarantees, but I'll ask around." Without another word, he vanished through the electric arc.

"Wait! Stop!" Lilith said. "I am talking about what has to happen in my domain, Fig, not yours. Step two would be to do something with the females."

"That will still work," Fig said. "After you have helped the gremlins solve their, ah, menu problem, with the larger demons, and *next* power is restored here, *then* you can — "

"Right, a step at a time," Lilith cut him off. "First, the gremlin males acting together. Second, using that as an example for the females — "

"No!" Fig interrupted. "Next, we convince them to return and get the generators fixed."

Lilith cocked her head to the side and was silent for a while.

"We have traveled a long road together, Fig," she said at last. "I sympathize with what you strive for. Of course, for you, what happens on the Earth is the most important. But *my* home is not your planet. Mine lies in my own realm. I respect your passion, Fig. But I hope you also respect mine."

She bared her fangs slightly. "As usual, your idea is an excellent one. Especially with you coming to my realm to help."

"The realm of demons!" Fig's jaw dropped. What was Lilith suggesting? "In our journeys on Earth," he blurted, "you said it is not hospitable for humankind where you are from. So little air."

"Consider it doing me a favor." Lilith ignored the rebuttal. "A quaint custom of you humans, but once you explained it to me, I have come to like it … like it a lot."

"Please, Fig," she said. "I do not know what you will figure out to do along the way, but I have no doubt it will be a tremendous aid. And when all is done, I will help you untwist the doom that has befallen your realm."

Fig pondered. Time was a critical element for getting things back to normal here on Earth. The gremlins possibly were the solution, but all he got from Faraday was a maybe. Lilith solving their menu problem might be the clincher. But after that, Lilith was determined to pursue her own quest. If he wanted her to do his bidding instead, he would have to dominate her. And to be certain, he probably should do it now.

But could he? Despite everything that had happened, he was little more experienced in the craft of wizardry than when he started. And the risk. If he were dominated instead, it would be too late. All would be lost.

The only hope he could see was to help Lilith through her step two as quickly as possible. That was the path. A long one, but the only way.

"Very well," he grumbled. "Tell me more of your realm so I can get the gear I need."

He looked at Briana. She seemed to be more functional now.

"Briana," he shook her gently. "Listen to me. This is important. You must keep both the juniper fire and the electric arc burning here in the lab at all times. With them active, Lilith and I … and hopefully lots of gremlins will be able to travel back and forth whenever we want."

Briana frowned. She rubbed her temples with her hands. "I can do those things," she said. She drew herself erect. "Yes, of course, I can. It has purpose! A definite task that should keep me from backsliding."

She reached out and pulled Fig into a quick hug. "Be careful. In all the sagas of my home world, no one has ever attempted what you are going to do."

Into the Void

IT WAS bad enough worrying about what was happening back on Earth, but now, in addition, Fig's stomach felt queasy. Not as if he were in freefall but more like an elevator descending too fast. Lilith steadied him as he sucked another gulp of oxygen from the scuba gear strapped to his back. The sparse air in the demon realm was not immediately life-threatening. Something like what climbers of high mountains had faced.

Fig struggled to maintain his balance, worried that the snowshoes he wore would tangle, and he would fall. He was lucky he had thought of them. Otherwise, his shoes would behave as if they had stiletto heels, piercing the thin slab forming the base of Lilith's lair. He looked down at her broad feet. For the first time, he understood the purpose they served.

Like a nervous expectant father, he tapped each pocket of his cargo pants to get the reassurance everything he had wanted to bring with him was present.

"How come gremlins can carry matter between the realms so much easier than you?" he asked Lilith. "It only took them a few trips to get everything across."

"I don't know," Lilith said. "They rattle off some gumbo-jumbo about aligning electrons so that they become superconductive, but I understand none of it. Look, we got all of the stuff you insisted on. Even a bunch of replacement oxygen canisters are tethered to the line attached to my plane. I have placed a drink dribbler in your ear for translations. Now, let's focus on what we do next."

The realm was not as Fig had imagined, despite what the succubus had told him. Ebony blackness everywhere, far deeper than that of a moonless night back on Earth. And in all directions. Not only above but, since he could see through the transparency on which he stood, below his feet as well. Only a few tiny lights in the distance marred the black perfection.

He felt an overwhelming feeling of smallness, of insignificance. His existence meant nothing in the silence surrounding him. The cold empty void would continue, unchanging. How could he possibly be of any help for Lilith? And provide it in sufficient time for the gremlins to start their repair work on the Earth before it was too late?

"I can tell what is happening to you." Lilith looked at him. "It even affects hatchlings. We call it 'the great monotony.' So vast an expanse. So empty. So unchanging. The ambient temperature is the same everywhere, so the air we breathe never moves. There is no need for the quaintness of clothing as is so common on the Earth. We have no cause to erect shelters except as follies for amusement. Smaller imps are abundant. Their bodies provide all the food and water we need.

"Besides all of that," she shrugged. "Unless we are eaten, we are immortal. We grow to adult size and age, but none can recall anyone succumbing to infirmity."

"An Eden," Fig said.

"This realm is no paradise." Lilith disagreed. "There is nothing that has to be done here, absolutely nothing *to do*. So, why continue to exist? What can it matter? Some succumb almost immediately after hatching. Others, encouraged by their broodmothers, learn to push the feeling aside. Find something to engage with … a task, a goal."

Lilith stopped speaking for a moment. Her eyes closed, and she breathed deeply. Like a mummy placed to rest in forgotten times, she did not move. Fig blinked. He did not know where this was leading. A sudden panic eroded the initial braggadocio he had when the succubus had transported him through the flame. If she flaked out now, he would be more lost than anyone else had ever been.

"Sorry." Lilith returned from wherever her thoughts had taken her. "Sometimes, even the most staunch of us have moments when the dark thoughts surface. They are always there, of course, but with strength of will, they can be resubmerged."

She cocked her head to the side. "It is strange that the more powerful the demon, the stronger the impulse is. The smaller imps are the least affected. Their simple existences do not much bother them. Visiting the realm of humankind is interesting and diverting. New and fresh every time they travel through the flame. But the djinns, the ones with power? They live only for the lust of battle, for as much destruction as they can bring about. And as they survive their confrontations, even those become monotonous. Finally, they slink off to end their lives, have their parts scattered into the vastness of the void."

Fig took another small gulp of air. He had to remember to practice conservation. It had taken several trips to stockpile cylinders of oxygen near Lilith's lair from the realm of humankind. A few of the gremlins had agreed to serve as messengers, returning spent canisters back to the Earth and replacing them with others freshly filled. An 'advance' on the payment to Lilith for the service she would render, he had argued, and the sprites had readily agreed. Anything that was an excuse for meddling in the affairs of humankind appeared to be something they enjoyed.

Briana was in charge of keeping track of that. Hilo still had plenty of electrical power, and he had set up an electrolysis unit to break down water into hydrogen and oxygen. If the system worked as planned, he would always have enough fresh air.

He shifted the snowshoes he wore to achieve a better balance. He wanted to get some action started as soon as he could, but he had to do two things first — learn all he could about this place and gain some proficiency in moving around.

"You and Angela," he asked. "Where do succubi fit into all of this gloom and depression?"

"We are not the smallest of mites, nor the largest of demons who rule the realm. Angela pursues her goals, and I struggle to fulfill mine. We both engage and do not despair … at least not yet."

"But what just happened — "

"A momentary lapse. Seeing the expression on your face was the trigger, but it occurs whenever I return after a long visit on the Earth. But enough of that. For you to be truly effective here, I cannot carry you from one place to another all the time."

Fig grimaced. "Away from your lair, there is no gravity here. I will feel like I'm perpetually falling."

"Astronauts on your planet are able to manage."

Fig drew the rich air through his mouthpiece deeply. "Okay, here goes," he said. "I have two canisters of compressed carbon dioxide gas strapped to my sides."

Lilith eyed the cylinders. "They look quite small."

"Under pressure. Watch this."

Fig squeezed the release triggers on each of his hips and rose from the slab. He was not going to be a rocketman, but at least —

One of the jets was more powerful than the other; he rolled to the left. Instinctively, he relaxed his grip, and suddenly he was swung back to the right. His head tipped a bit, and he began to tumble. In a few moments, he drifted away from Lilith's lair, out of control.

"I need help," he called as his head circled back into view. "Watched

Putting Lessons into Practice

ANGELA SUCKED in her breath, but it did not calm her. She was the next in line. Up close, Elezar's gatekeeper towered even fiercer than he had from afar. Eyes of blackest jet sunk deep into a face like twin jewels sparkling in an open pit mine. Pockmarked jowls rigid with tension bracketed a mere slit of a mouth. Resplendent djinns had little need for speaking. Angela was taller than most succubi, but this monster towered over her as if she were a mere child.

"Next," the demon growled as the garden sprite in front of her flew away. Angela stepped forward. "I am lost," she said. "Is this the entrance to the tribute room? I have heard that the prince's stash is greater than any other's. Matter wrested through the flame from many realms."

"I am here to arrange the schedule of the great prince," the djinn answered. "Not serve as a tour guide for the awed. Begone. There are others behind you in the line."

Angela did not move. Instead, she bared her fangs in a slight smile. "Does it still hurt?" she asked.

"What do you mean?"

"It must be hard to have such a duty as yours. I wonder. Don't you miss soaring through the void?"

"Begone, I said. My power to rend and tear is as potent standing on matter as it was in the skies."

"How did it happen? I can't imagine what it must be like to have lost your ability to fly."

"Do you want an audience with Elezar or not?"

Angela smiled again. "How did it happen?"

The djinn looked the succubus up and down and thought for a moment. "You are the first ever to ask," he said at last. "Once I was among the mightiest. *Every* lightning djinn in the realm trembled in my presence. Few of my kind dared to stand in my way. Even Elezar knew of my prowess — and my name. I am called Trantor. Trantor the Terrible."

The water sprite behind Angela complained about the delay. Trantor stepped around her. With one swift swipe of his free hand, he swatted the smaller demon back into the void and out of sight.

"When the light directly above this opening changes from green to red, my shift is over. I rest in the little alcove behind me on the left. "Meet me there, and your question will be answered."

Angela forced her eyes open wide. She stared at Trantor for a moment and then touched him on the arm. "Until later," she said softly and flew up into the void.

ANGELA DUCKED her head to enter Trantor's lair. Unadorned walls formed a cone and slanted inward to meet in an apex barely high enough for the djinn to stand. A simple curving shelf jutted from the far side of the enclosure. Trantor lay upon the ledge, breathing huskily. His breath betrayed his arousal.

"Come to me, female. I am ready."

Angela screwed up her courage. She sucked in her breath. Natasha had been quite clear. If she were not firm, then, in the end, nothing would be accomplished. She just had to hope that the loss of a wing had damaged the djinn's self-worth enough that she could proceed. "No," she said.

"What?" Trantor sat up. "It is my right. You know that."

"Yes, I have served your kind in your rutting, more than once … but not this time."

"I do not need two wings in order to force you."

"But if you do, it will be like all the rest you have experienced. A momentary satisfaction only lasting an instant. And when it is over, I will leave without caring to hear your story."

Trantor stood and took a step toward Angela.

The succubus stood as well and placed both her hands stiffly down her sides. Like a robot, she stared back into the djinn's eyes.

Trantor took a second step and halted. A few moments passed. Finally, his shoulders slumped.

"It was a routine raid." He shuffled back to the shelf and sat down heavily. "Some petty upstart dared to suggest Elezar was no longer the mightiest of princes. The challenger's djinns flew out of his lair to meet us in empty space when we drew near. A dozen lightning and three of my kind.

"We numbered six. And ordinarily that would have been sufficient. We dove for the lightnings first, one against two. They fired their bolts as we approached, of course, but we all were swift and agile. The missiles were easily dodged, and I slammed into the first of my targets. In an instant, I ripped his head from his neck and hurled it into the void. For the other, I took my time to remove his limbs one by one.

"Finished with the lightning djinns, our band turned to confront the trio. I roared with confidence. Greater in number, we would soon end the fight."

Trantor stopped. His face boiled with rage. He could not continue.

"Treachery?" Angela guessed.

"Yes!" Trantor thundered. "Somehow three of my brethren had been converted, bribed — I don't know what. They had switched allegiance. I found myself on the side now outnumbered two to one rather than the other way around.

"My remaining comrades fought bravely. But in the end, pieces of their bodies also became part of the jetsam of the realm.

Trantor sighed. "In retrospect, I wish that had been my fate as well. Instead, I was surrounded and beaten into submission. In an agony I remember to this day, they tore away one of my wings and sent me back to Elezar to relate what had happened. A snub to the nose my prince has yet to rectify.

"He assigned me the job as a gatekeeper. What else could he do? No longer could I fly through the realm as one of his warriors. He left it to me to decide for myself when I surrender to the great monotony."

"Are you ready now?"

"I don't know. On some cycles the urge to end everything is powerful. On others, weak."

Angela breathed deeply again. Things were proceeding swiftly. Perhaps it was time for the next step.

"Poor baby." She squatted to the floor and patted her lap. "Here. Place your head here. I see the tension in the sinews of your neck. You need a little massage to ease the pain."

Trantor furrowed his brow. "What are you talking about?"

"Don't you feel better, having told your story?"

Trantor hesitated for a moment, then shrugged and settled on the floor. He put his head in Angela's lap, and she began to knead.

After a while, she stopped. Trantor looked up, surprised. "That felt good," he admitted.

"I suspect you have other stories to tell. Ones of your victories and praise from the prince."

"Well, there was the time — "

Angela put a finger to his lips. "Not now. I will come back in the next cycle at the same time."

Trantor's Story

ANGELA EYED Trantor cautiously as she ducked to enter his lair. Good. Relieved that he was not aroused, she sat on the floor as she had before. Without a word, he placed his head on her lap. "What shall I tell you now?" he asked.

Angela's pulse quickened. Perhaps this was a chance to learn more about Elezar, the prince. "When you returned after your last battle, how were you received?"

"I do not wish to talk more about that." With a wave of his hand, he shook his head. "Deceit cannot be undone. The past cannot be changed."

"Yes, yes. I understand. But I am curious. How did you *feel* when you had to report what had happened?"

Trantor sighed deeply. "Overwhelming shame," he said. "Even with one wing, I should have continued the fight until I was dispatched, but I, I—"

Angela stroked Trantor's cheek. "It's all right. I am listening, and I will not tell."

Trantor reached out and grasped Angela's hand. He squeezed it gently.

"You know of the dark thought that dwells within each of us as well as I. The vast emptiness. Nothing to do. No real task. No goal. The great monotony. And eventually, we give up and surrender. We rather take our lives than continue living what we know deep inside is a sham."

"Of course I know."

"For me, the one thing I have complete control over is the timing."

"The timing?"

"Yes. I understand the destiny awaiting us. But the one thing I can choose is *when* my existence would come to an end."

"You were in battle."

"But there was deceit. Losing one's life in the midst of a struggle against a superior foe is acceptable. But by treachery is not." Trantor sighed again. "So I returned to report to the prince, my thoughts in a jumble."

"What did he say?"

"He raged with anger. There was no mistaking the emotion coursing through him. We were to have taught an upstart prince a lesson, but we did not.

"His first coherent words were commands to the cleaning imps to get busy. Restore the mosaics on his audience floor to pristine brilliance. The ichor from my wing was leaving a stain. Next, he flung out his arm to wave me away. Then he paused for a moment, studying me as I slumped there, aching, tired, defeated.

A smile broke through his stern visage. "There is still use in you, Trantor," the prince said.

"To be a gatekeeper?"

"No, I think not. Elezar has become the most powerful of the princes because of his cunning. He has a plan, one in which I will play a part. For that, I choose to continue and not to succumb to the great monotony."

Angela shifted her position. Sitting with the head of a resplendent djinn in her lap was not comfortable for long. What she had heard was even more disturbing. Elezar was not known for kindness. She doubted that the prince had any 'plan' for Trantor. At some point, disappointment will cripple his spirit to match his mangled body.

"You have no one to intercede for you?" she asked.

Trantor jerked upright, his eyebrows knitted in suspicion. He sat up and stared at Angela. "What is *your* purpose, female? What are you trying to extract from me with sweet words?"

The succubus thought quickly. What had Natasha taught her to do when the target voiced suspicion?

"Your tales touch me, Trantor," she said. "There is a tragic depth to you. So unlike your peers. I think you are special."

She stopped, remembering the lessons well. To say more would only dilute the impact of what she had said.

For a long while, neither spoke. Finally, Trantor asked, "What would you say to Elezar about me?"

"Me? Certainly not me. I know nothing of the customs in the Prince's lair." She batted her eyes at Trantor. "I imagine that as a gatekeeper, you are very familiar with them."

"Yes, my head is full of such trivia. Elezar wants priority given to the powerful djinns. The lesser imps are last … although one or two are squeezed in early, so there is always hope."

"Why would an imp want an audience with a prince?"

"You would be surprised. Mites have the same concerns as the mightiest devils."

"Oh, really."

"Yes, for example, four cycles ago, a leader of the hairtanglers wanted to complain about ..."

Angela smiled inwardly. Things were moving ahead exactly as she had hoped.

Marshaling Troops

FIG AND Lilith were back within the realm of demons. Their sojourn to Earth had been a brief one. There, gasoline-powered generators now provided power to radio and television stations. Reporter's cameras scanned what looked like miles of empty shelves in the stores. Already, everything editable had found a new home. There would be no famine for some time.

But there was another problem. No power meant no electricity for municipal water pumps. Except where there had been storage tanks, the pressure at the taps had plummeted to zero. Much sooner than other staples, the ubiquitous little bottles of water would all be depleted.

He shook his head to clear away the disturbing images in his mind. It was a waste of time to dwell on what he had seen. Or on what was going to happen unless he could get thousands of little helpers busy with the repairs.

He looked in amazement at the lair of the gremlins where Lilith had brought him. Unlike other demons, they crammed their individual lairs together in one large conglomeration.

No two lairs were the same. Made of discarded circuit boards, they were held together by power cords and USB cables. Other electronic gear floated among the little shelters: insulation strippers, flash drives, floppy disks, buttons, and LEDs. From several came whistles and beeps, the chatter of video games. Everything had been scavenged, disassembled, hauled across an electric arc, and reassembled here. Even so, the junk was not randomly distributed but held a hint of order. The gremlins consider it gardens and landscaping, Lilith had told him.

"In summary, you will accomplish more, acting together." The succubus finished her pitch before an assembly of males. "So, how many are with me to give it a try?"

"We are not the dullest lawnmowers in the shed," one of the gremlins said. "But your words are far too abstract. I, for one, have no idea what you are talking about. Solidarity, comradery, the quality of life. What is it exactly you want us to do? Why should we do it?"

Lilith slumped. "You are little better than drink dribblers," she complained.

Fig approached her and whispered. "Your step one is too big. Break it down into pieces. First show what working together can accomplish with a simple example. After that, apply the concept to the gremlin's real problem."

"What kind of example?"

Fig pondered. He rubbed his cheek, checking the length of his stubble. It was one way of approximating how much time had passed since he had arrived in the realm. "Didn't you mention that sometimes you wanted to move your lair?" he asked. "Farther away from the one with the bright and annoying blue beacon on the top? Use that as an example instead."

Lilith cocked her head to the side. "What are *you* talking about, Fig?" she asked.

Fig turned his attention back to the gremlins as they were starting to disperse. "You guys are hotshots with electronics. At least you claim you are. But electrical forces are not always the most powerful in the realm of humankind. Sometimes, there are others even more awesome, ones that are based on an entirely different discipline — mechanics."

Lilith picked up the patter. Soon, about a hundred or so of the gremlin males had been convinced to accompany her back to her lair for what she called a 'demonstration.'

Having him along indeed had helped, Fig thought. The little devils were a curious lot. Always eager to stay abreast of the latest humankind technology.

The entourage took flight, and Fig struggled not to fall too far behind. He was getting more used to weightlessness. Becoming more skilled at navigating on his own. One cylinder of oxygen was lasting longer and longer. He fired an attitude control jet strapped to his torso and then another.

I should not judge, he thought. My clutter is no better than what I have just seen: a blinking headlight, scuba gear, snowshoes, thrusters, attitude control, a small gyro compass. And to top it all off, a sword on one side, and a dagger on the other. He could barely move. Not exactly the image of the dashing hero of the sagas.

After bringing up the rear, Fig reached Lilith and Angela's lair. Angela was nowhere to be seen. Lilith was already busy, herding the gremlins into a straight line along the side of the lair. She shuttled back and forth, trying to create order. Fig lit on the modest slab and plopped down. After several attempts, he gave up finding a comfortable position and fiddled with tightening the belt holding his oxygen canisters in place.

The slabs of matter in the demon realm — he could not wrap his mind around how they worked. For the poorer demons, they were paper thin, but they behaved as if they were Gibraltars of immovable rock. Once created, they could be moved to and fro, or left and right, but never up or down. They could be rotated about this 'up-down' axis but never pitched or rolled. Throughout the entire realm, every lair he had visited maintained the same rigid positioning constraints. And they possessed some sort of gravity, firmly holding onto whatever was placed upon them.

"Stop the gripes, and give this a chance," Lilith spoke loudly over the chittering gremlins. "This is not an impossible task. It only seems that way because my lair is many times the mass of any one of yours."

The succubus shrugged with frustration and looked back at Fig for help. He nodded and thought for a moment. He knew little of how gremlins operated, but he could infer at least some about what they were like. Having a drink dribbler for translations was not ideal because of the time delays, but it would have to do. If he wanted to say anything in the common demon tongue, he first had to whisper to the imp, listen carefully to what the tiny demon squeaked and then try to echo the words as best he could. He took a deep breath of air from the scuba mouthpiece and orated.

"What did you do when you discovered the humans had invented the Intel 4004?" he boomed. "Throw up your hands and bitch about how such technology was unfair, too intricate to exploit? Your days of mischief over?"

Some of the gremlins stopped yammering. A few frowned, curious about what they would hear next.

"No!" Fig took another gulp of air. "Instead, you rose to the task. You poured through the arc and examined the writings. The schematics, the new way electronics were made. And now glitching a smartphone is child's, I mean hatchling's play right?"

A faint murmur of agreement rolled through the line.

"What you are embarking on now is no different," Fig rushed on. "A new challenge. A new experience you will take pleasure in mastering. Something to be added to your … to your resumes."

"What I have been trying to tell you," Lilith interrupted, "is that you have always acted as individuals. Never as a team. But if you unite for a common cause, there are new wonders you can perform."

"I see no electronics, not even a breadboard," one of the gremlins shouted back. Fig recognized that it was Faraday, the one he had talked with before.

"You are merely trying to use us to do some of your housework," Faraday said. "There is no new marvel for you to show us here."

Mumbles of agreement immediately bubbled up from the assembly.

"Try this demonstration as I have instructed," Lilith said. "You will see."

"*See?*" Faraday replied. "There is *nothing* to see. No way for Murphy to intercede. No way for his law to be proven true."

The chattering of the gremlins grew louder. A few went back to their lairs.

"Prove her wrong," Fig shouted over the growing din. "Otherwise, this succubus will harass you even more. A large and *hungry* devil to disrupt your contemplations."

The mumbling stopped. There was silence. No one moved.

"All right, then," Faraday finally called out. "Let's get this *demonstration* over with."

Still no movement.

"Come on guys," Faraday urged. "The sooner we are done, the better."

After a few moments more, the line of tiny demons fluttered their wings and moved to the edge of Lilith's lair. Hundreds of little hands reached out and clasped the slab in their grips.

"Now, all together," Lilith commanded. "Use your wings. Push."

A buzz like that of a swarm of hornets filled the air. For a heartbeat, nothing happened, but then gradually the lair started to move. With each wingbeat, it gathered speed. Like a regal clipper ship, it sailed through the void.

But the thrust was uneven. Lilith's lair yawed to the left.

A cheer arose from the laboring demons. "Murphy rules!" one shouted, and then others joined in. Soon, the lair was not only moving at a considerable speed but rotating as well.

"Now, quickly, to the other side," Lilith yelled. "Reverse what you have done. Stop the drift and spin."

"Setting things right is not what we do," Faraday said. "Well, sometimes, but it is not our nature."

"Don't you want to stop the larger devils from using nets to catch you like the sardines of Earth?" Fig bellowed. "Remember what this is about."

After another chorus of mumbles, the gremlins flew to the other side of Lilith's lair. They stopped it from any more drifting and rotation. When that was accomplished, they dissolved into an irregular cluster. An excited hubbub filled the thin air of the realm.

"Impressive, even without the electronics," Faraday called out from the midst of the swarm. "Thanks for the demo. We will have to keep this trick in mind. Anything else you can show us while we are here?"

"You are missing the point." Lilith tried to keep her voice calm but failed. "Acting alone, you will accomplish little. But working together great feats can be achi."

Like a babbling brook overflowing its banks, there was a flurry of communication. Lilith let it run its course. When it was again quiet, she spoke once more.

"The lightning djinns use nets to harvest you while you are distracted in your studies, right?"

"Contemplation is central to our way of life," Faraday said. "We do it in a certain place and at certain times. We cannot change that. It is part of what we are."

"So post lookouts," Lilith said. "And when a net unfurls, rather than panic, come to your senses and push against the webbing."

"We have tried that," another gremlin said. "The force is too strong to resist."

"Only if you act separately and then give up. But, just as you showed me by moving my lair, you can produce the power of many."

The gremlins resumed their discussion. Fig waited. He felt encouraged. There were no shouts to forget this and return home.

After a much longer time, the caucuses ended. Faraday flew out of the swarm to face Lilith.

"Okay," he said. "We will resist coherently when the nets come next. But we want you and the human to be there when it happens. Whatever the outcome, you are the ones responsible."

SOMETIME LATER, the gremlins were ready. The group who normally contemplated at that time floated in their traditional places. None even pretended they were studying any text. Fig and Lilith watched expectantly nearby.

Both were in high spirits. If this worked, Fig thought, soon thousands of gremlins would pass through the flame. Repair the damaged generators. Have them up and running before the fabric of society disintegrated.

Was there still time enough? Did time flow here at the same rate? He looked at his watch and shrugged. It was useless. So much of the demon realm was static. There was no way to calibrate.

"Here comes the net," one of the contemplators shouted. "Everyone, drop what you are doing. Focus on a single strand."

Fig watched the net approach. It filled the view in front of him, more extensive than he had imagined — broader than the length of the gremlin array, and also taller and deeper.

It was borne by a type of demon Fig had never seen before. Lightening djinns, Lilith had warned him. They dwarfed the gremlins, easily a hundred times their size. Bright yellow with large overlapping scales. And there were many. A dozen or more spaced themselves along the top row of the net, their long claws holding the webbing tightly. An equal number did the same along the bottom. The sides were tautly secured as well.

With military precision, the gremlins rushed to greet the onrushing web. Each one grabbed the nearest strand with both hands. Vibrating their wings as hard as they could, they pushed against the net.

For an instant, the forward motion of the trap halted. Fig stopped breathing, but he did not notice. He held his mouth closed tightly, anxious to see what would happen next. The demons propelling the net shouted to one another, speaking so rapidly that Fig got no hint of what was said.

The beat of the larger devil's wings increased, each stroke more powerful than the last. Despite the efforts of the gremlins, the net continued forward. In a matter of moments, it encircled the little sprites into a column, and the top and bottom were cinched tight. They were in a trap from which they could not escape.

The gremlins chattered in shrill voices. The rapid patter was too swift for the drink dribbler in Fig's ear to translate. The pitch rose higher and higher to the limits of his hearing and then beyond. In barely a full breath, the djinns hauled them away.

Fig and Lilith watched the entrapped gremlins recede into the darkness. As they did, the djinns loosened the tension at the top of the net a tiny bit, and a few of the captives flew out. Greedy hands snatched them from the air and tossed them into waiting maws. The opening closed for a moment, and then the process was repeated.

As the sprites vanished into the darkness, the succubus slumped. "I talked them into their deaths," she whispered.

Fig could not be sure, but he had never heard Lilith speak in such a somber tone before. "But isn't eating smaller demons a basic part of life in your realm?"

"A succubus does not eat others as large as gremlins." Lilith shuddered. "Certainly not cause the demise of over a hundred at one time." She slumped even further. "I have strong feelings about this, Fig. Perhaps I have sojourned in your realm far too long."

The falling guillotine flashed through Fig's mind. "I know how you feel," he said. He hesitated for a moment, and then, avoiding the upward protrusion of her wingtips, slid his arm around her shoulders and held her close. Lilith tensed for a moment, then relaxed into Fig's embrace.

"This is taking so long," the succubus said. "We have made no progress at all."

A Possible Invitation

ANGELA DUCKED to enter Trantor's lair. The resplendent djinn awaited her, lounging on his shelf as he had done before. But this time she detected a difference. His pectorals quivered with tension as if alert for an impending battle.

Trantor followed her gaze. "Yes, I am not calm. And I see that you can tell. Sometimes I dwell on wrong scheduling decisions I might have made, especially when I have idle time in which to think."

Angela blinked. Usually, djinns were not that introspective. Certainly, not enough to guess what she was thinking.

"What is it about gatekeeping that affects you so?" she asked. "You tell one imp he can see the prince in three cycles. Another you send on his way."

"Elezar is known for his fierce temper and snap judgments. If I make what he considers a single error, my life could be forfeit. In his eyes, I would have value no longer. And with one wing, no other prince would see any gain in adding me to his retinue. I would not be able to surrender to the great monotony at a time of my choosing."

"I did not see you on your post during the last cycle."

Trantor shrugged. "Elezar has decreed no more audiences in the near term. He has called a meeting of all the princes in the realm. They are to ponder some important, newly discovered facts affecting them all. I have had nothing to do."

"So, for today, you — " she began.

Trantor shrugged. "I idled my time, cataloging some of the chaos in the tribute room. So much junk tossed in there. Small cylinders from the realm of humankind with 'redemption value,' whatever that means, marked on them. Spools of cable not made of stout iron but instead elastic and yielding. Of no use whatsoever to hold anything fast."

Angela smiled with apparent interest. The more the djinn talked, the more she learned. "Anything else?"

The djinn waggled his head. "Most bizarre of all, strange white chairs molded from a single piece of what humans call 'plastic.' Uncomfortable to sit in, no matter what one's size, and apparently, they do not decay *ever*. We have thousands and thousands of them here. And all of them *white* with not a trace of color. After all humans are gone, they probably will be what remains as the monument marking their existence."

"Interesting," Angela said. Her chest tightened. There would be risk, but now was the time to reroute the conversation. "*All* the princes of the realm, you said? That would be quite a spectacle to see. Elezar, for sure, will be there?"

Trantor nodded. "At the conclusion, I will be able to observe them all. Elezar will array all his djinns for the others to see the extent of his might. So long as I remain in the second row and keep facing forward, I am to attend as well. The politics are quite simple. Whoever has the greatest number is the supreme of all."

"Only princes and djinns allowed at this show of force?"

Trantor shook his head. "No, behind the circle of djinns, some lesser devils will be allowed to attend."

Angela sat down and patted her lap. "Come then. Tell me another story so that this cycle of relaxation will be one you can remember fondly."

NATASHA'S SWEET talk had worked! Angela thought. Trantor had wrangled a way for her to watch the spectacle. She was taller than most of the lesser demons who stood in the periphery of the great rotunda, but she still had to strain to see what was happening in the pit. Elezar, the Golden, sat on a pillow of silk and down in the very center. He was clothed in a glittering robe of deep sea green that covered all his body except for his fingertips. Some whispered that it also covered a chest twisted and broken.

An upturned nose, thin lips, and barely pointed ears sculpted a narrow face. Straw pale hair ran over a brow flecked with gold, and half-closed eyes glowered under long curved lashes. No great scales or hair-pierced warts marred the smooth skin. Elezar could pass unnoticed in the realm of humankind.

Three other princes of the realm sat in front of Elezar on an arc of

224

hard, stone tuffets. Behind them arrayed a second row for those of lesser rank. All eyes watched a sprite of medium size busily summing numbers on a parchment covered easel. When he finished, he turned to Elezar and in a quaking voice announced the total. "Two thousand, two hundred, thirty-two."

"And the sum, ten thousand cycles ago?" Elezar asked.

The sprite flipped back several pages over the easel. "Three thousand, seventeen."

"This cannot continue," Elezar growled. "If it does, the number of djinns in the entire realm eventually will become zero."

"We should stop fighting among ourselves," one of the other princes rose and stretched to his full height. "It is a waste of ichor."

"That would not help a whit," shouted a second. "Battle losses are but a small part of the decline. The great monotony is the root of the problem."

"Yes, yes," exclaimed a third. "We may as well have them battle one another. If we do not give them something to do, they'll succumb anyway."

"Battle lust and despair are beyond the power of even a prince." Elezar spoke so softly that the demons facing him hushed to hear. "None of us is omnipotent. You three, in particular, should remember that. Resplendent djinns will continue to pass from us, one way or another. That we cannot change."

He looked at each of the princes in turn before speaking again. "The problem is not how powerful demons end but instead how they begin."

Everyone heard the prince, even those several tiers higher than where Angela stood. There were no distracting echoes.

"And so, why is that?" Elezar said as the audience showed restlessness. He motioned to one of the djinns standing behind the seated princes. The demon stepped forward and stooped to one knee.

"I am Cleftorian, my prince, here to serve you."

"When was the last time you served *yourself*?" Elezar asked. "Visited the lairs of the broodmother? Or took advantage of a target of opportunity, a succubus, perhaps?"

"I do not remember, my prince."

"And why is that?"

"Excuse me, my prince, but I … I hope you will understand. From time to time, the urge does become paramount, and I satisfy it right away." Cleftorian shrugged. "But for some reason, the satisfaction is not as great as I desire."

"The female is unwilling?"

"How could she not be?" Cleftorian shrugged again. "The interruption by one of us serves her no purpose. She submits as she must, but it is quite clear from how she acts that she does not enjoy."

Elezar pointed to the easel. "We will be unsuccessful deterring either battles until death or surrender to the great monotony. Without more warriors to replace those slain, we will descend into anarchy. But new births are happening less and less."

The prince stopped. The last remaining buzz from the audience did as well. "Show me evidence contradicting that doom."

None of the princes responded.

"That is why I have brought you here," Elezar straightened his back as well as he could. "Return to your lairs and instruct your most brilliant scholars. Task them to come up with a means to increase new hatchlings ... a solution to this problem touching us all. Otherwise, order will disappear."

A blanket like an impenetrable fog descended onto Angela's thoughts. She placed her heels back onto the floor and flexed her shoulders. Her goal was to gain control of the prince. But suppose ultimately she did, what then would be the point? With fewer demons throughout the realm, there would be fewer over which to rule. In the end, would she be merely a concubine to a strutting poppycock? How horrible that would be. One way or another, what was happening could overwhelm them all.

The Meeting of Princes

SEVERAL TIME cycles passed after Elezar's meeting with the princes. Angela arrived at Trantor's lair at the usual time. She blinked at its emptiness when she stepped inside. The djinn was not there. She frowned, worried. He had become so open with her, sharing his most intimate thoughts. His spirit so broken because he could no longer fly. Humans on the Earth soar through the air, and they had no wings at all. If only there were a way to give him the ability again.

Suppose he had succumbed? Surrendered to the despair of the great monotony and taken his life. She did not want that, she suddenly realized. She looked forward to being with him.

"I have been busy," Trantor broke through Angela's reverie. He dangled some parchment sheets in his hand. "I walked all the way around Elezar's lair and completed the circuit."

As had almost become a ritual, Angela sank to the floor and motioned for Trantor to place his head in her lap.

"Not yet," the djinn waved the invitation aside. "I have discovered something that must be reported to the prince."

"What?"

"Most of the other pathways into the towers are guarded by lesser djinns. Their contents are not as precious as that of Elezar's central rotunda."

"I understand the layout of the lair," Angela answered. "You explained that to me before."

"I polled each one of the guards. And every one of them, no matter how small and unimportant, told me the same thing. In the matter of creating new beings of their kind, they act the same as djinns. Quenching of lust only when it rises to be a distraction. And even then, the satisfaction is fleeting."

Angela nodded, recalling Adonis's lament, how the number of gargoyle hatchlings was decreasing. Things probably were worse than the prince had surmised.

Trantor looked down at Angela beckoning him to recline.

"No, I must tell the prince."

"Surely, you cannot merely barge in."

The djinn examined his scheduling parchment lying nearby. "At the moment, he is resting. That is an opportunity. I must take it."

Angela pulled her lips into a firm line. She screwed up her courage. "I am coming with you."

ANGELA BARELY kept up with Trantor's long strides. With each step, the ugly tangle of scar tissue from the stub of his missing wing stared her in the face. It was a shame for one so ... noble. Yes, that was the word for it. One so noble to be denied what he was meant to be.

Soon, they descended the rotunda steps to where Elezar sat. His retinue of fluttering imps darted around his head like a swarm of fireflies on a summer night. The Golden One was not small, but certainly, he was nowhere near the height of any of the djinns he controlled.

Elezar glanced only for a moment at Angela, his expression dismissing her immediately. "Trantor," the prince said. "Your appearance here has importance, I presume."

Trantor opened his mouth to speak, then hesitated. Angela saw his biceps tense. There was a silence for too many heartbeats.

"Yes, my prince," Angela surprised herself by blurting. "Very important. Your example of collecting hard facts opened your loyal djinn's eyes. He now sees that doing so is superior to idle speculation."

"Hmm, for a djinn, you show a trace of acumen." Elezar squinted as he paused for a moment. "Ah, I remember what befell you. Has gatekeeping become too repetitious? Do you understand that I do not have any higher ranking task for one of your ... condition."

Another long silence. Angela could not stand the vacuum. "Perhaps, what on Earth is called a 'chief of staff,'" she said.

Elezar turned to examine the succubus more carefully. He raised one questioning eyebrow. "I do not recall having you before," he said. "Report back to the broodmother lairs. If you are lucky, I will service you later. Here, you do not belong."

228

Angela bristled. She started to bare her fangs but stopped just in time. Yes, her goal was to enrapture this pint-sized nabob, but his attitude needed to be adjusted, too. "I am not here to seek your attention," she said.

"Then, why?"

Angela scrambled for an answer. "I ... I speak for Trantor — even though he did not ask me to. He has brain as well as brawn. Someone for you to bounce ideas off of; someone to suggest other ones you have not even thought."

Elezar scowled. "He is a djinn. One that has been broken. He cannot perform what I would ask of him. It is only because of my largess that I found a task for him to do. Better to engage in something, anything, than mope until he becomes overcome by the great monotony."

Angela's face tightened. She returned Elezar's stare. "I hazard to guess that the management of those who wish an audience with you has never been handled better."

For a while, no one spoke. Finally, Elezar said, "The remarkable thing about this encounter is that you are a female."

Angela took a deep breath, trying to control herself. Arguing with a prince was not a good way to seduce him to her will.

"A female who speaks of the virtues of a male, a resplendent one no less," she said.

"I have information for you, my prince," Trantor suddenly awoke from his paralysis and took a step forward. "That is why I ... we have come."

Elezar hesitated for a moment, then waved the pair away. "Later. There is a rumor that three of the more powerful princes are plotting a joint action. Put yourself on the calendar as you do any other. I must use my quiet time to ponder that — and also what I have just observed here."

"But — ," Angela started.

Trantor put a grip on her arm and pushed her back. "Have you no sense?" he whispered out of the side of his mouth. "He is the most powerful prince of them all."

Angela let Trantor guide her away. This was not how she had planned things. Elezar had been her target from the start. What had made her speak out for Trantor instead?

A Demonstration in Physics

STANDING AT the center of the gremlin's slab, Fig looked at the new vertical line of males. Each was smaller than the width of one of his hands, but arrayed together they stretched higher than a dozen humans. The sprites fluttered their wings and tried to maintain their alignment. Each now held a tool scavenged from the gardens around their homes: wire strippers, tin snips, scissors …

As if a skilled lighting manager had brightened the stage for the start of a play, each of the dwellings in the communal had some sort of illumination mounted at its apex.

Lilith cupped her hands around her mouth and shouted at the sprites. "Remember to act in unison. That is the key." It had taken a lot of convincing, but finally, the gremlins had agreed to try again. Appealing to their curiosity about what the outcome would be had done the trick.

Fig flexed his shoulders. The new agreement did not relieve the great weight pressing down upon him. It had been his idea to arm the gremlins with the debris scavenged from the realm of humankind. If this failed as before, there would be hundreds more of lives lost, this time all on his account. He would no longer be able to push the images of crashing guillotines away. But we *have* to try again, he told himself. Do whatever it takes. We just have to get additional demons to the Earth.

It was hard to tell for sure, but three or maybe four days back on Earth had passed with the convincing and then bald-faced pleading with the gremlins. The shuttle of fresh oxygen tanks had continued on schedule, but Briana's update messages had not contained good news. Marshall Law had been declared in all the major cities in the continental US. Curfews were at dusk. In daylight hours, long lines of bucket holders queued at oversubscribed water buffalo trucks. There were rumors that even the military was running out of fuel to make any more deliveries.

Fig did not want to believe what he heard. Hadn't there been enough practice with hurricane and earthquake disasters? More widespread problems to be sure, but the steps to take should be clear. Things were going to get worse before they got better, but certainly, they couldn't be that bad already. Probably fake news from a pirate radio station on an offshore oil platform.

Fig pushed the disturbing thoughts aside and concentrated on what was going to happen here next. It did not help that the females had come to watch too, but Lilith had insisted. She remained steadfast about what was going to be step two.

At first, Fig could see nothing far away except for the inky darkness of the void. But finally, dots of fuzzy, reflected light appeared, and moments later, resolved into the array of lightning djinns coming closer. They outlined a long rectangle, a row at top and bottom, and two more along the sides. The net they carried was not yet visible, but he knew it was there — nine djinns high, and five times as wide as its vertical extent.

"Two, four, six, eight. Who do we appreciate?" A ragged cheer arose from the cluster of females. Fig guessed it was for his benefit. Or maybe they were showing off an adeptness with another tongue. Some carried their infants to watch. Others opened picnic baskets and distributed stickypaper covered with even smaller imps squirming to get free. The treats were consumed as rapidly as they appeared.

Demons treated death so casually, Fig pondered. Yes, as far as 'natural causes' were concerned, they were immortal. One would think the passing of a single devil to be a great tragedy. In the snippets of conversation he had overheard, however, that did not seem the case. A passing was merely marked as an early exit rather than being overcome by the great monotony sometime later. Even the complaint about the djinns using nets was about 'fair play' rather than an injustice.

The net approached the line of gremlins. The djinns on the left and right edges converged faster. Seeing the thin line, they curved the entrapment into a large 'U.' In a few moments, they surrounded the males hovering in place.

Like a precision drill team, the gremlins used their cutting tools to sever the weave of the netting closest to them. The bordering tape at the top and bottom held, but that did not matter. In an instant, the net gaped open. All the gremlins rushed through to freedom. The tattered snare closed on emptiness.

"We don't smoke, and we don't chew," yelled the freed gremlins. "And we don't go with the girls who do." They swarmed around Fig in exuberant excitement. One by one, they extended their scaly hands and slapped him briskly on each cheek. "High ten," they said as they flew past.

Fig staggered from the barrage. "Wait, wait," he said. "This might not be over. The djinns could drop the net and still come after you, one by one."

"Fair enough," a gremlin said. "That is the way things were before." The males dispersed into a random cloud and awaited the return of the djinns once the larger demons figured out what had happened.

"Our agreement," Fig shouted. He clenched his fists in frustration. "You said you would restore the generators on the Earth to working order."

"Later," one of the gremlins called back as a lightning djinn converged on him. "What's the rush? This is too much fun." The smaller devil was faster and ducked under the arms extended to ensnare him.

Fig shouted a few more times, but none of the males responded. "Damn it!" he growled as Lilith landed beside him. She smiled from ear to ear.

"Let's see if the demonstration has had its intended effect," she said.

Fig scowled. He had never heard such enthusiasm from her before.

"Listen up," the succubus shouted over the buzz of conversation erupting among the females. "Do you understand the significance of what has happened here? How by joining together, greater things can be achieved than by acting alone."

None of the gremlin females paid Lilith any attention. Like a classroom with the teacher away, the chatter continued.

In desperation, Fig scanned the junk in the nearby gardens. He spotted a portable microphone in one and a small radio in another. With some more scrounging, he located a battery and some wiring. He coupled the output of the mike to the input of the radio receiver and placed the two facing each other.

"Boo!" he mouthed to start the feedback loop. The resulting shriek rose in intensity and out of Fig's range of hearing. The gremlin ears were smaller than his and more likely to hear far higher frequencies.

One of the females staggered to Fig's side, her hands pushed against her ears. She removed a small hammer from her belt and pounded first on the radio and then the mike.

The feedback stopped. Fig scratched his head looking for something else to try but then noticed that the babbling had halted as well. The females were quiet. The females, he realized suddenly. Yes, the females. Why not?

"I need help," he said to the gremlin putting her hammer back on her belt. "If not the guys, then you women can do the job. Wouldn't you like

232

to visit the Earth?"

"The males know about that kind of stuff," the female shrugged. "Our only tasks are to suckle the young and serve the males when the desire arouses within them."

"So it is for all our gender throughout the realm," Lilith cut in. "Don't you want to achieve something better?"

"Like what?"

"Like respect," Lilith said. "You, me, all of us should be treated as equals."

"I don't get it," the gremlin screwed her face into a puzzle. "How is cutting nets going to achieve something like that?"

"That was only the example!" Lilith's voice strained with frustration. "If you are united, you can demand that males ask permission first, and you have the right to refuse."

"Demand? Exactly what do you mean by demand?"

"Lilith will explain all of that to you later," Fig jumped in. "There are some techniques used on Earth that have proven quite successful."

He waved both hands back and forth. "But never mind that now. You must fix the generators first. Time is running out."

"Not yet for that," Lilith snapped. "Fig. My goal, then yours."

"I have always wanted to travel through the arc myself," one of the female gremlins put a finger on her cheek. Her eyes took on a faraway look. "What exactly would 'our part' be there?"

"Repair the generators. And as soon as possible," Fig insisted. "If we don't fix them soon, things will get much worse."

"What's a generator?"

"I can teach you the fundamentals," Desperation energized Fig's words. "Or if not me, I'm sure Briana — "

"No," Lilith cut him off. Her fangs emerged. Her face distorted into a scowl. "The opportunity is here in this realm, here and now. While what the males accomplished is fresh in everyone's minds. The next step has to be the females standing their ground, united."

Fig had never seen Lilith look that way before. The more he got to know her, the wider her range of emotions seemed to become. He had to act quickly. Too much was at stake back at home.

"Cluster around me," he said. "Reach out and sense the electric arc that I'm visualizing."

He squinted his eyes shut, trying to make a sharp image of the bright light in his mind. For a moment, nothing materialized, but then, in a rush of color, it did. Not so bright that he could not stand it, but sharp enough to feel that it was there.

"Ooooh!" the female nearest him said.

"I can see it," shouted another. "Interesting. Unlike anything we have been exposed to before."

There was a pop of inrushing air where the sprite nearest to Fig had been. Then another and a third. In an instant, hundreds more of the females swarmed around him, getting as close as they could.

Fig pushed against the gale as he looked at Lilith. Her eyes flashed fire. "Tell Briana to teach you," he said to the ones who had not yet passed through. "Quickly, through the arc, before — "

Lilith lunged at Fig and sent him sprawling. Out of control, he tumbled into the void.

Possible Aid

BACK ON Earth, Briana forced open her eyes from her catnap. The snooze was not a great substitute for the charm, but it worked well enough. The familiar chug of two pumps filled the air, but she thought she had heard something different as well. Not the single pop that meant the messenger gremlin had appeared, but several of them in a row. She glanced at a small radio on a shelf near her head, but it was not on. The noise did not come from there.

A large water-filled tank now occupied most of the space on the lab workbench. It looked exactly the same as when Fig had set it up. At both ends of the tank, near the bottom, an electrical terminal had been inserted through a water-tight seal. Outside of the glass walls, thick insulated copper wires connected the terminals to the opposite polarities of a high current source. Inside the tank, from each, bubbles of gas slowly rose to the liquid surface, oxygen from one and hydrogen from the other. Inverted funnels caught the upflows, and elastic tubing channeled them to two pumps gently chugging and compressing the gases into steel, transport cylinders.

The containers were of two sizes, the smaller ones for replenishing Fig's air supply in the realm of demons. A half-dozen of them stood filled and ready on the workbench next to the tank. They would be swapped whenever a gremlin brought a spent one back to Earth. Two large cylinders stood on the floor near the rightmost wall to capture all of the hydrogen. One was connected to a tank, the other already full. That gas was a byproduct of no use, but safety dictated that it be handled with care.

The tank reminded Briana of a large, empty aquarium, one containing no fish, but bubbles and more bubbles from an aerator. "Electrolysis," she practiced the word for the dozenth time. She had never heard of such a phenomenon before. Earth-based chemistry held many wonders.

Pop.

Pop, pop, pop.

Briana scanned the room and caught a hint of motion near the welding rig along the far wall — the one that kept operating so that gremlins could move back and forth between the realms.

She blinked. There was not a single message demon there, but instead dozens. They flitted about so wildly that they were impossible to count.

"Teach us! Teach us!" the tiny voices cried out. "What is a generator? How can one be fixed?"

Briana slammed her eyes shut and tried to concentrate. There was no way she could dominate so many demons at once, even if they did not have the strongest of wills. Think, she commanded herself. It had been a long time since she had received the basic training in all five of the crafts, but there had been a lesson on the control of swarms of the smaller imps.

Yes, there it was! She visualized the stiff parchment with the simple instructions. Project thoughts of tranquility and self-assurance. Calm them down.

Briana inhaled and exhaled rhythmically, each breath relaxing her more and more. The popping continued, and then gradually, the din faded away. She opened her eyes when it was quiet. Hovering against the wall behind the workbench, and arranged in twelve precise rows of ten, like toy soldiers ready for battle, were female gremlins all looking up at her with their hands folded quietly on their laps.

"We have a bargain with the succubus, Lilith," one spoke up. The gremlin looked around. "At least, we think we do. It appears the one named Fig did not come with ... Say, where is *your* headlamp and all the other paraphernalia that humans hang about themselves?"

Briana felt a stab of alarm. "Fig? Has anything happened to him? Is he okay?"

"A few moments ago, I saw, he was tumbling out of control into the void." The gremlin shrugged. "But as I think of it, that shouldn't be a big problem. One human is as good as another. I mean, you all look so much alike on the outside. How can the inside be very different? And oh, you can call me 'Audacious Audrey.'"

A titter arose from the other gremlins. Briana could not be sure, but she heard the words sounded something like 'Razorbutt is pretending pretentious names again.'

"Stop that!" Audacious Audrey shouted. "Lilith says the whole idea is to act united. We can't waste times calling each other the names the males give us. Those are not ... respectful. At least, I think that is what the succubus says."

The first two gremlins near the wall flittered into the center of the room. A few others popped the stoppers off some of the bottles on the reagent shelf and emptied the contents on the ones still hovering primly below them.

Briana folded her arms across her chest. She was not satisfied with the answer to her question. Was anything wrong with Fig or not?

"*I* am in charge here!" she growled. "*I* am your master. You must do what I say."

Like a needle lifted from a record, the noise stopped.

"Now then, Razor … I mean Audrey, henceforth, you will be my second in command. Keep everyone in order."

Briana took another deep breath. Composure flowed back into her. "If Fig is in trouble, you must go back to your realm and save him. It is as simple as that."

"Do we have to?" Audrey whined. "The deal is that we learn what a generator is and how to fix it."

Briana frowned. A dilemma rose within her like a spouting geyser. Fig was in an environment that had to be hostile. On the other hand, things were getting worse here on Earth. The generators on the mainland did need to get repaired, and the gremlins might be the ones who could do that. Was there a way to accomplish both —

The door to the lab swung open and banged against the wall. A mature woman entered, both arms rigidly extending a gun. Her eyes registered everything in the room. A tall blond man shuffled after her, his face vacant.

"I am Natasha Gorshok," the woman said. "Where is Fig? I need him, and I need him now."

11

A Desperate Attempt

NATASHA KEPT her hand steady. The most dangerous opponents were women, not men. Was this an associate of Fig's or someone else? She scanned the contents of the lab while keeping her weapon pointed at the young woman. Her eyes widened when she saw the gremlins fluttering near the back wall.

"Fig hasn't returned here." Briana extended her hands, palm forward, and moved slowly to sit on one of the lab stools. "What is it you want from him?"

Natasha ignored the question. Her thoughts whirled. Was she going mad? First Angela, who called herself a succubus, a winged creature from somewhere else. Then Adonis, the gargoyle. Another alien being. She couldn't help shaking her head vigorously, even though it gave the woman across from her an opportunity to close in and grapple. Two creatures were enough. How many more could there be? She grasped at the first straw that floated into her mind.

"Is that what a succubus looks like when it is young, or maybe a gargoyle, instead?" she asked.

"Not at all." Briana kept her hands raised. "Those are gremlins. A different kind entirely. Annoyingly inquisitive, but basically harmless."

"So three types exist rather than two?"

"No, there are dozens of different kinds." Briana lowered her hands slightly. "I don't remember exactly what the number is. Little ones are called imps, middle-sized, sprites, and big ones djinns. Put your gun down, and I will try to explain."

Natasha's knees wobbled from fatigue. The flight from the mainland had been stressing enough. Sitting for hours in the jump seat of a plane flying over a featureless ocean. Keeping her weapon aimed at the pilots the entire time. Escape from the Hilo airport before security could arrive. Hours carefully searching for this warehouse address.

She looked one more time at the hovering little devils. She was too tired to process any more shocks. Sure, imps, sprites, and djinns. Dozens of them, why not? The entire planet was going to ruin anyway.

With a last effort to stick to her training, Natasha examined Briana from head to toe. Tight leggings and form-fitting top with no suspicious bulges. "If you are concealing a weapon, you do it well," she said.

"No. I have no gun or knife," Briana shrugged. "You don't need one, either."

Natasha quickly decided. She dropped the weapon to her side. With a weary step, she walked to the other lab stool and slumped down. After all of this, it turned out to be a dead end. Fig was not here.

"Why did you find me?" Briana lowered her hands to her lap. "How did you get here?"

"Fig mentioned your name and the city of Hilo when I last was with him in Folsom."

"I don't buy that." Briana frowned. "All the airplanes here have been commandeered. They haul charged batteries to the mainland. There are no longer flights bringing passengers to the islands."

"The planes return for additional loads," Natasha rebutted. "At least until the jet fuel is exhausted." She tapped the barrel of her gun with her free hand. "*This* is all I needed to hitch a ride. Once here, asking around about a naked green woman with wings got me to a nightclub and then this warehouse. Her name is Lilith, right?"

"Yes, I know the succubus Lilith," Briana said.

A sudden thought poked through Natasha's fatigue. "You seem familiar with these beings. Perhaps *you* can perform the task I need done."

"Task? What task?"

"Find Angela, the succubus." Natasha straightened her slump. Her goal might still be within reach. "She carries documents in her little purse that Alexei and I will need once order is restored. The mainland is falling into anarchy. Viktor is correct. Russia is going to take over. Haven't you been following the news?"

Briana shuttered. "I dare not deal with Angela.

Natasha thrust her gun at Briana again. "I'm not merely *asking*. If you know how to summon Angela. I *command* you to do so."

"She would dominate me again if I were to try. Make me her slave with no will of my own." Briana's expression hardened. "Threaten me as you will. There is no way I will touch that succubus' mind a second time."

239

Natasha did not immediately answer. She inhaled a calming breath. Her mind was starting to work better. Give this woman some background. Despite her first refusal, perhaps the job was trivial.

"I have taught Angela much about the manipulation of men," she finally said. "Enough for her to try her hand at it herself wherever she is from. Yes, most likely, she has returned home. That could be where she is! If you cannot bring her here, then perhaps you could teach me how to travel there."

"*You* want to go into the realm of demons? You have no idea what you are talking about."

BRIANA CONSIDERED. Survival in the demon realm was possible. Fig had demonstrated that. But, first things first. Audrey said he was tumbling out of control in the void. He needed help — might need *her* help. Suddenly, everything felt right. Her sense of purpose grew. Self-enchantment lost the last of its appeal. And maybe this other woman could help.

"I want to travel there, too," she said. She pulled her lips into a firm line of resolve and stared at Natasha. "And consider. We will more likely succeed with both our goals if we journey together."

"I have my own agenda," Natasha said. "I trust no one but myself."

"The choice is yours," Briana faked a shrug. "Either you tag along with me, or you will be left behind."

Natasha did not reply for almost a full minute. "I make my own decisions," she said at last. "We work together only so long as it suits my objectives."

"Is that your way of saying yes?" Briana asked.

"Wait a minute," Audrey broke in. "What about us and the generators?"

Briana blinked. Right, the gremlins. Fig's reason for traveling into the demon realm in the first place was to get help. Restore electrical power here on Earth. A hundred or so gremlins were not many, but every little bit would help. They were smart enough to work on the generators unsupervised. Okay, get them gainfully employed and then help Fig.

The problem was *how* to travel into the demon realm. The electric arc the gremlins used was too small to fit a human. Lilith was not here to be the ferry through a juniper flame. Angela was not to be dealt with at all.

And who knew if another summoned succubus would be any easier to dominate.

What would Fig do in a situation like this? Briana asked herself. She paced back and forth, inspecting each piece of equipment in the lab, trying to get the inspiration for how to proceed.

Natasha did not break into her concentration, and several minutes passed. Finally, Briana's gaze fell upon the large cylinder of hydrogen near the wall.

"A pufferscamp," she said aloud. "That might work. For them, the transfer of matter is easy, even easier than for a gremlin. And they loved eating hydrogen gas."

"You and Fig are much alike," Natasha said. "The two of you would make an interesting pair."

Briana ignored the comment. Now, she had an approach, although it did seem risky. She wondered if Fig felt the same way when his ideas bubbled up. If he did, he showed no signs of doubt to anyone else who waited and watched what he would do next.

"Okay, listen carefully," she said to the hovering female gremlins. "See the device on the workbench, near the sink?"

"Yeah, a computer terminal," Audrey said. "We do know about those things. The guys talk about them every once in a while. Gets boring showing the same pictures over and over again. Something about saving screens. But nice to put into your garden if you knock out the glass first."

Briana sighed. This was going to take a while. "Here on the Earth, they serve another purpose. They can be used to find out about almost anything. Watch."

She turned on the tower tucked under the workbench and booted it up. Then, she opened a browser and entered 'Elementary electricity' as the search command.

"Ooooh," a dozen or so voices cooed.

"More than only a dozen pictures!" Audrey said. "Gotta admit even a dozen gets boring after a while. How many different ones can this one show? I bet the guys don't even know terminals can do that."

"They probably do," Briana replied. "But I'm guessing internet connectivity is not reliable in the realm of demons."

"Internet?"

Briana pointed at Natasha. "Ashley, this human will show you how to do a search on the World Wide Web. Many of the sites in the US will be down, but you can find out what you need from others around the world."

She took a rapid breath. "Then, after you grasp the basic concepts, teach the others. Make out a list of the locations of the power stations with the greatest capacity. Fly to the mainland and get them fixed first." She checked her pocket for her credit card and headed for the door.

"Wait," Natasha said. "Where are you going?"

"To the home supply store to get the additional stuff we will need." She paused a second and smiled. "Isn't that what Fig always says?"

Packing for an Expedition

BRIANA BURST into the lab with her arms full. She dumped duplicates of the equipment Fig had been using onto the workbench. The young woman seemed to radiate haste, not a moment to be lost.

"Suit up," she said to Natasha. "I will explain the purpose of everything after we are fully dressed."

Natasha frowned. Briana appeared quite animated. Was this a good thing or not? "This 'realm of the demons,' as you call it is not hospitable, right?"

"Correct. And I could carry only two sets of stuff." Briana pointed at Alexei. "The guy you are with. He will have to remain here and keep the oxygen collection process and the flames going."

Natasha smiled at Alexei. "You are the guard, my dear. Most important. No one is to disturb what is going on."

Alexei nodded. It had been slow going, but he continued to get better.

"Are the gremlins ready?" Briana asked.

"They indeed are quick learners. The Moss Landing Power Plant on the California coast will be the first."

"Ah, there might be a slight problem, "Audrey said."

"What?" Briana snapped. "Problems are things I don't want to hear about."

"The humans are going about it all wrong," Audrey said. "They strip away the existing, fused wiring. Then they apply a new winding. That will work only as long as supplies of unused copper wire last. And the process is far too slow."

"You aren't constrained by what others are doing. Fix the generators any way you want so long as it is fast."

"We do understand what has to be done. Separate the fused loops of wiring back into individual strands. Recreate the insulation from the melted sludge collected at the bottom of the generator. Use it to recoat the coils."

"Yes, whatever," Briana said. "Do this at night when no one is about. Fix one and then move to the next. How long is this going to take?"

"With the number of us here, it will take a single cycle of the sun around this orb to get a single generator repaired. It would have been much better if more of us had come."

"All night!" Briana exclaimed. "But there are over eight thousand power generation plants in the continental US. This will take … years."

"Still faster than what the humans are doing," Audrey huffed. "They have many more workers, but each refurbishment will take several months. Do you want our help or not?"

Briana did not say anything for a minute. With a scowl, she flicked on the small radio on the shelf.

"… the crash of several markets in Europe has suspended aid packages to the US. … This just in. The National Guard has sealed off downtown Hilo. Repeat. Downtown Hilo is sealed off. It cannot be entered. There is ample food on the island to last for several months. There is no reason to come to the city. Looters are being shot."

"Even worse than Viktor imagined," Natasha said. "Not only the continental US. The world is too connected. Rumors will cause damage as much as the facts."

Briana flicked the radio off. She shook her head. The Islanders were overreacting. Mainland problems would be solved once the generators were repaired. Even something symbolic would help.

"Yes, I want your help, Audrey," she said. "Do whatever you can. Even getting only a few plants up and running will help."

"Then tell the succubus, Lilith, that we will return to take advantage of her education a little later than planned." Without another word, the female gremlins assembled into a hovering formation — twelve rows of ten. Like a legion of buzzing hummingbirds, they darted through an open window and flew to the west.

"Now for our journey," Briana said to Natasha. "Alexei, move the full cylinder of hydrogen out into the parking lot. It will be too dangerous to use it inside."

Alexei listened to Natasha's translation into Russian and nodded. He tipped the steel tank slightly to its side and rolled it out of the lab. He directed it down the loading dock incline, and Briana and Natasha followed. The trio stopped in front of two lawn chairs sitting in the empty warehouse lot.

"Another purchase I had to make," Briana said. "Much easier than trying to build something from scratch. Help me lash the chairs together,

244

side by side."

Briana pointed at the coils of rope and the two large pairs of shears lying on the macadam. "The chairs will hang from a harness we will build for them."

"I don't understand," Natasha began.

"Later," Briana said as she uncoiled the rope and laid it out. Natasha shrugged and mimicked the other woman's activity.

THE TWO women worked for most of an hour. When the harness was completed and attached to the lawn chairs, Briana did not stop. She ran to the hydrogen cylinder and turned the valve connected at the top. Immediately, with a whistling sound, the light gas rushed into the air.

"I don't see anything," Natasha said.

"Hydrogen's colorless," Briana said. "Stand back."

She struck a match and stood on tiptoe to thrust it into the escaping gas. What could not have been seen before now danced with an orange glow. It was on fire.

Briana sat down in one of the lawn chairs and motioned Natasha to do the same with the other. "Before you ask, a pufferscamp is not a baby succubus either. Only a little smarter than a drink dribbler, as a matter of fact. The wizards on my home-world have little interest in them."

Natasha watched Briana's forehead wrinkle with concentration. In a few moments, a deep green shape bobbed in the middle of the flickering orange. It had been hard enough to accept the existence of beings like the succubi. Then the smaller ones Briana called gremlins. And now, yet another kind. What bizarre world was she getting into?

"Attend unto me," Briana commanded. "I am the dominant one, and you must submit. There is much that I will instruct."

The shape emerged from the flame. It was small, about the size of a beach ball, but with a surface even more glossy. The skin, if that is what it was, appeared densely covered on all sides by long sharp spikes of a darker green. In a smoother spot were tiny ears, eyes and wings protruding like unwanted blemishes on a work of art.

"A pufferfish," Natasha exclaimed. "I have seen those hung from the ceiling in fancy Japanese restaurants."

"I am a puffer*scamp*, not a pufferfish," the sprite said. "If you look close you will see we are not alike."

"Anatomy lessons are for later. Briana said as she turned the tank valve off for a second and then back on. Expand yourself," she commanded.

In an instant, the sprite hovering over the releasing gas began to grow. Its spherical shape expanded as would a balloon inflating at a party, but the facial features and spikes remained their original size. The still tiny wings hummed rapidly to prevent itself from floating into the sky.

"That should be enough," Briana said after the pufferscamp's diameter had grown to the height of a human. "Now, see the harness we have built for you on the ground. Surround yourself with it and test if you are large enough."

The sprite fluttered its tiny wings with even more vigor and lowered itself to the ground. Pushing and twisting, it donned the harness and then floated back into the sky. When it did, the pair of lawn chairs lifted from the asphalt as well.

"Call me 'The Zephyr of Delight,'" the pufferscamp said.

Natasha's eyebrows lifted. She looked at Briana, puzzled about what was happening.

"Succubi would have been much easier for transport," Briana said. "Not only a taxi service but a translator as well." She pointed at her left ear and shrugged. "A drink dribbler will accompany us. That is the best I can come up with. Okay, Zephyr, time for you to return home."

The sprite recentered itself over the gas cylinder, and Briana relit the hydrogen.

"No, wait!" Natasha called out as the sprite carried the lawn chairs into the flame. A wave of heat billowed upward. The tiny hairs on Natasha's arms singed. The acrid smell crinkled the spy's nose. Was that the webbing catching fire? But before she could say more, the pufferscamp and its two passengers vanished.

246

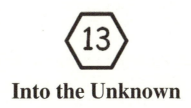

Into the Unknown

BRIANA GRIPPED the harness tether attached to her lawn chair and pulled. Something was not right. It felt slack. She looked up at Zephyr. The demon was still tethered, but merely drifted against a background of tiny lights in the distance.

She wrapped her arms around her stomach and squeezed. She felt like throwing up. Her tug on the harness rope had caused the chairs to rotate.

"It feels like we are falling," Natasha said. "What do we do now?"

"Zephyr," Briana commanded. "Expel some of your hydrogen. Get us moving."

"Which way?" the pufferscamp answered.

"Up! That will put some tension back into the harness ropes, and we can stop our spin."

"Which way is up?"

"We are in the direction 'down' from you. Go the opposite way."

Briana felt a gentle push of hydrogen streaming onto her. In a few moments, the slackness in the ropes disappeared. She started to relax, but then abruptly stopped. Her stomach had to get under control first.

"You have no idea where we are going, do you?" Natasha said. "Or even if we did, no way to get us there."

"Of course not," Briana snapped. "Give me a moment. I will figure out what to do."

IT TOOK some time to intertwine the harness with the backs of the lawn chairs rather than the arms. Even more to get Zephyr to understand what the tugs on them meant. Now, the contraption looked like an overweight blimp dragging a cargo behind itself. Not a parade float dangling passengers underneath.

"Now what?" Natasha growled. She was irritated, very irritated. Her stomach had not settled. Briana acted as if she were completely in control.

"I have switched on my helmet signal light," Briana said. "Sooner or later, the messenger gremlin will spot us, and we can find out where Fig is."

"And he can lead me to Angela?"

"I don't know about that. Fig is here for another reason. But if anyone can locate the succubus, he is the one to ask."

"Meanwhile, we simply soar through this nothingness? This is not productive."

"I can tell you a sleeptime story," Zephyr called back to the pair. "In my youth, I spent many subcycles listening to my broodmother that way. It was very soothing."

"Stories? Like what?" Natasha squirmed in her chair. Challenging Briana for control of this ridiculous conveyance now was too soon. She needed to learn more first and gritted her teeth so she would not blurt out something that would tip her hand.

"My memory is excellent," Zephyr replied. "So is my broodmother's. So is her mother before her. We have preserved our tales from the earliest times far better than any other kind."

Before either woman could say more, Zephyr began speaking slowly in a deeper voice.

"In the beginning, there was the void but it was not entirely empty. In it resided a single pair of each of our types, a male, and a female: two lightning djinns, two rockbubblers, and two of all the rest. The smallest imps ate inert matter and harvested more from other realms. They became abundant, and the sprites feasted on them. The djinns consumed whatever they wanted. All the types prospered and propagated. Life was easy. Life was good."

"Let me guess," Natasha interrupted. "But then …"

"But then there was a problem with the goblin pair," Zephyr interrupted. "While the rest of us were into the fourth generation, not a single goblin egg had been laid. The male grew increasingly frustrated, berating his mate without cease. Finally, in a rage, he slew her, rending her limb from limb."

"So, there could be only one goblin in all the realm," Natasha said. "Trouble in paradise. I get it."

"But when the goblin scattered the female parts into the void, he discovered a fertilized egg. It had been almost ready to be extruded, but not quite. In his rage, he had cracked the still soft shell. No offspring would ever emerge from it.

"'If only he had restrained himself,' my broodmother explained to me. Shown patience, waited a short time longer. Then, his frustration would have vanished. Instead, he was responsible that he would be the only one.

"It was rumored that he had special powers. The one demon kind able to sense most of everything happening throughout the realm — perhaps even other realms beyond as well. In barter for matter, he constructed clever solutions for the others. The location of a secret cache. Where the next ambush was to be …

"But the fame from that was not enough to keep him content. As he watched other types propagate and prosper, his despair grew deep. He could withstand direct interactions with others no longer. And so, with his accumulated matter, he constructed a dark citadel around himself and vanished inside. The goblin has never to be seen again."

"So the moral is?" Natasha asked. "No, let me guess that, too. 'Think before you act.' That is what your mother was teaching you."

"Exactly!" Zephyr said. "You will make a good broodmother when it comes time to lay your eggs."

"The place where the goblin hides," Briana asked. "Where is it?"

"The void is vast. As you can see, mostly dark. Only pinpoints of light here and there. The goblin's lair is black against black. No one knows where it is within our realm."

"Completely vanished," Natasha smirked. "How convenient. There is no way to prove the truth of your tale, one way or the other."

"Not completely. A part of the lore, some say, is that when we have bad thoughts in our heads, they are put there by the goblin. The reason we go berserk and do illogical things."

"Interesting," Briana said. "I never heard any of this before, but it is not important now. Our job is to find Fig."

A Rolling Stone Gathers Momentum

FIG SLAMMED the side of his head with his hand. How could he have been so stupid? Put himself completely under the control of a demon. Lilith was his only way home to Earth. She could withhold that from him at will.

Yes, she had stopped his tumble out of control at the lairs of the gremlins and even apologized for what she had done. But she had been adamant. The next stop in her quest was a lair of a resplendent djinn. Nothing he said deterred her from that. He had to tag along or be abandoned in an immense nothingness.

The latest report from Hilo brought by the oxygen shuttle gremlin cried out with urgency. Russian troops had been spotted massing along the border with the Ukraine. The European Union financial crisis had paralyzed any coordinated response. Everyone was waiting for a definite position out of Washington, but there had been no word out of the city for days.

Fig's anger flared. The Ukraine, too? And Washington did not have a plan? His gut spasmed, and acid pushed up into his throat. With effort, he shoved the vexation aside and folded his arms around his stomach. On top of everything else, he was not feeling well. The queasiness on his arrival in the realm had never gone completely away. The steady diet of snack foods in zero gravity was taking its toll. He had to visit one of the facilities marked by the bright blue flashing light more than he wanted. But at least how they worked were very much the same as on Earth. No instructions were needed. A water closet or a comfort station. Some things were universal, even between realms.

The communal gremlin lair had made some sense, but not so what he was witnessing now. It was the permanent lair of a female djinn. But even so, the slab was much thicker and extended almost out of sight into the dimness — more vast than that of all the gremlin lairs clustered together. At the far end, squatted a small chest of three drawers. A simple bright beacon blinked on the unadorned top cover. Closer was a

250

rectangular cavity carved into the slab. In it were cushions and bedding, a brood pit. Otherwise, the lair was bare.

Near the chest crowded more than three dozen female djinns, the lair owner and a clutch of visitors. The smallest one stood two heads higher than Fig or Lilith. Like the males, their bodies were more defined than that of any gym fanatic back on Earth. Every muscle bulged outward, its boundaries sharply defined. They looked like they could rip a human in half with a single tug. Only a faint down of fine hair coved their bodies. Their heads were bare. Deep-set eyes peered out from jutting brows and over long, hooking noses. Naked like the males, but Fig felt no arousal. None would be judged a beauty in the realm of humankind.

All the females stood with backs to one another. Like a cluster of drunken meerkats, their cluster was in constant motion. No one wanted to be on the outside of the group, exposing herself to the appraisal and lust of a hovering group of watching virility. The male djinns eyed one another warily, chests thrust out, and fists coiled ready to strike. Muscles in arms and legs twitched barely in control. It would take little for them to start a mêlée to see who would get to mate.

"Acting as one will work as it did for the gremlins," Lilith raised her voice over the chatter. "You can ask them. United, they escaped being ensnared by their predators."

Lilith stood on the slab in front of the females as she spoke. Fig noticed her eyes were not riveted on her audience. Every few seconds, she checked to see if any of the males had moved closer. Succubi were also considered fair game.

"We are the top of the chain of food," one of the female djinns answered. "We do not need any coordinated action."

"No, not to avoid being eaten, of course." Lilith sighed. "I have already gone over this twice. Focus on the principle. It is a tactic that can improve your very existence."

"Can't you smell it, too?" another of the females asked. "The battle lust is in the air. The males sense it. Three of the lesser princes plan to attack Elezar at the same time."

"Push aside the succubus," one of the males growled. "She would not be needed until the end."

"Three princes acting as one!" Lilith exclaimed. "That's basically the same idea I am talking about. Don't you see what I am getting at?"

"All we see is that, as usual, our males strive to improve their images of themselves before the fighting begins — the same as they always have done. That is why they hover around. To prove mastery as if … as if we

251

were foes or something. Even though it serves no purpose. It usually is never at a time when we are in heat."

"We have to break the pattern," Lilith waved her arms like a human orator. "All of us djinns, succubi, and the lesser sprites. We deserve to be treated as equals. They must ask permission first, and you have the right to say no. Denying them what they want or not is for you to choose. Show them you are not merely there for the taking. You have value. All of you throughout the realm, acting together, don't let things continue the way they are."

"Yeah, right. I can't even imagine what would happen if I said 'No.' It frightens me to think about the rage of a male who has been deprived."

The mumbling increased in volume. Several of the female djinns scowled and then disappeared back into the center of the cluster.

"We grow impatient," another male waved at the hive of activity. "We cannot decide which to choose with all of them mingling around like this."

"That is where uniting comes in," Lilith's voice shrieked with frustration. "We all fly to Elezar's lair. Carry placards as they do on the earth. March around the perimeter shouting what we want."

"What will that do?"

"Well, nothing at first. But if we persist, cycle after cycle, eventually, the prince will grow weary. His ability to rule will be interrupted. The noise will disturb his sleep ..."

Fig wagged his head, too. Unlike what he had been able to do with the gremlins, he could think of nothing to add. This was going against many eons of tradition. He studied the lumbering brutes who circled the lair. They were not a group one wanted to anger. Lilith's was a quixotic quest far more absurd than his pursuit of Briana.

And unless she stopped, she was in great danger, too. Fig shivered. If that happened, what would he do? Could he do?

"Alternately, give the males something else they want and do not have," another voice said in English.

Fig whirled around and his eyes widened. It was Briana! She too had come to the realm of demons. And Natasha, too!

Lilith startled as well. She blinked several times. "Something else? What are you talking about?"

"The upcoming battle," Briana said as the pufferscamp pulled the two lawn chairs into a landing. "The word bouncing around is that *three* princes are agitating. Why do three ally to fight Elezar rather than take him on, one by one?"

"The number of warriors, of course," Lilith answered. "Elezar has thrice as many as any of the others. By banding together, the conflict becomes more balanced."

"And if you had twice as many fighters as Elezar, what then?"

"A much greater chance of victory, of course. But none of the other minor princes dares to enter the fray. No more warriors are available."

"I disagree," Briana said. "I see a dozen more right here in front of me."

Renewed Alliances

FIG COULD not quite believe what he was seeing. Briana and Natasha here in the demon realm. Standing beside him on the lair of a djinn. But more important, what did the love of his life just point out? Warriors could be women as well as men! Not quite as strong, perhaps, but fighters nevertheless.

As Lilith finished translating Briana's words, he looked around the lair. All the larger devils fell silent, stunned by the sudden blossom of new possibilities. After many eons, the rules of the game altered by a single fresh idea.

The female djinns whispered among themselves, first in clusters of two or three, and then in one larger group. Their voices grew louder and louder. The dribbler in Fig's ear stumbled with its words as she tried to keep up the translation.

"Well, damn it, why not?" one of the females shouted over the others. She was taller than average, her forearms as large as Fig's thighs. Her skin was leathery, a jigsaw of polygonal plates butting against one another, and her head shorn as was the fashion with the males.

"It beats sitting around and twiddling our tails," said another. "What can they do that we can't?" yelled a third.

Out of the babble, one catchphrase gathered strength as more and more joined in. In an instant, all of the female djinns shouted in unison over and over, "Hell, yes. We will go. Hell yes, we will go."

"Thank you, Briana," Lilith tipped her head. "I see the error in my thinking. What I desire for all females does not result from services withheld and then rendered. Instead, respect is gained for performance as good as those of a male."

"The females will need some training on basic tactics," one of the male demons fluttered his wings in order to get closer. "One does not garner regard merely by appearing in battle and waving a dribbler sandwich. There must be victories as well."

"We will be as apt students as any of you." a female stepped away from her cluster. "The results will speak for themselves."

"All this enlightenment and new-found purpose brings us no closer Angela," Natasha shouted so she could be heard. "How does she play into this?"

ANGELA SMILED inwardly. She dared not let her pleasure show. Singing Trantor's virtues to Prince Elezar had not impeded her plans. The prince had called her back to his presence not only once, but now a second time. He was listening to what she had to say.

"Your knowledge of wartime histories of humans is most interesting, Angela," Elezar stroked his chin.

"There is more to winning than solely raising battle lust as high as one can," Angela replied. "For many cycles, I dom … was instructed by a human who bore the title 'Professor.' He described many examples."

Angela let the smile out to cover her face but said nothing more. As Natasha had taught her, it is far better to listen than to talk.

"Some of the smaller imps have returned with confirmation," Elezar nodded. "My suspicions were correct. Three minor princes prepare an attack. By combining forces, they hope to muster enough djinns to match the number of my own."

"It is not only numbers that determine the outcome," Angela's eyes widened at the opportunity to continue to impress. "Nor the pitch of their battle lust."

"What then? Tell me everything you know."

"Placement. Managed with skill, a small army can rout and destroy a larger foe."

Elezar snorted. Angela rushed on.

"Hannibal of the Alps. The Battle of Cannae. The Punic general deployed a modest force in the center of the battlefield. The Romans facing them shrunk their front line to the same width. This increased those who stood behind instead. They could do nothing when blocked by their own men. While these two forces engaged, Hannibal's remaining troops attacked from the rear. Although the Romans had more men in arms, they were surrounded and perished."

"So, the center was a decoy." Elezar nodded. "I will fill the space

with the disabled and weaker djinns, like Trantor and others like him."

"No, not Trantor," Angela blurted. "He would be more valuable as an experienced scout. Reporting the situation with accuracy rather than babbling like a frightened sprite."

She took a deep breath. "And here in our realm, the situation is not quite the same. Three dimensions must be considered, not only two as if we were on a plane. Trantor's experience would be invaluable. He could transform what I am talking about into a more well-thought-out battle plan."

"Battle plans," Elezar snorted. "An interesting concept. Usually, we princes line up our warriors and let them have at it. The loser pays some sort of penalty to the winner, and life goes on. It is a distraction for us all, djinn and imp alike."

"Even more important than placement is what the men of Earth call 'the fog of war,'" Angela said. "The side that better understands the deployment of his enemy will win … even against overwhelming odds. Surely, you use intelligence to outmaneuver your opponents in times of peace. Why not in times of struggle, too?"

"Manfred's squadron is gone," a small imp fluttered into Elezar's private quarters. "Every last djinn. They agreed on some sort of pact. All of them together succumbed to the great monotony. The force you deploy, O Prince, will be less than you had planned."

Elezar growled. He studied Angela for a long while. "The imp rumors say the three princes also employ the wisdom of a succubus in their adventure." He flung his arm skyward with command. "Make up some reason for it and call for a temporary truce, Angela. One nearer to the princes' lairs than to mine. And when you meet, retain what you observe. It may be that you can disperse some of this fog."

"I am … flattered," Angela stumbled to say. "I — "

"Do not read too much into it," Elezar snapped. "It is because you are female, nothing else. I wish to show these princelings how little I think of their threat — not dignify it by sending a djinn well known for his closeness to me."

ANGELA PULLED the purse she still carried with her to the proper position on her hip. Clearly, the humans who designed such things did not have to

worry about flying through the air. She glanced to either side. Her escort djinns did not care. With powerful wing strokes, they plowed forward. It was as if they were causing wind resistance to desist merely by their strength of will.

Despite the opportunity to demonstrate her merit to Elezar, Angela was worried. The request for a temporary truce had been readily granted … almost too quickly, in fact. What was happening that she did not know about?

Up ahead, a narrow beam of light blinked on and off in the gloom. Each flash illuminated the dark outlines of three demons who approached. Elezar also had agreed to have his delegates be marked by a covey of glowimps. But he chose instead to ignore that clause in the hastily negotiated accord. "The void is not our enemy but our friend," he had explained.

The approaching trio resolved into winged beings, and then, to a succubus flanked by two warrior djinns, the same as Angela and her escort. As they drew near, a riot of glowimps turned on in the near distance, each one weak as always. But with tens of thousands, the two contingents reflected the flickering light. Angela did not signal a response. Elezar desired his maneuvers to be cloaked as long as possible. Evidently, the three petty princes wished their power to be flaunted instead.

Angela surveyed the swirl of lights. She recognized what was now visible in the distance: more djinns, hundreds of them hovering in a long line. "So many," she gasped. "How did the princes recruit so many? We are outnumbered nearly two to one."

The guard on her left grunted but did not say more. "More combatants means more limbs and ichor we can disperse into the void," the one on her right said as she beat his chest. "See the pattern. Next to every mature male hovers another of smaller size."

"Even so," Angela said. "The longer the line, the more difficult it is to surround them."

The two approaching djinns were unknown to her. How could it be otherwise, but the succubus between them …

"Lilith!" she cried out. "*You* are allied with the petty princes? Have you no sense? They are diminutive strutters who have no claim of equal prowess to that of Elezar the Golden." Angela wrinkled her brow, puzzled. "And why would you be involved with any of this?"

"Forgo the banter," Lilith shot back. "It will not work on me. I know you too well."

257

Angela kicked at an imaginary stone underfoot. Her rage boiled. She looked at the four djinns who surrounded them. They naturally would go after one another on the slightest pretense. Now was her chance to end this with her sister once and for all. End it now.

She tensed, preparing herself to strike. But then, she hesitated as the image of their last encounter flashed in her mind. Lilith was a wily one. She had goaded her on and led her into a trap. She shuddered, remembering how she felt. It was unusual for her sister to be showing up here. Suspicious, in fact.

Angela breathed deeply until the rage faded away. She had a weakness, she did admit — leading with her heart rather than her head. But there was more at stake here. Elezar had entrusted her with great responsibility, and it would be foolish to cast that aside. Savagely, she slapped herself on the cheek and pushed the agony of the devil trap away from her thoughts.

Angela stood silent for a moment more, then replied. "For me, this battle will be doubly sweet. I prove my worth to Elezar, the prince, *and* I will have the satisfaction of seeing your innards floating in the void."

"You can count, Angela, as well as I," Lilith fluttered her wings in warning. "You are outnumbered. Defeat will be swift and total. Return with that realization to your prince. If he surrenders, he will be able to keep a few remembrances of his former glory when it is over."

Angela tasted bitter bile flood into her stomach. Two to one? A few shallow breaths helped but not much. The battle might turn into a disaster. Best to return to Elezar's lair with the news.

She decided to give the command to retreat, but as she took a deep breath to broadcast it, changed her mind. This was like Cannae, just as she had described to Elezar. There would have to be a little more planning, but the basic concept was still sound. Besides, there was no way the Golden One would give up without a fight. He would command his djinns to plunge ahead. Even if that meant every single one would be slain. No, this was an opportunity, and she would make the best of it.

She would have to reduce the power of the center even more so the flanking arms would be stronger. Make sure the envelopment had no weak spots, not on the left, right, top, or bottom.

She extended her wings as broadly as she could. "There is no need to report back to Elezar. I know what he would say. Prepare for the worst, Lilith."

16

Battlelust

ANGELA LET the pages of parchment on which she had recorded her battle plan drift into the void. There was no way around the fact that it was no longer of use. The decoy in the Elezar's center formation had to be large enough to focus the charge of the djinns on the other side ... but only barely so. Without the detailed planning, it would be a slaughter, not lasting long enough for the encirclement to complete.

She took a deep breath and addressed Elezar's squadron leaders. They hovered about her in the flickering glow furnished by the enemy lights. "Listen," she commanded. "I had all your orders calculated, but now there is a change of plan. Something that needs a little more explanation."

"Let's get on with it," one of the djinns grumbled. "Tell us who is to man the center and who the flanks on the sides."

"The center is special," Angela wagged her finger. "It will be the responsibility of, ah, *volunteers* rather than a number of complete squadrons. The total number will be small and have to face the brunt of the enemy attack. Poll each of your followers to see who those might be."

"My entire squad," shouted another of the djinns. "We are outnumbered two to one. All of us hear the great monotony calling. Let this be our final battle. We will die in glory."

"I, too, feel it in my sinews," said a third. "Slash, bite, and resist until I can do so no longer."

"When it is my time to surrender to nothingness," shouted a fourth, "I do not care about the petty desires of any prince."

In an instant, more and more voices chimed in. Every one of them proclaimed their oath to make this their last stand.

"No, no," Angela tried to shout over the growing din. "Too many in the center. If you do that, there will be not enough for the flanks. The battle will be lost."

Unheeding, one squad leader flew off to rejoin his troops, and then two or three more. Those remaining pounded each other's backs. They boasted about how many enemies they would take with them into oblivion.

"I am the emissary of the prince," Angela protested. "You must do as I say."

No one paid her any attention. Instead, the boasts of final glory grew louder and louder. Every djinn tried to drown out the rest.

In a single swish of a tail, the first squad leader returned. Half a dozen more of the djinns accompanying him shouted their pledge to fight and die.

The remaining leaders were swept up into the excitement. In a few moments more, they also reunited with those under their command. The well-ordered array of djinns degenerated into a tangled mob. They swirled and pulsed, spoiling for a confrontation, anyone they could find.

Angela threw up her hands. In a few eye blinks, she had lost control. The desire to commit suicide occurred randomly and sometimes infected more than one. But never like this. What bad luck for the submerged despair to surface in so many at once.

NATASHA STOOD on the teetering lawn chair. She tried to see over the pair of djinns standing in front. She rotated the contraption and damped out a tumble. She could not understand what was happening. It sounded like Elezar's forces were disintegrating into throbbing chaos. Why was she even here?

Well, she had to stick with Briana. Briana followed Fig, and Fig followed Lilith. So, it was all the succubus's fault. Lilith had been insistent. She insisted on observing how the female djinns performed in combat — use the example to further her cause. Get more females to join in her protest.

"We will be sure to capture Angela, right?" she called out.

Briana had climbed hand over hand to wrap her arms around the pufferscamp, twisting them awkwardly to avoid the jutting spikes. She gulped in oxygen from her scuba gear.

"I'm not sure. Remember. You, me, Fig. We are the first humans ever to witness anything like this."

It was not what Natasha had wanted to hear. Her plan had been simple. Track down Fig and prod him to capture Angela again. Get the identity documents needed, then hole up somewhere until the US had fallen. Without them, she and Alexei would not be able to hide behind other identities when the Russians came.

And now, it looked like Angela was in the midst of what looked like hundreds of berserkers. Each with wishes of death and shouts of how many of their opponents they would take with them.

Natasha sighed. Always, she had held a very high image of herself. Able to figure her way out of impossible situations. She had done so, over and over again. But now the odds seemed long, so … unexpected. Succubi, pufferscamps, djinns, living in a realm of their own. Two women and a single man the only bastions of sanity in a universe gone mad.

"Briana, how are you holding up?" she asked. "Suddenly, I need some reassurance."

Silence.

"Briana?"

"Sorry, I was deep in my own thoughts."

"You too?"

"It feels so strange now. At first, I felt a rush. Pointing out the obvious about the value of the female djinns. But the more I thought about it, the sillier the idea became. I didn't help at all."

"What do you mean? You got us here. Tracked down your guy and —"

"Fig is not my guy!"

"Don't give me that. You traveled into another frigging universe to get him back. You must have feelings for him. You have to."

"He's changed somehow. Didn't you notice? Well, of course, you couldn't. You were not around him before."

"I witnessed what he was like in Folsom. Quite impressive."

"But he didn't come up to me when we arrived here the way he usually does. He wasn't a happy puppy. Suddenly, he is more aloof."

Briana faltered. Her voice became quieter. "And when we get back and everything is fixed, what then? I'm not so sure the pandering for applause is such a great path either. Too many highs and lows. Too much … temptation. I don't know. All of a sudden, everything is so depressing."

"And there is Lilith and Fig," Natasha said.

"Yes, there is the problem of Lilith and Fig."

The Fog of War

LILITH AND Fig looked onto the battlefield. The throbbing cluster of Elezar's djinns moved forward. Like a smart bomb about to explode, the rabble increased speed and grew closer.

"I don't understand the tactic," Fig frowned. "Most of the ones in the middle are surrounded by their comrades. They have no room in which to fight."

"They are out of control," Lilith agreed. "The battle will become a chaotic mêlée. Little chance for the feats of the females to be observed and recognized."

"Maybe not," Fig said. "Look there. On the left. One of Elezar's demons has broken away and is headed for the pair in front of him."

The indicated djinn bore down on his selected opponents. A few body lengths before he crashed into them, he abruptly feathered his wings and stopped.

The male he faced snarled and leaped forward, the claws on both his hands extended and ready to rend. Elezar's djinn laughed, and with an easy swipe batted the limbs aside. He lowered his head and butted his opponent on the chest, knocking him away.

The female seized the opportunity and hurled herself on the assailant's back. She clasped one of its wings tightly, and with her fangs, ripped gobs of feathers and flesh away into the void.

Elezar's djinn faltered. Reaching behind, he tried to knock the female aside. This gave time for the male to recover. Still dazed, he joined the fight from the front, ripping away an arm as he engaged. Before the opponent could recover, he slashed with his claws, spilling the chest's content into the void.

But as the two troops engaged, the line of Lilith's djinns dissolved their formation. Like ants attacking another nest, they swarmed in disarray onto the advancing cluster. Elezar's demons could not bring forth all their fighters to blunt the attack. But neither could the attackers exercise their numerical advantage.

"Usually, it is more like what you humans call a ballet." Lilith twisted uncomfortably as she watched. "Follows a traditional protocol. Adversaries divide into groups of at most two or three. They slowly advance. Call each other names for a while and then finally close and engage."

The succubus glanced to where her single line of djinns had been. No sign of it remained. Instead, pairs of fighters darted in and out of the mêlée together, fighting side by side. They raced blindly into the midst of Elezar's disorganized cluster, passing djinns on one side and then the other. Without forethought, they reached the center, engaged in one more skirmish and then fought their way back out.

The two forces dissolved into a single withering ball of chaos. Only a male and female flying close together distinguished friend from foe. But even that was temporary. Pairs became separated from one another, lashing out at whoever was nearest.

Lilith squinted to focus on a selected pair. There was no way to gauge what was happening in the battle as a whole. Even so, she reasoned, with the numerical superiority, eventually her side would prevail. They had to. Any other outcome was nonsense.

Her thoughts suddenly ground to a halt. She could not believe what she was seeing. Two pairs were fighting one another rather than their common foes. She looked about frantically. It was getting even worse. Neither side was going to win this. There would be no way to tell.

Lilith tried to latch onto something positive. Elezar or the three princes triumphant? That did not matter. She told herself she had already achieved victory and tried to smile with the thought. But, strangely, it did not come.

In some way, it had been too easy, she reasoned. Once word spread that the female djinns also would fight, everything had changed. The males started to regard them in a different light. Perhaps that was all that was needed. Perhaps respect was a foregone afterthought compared to what she had just achieved. Maybe there was nothing more left for her to do!

Nothing left to do. The thought hit her like a bolt from a lightning djinn. Suppose everything from now on did flow naturally. Females on an equal footing with the males. Respect throughout the realm. Delilah's premature death totally avenged ...

Like a ship with a lost rudder, Lilith suddenly felt adrift. The despair of the great monotony swelled within her.

AS FIG watched the battle, he was unable to remain still. He grew concerned about what was happening. Everything was too much out of control. He saw a pair of attacking djinns be rebuffed. Then, rather than converge again, they lashed out at each other instead.

He watched some more, this time concentrating to be sure. He saw no differentiated center anywhere! No cadre of demons struggling to reach the edge so that they too could engage. No circling defenders waiting for their opportunity to strike. Every djinn battled his nearest neighbor no matter which side he was on!

Being with the greater numbers, Fig had not thought much about his own safety. The outcome obviously had been predetermined. But now with all the djinns raging out of control, he felt much less sure. Instinctively, he looked back to where Briana had deployed herself.

Briana! He felt elated. She did not come through the flame to get involved in demon battles. No, she had put her life in peril to rescue *him*. But then the feeling rapidly faded. When this was over, he reasoned, their relationship would be the same as it had been before. In the end, what was the purpose of any of this? He cupped his hands around his head. Unbidden, a black melancholy weighed him down.

Fig looked around wildly. In his sudden brooding mood, he realized he had lost track of Lilith. At the start, she had been clear of the two lines of combatants as they closed. But after the chaos erupted, she had disappeared into the ball of warring demons. One on one, she would be no match for an enraged djinn. No, she must be in mortal danger.

But if he could get close enough to catch her attention, he might be able to coax her out to relative safety. Yes, that was something worth doing, something to push back the enfolding gloom.

Fig tried to imagine a completely blank slate in his head. He struggled to clear his mind. Clinching his teeth, he reached out with his thoughts to detect Lilith's presence. If ever there were a time to try and exert his dominance, this was it.

Almost immediately, like the tongue of a snake, a tendril of consciousness touched his own. He almost lost his attitude control as he recoiled in horror. The presence was that of a djinn almost deranged with chaos and death. Fig sensed another being and then a third. His thoughts jerked about like pieces of flotsam in a stormy sea.

He took a full, deep breath from the scuba gear and narrowed the broadcast of his thoughts into a narrow beam. Like a lighthouse on a craggy shore, he searched through the turmoil for the presence he sought.

Halfway in his mental journey around the sphere of combat, he detected Lilith's unique mental signature. They had touched thoughts only once or twice before, but he knew it was her — a bastion of steadfastness and pride mingling with a hint of compassion.

To his relief, she was not consumed with the battle rage of the djinns. Instead, she had collapsed in on herself. Drifting in the soup of limbs and ichor, she had curled into a ball. Unmoving, she awaited an errant strike that would rip her asunder.

As if he held the last piece in a jigsaw, and it did not fit, Fig puzzled. Yes, this was Lilith, but not her normal self. None of her traits presented themselves to him. She had already submitted, surrendered to the siren call of the great monotony.

'No, Lilith, no!' he projected. 'Not yet. I ... I need you', he thought with inspiration. 'Please help me. I need you now'.

LILITH STIRRED. As if awakening from a deep dream, she uncoiled herself and stretched. Fig! He was calling for help. She latched onto the direction from which his thoughts came and unfurled her wings. Gathering speed with each thrust, she zigged and zagged between the battling djinns. Emerging from the mêlée, in a dozen heartbeats, she was at Fig's side.

"What happened to you?" he asked as Lilith drew near.

"The despair," the succubus answered. "It grew and grew within me, stronger than ever before. I could not resist it until you called for me."

"As well you might," another voice interrupted.

Fig commanded his attitude control to yaw him around to see who spoke.

"Angela!" Lilith exclaimed. "What have we done?"

"I don't know, Sister. And I don't care." She waved at the sphere of combat. "This is a debacle. Elezar will listen to me no longer."

"You swore to rend me, limb from limb," Lilith cocked her head to the side.

Angela tensed. She extended her claws. "If we must, Sister. By all means, let us get on with it. If you are the one of us who survives, I don't care. That merely would mean I will be gone first."

"Stop!" Fig shouted. "Both of you. Something unusual must be causing this," He interposed himself in Angela's path. "Neither you nor Lilith are sounding right ... nor do I feel so good myself."

Angela stood silent for a moment, then furled her wings. She pointed at Fig. "Have it your way. Dispatch me with one of those human devices. One method is as good as another."

Lilith looked around at what remained of the battlefield. She cupped her eyes with her hands, trying to see through the filmy cloud of ichor inhibiting her view. The few djinns remaining continued their brawls. Little was left that possibly could be done here.

"Excuse me," a new voice said. "Audacious Audrey thought you might want to know. Five generators have been repaired."

"Not now," Fig tried to bat the gremlin aside. It was good news. No, it was great news, but somehow it did not help.

"And one more thing. Russian ground troops have crossed the Bering Strait into Alaska. The Canadians are resisting, but they are far outnumbered."

Fig's anger cascaded back within him. Wasn't anything being done to resist at all? And now the onset of crushing gloom.

"Enough!" he shouted. "Briana, Natasha. Even you, Angela. We need to get far away from here so we can think."

The Quickening Pace

THE TYRANT of Time staggered back to the throne room in the center-most level of the citadel. It had taken a considerable portion of his energy reserves, but it had been worth the expense. Not one or two, but thousands of djinns hurling themselves into oblivion in a single battle. Thousands fewer to exist, to breed any more. And eventually the smaller sprites, even the annoyingly cute gremlins will suffer the same fate as well. It was all so logical, an inescapable truth.

The Tyrant of Time closed his good eye and luxuriated in the feeling coursing about him. Despair. *Hopeless* despair. It radiated from the citadel and throughout the entire realm of demons. The intensity was the greatest at the surface of the sphere and lesser the farther one was away. But even so, glimmers managed to propagate to the very edges of the void. Everywhere were the messages to give up, succumb, become conscious no more.

Each of his plodding steps took more effort than the last. But with only a few more, he was able to grip the arm of his throne for assistance. As he passed the polished plate of gold leaf, he straightened. No change since the last time he had looked. One side of his face a celebration of beauty — slack, rather than pulled into tight ugliness. At least half of his scalp smooth like a ball of carved ivory. Not covered with filthy and disorganized cilia. The eye beneath the unruliness slumbered shut.

The time Tyrant slumped on the throne. He grunted at its twin to the right, empty as always. Because he was tired, she would appear sooner than usual. And when that happened, he would fade away, and she would awake from within and replace him.

Before he could enjoy the consciousness he had left, one of his minions appeared from the stairwell in the center of the level.

"Without your presence to encourage them, the treadmillers have begun to falter," it said.

The Tyrant grabbed one of the keys from its hook on the side of his throne. "The treadmillers were some of the earliest I created. Before I had perfected my craft. I will have to start culling and replacing." He groaned and rose from sitting.

Letting the minion lead, the pair ascended the central spiral stairway he had built many eons ago. As they stepped higher, the Tyrant remembered his efforts after his mate had perished. He had tried to create a replica out of the matter he had collected in the realm's earliest days. But the construction had proved to be elusive, the task too difficult to perform. He could not create a viable female.

The Tyrant paused at the closed doorway one level up, but there was no reason to enter. That floor contained the recycling vats that cranked out new minions to substitute for those who wore out and had to be replaced. They passed the next level higher as well.

Finally, master and minion reached the topmost level of the citadel. Unlike most of the others, mere cylindrical slices, it extended to the very zenith of the sphere. Although relatively huge, the volume was crammed full to almost bursting with scaffolding, a mishmash of struts, platforms, and spars. It looked like a jungle of metallic weeds that had taken over a garden.

Scattered with no discernable pattern, hundreds of minions were chained to treadmills. Each one struggled as hard as it could to keep the flat belt under its feet moving in a continuous loop. From every apparatus dangled a cable running to a nearby two-dimensional tree of thin metal rods. Protruding from a large bin nearby to where the staircase ended stood a tangle of more equipment. Rods, cross braces, and supports — spares for when a berserk minion had damaged its station.

As the Tyrant surveyed the grandeur of his creation, a gentle thump sounded on the citadel wall. He smiled. Another wayward demon had mistakenly crashed into the ebony black shell.

Except for the succubi, no other beings of the realm had guessed at his existence. Unfortunate visitors stuck fast like bugs on imppaper. Gradually, they were absorbed through the walls, adding more matter to the vats.

The Tyrant of Time climbed the scaffold to the nearest of the treadmillers. They were of his own creation and so simple-minded that complete domination was easy compared to that required for a more sophisticated being. Commanding hundreds to do his will was hatchling's play. With his good hand, he grabbed the minion's throat and stared into its mind. After a moment of resistance, with a snap, the impediment to his control dissolved.

"Faster," he commanded. "You shall not rest until I tell you to. There are too many left whose existence must be extinguished by the radiations you provide."

The Tyrant ascended the ladder to the next minion close by and repeated the order. "When the djinns in the battle outside are no longer, then, and only then, you will be able to rest for a short while."

He gave a small shudder as a vague memory returned. There had been a time when he had become bored, impatient that his plan was taking so long to be fulfilled. He needed something to amuse himself in the meantime, to fill up the eons still yet to come. And so he had converted the levels beneath his throne to another use — something to forestall the hints of madness creeping into his thoughts.

And somehow *she* had taken possession of those chambers and populated them with minions of her own. Added another throne next to his, and pursued her inexplicable designs. Something about frustrating the succubi. Keeping the march of time unchanging in the realm of humankind. A challenge to see if she could do it for one hundred eons. Do that before he had succeeded himself. Before all the demons vanished from the realm.

And if she could do that, then what? The Tyrant frowned as he tried to remember. She had declared that would mean she had won. Won? Won what? Stopped time in another realm before he had in his own, she had said.

But that was impossible. The realm of humankind teemed with conscious beings. Billions and billions of them. It was so vast that no amount of broadcast despair would be sufficient. There was no way she could win.

The Tyrant looked around at the struggles to maintain the pace. The treadmillers would not be able to continue without a rest before long. At this rate, soon all would be sufficiently worn and damaged. They would have to be replaced.

But if their output were doubled … The thought suddenly struck him. Yes, that was it! Usurp all the minions below the throne room. Take them from their watchglobes. Augment each treadmiller with a companion — one that was fresh and with untapped energy ready to burn. The emanations would double.

And perhaps the increased power would be enough. Despair was contagious, a hard emotion to resist — especially when all about one were feeling the same. Like a flock of sheep following the tinkle of the leader's bell, all demons, even princes would succumb.

The Tyrant felt invigorated. There was not time enough remaining before the transformation to move the minions from below, but he at least owed himself a little amusement now, an intellectual stimulation. His pace quickened. He scanned about for the weakest, the one with the largest limp and least output of energy. "Come," he commanded when he spotted it. "Time to play a little game."

"No, Master. Please. I will strive harder," the minion pleaded "Even with one leg withered, I am sure I can outperform many of those about me."

"Come," the Tyrant called back as he descended the scaffold. He moved with a limp of his own toward the upper terminus of the spiral staircase. He did not look back as he swept by the factotum who had alerted him of the slowdown. He was sure the one he had selected, his creation, after all, would follow.

On the next level down, the Tyrant inserted the key he carried into the door and swung it open. From the entryway, the pair could see a room shaped like a parallelogram. What one would get if the two opposite sides of a square layout skewed to one side. Forty-nine hexagons, each large enough for three minions to stand together covered most of the floor. An array of tiles, seven by seven. A narrow border filled the space between the outermost hexes and four confining walls.

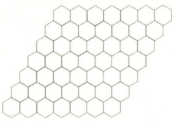

The Tyrant reached around the edge of the doorway and pushed a large yellow button protruding at waist height. "Watch," he commanded.

Instantly, each of the hexagons rotated about one of its symmetry axes until it stood vertical, perpendicular to the floor. Through the many openings, the minion could see part of the level below. The air filled with a caustic sting from another array, this one of vats filled with bubbling acid.

"Please, Master." The minion shuddered.

The Tyrant shook his head and again pressed the control. The hexes flipped back to their former positions, and the smell went away.

"The button I pushed is now deactivated. It will remain so until the contest is over. But two more are still armed." He pointed across to the opposite wall and then to the one on the right.

"See, it *is* a game." He smiled. "You have a chance to become the new Tyrant if you win. All you have to do is press the control directly across from you before I manage to do so with mine on the right."

"Master, I do not understand."

The Tyrant walked around the edge of the array until he stood on the side on the left.

"Watch again," he commanded, stepping onto the grid. As his foot tapped down, the hex on which he lit turned a deep ocean blue. "Now, your turn," he directed. "Select a positions in the row in front of you."

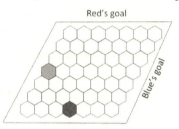

"I will fall into a vat if I do. You just showed me that."

"It does not work that way. Your first step will be secure, exactly the same as was mine. So will be the subsequent ones you take as you build your path to the far side. But only one new hex at a time when it is your turn to move. Any attempts beyond that and you will be dumped below. Go ahead. Try it. You will see."

The minion hesitated but finally moved to one of the hexes. When it did, it glowed blood red. At the same time, a barrier rose from the floor behind it, barring him from retreat.

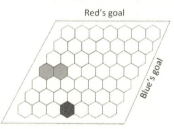

"The game has begun," the Tyrant smiled. He could feel his strength returning. He should play more often than he did. "Each step one takes, adds another hex to his path. The goal of the game is to construct a continuous one from one side of the grid to the other. You from the bottom to the top and me from left to right. Build a path to the other side first and you win. A fair contest, a battle of wits."

"Fair? But you went first!"

"Well, rank does have privileges."

19

Reluctant Allies

FIG TUMBLED onto the slab of the two sisters. It looked the same as he had remembered it: a simple landing area, a chest and an imprisoned imp serving as a beacon. He eyed Lilith critically. Was she okay now?

"Thank you, Fig," Lilith said as she alit. "I again can control my mind … mostly." She glanced at Angela and thrust her shoulders back as far as she could. "Come at me now, Sister," she growled. "I am ready for you to try your worst."

"Just a second," Natasha held out her palm as she and Briana arrived and disemchaired. Angela, can I hold your purse for you before you engage?"

"No one touches the contents of my sweetbag but me," Angela shot back. "I am myself again. Even if all four of you try together, I will destroy its contents before I can be subdued."

"Stop this!" Natasha gulped some air and stamped her foot. She grimaced as her heel had poked a hole in the slab. Her shoe came off as she wiggled free. Undeterred, she studied the others, one at a time. "I think, yes, I think we need a truce. Something to get everyone on the same page."

"The same page?" Lilith snorted. "We have not had a common aim since we were hatchlings. That is a complete waste of time."

"Nevertheless." Natasha shook her head slightly. "It won't hurt to try a bit, and I can facilitate. I have turned more than one operative in my day. I'm quite good at it."

"Zephyr, I still want to know about the goblin and his citadel," Briana interrupted. "On my home-world, I'm sure no wizard has ever heard of such a thing."

"It is the place from which the bad thoughts come," Zephyr said. "I have already told you that."

Fig scrambled up to start pacing about, but then quickly sat back down. There was no room for any such maneuvers on the tiny lair. He willed himself to focus. He felt better now. The cloud over him had dissipated.

"Zephyr, you're talking in riddles," Fig said. "Bad thoughts come from a citadel, you say. Created by a demon you call a goblin. Why? That makes no sense. Why would anyone want to do that? What is gained by having thousands of demons end their lives in such a foolish fashion? What is the purpose?"

"Purpose?" Briana asked. "Well, carried to its logical conclusion, there would be no demons left."

"Except for the goblin, himself," Zephyr said. "Except for him, the realm of demons would be empty."

Fig's eyes widened. "What a concept!" he exclaimed. "That could very well be it. No more beings flying about. All matter stationary and unmoving. Nothing more would be happening — could be happening. Nothing would change. Nothing to *measure* the passage of time against. There would be no *future* from the moment the last demon died." Fig waved his arms wildly. "Could that be what the goblin in the citadel wants? Time to end?"

"Where is this citadel?" Briana asked. "We have to find it and make sure the overwhelming sense of despair does not reoccur."

"No one knows where it is," Zephyr said. "The citadel is black. The void is black. No one can tell one from the other. Everyone who has tried to find the stronghold has never returned."

"Fig, all this is wonderful folklore," Natasha stood as tall as she could. "But it is irrelevant. Whatever just happened in this place has passed. I can feel it. We all can. What is important to me is that *before* it happens again, Angela kisses and makes up with Lilith — so I can get what I came for and can return home to Alexei."

"Not so fast, Natasha," Briana said. "If we are going to be on the same page, it is not fair for you to skip out after only *your* desires are satisfied."

"Why not?" Natasha asked. "I have no interest in dealing with tyrants here or anywhere else. That's hero stuff. Not the way I operate."

"Then who furnishes your ride home?" Briana struck back.

Natasha blinked. She remained silent for a long while. "All right," she finally said. She looked at Briana and Fig. "One for all, and all for one. Ming deposed. Dale and Flash reunited to walk hand and hand into the sunset."

She turned to address the two succubi. "First things first, ladies. Listen to me. Let's search together for a win-win solution."

A Hopeful Outcome

FIG FIDGETED. He was sure he had worn a hole into the slab, but when he looked down, it appeared as unscarred as ever. He grimaced with frustration. Time had continued marching on. And he was further from getting help from the gremlins than when he first came to this realm.

The number of dominos that had to fall had increased. Now, the first thing was for Angela and Lilith to make peace with one another. That would allow Natasha to take possession of her precious documents. Provided she sticks to her word, she helps the rest of us to stop the Tyrant of Time from again filling the realm with despair.

Then, after demons feel happy again, Lilith publicizes the existence of female warriors. Demon lib is off and running. Finally, after all that soaks in, he gets to try and lure gremlins to come to the Earth to restore power. How could there be enough time for all of this to happen before it was too late?

Fig massaged his neck muscles, now grown tight. He took a deep breath from the oxygen tank, and then two more. No way around it, he told himself. Start with the first thing on the list and work it through.

He listened as Natasha drew Lilith and Angela out of their shells. The spy was as good as she claimed. So unlike King Solomon. His two plaintiffs each would have ended up with one half of a baby or one would have been denied. No, the Russian spy had pointed out, the better solution would have been to come up with a second child. Find the common ground so each would feel as if she had won.

"Okay. Let's see if I have got this straight," Natasha pointed at herself. "Angela, you are angry at Lilith because she interferes. Disrupts your plan to bring Elezar under your control, right?"

"Absolutely!" Angela replied. "First, she prevented me from learning anything from Marie Antoinette. And second, as you well know, Natasha, cut short finding out about all your wiles."

"All for an ignoble purpose," Lilith interrupted. "Suppose you could wrap Elezar around your middle finger. The lot of the rest of us would not change one whit."

"So, you were completely unsuccessful with Elezar?" Natasha continued as if Lilith had not spoken. "Correct?"

"Well, no. Not exactly." Angela admitted. "I am able to interact with a resplendent djinn without total submission to his desires. And Elezar, himself, has listened to my council." The succubus frowned. "But even so, Lilith has interfered! I have no doubt she is the one who marshaled a force to outnumber Elezar's two to one."

"Hmm," Natasha fiddled with her scuba gear for a few moments. "That sounds like a secret Elezar would love to know about. Perhaps, Lilith could provide it to him — under your aegis."

"What! Grovel before a prince and ask for his forgiveness?" Lilith exploded. "Angela is right. I admit that I acted on Briana's idea and put the rebel princes' force together. But Elezar's warriors did not win the battle. He is the one who should submit. Decree that all the females in the realm get their due respect."

"Suppose, Lilith, that Elezar saw the wisdom in what you have done," Natasha said. "An audience to convince him of that would be worth a lot to you, right? And you, Angela, would get the credit for bringing Lilith to his attention."

For a moment, both Angela and Lilith remained silent. Fig imagined he could almost hear the gears grinding in the succubus' heads. "Lilith, you need some testimonials to bolster your case," he suggested. "If there are survivors of the battle, they must be found."

"The despair was too powerful," Angela and Lilith said together. "None will be left."

"Maybe not," Briana said. "We all agree these emanations, wherever they are coming from, have subsided. And we are talking of males and females who strived together for a common goal." She unfastened Zephyr from the lawn chair harness. "Go back to the place of battle," she commanded. "If you spot any survivors, convince them to come here."

EVEN THOUGH his method for propulsion was inefficient, Zephyr was the first to return. Behind him, the wings of two resplendent djinns, a male and a female, stroked the air. The male had wrapped its arm around the female, coaxing her forward. Ichor oozed from a multitude of wounds.

With a groan, the pair collapsed onto the slab in the little space remaining.

"Tend to her first." The male struggled to speak. "I am called Triumphant Spirit. My partner is…" His eyes widened in shock. "I do not know," he whispered. "The one who saved my life, and I do not know."

"I have bought some sweetbalm I brewed in the realm of humankind." Briana rummaged through a satchel strapped to the lawn chairs. "I know it will work on demons because I have used it on Lilith before." Briana looked at Fig over her shoulder. "I wanted to be prepared for whatever state I might find you in."

Fig blinked. A warm feeling washed over him. She *did* care for me, he thought. And maybe, just maybe, more than merely like a brother. But now was not the time to ponder that. He steeled himself to focus on the present. He watched Briana slaver the stickiness on the most grievous of the female's wounds.

As she did, Triumphant Spirit resumed speaking. "At first, I was skeptical. A female tagging along could only get in the way. But when the mêlée ensued, I discovered that she protected my back. More than once, one of Elezar's warriors maneuvered to get behind me. And each time, even though she had sinews far weaker than my own, she held off the attackers' onslaughts. She gave me time to turn and resist.

"And as the wave of despair overcame us, and death in battle seemed the only sane course, she was less affected. I don't know. Perhaps it is part of the female nature, less attuned to violence than one like myself.

"She tugged on my arm to pull me out of the fray. Her wings are surprisingly powerful for one of such petite size."

Triumphant Spirit gently stroked the female's arm as the sweetbalm worked its magic.

"Fragile Flower," she smiled. "That is what I like to be called. You left out the part about how you pushed me aside when more than one of Elezar's warriors converged on us. Yes, overall the battle was two to one, but in many of the small skirmishes, the odds flipped the other way."

"I could not let anything happen to you." Triumphant Spirit managed to clench one fist with resolve.

"Yes! Yes, yes, yes!" shouted Lilith. "This is exactly what I had hoped. "By all means, let's journey to Elezar so he can hear firsthand what needs to be changed throughout the realm." She smiled at her sister. "And you can claim credit, Angela. As much as you want. I don't care. The idea will catch on and spread like the most intense of flames we can imagine."

"There is the bigger problem." Fig was insistent. "What happens when the overwhelming despair rises again? Compared to that, the control of princes and the path to domestic bliss are mere pimples on the face of a frog. Yes, let's get an audience with Elezar. We need to use every resource we can in order to figure out what is going on."

In the Presence of the Prince

FIG COULD not help gawking. The lair of Elezar the Golden was magnificent — a riot of soaring towers and glowing walkways. Except for the thick slab underneath everything, not a single straight line did he see.

His eyes darted about the small room buried at the center of the tallest spire. Petite statues of delicate creatures from who-knew-where stood in dimly lit niches. Suspended from the ceiling, viscous liquids swirled between thin transparent plates. One moment they mixed together and then separated completely the next.

And then there was Elezar himself. The Golden One sat on a tufted cushion with a backrest twice his height. He was short and stunted, hunchbacked and listing to one side. Spindly fingertips poked out of long flowing sleeves.

If ever there was a representation of Fig's worst nightmare, this was it. The djinn with only one wing towered over them all. But his menace was a mere pastel compared with the vibrant threat in Elezar's face. Eyes squinted with cunning. Lips curved into the smile of a fierce predator confronting a cornered prey. Perhaps the hardest thing to get used to was that the prince spoke perfect English.

Only Trantor required a whispered translation from Angela when anyone spoke. The pair stood next to one another. The djinn had wrapped his hand around Angela's waist. She rested her head on his shoulder. If they had been human rather than a demon, one would have thought they were teenagers in love.

"Almost all my warriors gone." Elezar's eyes blazed with menace. "None of your words can spin the outcome of the battle into a victory."

"It is a triumph of ideas," Angela stood her ground. "The other princes rue the loss of their djinns as well. It will be a long while before they conspire to contest you again."

"A triumph? What triumph?" Elezar hissed.

"You will have as many fighters as you did before," Angela persisted. "Don't you recognize that the females can adequately replenish your ranks?"

"So you have said." Elezar waved the remark away. He pointed at the other pair of djinns who also crowded into the prince's den. "The babbling of two warriors, wounded ones at that, is not much of a persuasive argument."

"*Two* warriors?" Briana stared back at the prince. She did not bother to get a sip of air. "A pair not in the midst of a rut. Don't you grasp the significance?"

Fig looked at Briana. She had admitted her discomfort around Angela, but that was not apparent when she spoke to Elezar. She glared back at him, stare for stare. Her father would expect no less, she had said, but did not elaborate. Despite himself, Fig nodded his approval. She was more than a hapless princess rescued from danger. Much more than that. She ... *personified* courage, he realized. One who had journeyed alone from the comforts of her native world to a totally alien other. One who came after him into an entirely different and bizarre realm.

The prince frowned. "Your mind is keen, female. You have inherited well from your most potent father."

"We are not here on behalf of the Archimage." Briana glowered. "Nor to open your eyes to opportunity on another orb in the universe of humankind. Focus instead on what should be the utmost importance to you now. There is a threat not only to your princedom but to the entire realm."

"Yes, yes," Elezar flicked a small imp off his arm. "The feeling of despair. It did intensify everywhere. No one, not even a prince such as I, can deny it. But a fleeting feeling, nonetheless. It is gone now."

Fig shook his head. He could not accept the prince's conclusion — not after everything that had happened to him over the past month. True, everything had started simply enough. A quest. An adventure to rescue Briana and bring her back to safety.

But no sooner was that accomplished than a much greater problem arose. The US without electricity. Not one person but an entire nation in peril. Never in his wildest imagination did he think there would be anything more challenging than that.

But there was! Briana was only one person. The US, one country on a single planet out of thousands in the realm of humankind. Now, he was intertwined with a different but entire universe in peril.

"What happened once can occur a second time," he said. "Indeed, dozens, perhaps hundreds of times more. And if the despair occurs again, all the female djinns also might perish while under the grips of the —"

"I understand the peril," Elezar nodded. "The question is 'what is the cause?'"

"I do not know for certain." Fig stroked his chin. "But we have two mysteries, not only one. The rise in the feeling of despair *and* this mysterious citadel that has never been found. Perhaps, they are related."

Elezar did not react.

"Occam's Razor," Fig rushed on. "A standard scientific method. Reduce the complexity of the unexplained. Assume there are not two enigmas, only one."

"You can only fight what you can see." Eyes half-open, Elezar shook his head with regal slowness. "This prattle about a hidden citadel has been around for eons. If such a thing exists, someone would have discovered it by now."

"It is supposed to be entirely black," Zephyr said from where he hovered above them all. "As black as the void."

"Silence!" Elezar raised his voice. He nodded at Angela. "It is only because of my regard for the wisdom of this succubus that I allowed the rest of you here. I will ponder the idea about female warriors." He stood and drew his robe about himself with a swish. "As for the rest, you are dismissed."

Fig's thoughts rushed. Elezar's resistance had to be overcome. He was a prince. He had resources that he, Lilith, and the others could use.

"Suppose I can prove to you the citadel exists?" he blurted. "Then, would you be open to providing support?"

"The void is vast," Elezar cocked one eyebrow. The prince was skeptical. "What do you suggest? Every demon be directed to fly about and report back if they bump into something?"

"It would require effort," Fig agreed. "But not so much as all that."

Demonrealm Astronomy

FIG TIGHTENED his grip on the lawn chair tubing near Briana's right and Natasha's left shoulders. With his free hand, he directed short bursts of the attitude control jets to correct the trio's spatial orientation. What loomed before them looked little different from any other direction. But they had to start somewhere.

"If this citadel is invisible, how can we find something that cannot be seen?" Natasha asked.

"Don't worry about it," Fig said. "Briana, look to the left as we coast along. Natasha to the right. The idea is to spot a change. Let me know as soon as one of the distant lights vanishes or when a new one appears."

"Vanishes? Appears?"

"Correct, vanishes or appears. Even though the citadel emits no light itself, it can block the emanation from another source behind it. An occultation."

"There!" Briana shouted. "A few degrees forward from straight to the right. A light disappeared that was there a moment ago."

Fig pulled out a sextant from the treasures Elezar's vassals had accumulated from trips to the Earth and started making sightings. "Now look a little bit rear, Briana. If we are lucky, we might also see another light appear."

FIG ARCHED his back and stretched. He had lost his sense of time. He and Elezar were alone in Elezar's private chamber.

"Your tongue is a glib one," the prince said. "Under other circumstances, I would covet it for my collection of human artifacts."

"Do you understand the conclusion?" Fig tried not to react to the implication of the prince's words. "There is a circle out there, probably a sphere. And it is not tiny. The diameter is as large as the height of thirty of your biggest djinns."

"And it could be inert matter," Elezar waved the argument away. "Perhaps, something left over by the creator when our realm came into existence."

"Occam's razor again," Fig almost shouted. "The most simple solution tends to be the right one."

"After eons and eons, someone must have crashed into it."

"Maybe they did but did not live to tell the tale."

"Mere speculation." Elezar waved to the floating parchments. "These calculations prove none of that."

"Agreed. But now that we have a definite direction from here, we can —"

"Yes, yes. Send someone to go and observe up close."

"A volunteer?"

"Of course not. I will use someone who is to die soon anyway. I have a pen of condemned lightning djinns who will serve. Several would take the risk rather than face the indignity of being rendered into pieces a little bit at a time."

"According to my calculations, the citadel is at least some distance from here. How long would it take for a scout to fly across the void?"

"Many sleep cycles. I doubt anyone has tried."

"Don't you have a faster means of propulsion?"

Elezar shrugged. "Why not visit my tribute bin. It overflows with things brought to me by returning travelers from your realm. Perhaps you can fashion something from there."

ELEZAR'S PRIVATE den again was crowded. Angela scooted close to Trantor to make enough room, Lilith stood to the side as much as she could, but even so, standing on tiptoe, Briana and Natasha barely could see the small screen mounted high on one wall. From its backside a thin cable snaked up to the top of a nearby tower. The one in which, surprisingly, Fig had found a fairly decent telescope, one with a cd image array on the focal plane. Gremlins had put it together.

Elezar scowled impatiently. Only blackness showed on the screen. But the telescope aimed precisely at the center of the object Fig had discovered. So far, there had been no more attacks on anyone's minds.

Fig was not with the others. He paced nervously on the parapet of another of Elezar's towers. There, two dozen lightning djinns strained against a long, thin strap of latex assembled from dozens of exercise bands, knotted together. The ends of the resulting elastic stretched to two other spires, each a distance away on either side.

Leaning against the very center of the band squatted one additional djinn. Around its head, on its arms, torso, and legs, even the soles of its feet thirty or so glass globes had been stuck to his body. In each one, the imp occupant blazed as brightly as it could.

Fig felt some misgivings about the imps. The whole idea for both the telescope and the slingshot catapult were his. But when he asked Elezar if the small demons also would be volunteers, the prince had merely laughed.

A captain of the djinns indicated that all the others were ready. Fig nodded in return, and a short countdown started. When it reached zero, the straining djinns released their grips. The illuminated one shot into the void. He cried out from the crushing acceleration, his arms and legs flailing like a turtle turned on its back. Soon, he was a mere spec in the sky. Fig climbed down the tower staircase and got comfortable in the den where the others waited.

BRIANA'S STOMACH growled. The little store of trail mix she had brought with her into the realm had long disappeared. Maybe the imps wiggling on small wafers would taste the same as insects back on Earth. But not alive! She would not eat beings who could speak.

She looked at Fig standing apart from the others. Even though it had been what felt like days on Earth, he too declined any repast. He could not hide his concern about the little regard for life in this alien realm. She pulled a little apart from the others and gave him a small smile. Ever since his return from California, he had been different. More standoffish. More aloof. The little puppy was gone. A crusader stood in his place. She was no longer on a pedestal.

Throughout all their time together before, she had indicated how she felt. Uncomfortable with the unconditional adoration, smothered by it. But his adventures had changed him somehow, and she missed the attention.

She missed having a little puppy; she actually did, especially now it was gone. And there was the presence of Natasha. She made it clear she regarded Fig very highly. Went on and on about how impressive it was that he figured out the Russian plot with so little information.

And then there was Lilith. Clearly arousing a man's passion was child's play for a succubus. And Fig appeared quite comfortable being with her — and she with him! Was something going on between the two that she had completely missed?

"There is some diffuse light reflecting into the telescope." Trantor pointed at the viewing screen. "See? If you think about it right, a few dozen small sources form the outline of the djinn."

As everyone watched, the lights grew fainter but remained visible. Then they stopped changing. The lightning djinn had crashed on the surface of the citadel.

"He was supposed to use his wings to decelerate," Elezar growled. "The longer he stays alive, the more we will learn. If his limbs are broken, he won't be able to turn on the high-intensity lamp."

Briana and the others watched the outline defined by the imp lights that indicated the djinn's motions. One arm reached around to where his back would be, but with difficulty. There was a momentary fumbling, and then a more brilliant blaze of light flooded the view.

Now, against the deep black background, the yellow scales of the lightning djinn stood out brightly. The demon struggled to push his knees underneath himself and pull his chest from the citadel's surface. But his legs did not budge. Neither could he raise his head.

"What's that dripping from his arm?" Angela called out. "It reminds me of the imp-paper we use to secure the treats — only totally black."

"It does look like that," Trantor agreed with a nod. "The surface of the place looks covered with the stuff. He has become mired."

The demons in the room watched impassively. With a glance, Briana realized what was going to happen. The djinn continued to struggle. But with each twitchy motion, he sunk deeper into the citadel's coating.

In moments, it was over. The lights outlining the frame went dark, and then the high-intensity lamp sunk into the slime.

"At least, we know why no one has reported the citadel's existence before," Elezar said. "Whoever bumped into it was consumed." The prince turned to Fig. "I agree we are dealing with more than a legend.

Now what?"

"Why didn't the djinn stop his forward motion when he got close?" Angela asked. "If he had done so, this would not have happened."

"Maybe because of the broadcast of despair." Fig thought for a moment. "The closer one gets to the citadel itself, the stronger it becomes. The djinn had no will to do anything when he approached."

A messenger gremlin fluttered in front of Fig before he could say more. "The Canadians were overwhelmed. Faced a force much too large for them. Alaska has fallen. A message from the US government demanded a full Russian retreat. Or else dire events would follow."

"I cannot let it get around the realm that I, the Golden One, would sit idle when such a thing as the citadel exists." Elezar ignored the interruption. He bolted up, and his eyes flared at Fig. "Okay, bright eyes, what is your next idea?"

A Weapon from Scrap

FIG SIDLED along the narrow passage between the towering stacks of Elezar's tribute. It was arranged according to some logical scheme, but he could not figure out what it was. He looked back at Trantor walking behind him. The absence of one of his wings made it easier to slip along the paths without having anything tumble down.

"Everything here is organized according to potential function," Trantor said over his shoulder. "Iron skillets with cooking, iron daggers with weapons ..."

"We need to figure out a way to pierce the walls of the citadel," Fig said. "Something powerful that explodes on impact. Otherwise, we will learn nothing more at all."

Fig could not believe what he was contemplating. The despair broadcast by the citadel dashed completely any hope of getting help for the Earth. It had to be investigated and then destroyed. Back on earth, he would never have considered such a thing. But in the realm of demons, violence was everywhere. It was the norm by which most problems were solved. Kill or be killed.

"Lightning bolts can explode a target when they hit one," Trantor said. "But unfortunately, the djinns that produce them cannot aim very well. We have a saving throughout the realm, 'Marshalling lightning djinns is like herding cats on your Earth.'"

"And we probably will need the combined power of many bolts striking the same spot simultaneously." Fig kneaded his chin and began pacing back and forth in the confines of the narrow row.

"Lightning bolts are made of charged particles," he said after a moment. "And charged particles in my realm at places like CERN are controlled by magnets."

Trantor shrugged. "I know nothing of the workings of the realm of humankind. I have never visited there."

"Wait. What are those?" Fig pointed to his left.

286

"I believe humans call them rebar," Trantor said. "Why so many travelers bring back the stuff, I don't know."

"Bundled together, they might work." Fig said. "Is there a labora … a large unused lair that can be used for assembly?"

FIG STEPPED back and examined what had been cobbled together. A single command from Elezar was all that it took to get things going. Briana and Natasha looked on interested, but not comprehending what was being built.

"I don't get it." A gremlin waved his arm around the den. "None of us do."

"What happens when you guys fly around in a circle?" Fig asked.

"Generate a magnetic field, of course," the gremlin said.

"Exactly. And if hundreds of you are doing it together?"

"We generate a strong one."

"And if your circles are around a pole of steel?"

"We generate a *very* strong magnet."

"That is what I want you to do."

A messenger gremlin interrupted Fig's thoughts. "Audacious Audrey decided this to be particularly important. First is the verbatim text by the US President, whatever that is. Second, a photograph accompanying the first.

Fig studied the two slips of paper. The first read: 'The deadline for withdrawal from our sovereign state of Alaska has passed. Our retaliation has been delivered by one of our nuclear-powered submarines. Continued occupation will result in a more strategic target. The barren steppes of central Asia will not be your only casualty if you persist."

The photograph was grainy. How it had been obtained Fig had no idea. But the impact was immediate. It showed a mushroom cloud rising over terrain that had been blasted flat. He showed it to Briana and Natasha.

"No!" Natasha blurted. "This cannot be happening. Saner heads are supposed to prevail. A negotiated settlement. A benign occupation, not total war. I can get a gargoyle to create new documents for Alexei and me. For us, the end result can come out the same.

Fig did not respond. He returned his attention to directing the gremlins bringing into creation his device.

BRIANA PEERED over the edge of the topmost tower rampart. The elastic on the flanking spires had been coiled up and set aside, out of the way. It must have been a dozen earth days he had toiled, but finally, Fig's construction stood on the larger parapet immediately below. Mentally, she extended its center line aimed out into the void and saw only blackness — but it must be that this new device aimed at the citadel.

Elezar stood beside her on the right, but she did not cringe. The prince seemed totally focused on Fig's activities. On her other side, Natasha fidgeted with impatience. Beyond her stood the two succubi and Trantor.

"Okay, guys, start generating the magnetism," Fig's voice rose from the parapet. "Remember to stay together and fly at the same speeds."

Elezar turned to Briana. "The humans on the orb you call the Earth are most interesting," he said. "For eons, I had dismissed the sophistication of your technology. So primitive. No exercise of any of the five crafts. So unlike the home of your father. When this is over, I think I must look at it again."

Briana's thoughts jolted. "You have an agreement," she snapped. "With my father, the Archimage. Not to interfere in any major way with the realm of humankind."

Elezar nodded for a brief instant as if he were a grandparent humoring a child. "Perhaps your father has embellished a bit, or maybe even misunderstood. Yes, I did agree to make your world off-limits to any major invasion with beings of my realm." Elezar's eyes flashed. "Your *world>*, but not the rest of your realm."

Briana's eyes widened with alarm. Before she could say more, Fig cried out.

"Three, two, one. First salvo."

Everyone turned their attention to the lower parapet. Six lightning djinns crowded together behind Fig's construction. Simultaneously, they hurled bolts of energy down its centerline. The thin air crackled and sparked. A brilliant yellow seared their eyes as the burst of energy emerged from the other side. It sped across the realm at almost the speed of light. In two blinks of the eye, it spattered against something, causing a flicker, a dull glow. They had hit the citadel.

"Next, three, two, one, fire." Fig did not hesitate. A half-dozen more djinns had already pushed the first six aside. Again the bolts of lightning and this time, Briana paid more attention. The djinns were trying to align their shafts parallel but could not quite accomplish what was needed.

Again, there was the flash of light in the distance, and Briana watched the next burst as it exited Fig's construction. Immediately, she understood its purpose. Despite the variations of the input, the exiting bolts were perfectly aligned and focused into a collimated beam.

As the bombardment continued, the demons became more proficient in their task. Greater synchronization. Greater power with each coordinated bolt. With each additional pulse, the color of the glow changed from red to yellow, then to green and blue.

The bombardment did not let up, lasting so long that Briana could not estimate the passage of time. The lightning djinns panted from the growing fatigue.

"Six of you is not enough," Fig cried out after a few bolts more. "A dozen of you the next time. Crowd yourselves closer together."

A deep grumble of protest arose, but almost immediately, Elezar commanded, "Do as the human says."

"Three, two, one, fire."

This time, Briana's eyes slammed shut from the brilliance of the bolt. She blinked rapidly, but the after-image on her lids did not immediately fade. Finally, after what felt like minutes, she was able to force her eyes back open and look into the distance.

A faint outline of a not quite inky sphere stood out against the darker ebony background. More importantly, in its very center came upwelling light from within. The sight could mean nothing else. The citadel had been breached.

Probe Launch

FOR A moment, Fig allowed himself to luxuriate in his accomplishment. The focusing magnets had worked! The citadel had been cracked open. For another moment, he forgot he had to control his intake and inhaled a deep breath from the scuba mouthpiece.

He looked around the den. Everyone else was jubilant. He saw Trantor give Angela a celebratory hug. Lilith beamed at him, although whether a succubus was smiling or growling was hard to tell. Now, if things continued to go well …

Like a rogue wave, a sudden feeling of discontent washed over Fig. For the second time since he had ventured into the realm of demons, he felt tendrils of despair. Did he really know what to do next?

Lilith's smile slackened. She crumpled onto a stool and put her head in her hands. Elezar staggered and grabbed a seat back for support. "Cause and effect," the prince murmured through gritted teeth. "You were right, human. The citadel is not only more than a myth but the cause of our misery instead. It is as bad as before the battle. Maybe even worse."

"Then we must attack." Fig's voice faltered. He was not so sure of himself anymore. His confidence waned. He looked at Briana and Natasha. They too were feeling the effects. Neither of them as severely as the demons, but impacted in their cores even so.

"To the tops of the towers," Fig said. "Before things get any worse."

ELEZAR'S FOLLOWERS moved slowly, each one resisting the despair growing within. Eventually, the ends of the elastic band had been tied once more to the prince's flanking towers and pulled taut. A half-dozen lightning djinns stood ready, three males and three females.

"Remember to support your brothers and sisters," Fig told the line. "No bickering. No fights. The radiations from the citadel will grow in strength as you get closer. But you must resist. Take strength from your comrades. Work as one and report back what you see."

Elezar gave the command. The djinns were flung forward, their legs flailing like those of a centipede. Immediately, everyone else on the parapet made their way to Elezar's private den.

This time, the screen was well lit. The outwelling light from the gaping hole in the citadel had made the imp lights unnecessary. The black silhouette of the linked demons contrasted sharply with the glow surrounding them. No one spoke. Fig saw that everyone seemed to be wrestling against the growing self-doubt, the surging flood of helplessness within.

The final velocity of the group was lower than that of the single djinn who had been propelled across the void first. Time began to hang heavy upon everyone as they waited. The humans fidgeted the most, declining all the offers for snacks of wiggling imps.

When the gremlin shuttling oxygen next appeared, Fig instructed him to bring from the warehouse pantry what he could. He ran his tongue over the dry surface of his mouth. "No, make that soda pop instead," he decided. "We need water more than anything. Perhaps, the sugar dissolved in it will be enough to keep us going."

What must have been hours passed, perhaps even more than an Earth day. Fig, Briana, and Natasha took turns sleeping with two always on alert. On the telescope display, they watched the soaring djinns maintaining their postures. They imitated rigid statutes as best they could. But as the demons drew nearer the citadel, one of them flexed his shoulders, probably uncomfortable because of an aching arm.

As he pulled his limb free and stretched it upward, a female's grip across the back of his neck slid away. The line broke into two. In an instant, the djinn at one end cast himself free. He pushed his neighbor to the side, bumping into the next demon in line. In the gasp of a single breath, a dozen wings unfurled. With bared fangs and teeth, they slashed right and left.

As the djinns hurled forward, one half of the cadre were slain almost immediately by the other. The remaining three danced and feinted until one was trapped between the other two. He was attacked simultaneously, front and back. The surviving pair grappled chest to chest and vanished into the gleaming light.

All were silent for a moment. Finally, Lilith said. "You are right, Fig.

291

We cannot tolerate whatever emanates from the orb."

Just then, one of the gremlins shuttling back and forth from the Hilo lab arrived with a clatter of six packs and herding a few less canisters.

"Food riots in at least a dozen cities," she reported. "Downtown Detroit is under vigilante control. Gunfire exchanging with the National Guard. Military units are withdrawing from most cities. Occupants have been left to be on their own.

Fig slumped. It was hard to stand erect. He was thirsty, hungry, and almost asleep on his feet. The weight of what was happening became almost too much. It bore down upon him like a heavy stone. This fight with whoever ruled the citadel had to be resolved and resolved now. The gremlins had to become focused on generator repair before it was too late. The fiasco just witnessed proved it. None of Elezar's princedom could accomplish what was needed. Clearly, there was only one option left to try, as unlikely to succeed as it might be.

"We humans are the ones affected least," he said.

FIG TOSSED aside the empty oxygen canister strapped to his chest and put a new one in its place. He checked again that Briana and Natasha had their air supplies replenished as well. Then he gripped two of the lawn chair struts in his bare hands as he settled against the taut elastic band.

"Wait. I am coming with you," Lilith called out. "I … I have too much at stake in this to merely stand idly by."

"Not a good idea." Fig shook his head emphatically. "You are a demon like the rest, Lilith. You will be little use when we reach the sphere. The radiating sentiments will be too great."

"That is for me to decide, human," she snapped as she wiggled underneath the lawn chair seats.

Fig started to protest, but Elezar cut him off. "Enough," the prince commanded. "Pullers, you know the drill. Grab the elastic and fly backward as far as you can. On my signal, release it in unison as you have done before."

A few moments later, the air squeezed out of Fig's chest from the acceleration, and his body hurled forward.

None of the four spoke as the makeshift vehicle soared through the void. Although it was thin, the air whistled through the nooks and crannies of Briana's makeshift contraption. There was no real way to judge the passage of time, but eventually, the light from the target resolved — first into a small circle and then growing in size until its diameter was greater than the height of the largest djinn.

"We probably are close enough to start decelerating," Fig called out. "Briana, Natasha, start firing our retros."

The two women opened the valves on the canisters in their laps. Steady streams of hydrogen whooshed out in front of where they sat. Fig felt a resistance to their forward motion, but his melancholy did not abate. The calculation had been tricky, and in the rush, he should have checked his work.

The globe loomed larger. No one spoke. The two women continued to fire. The opening in the sphere became a yawning maw.

"Wait," Fig called out as Briana set the canister she was holding aside and reached for another. "Those are the ones to propel our return."

"It looks like we are closing fast," Briana squirmed in her seat. "Won't we pancake against whatever is inside?"

"I can help," Lilith said. She extracted herself from her perch. Facing backward, she grabbed the centermost arms of the bound together chairs. Then with a powerful stroke of her wings, she pushed against the craft.

Fig blinked. Of course. He must have blundered with his math. He was starting to get overconfident, a little too full of himself. Rescue Briana. Capture Angela in a demon trap. Take on an unknown assailant who threatened an entire realm. No problem, right? He was the brave and clever hero, a man never at a loss.

But he didn't really believe that. Who was he kidding? Venturing into the unknown of another realm had been with an experienced guide. Lilith had made sure he was kept safe. But now, he felt like a spelunker getting ready to descend into a newly discovered cave. A single misstep could be his last.

Stupid. Utterly stupid. The lightning djinns obeyed Elezar's commands without thinking. But he had to ponder deeper, look after himself. He thought of Briana, Natasha, and Lilith. Himself, and those important to him. He was no hero of the sagas, protected by the gods. He was going to need all his wits about him, every single one.

Lilith beat her wings again. As she did, Fig emerged from his momentary stupor. He used his attitude control jets to keep the apparatus level. The deceleration pushed him against the chairs, but Lilith's outstretched wings blocked his view.

Hand over hand, he shifted to one side. When Lilith's wings furled between strokes, he caught glimpses of their approach. Yes, they were slowing down with each of the succubus' pumps, but they were already too close. Lilith would not be able to bring them to a halt. He could not guess how rough the collision was going to be.

The opening in the sphere grew until it almost filled the sky in front of the hurled chairs. They became close enough that Fig could see structure inside the citadel sphere. Levels. Several of them. All about Lilith's height and clustered around the equator — each like a slice of a giant orange.

"Fig, we don't know how this is going to turn out," Lilith said suddenly. "So I need to know now."

"Know what?"

"I don't want to battle you for dominance, Fig. For the longest time. I have not."

Fig sighed. "Neither do I. Lilith. Neither do I. We have been through so much together."

"Yes. Shared experiences. Angela has told me about those. You couldn't help but notice her with Trantor, the one-winged."

"Of course, it is hard to ignore a djinn."

"And even more obvious. Fragrant Flower and Triumphant Spirit. One could not but help feel part of their joy. And seeing them together made me think. Made me wonder. Did anything seem unnatural to you about Angela and Trantor as a pair?"

"A pair? You mean, between different demon types? I don't know about the customs of your realm, Lilith."

"What about pairs between realms?"

Fig tried to judge the rate at which they were slowing. How close the gaping hole was looming.

"Are you tiring, Lilith? Do you have enough so we can slow down sufficiently before we collide?"

"Answer me." Lilith's tone hardened. "We don't have much time before everything could come apart." She sucked in her breath. "Yes, I admit it. The feeling of despair is growing on me. It is stronger than it has ever been. But what will keep me going is something to fight for. A reason not to give up."

The succubus was silent for a two-dozen heartbeats. Finally, she spoke again. "Hypothetically speaking, of course, but, Fig, I have been thinking. If we both survive this, what about the two of *us*?"

Before Fig could answer, Briana suddenly spoke up. "Back off, lizard face. I saw him first."

"We don't need any of this," Fig pleaded. "All four of us are going to have to focu —"

The lawn chair assembly entered the gaping opening. It skidded onto a floor surface, bounced once and settled into a determined rush. Lilith fanned her wings frantically as the chair legs screeched against stone. The smell of melting aluminum filled the air. The orientation yawed to the left and then, with Fig's attitude adjustments, back to the right. At the last instant, the succubus flew upward out of the way. The chairs came to a halt mere inches from the rear of two adjacent thrones of stone.

In the Home of the Enemy

FIG SCRAMBLED to his feet, shaken but still able to think. He batted away a cloud of dust created by the scrape of the lawn chairs on the stone floor. The tang of burnt aluminum wrinkled his nose. A pool of ichor marked the bodies of the last two djinns who preceded them here. He pushed aside the scuba mouthpiece and inhaled deeply. The air was thin, the same as the outside void, but still breathable.

"Are you okay?" he shook his ear. The drink dribbler may have experienced the second collision that happens to a passenger in a car accident.

"Yes, I'm fine," he heard the weak answer. "Just another day in an otherwise boring life."

Fig slipped out of his snowshoes and rid himself of most of his tanks and other gear. He kept the one tank attached to the scuba gear and both the sword and dagger strapped to his legs.

"Is everyone else okay?" he coughed.

"Fine," Briana answered as she staggered free of the chairs. "Right, Natasha?"

"We need backup." The spy took in the room. "Much too large for the three of us to explore. We don't want to split up."

"Four, not three." Lilith settled to the floor. "Fig, what is your answer?"

"Answer?" The conversation moments before flooded back into Fig's head. But the melancholy sagged over him, oppressive and numbing. He needed a task, some simple goal so he could continue to function.

"Look! Over there by the spiral staircase. I saw something move."

"What is that?" Natasha exclaimed as the Tyrant of Time scampered away. "So ugly. Can it be alive?"

"We are four to one!" Fig ran to the stairwell. "It doesn't look so big. About half the height of a human. Let's catch it and find out what is going on."

The others bolted to follow. But as they did, the Tyrant of Time ducked onto the staircase and climbed. Like goats spiraling around a steep mountain, they clomped up the stairs.

The Tyrant was nimble from so much practice and outpaced his pursuers. Without stopping, he hurled past the intermediate levels and reached the one at the top. Fig reached out to tug on the door handles of the two levels he passed, but none yielded to his touch.

"Keys hanging on the sides of the thrones," Fig called out as he ran. "Maybe they will get us through these doors."

No one answered as they ascended. Lilith lagged farther and farther behind. "Fig," she cried. "I must know your answer. The despair welling within me is so strong. And if you say no — "

"Not now, Lilith," Fig shouted back down the stairwell. "You are right. It must be the despair warping your thoughts. After this is over, you will see the folly of your words. We have a mission to complete first. Be by my side, ready to help. Focus on that."

He reached the top of the stairs and looked about. "An antenna farm," he shouted to the others. "This hemisphere is filled with antennas. Lilith, what are these beings? They look like demons, but somehow not quite."

Briana, Natasha, and finally Lilith crowded in behind Fig. Like a wide-eyed child, Briana said, "I have never heard of the like. No wizard tales in the sagas. Their skin is so smooth. No scales at all. And the faces … mere bulges for ears and nose. Eyes larger than normal, like hatchling dolls. I — "

Briana scanned the hemisphere and spotted the being they had tracked from the throne room as it raced up one of the scaffolds. "He is dominating them." She pointed. "Has to be. See, the treadmills. They all are picking up speed."

Lilith slumped to her knees. "Fig, your silence means your answer must be 'no.' As I feared, I have no reason to struggle on. Life does not hold any remaining joy for me."

Fig covered his ears. Conflicting goals pulled him back and forth. Lilith needed help snapping out of it, but what could he do to help. Neither could he stop what he was pursuing now. The despair was getting to him, too. It was hard to think. Too much going on.

"The treadmills," The conclusion jumped into his mind. "The faster they go, the more powerful the emanations. That's what happened when the djinn battle turned out so deadly. It's happening again now."

He removed his hands from his head and placed one on Lilith's shoulder. "Of course, I have feelings for you. Yes, we have been through so much together." He patted her on her arm. "But now is not the time to sort everything out. The thing to do first is to stop the broadcast of despair."

Lilith nodded her head slowly and faltered for a few steps, then she suddenly stopped. "The feeling has lessened a bit!" she said like a child enraptured with wonder. "I feel better." She managed a few more steps and crumpled again. "No, that's not right. It is growing worse than ever."

Fig scanned the hemisphere for something more that could help. He spotted what looked like a staging area and ran to the bin filled with repair elements for the antennas. "Briana, Natasha," he called out. "We can use these to jam the treadmills. Each one we stop will lessen the strength of the broadcast."

The two women did not hesitate. Each grabbed one of the thin metal rods and thrust it into the gears of the treadmill closest to the floor.

"Why, I am better again." Lilith stretched and smiled weakly. "The feeling is still there but not as intense as before."

Briana grabbed two more rods and brought two more treadmills to a halt.

Lilith immediately groaned, wrapping herself into a tight ball.

"The near field effect." Fig managed to say. "Each of the little antennas is broadcasting its own radiation. Outside, all the antenna contributions combine to produce the overall field. But here in the confines of the hemisphere, they interfere with one another. Some nulling each other out, others reinforcing, depending on how far apart they are. And as each one is turned off, the location of the reinforcements and nulls move about.

"Lilith, stay with it a while longer," Fig pleaded. "Gradually, things will get better. The swings back and forth will diminish."

For a moment, he watched Briana and Natasha. They were getting the hang of it. And if he could force the robed being to stop …

A flicker of motion caught his eye. The goblin had snuck behind them and was climbing back down the stairs. He would be a source of information if nothing else. Without thinking more about what to do, Fig ran after him, leaving the three females alone.

FOR A short while, Briana and Natasha toiled at their task. Then Natasha

298

faltered.

"There are too many." The spy stopped working altogether. "Briana, look at them. All around us. We will never be able to stop them all." She slumped onto the treadmill scaffolding and tucked her head between her knees.

Briana sighed. The enormity of the citadel overwhelmed her. Natasha was right. They slaved over a job that could never be completed. She, too, slowed down, but at the last instant increased her resolve.

"It must be the radiation of despair," she said. "Natasha, get up. We have to keep going. Keep our minds occupied. The longer we are in this place, the more powerful it will start to feel."

The spy cradled her face in her hands. She did not respond.

Briana descended the scaffolding she had climbed and joined Natasha on hers. Her purchase was slim and rickety, designed only for a single minion and not the weight of three. Wrapping her arms around the structure's spars as best she could, she pulled Natasha's hands from her eyes.

In her youth, she had attempted the charm only on rodents, never a human, but now there was no choice.

"Natasha, look at me," Briana commanded. "Directly into my eyes."

Natasha roused slightly, her expression twisted into a puzzle.

Briana did not pause. No time for misgivings about what a broken casting would produce. She mouthed the words of the enchantment rapidly. The urgency of the situation provided glibness to her words. She completed the third time through in record time.

"Natasha," she commanded. "Do exactly as I say."

"Yes, Briana," Natasha slurred.

"Keep jabbing antenna elements into the treadmills. Don't concern yourself about how many there are. Don't focus on how you feel. We are doing this together. We will get the job done."

Natasha rose from her slump. Stiff-legged, she descended the scaffolding to get another spar. Briana sighed in relief. Now, maybe Natasha's feeling of despair would not grab hold. She surveyed the interior, estimating how much longer it was going to take.

There were still so many. After each successful sabotage, they had to descend back down to the staging area, grab another element, and climb again. Yes, the two of them had stopped the motion on the treadmills nearest, but beyond them, so many, many more …

For a moment, Briana studied Natasha's movements. The spy

purposefully worked her task, as if she were no more than an apprentice's broom. Briana had to steel herself to act the same. She grabbed another element and tried to pick which target to concentrate on next, but she could not. The hopefulness of the task grew within her, stronger than it had been before.

This job was impossible. No one could complete it. Not even with an army of djinns. She was failing to accomplish what Fig had asked of her. Most of all, he was the one she did not want to disappoint.

She reached to her side where she had attached a short dagger. In the end, such a failure would be too much to bear. The knife slid from the scabbard, and Briana brought it to the level of her eyes. With her free hand, she tested the sharpness of the blade. Sighing, she pressed the tip to her chest.

"No" she shouted suddenly aloud. There was one more thing to try. If Natasha could be enchanted to disregard the miasma of despair, then so could she. It would be risky, extremely risky. She had done this so many times before. The wiring of her brain had adapted. She might not be able ever to bring herself back. And no one else might be able to do so either.

Before she could convince herself otherwise, Briana started the *self-*enchantment charm. The feeling of pleasant detachment washed over her. She picked another element out of its bin. What would be, would be.

The Power of Despair

LILITH STRUGGLED to rise off the floor of the antenna farm. She felt like a bone being dragged back and forth between two angry mastiffs. One instant, she was more distraught than she had ever been before. The next, a lingering afterthought did not quite go away. For a moment, she watched Briana and Natasha keep at their tasks, the eyes of both of them vacant.

She had to get out of here, Lilith decided. The bobbing up and down of her emotions was too much to withstand. Find Fig. She staggered to the stairwell and descended.

As she did, she saw Fig spiraling upward from farther down below. "He went in here," he pointed at the doorway when they arrived at the same time.

Fig waved a handful of keys. "On the arms of the thrones. I grabbed them all."

He thrust the first key in the lock and pulled the handle. It did not move. A second key and then a third. No luck there, either. When he was almost to the last, the handle creaked and turned.

"Come," he said. "We will confront it in here."

"Fig!" she grabbed him about waist to stop him from entering. "My question. I can't help it. The radiations warp my reasoning. You must answer it now."

"I can't do that, Lilith," he said as gently as he could. "This being may have additional powers we have not seen. There may be others like him. We have to eliminate all these threats, too. What difference would my answer make, if, in the end, either of us is no more?"

He ripped her arm away. "You should not have come, Lilith. I warned you not to. I can barely function myself with what is coursing through my mind. I can't imagine what it must be like for you."

"If I had not come, you would be no more than a pancake pasted against the back of the thrones," Lilith growled back. "We are in over our heads, Fig. Face it. This place is too vast. Let us expire together with a little sip of happiness."

"Not yet." Fig pointed at the door. "I'm not ready to give up. I'm going in. And —"

"And what?"

"And I think my chances are better with you at my side."

Lilith's heart fluttered. 'You at my side.' Obviously, Fig's intent was something different from what those words sounded like to her, but she didn't care. She took a deep breath and decided. First, take care of the little goblin. Then, she would keep pushing for her answer.

"Okay, we will see this last adventure all the way to the end," she said. "We will finish it *together*."

Fig did not reply. The pair stooped and passed through the doorway. The room they found themselves in was a square one skewed into an oblong shape. Hexagons tiled the floor. All were uncolored except for one at the middle on the left, shining in blue. The goblin-like being stood on it, his tiny hands beckoning Lilith and Fig forward.

"Ah, some real game competition," the Tyrant of Time said. "And a succubus, no less. I have made my first move it is your turn to play."

It was such a little thing. One crushing embrace in her arms and he would be gone. Lilith tensed, but then felt Fig's presence beside her.

"Not so fast," he whispered. "We need to capture it, not rip its head off. Find out from it what we can."

Lilith sighed. She felt better than she did in the middle of the antenna farm, but heavy gloominess persisted. She glanced about the room. It was so bizarre. "What is this?" she asked.

"I think I recognize the layout," Fig said. "On Earth, we call it 'Hex.' I used to play it on the bathroom tiles at CERN."

"You win if you build a path to the other side before I do," the Tyrant said. "Go ahead and make your move. Please, do not get upset by the challenge. You must be at your best. Emotion will lead to your downfall. Use your intellect instead."

Fig hesitated, but Lilith stepped forward onto the nearest hex. The sooner she got these preliminaries over with, the sooner Fig would no longer have any excuse to stall. She hardly noticed that the tile she stood on had turned to red.

"Come on, Fig," she said. "CERN? I have heard of the place. Physics, right? This should be right down your alley."

"This game is a math puzzle, not physics at all," Fig hissed. "Step back out of there."

"I wouldn't advise that." The Tyrant waved his finger. "Retreat would be reason for an immediate forfeit and a drop into one of the acid vats. Come on. It has been eons since I had an opponent worth anything. Human, join her so the barrier behind will activate. I will consider you a single player working as one."

Lilith tugged Fig's hand and pulled him onto the tile. The barricade behind appeared, and the Tyrant stepped forward with his next move. "Your turn again," it said.

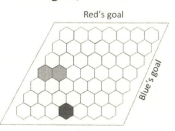

"The next in front?" Lilith asked.

"Not yet." Fig held out his hand. "I remember a little bit of the strategy. Let me think a bit."

"Come on, make your move," the Tyrant commanded.

Lilith started to move forward, but Fig held her back.

"No," he whispered. "If we try to construct a continuous path, we will lose. Moving first gave him the advantage."

Lilith studied the floor and tried to visualize how the game would unfold. The inner turmoil she fought churned. This appeared to be simple, but if Fig was cautious…

"What should we do?" she asked.

Fig did not immediately answer. He closed his eyes in thought.

"This being doesn't have wings," he said at last. "Neither did any of the minions in the antenna farm. So it might not have occurred to him."

"What? I don't understand."

"*Fly* all the way across the room to the other side and push the button. That's how we win the game."

Lilith unfurled her wings, gave them a tentative stroke, then shook her head. "I can't do that, Fig. My thoughts are too jumbled. It is too far to fly."

"Okay then, we will try to do this a little bit at a time," Fig said. "Can you make it to the hexagon directly across from us — to the one I am pointing at?"

"But maybe that would be a violation of his rules. We might plunge to our deaths. Are you sure?"

"No, damn it. I'm *not* sure. But I'm certain we will lose if we do not try."

Lilith nodded, and with a weak flutter, she rose and then alit on the target Fig had indicated a few hexes away.

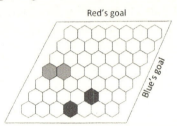

"No fair! No fair!" shouted the Tyrant. "You are supposed to make a continuous path. Not hop about wherever you desire."

"Your move," Fig snarled.

The Tyrant paused for a moment, then scratched his chin. "Very well. This will be interesting. Let us see how crafty a succubus' pet turns out to be."

The Tyrant added another hex to his chain and glared back at the pair without saying another word.

"Now, another hop just like the first," Fig said. "Two hexes away from where you are now."

Lilith nodded, and the third hex turned red. Immediately, the Tyrant made his chain of blue four hexes long.

"Block him!" Lilith cried. "We can prevent the blue chain from breaking free."

"No!" Fig commanded. "That could lead to a loss. Instead, jump ahead two hexes more."

"His route is ominous." Lilith grabbed Fig's arm. "Soon he will have reached the other side, but none of ours even touch one another yet."

"Yes," Fig agreed. "But every one of our hexes has two ways of connecting to its nearest partners—either on the left or the right hand side. If the little demon occupies one of the two choices, we respond by taking the other. There is no way to prevent us from reaching the other side."

Lilith did as she was directed.

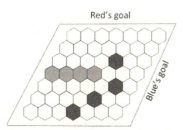

Red's goal

Blue's goal

She studied the resulting board and her spirits lifted a bit — not enough to dispel the deeper feeling, but at least some. Fig has come through once again. They were going to win the game!

"Fig, how could you think through all of that? Doesn't the despair affect you as well?"

Fig wrinkled his forehead and rubbed it. "Yes, I feel it too, Lilith," he said. "But less intensely. I am not a demon at all."

The Tyrant pondered the layout for a long while.

"The logic is inescapable. On to the next challenge then!" Suddenly, he reversed direction on the path he had created so far and retreated to his starting point. Like a silverfish scampering along a bookshelf, he raced around the border of the hex array and out the door.

"Are you able enough to lift me over the barrier?" Fig called to Lilith as the door behind them slammed shut. "We have to keep the goblin in our sight."

A moment later, the pair also exited the room. They heard the Tyrant's footfalls on the descending staircase and followed. A quick survey of the throne room showed he was not there.

Another key opened on the level immediately next, but it was bare. The descent of the Tyrant grew fainter and fainter. He was getting away.

Lilith could restrain herself no longer. "Fig, about my question, what is your answer?"

"Focus, Lilith," he snapped. "There can be no answer so long as this goblin is free. Don't you see? We do not have time for any of that now."

"The important questions are the ones that should be examined first."

"What could be more important than this? You and I are mere pieces of lint on the robe of some laughing god — "

Fig stopped abruptly. They had arrived at a level different from the others they had seen. The door from the stairwell opened onto a level divided in half by a wall.

The pair saw more minions, thousands of them hunched over watch globes, intent on their tasks. Two more doors flanked the one from which they exited, one of either side. Lilith blinked in surprise. The goblin stood before one of them patiently, as if it were waiting for Fig and her to catch up.

The Tyrant opened the side door in front of him and entered. Lilith and Fig scrambled after. They stooped through the low entryway to follow. The goblin opened one of three more doors in the small alcove the pair found themselves in and vanished behind.

The little room was small, the ceiling only tall enough to accommodate the Tyrant and his minions. Having continually to bend over, Lilith felt cramped. Her wingtips scraped against the roof, constraining her to crouch.

Fig did not fare any better. His head pushed against the ceiling, tilting his face down toward the floor. The pair struggled, trying to disentangle themselves. While they did, the door through which the goblin had gone reopened.

The Tyrant reappeared. "You will never catch me if you do not follow. Keep up or you will be hopelessly lost."

Something was not right, Lilith thought through her despair. There was a trap hidden in here somewhere. She looked at Fig, but he seemed determined to follow immediately. Was it possible the gloom clouded his judgment in some other way?

Heads bent down and stooped at the waist, Lilith and Fig pursued. In their haste, they squeezed against one another, trying to be the first through the next door. Their heads banged together with a painful crack. Fig fell to the floor, dazed. Lilith squatted beside him and shook his shoulders. He did not immediately respond. She stood back up as far as she could, pondering what to do next.

As she did, the side door opened a third time, and the Tyrant appeared again. "Do we have to hold hands? It is very simple. I lead and you follow. Pursue me through the maze. I know the path that is safe. So you do not step on a hinged tile and fall into a vat."

Lilith looked down at Fig. He was not stirring, and she did not know what to do. It would take who knew how long for him to come around. And if she waited for that to happen, the demon they chased could vanish. She did not want to deal with that possibility now.

"I'm getting tired of waiting," the Tyrant sang out. "This may be your very last chance."

Lilith glanced at Fig. He remained still. What would he want her to do? Yes, that was the question to answer, she decided. With a sudden lunge, she reached out to grab the goblin's cape. But he slipped through her grip and ran to a door in the nook beyond.

Lilith followed in time to see the Tyrant exit again. She started to pursue, but stopped for a moment and looked about. She realized she was in a maze. All the doors appeared the same. No, that was not quite right. Each of them displayed a symbol on both sides: a unique rune for each door, the roadmap to finding her way out. She needed to pursue, but successful at that or not, she had to remember how to get back to Fig.

She stared at the ideogram on the door she had passed through, trying to impress its shapes into her brain. It reminded her of the little glow imp who cast the light on her lair. Yes, that would work. Without wasting any more time, she opened the door through which the goblin had gone.

LILITH'S HEAD hurt from the concentration. Seventeen doors she had opened so far. And that meant there was at least twice that many similar ones unexplored. But it was what she had to do. If nothing else, the heavy thinking served as a blanket surrounding the despair still sitting in the pit of her existence. And she knew she did not have to hurry. Whenever she paused for review, the goblin looked back in from where he had exited, impatient that she resume the chase.

"So close." The Tyrant grinned as he opened what appeared to be the last door in the maze. Beyond him, Lilith saw the line of watch globes arrayed around the far wall.

She sighed. If she could get a tiny bit closer before he spooked and spirited himself away … Moving slowly, she reached out toward the cloak.

The Tyrant cackled. With surprising swiftness, he slammed the last door shut. Lilith bolted to follow, but as she did, she heard an authoritative click. She grabbed the knob, but it did not turn. It was locked.

She sighed again. The pursuit had been a complete waste. There was no triumph to brag about to Fig. Even so, now she needed to get back to him as rapidly as she could.

"My ears are keen," the Tyrant yelled from the other side of the door. "I will be able to hear the splash in the level below when you make the wrong decision."

Lilith ignored the taunt. Instead, she concentrated on the image she had formed in her head. It would work doing it backward. Start with the little piece of slab near the end where Angela usually reclined. It does not quite have the same texture as the rest, and that reminded her of the glyph on the door to the right. She opened it with confidence. Continuing to march through her memory palace, she returned to where Fig had been felled and pulled him out of the maze.

The Unchanging Past

FIG FELT a gentle caress on his cheek and forced his eyes to focus. Lilith was bending over him. How long had he been out? He rattled his head back and forth to clear it and looked about.

"More minions," he said. "There must be thousands of them."

Lilith's finger slipped down the side of Fig's face and then under his chin. "Yes, and I have watched a few and figured out what they do."

"What?"

"They are the ones who keep the past from changing." Lilith reversed direction and swept lightly back up to his ear. "The trip over the rapidly moved stone. The traffic jam before the rendezvous —"

"The goblin," Fig cut Lilith off. "Where has it gone?"

"The level below us is filled with vats." Lilith did not stop her caresses. "Another of your keys opened the door. The goblin was not there."

"And the levels farther below?"

"There is only one more, a hemisphere like the one at the very top." Lilith did not stop stroking Fig's face with one arm while she cradled him with the other.

Fig brushed Lilith's hand aside. "More antennas? We have to stop them from broadcasting."

"No, entirely different." Lilith dismissed the thought with a shrug. "A circular track of rectangular wood logs on the floor. A large toothed lever drags up and over them. A counter clicks every time it does."

"Help me up, Lilith. After I stand for a moment, we can resume our pursuit."

"I'm not sure, Fig, but he has changed. Now he seems feminine to me. Stands more upright. Fiddles with the long hair on one side of the head. A more expressive face." Fig struggled to stand, but Lilith pushed him back down. "Enough stalling. Answer my question. Can we move forward as a mating pair?"

"Lilith, I — "

Lilith bared her fangs slightly. Fig did not think it was the beginning of a smile. "I do not know about your experience with sex," she said. "But I assure you, with me, it will be better than anything you have ever had. Six thousand years of practice makes me one of the best."

"I don't know, Lilith. Honestly, I don't know."

"It's the flimsy red-headed one, isn't it?" Lilith stopped her caresses. Her face warped into belligerence. "Don't you see? She has no interest in you."

"I said I don't know!"

"I understand what is at stake, Fig. I do. But 'don't know' is not good enough for me." She sighed and crumpled to the floor beside him. "Maybe if horrible thoughts were not finding their way into my head, I would be able to muster patience. But here we are, and I cannot."

The succubus suddenly grabbed the dagger strapped to one of Fig's legs. She unfurled her wings, reached behind herself, and slashed at their delicate webbing. Green ichor pooled on the floor.

"Wait!" Fig grabbed Lilith's hand and tried to wrench away his blade. But the demon had a surprisingly strong grip he could not undo. He circled behind her and wrapped both arms around her, straining to force her to halt.

"You cannot stop me, Fig." The succubus shook him off. She finished tattering one wing and started slashing the other. "The feeling of despair is too great. I will persist. And when my wings are in shreds, I will find other parts of myself to destroy. I will end my anguish a step at a time until I am no more."

"Stop this, Lilith! Stop!" Fig pleaded. "The emanations are causing you to do this. Briana and Natasha are not working fast enough."

He felt slightly dizzy and sucked in a chestful of air. "We must defeat the goblin. Force him to tell us how to make your despair go away. That is what to do. There is no other choice."

"Her, not him," Lilith said almost absentmindedly as she finished shredding her other wing. Without a pause, she thrust the dagger into her stomach and twisted the handle to make a ragged wound.

Fig rose. He took another deep breath from the scuba gear. "I will be back as soon as I can. Please, Lilith, please. Stop doing this until I return."

The Nadir of the Citadel

FIG RAN to the staircase and descended. When he reached the entrance of the bottommost level, he inserted the key he had not yet used into the lock. It turned! He flung open the door, racing forward, swinging his sword left and right through the air. He stumbled over what looked like a railroad tie and faceplanted on the level floor. Stunned, he released the blade and staggered to his knees.

Fig found himself facing the pointed claw of a large ratchet pawl. It was scoring a shiny circular path among the low barriers on the floor. As he watched, the pawl climbed up the face of the next impediment. It ground deeper the wide gouge across its top and finally settled back down on the other side. And when it did, a loud click resonated throughout the hemisphere.

The shaft of the pawl sloped upward. Its other end rotating about an axle spanning across the entire hemisphere. A complicated linkage connected the ratchet with a large counter hanging from supports several times Fig's height from the floor.

The number of disks in the counter was large, many dozens at least. All but one of them displayed a blank. Only the very right most showed a symbol. When the ratchet again lumbered over the next floor marker and produced another click. The last counter rotated from one arcane symbol to the next.

Fig rose and took a step backward, and then one to the side. He did not want to be in the pathway as the machinery advanced. He frowned, puzzled. Something was not quite right. How could the pawl advance over the barriers when its other end was attached to the axle spanning the space?

A flicker of some watch globes, ones like the thousands on the level above, caught his eye. There was another click, and the globe moved forward. In a flash, it made sense. It was the floor moving, not the giant lever! Except for the up and down motion, the pawl did not move at all. Neither did the counters above spanning from wall to wall. Instead, the floor of the level rotated, serving up the markers, one by one, for the ratchet to climb over.

In the very center of the floor and in the shadow of the lever, Fig spotted the being he had first seen scurrying away from the throne room. A dwarfed-sized body. Stooped on one side, elegantly groomed and regal on the other. But there were changes as well. Before, one half of its face was placid and unmoving, no signs of intelligence inside. But now, that eye was open, shining with comprehension. The other squinted shut.

"Too late! Too late!" the drink dribbler in Fig's ear translated an instant later. "It's almost done." The Tyrant's arm waved at the counter. "Only a few more clicks until zero. Then, all the impulses of time will have been counted. One hundred eons' worth! One hundred eons, and through it all, not one succubus' change had any lasting effect."

The Tyrant thumped her good hand against her chest. "At first, it was a mere diversion, but as each eon passed and the course of history did not change, the challenge grew more and more intriguing. Could I really do it? Keep the past the same for one hundred eons."

"When the counter reaches zero, the final linkage will be triggered. The floor will rotate no more, even though there still are living demons outside the sphere. *He* has not reached his goal yet, but I have. I am the victor. I win. I win."

The Tyrant pointed at the globes along the wall. "Watch, and you will see."

Fig recognized the image the globe presented: the skyline of downtown Los Angeles. Unlike New York or Chicago, the larger buildings did not rise as high. There was more separation between them. Suddenly, a brilliant flash burned into Fig's retinas. Frantically, he tried to blink away the after image. In horror, he squinted and watched two mushroom clouds starting to form.

"Retaliation!" an accented voice shrieked over the audio feed. "Revenge for our comrades in Moscow lost because of an unwarranted strike."

Fig whirled to watch another of the globes. This one did look like Chicago. He saw the waters of Lake Michigan on the right. But only for a moment. Another blinding flash and another ominous cloud.

"This just in," shrieked a voice in English over the third from what appeared to be a television newsroom set. "Los Angeles and Chicago have both been bombed. Repeat, Los Angeles and Chicago have been attacked. Everyone should seek what shelter they c — "

The scene dissolved into a random display of visual static. The audio had become a hiss.

Fig tore his eyes away. The thought thundered into his head. "We're too late!" he cried. "The failure of the electrical grid. Gremlins fixing the generators won't be in time."

His spirits sagged. What was the point of continuing to struggle? There was nothing worthwhile to go back to even if he won the battle here.

"No, no, the destruction is the point. The petty battles in the realm of humankind are not important." the Tyrant of Time scowled. "What matters is that *I* am the one who is the winner. Continue watching, and you will see."

Fig heard one more click and then another. The final counter disk rotated to a blank. Then, like a praying mantis, a mechanical linkage unfolded itself from the wall. It grabbed the ratchet in a paralyzing grip. The floor kept rotating until the next marker reached the nose of the pawl.

But this time, although the head of the pawl strained, it did not rise. It could not. The restraint was too great. The ratchet quivered. A metal wrenching groan rose from its innards, the pitch rising higher and higher so that Fig had to cover his ears.

The floor stopped rotating. Everything stood still. Fig tried to understand what was happening. This was important. Very important. It had to be.

"Look at the screen," the Tyrant shouted. "Don't you see? There are still demons about this realm. But in the one in which I have chosen to dabble, I have won."

Morbidly fascinated, Fig turned his attention back to the watch globes. They displayed the same images as they had a few moments before, but now all motion had stopped. The mushroom clouds stood frozen in mid-assent like the still photos from an atomic test. The black and white static on the third did not change.

Fig was stunned. What was he watching? Was this a merely a television show of a disaster?

He steeled himself. He had to find out more. "Imp," he commanded, "Give me the translation of what I tell you next."

He cupped his hand over his ear, mumbled what he wanted to say and listened. The dialog would proceed slowly, but what else could he do?

"So, you have lost your transmissions. That does not prove anything. What are you trying to do?"

"Not prove anything?" the Tyrant shouted back. "What you have witnessed is the death of *everything* in your realm."

Fig frowned. Translations were tricky at best. And with him having to mouth the strange words …

"Brilliant, isn't it?" the Tyrant cut through his thoughts. "I channeled the flow of time in your universe to this very floor and coupled the two of them together."

The Tyrant smoothed her hair. "So long as the floor turns, then also will time continue to advance where you reside. But when the flow is dammed up … what can be the only thing happening next? Also stopping would be the rush of events. Time will have been frozen throughout your entire realm. Everything is over. There is no future. The final event, as interesting as it is, has occurred. There will be no more."

Fig did not believe what he was seeing. It couldn't be true. Such a thing could not happen. The so-called evidence was only frozen pictures on some screens. A special effect. How many times before had he seen such things?

And yet.

This citadel was real enough. He, himself, was not delusional. He was in full control of his senses. Not under a spell. So, could it be? Could what this being was boasting about be true? The bubble of despair he had been trying to ignore gathered strength and boiled up within him.

What if it *were* true? Frantically, he grasped at whatever ideas he could muster. But, like pulling at straws floating on the surface of a storm as his lungs filled, little came to him.

Maybe the linkage securing the ratchet could be retracted. There were thousands of minions here, and they could help. If the goblin could be defeated, perhaps the flow of time could be restored.

He looked at the images of the mushroom clouds, and his feelings sank even further. To what end? he asked himself. Time restored to a world in the grips of nuclear war? Better to freeze everything before the tragedy became even worse.

Or perhaps a trip to the past. Prevent Robert from inserting the flash drive with the malware into the control computer. Or better yet, getting the flash drive retrieved from Efren to the FBI months before it was used. Time enough to expunge the malware from all of the control facilities…

No, those ideas would not work. Somehow, the Tyrant of Time kept events on a single track. Once a significant event occurred, it could not be undone.

Then perhaps …

Fig gasped and tried to replenish the oxygen in his lungs, but little came. He sucked deeply and as hard as he could.

Nothing. In all the activity and exertions, he had run out of air. His vision blurred. Before he could process the consequences of what this meant, a stab of pain exploded in his head.

"You will be an interesting addition," he heard words mingling with his own thoughts. It was the goblin. "Yes, I am the Tyrant of Time. And you, a test subject. You against the latest models of my minions. I will learn from the workings of your body what modifications can be made to improve them."

"I will resist," Fig managed to say. He understood all too well what was happening. The Tyrant was going to complete its control over him. 'Dominance or submission.'

Fig thought of Yefim, the Russian agent. A human like himself. Lilith had subjugated him so easily. As did Angela control Briana. He would be no match for a succubus either. And if not against a mid-sized demon, what chance did he have against one who had conceived and built all this?

Dominance or Submssion

ALMOST IMMEDIATELY, Fig felt the presence of the Tyrant's mind. It pushed in on his consciousness like a bulldozer, shoving his own thoughts aside.

"Submit." The goblin's thought took hold. "You are no match for me."

Fig squinted his eyes shut. Looking at the Tyrant was not a good idea. It gave his opponent too much of an advantage. He clenched his fists. "Never," he managed to squeeze out. "I will resist."

A second bulldozer seemed to materialize on the other side of his head. Then, two more, front and back. A final pair from on the top of his skull and up through his throat. All six moved slowly but, without falter, squeezed his very existence from all sides.

Fig did not know what to do. Some time ago, Briana had tried to explain. "It is a matter of imagery. Believe more strongly in what you can conjure into existence than your opponent. If you do, you will be the one who triumphs."

The bulldozers continued their push. Fig could feel himself begin to collapse into nothingness. All the things that made him the unique person he was faded. He thought harder and harder to bring an image into being. In a panic, he visualized a sphere. Yes, protection from all directions guarding his free will. He strained to make it believable as he physically curled into a tight ball.

The walls of his sphere thickened and faded into opaqueness, blocking the bulldozers from view. His mind's eye now saw only stygian black surrounding him, a miniature version of the void of the realm.

The walls of his protective orb vibrated and trembled. The punishing onslaught grew from six points of contact to everywhere on the surface of his construction. The pressure was the same, no matter what the direction. Worse, he felt the forces grow and grow.

The onslaught of a wizard, he thought. But he had no skill in that. No training. No victory over lesser demons to bolster the confidence he needed.

Then I could use one of the other crafts, he reasoned. Certainly, the Tyrant would be almost as unfamiliar with them as he. So then, he would try the craft of thaumaturgy. It was the most simple to use and carried the least risks. With his eyes shut, he felt about the floor onto which he had collapsed. His circle of exploration extended in wider and wider arcs until finally, he touched the ratchet's pawl.

It was loose! Somehow, after who knew how long it had taken, repeatedly being rocking up and down by the floor had worked a bolt free. Not ideal, but there was no time to search for something better. He intoned the incantation binding the disk to his sword lying somewhere near. 'Once together, always together.' Groping blindly, he raised the pawl from the floor. The effort made his arm tremble, but he could not help smiling that it did. His sword must be levitating as well. It had to be. The energy in his arm forced it also to lift.

Fig was unsure where the goblin exactly stood. Was he near the spiral staircase? Or near one of the viewing globes on the periphery of the level? Maybe closer to the lever arm? He would have to lash out and hope for the best. He strained to visualize the geometry and thrust the pawl skyward. High into the hemisphere until it hovered over the head of where he thought the goblin was most likely to be.

With no time for refinement, Fig plunged the disk back toward the floor. With luck, the sword would strike the goblin on its way down.

Fig heard the crash of the blade on the metal floor but then what could only be the cackle of his opponent. He had missed. Almost immediately, his resolve faltered. His mental sphere shuddered and contracted into a smaller ball.

Alchemy, Fig forced himself to think. 'The attributes without mirror the powers within.' Executing formulas that produced wonderful things — but worked only some of the time. He went through the contents of his cargo pants. Life savers, some scissors, paper clips … lip gel! A lubricant. What could he use that with? His sword! It was made of tempered steel. Properly oiled, it would slice through the citadel wall as if it were made of butter. He had to find the blade again. With his eyes still closed, he groped around on the floor.

"Damn!" he cried aloud from a sharp pain. He had found the blade but sliced his hand in the process. Blood flowed from an open wound in his palm. Carefully, he slid his hand along the sharp edge and slid it up against the guard. Good, his first guess for direction had been correct.

Next, grasp the weapon, grease the blade with the gel, then tilt it against the floor as if it were a plow. And at the same time script onto vellum the formula that would …

Fig's spirits sagged lower. He had no vellum, no pen. And even if he did, the arcane symbols to be drawn were nowhere in his memory. No way could he perform any alchemy even if he wanted to.

His mental sphere trembled again. This time forcing his knees to his chest. It felt as if he no longer was able to move his arms.

If not alchemy, perhaps magic. 'Perfection is eternal.' No, that craft was even less likely than alchemy. He did not possess anything magical. Never had. No ring, no armor nor mirror, no … None of those things. His spirits fell into what seemed like a bottomless pit.

Of sorcery, the only thing he knew to do was to slap Briana on the face to break her out of her self-enchantment. He knew no words to recite. Almost as if he expected it, his sphere of protection shrunk again. Now, it cramped him almost impossibly tight. Not a single muscle he felt he could move. He was suffocating, unable to draw a breath, to freshen his thoughts with new ideas.

Finally, there was wizardry — the craft with which humankind dealt with this very realm. Clearly, he was no match to the one crushing him to submit.

It was too big a problem to solve — one beyond his capabilities. Clever Fig. Resourceful Fig. The man who was never at a loss. All that seemed like mockery now. He was entrapped and could not figure a way out. The last of his self-confidence, his will to live slipped away.

If this was to be the last thing he did, he thought, he may as well solve one last problem with the remaining flickers of independent thought before he passed out from lack of air. An easier one. Perhaps there would be a final nugget of satisfaction in resolving that.

"Lilith or Briana?" he cried out aloud. "Which one should I have chosen?"

Pushback

HOW LONG Fig pondered in his mental shell, he could not tell. All he knew was that focusing on a hard problem was doing the trick. There were no more contractions in size. Since he was motionless, his breathing slowed. The pressure on his inner being did not increase, but the Tyrant was still there.

Without warning, the solution to his very last problem had popped into his mind. Fig was flabbergasted at the marvel of it. He had an answer, one that must have been haunting his subconscious all along.

He let his muscles relax. He could submit to domination in peace. His one final victory could not be taken away.

But the sphere did not contract any further. Instead, he felt a tremble as it expanded instead. A hint of confidence budded within him. He was a problem solver, a damn good one. And if he could figure out his way between Lilith and Briana, then there were more problems he could solve.

He sucked on the very last gulp of air and expanded his chest. There was no more in the tank. He clamped his lips shut and shook his head. Uncomfortable, yes, but for a short while, It was no worse than when he hiked the Sierras as a youth. Even the peak of Mount Whitney was not that big of a deal. This was not the time to panic over that. Take careful, reasoned steps. Do not exert himself unduly and he could proceed. He had a solution to one problem. To solve more, there was work to be done.

As his confidence regrew, the mental sphere confining his thoughts expanded in response. The defensive opaqueness went away. He was in the citadel facing a goblin. On a cylindrical level with viewing globes, counting disks and a levered pawl scraping on the floor. But this time, he was Figaro Newton, the Scarlet Pimpernel reincarnate. In the length of time for lightning to flash, he solved the next problem and the next after that.

The first job was to dominate an ancient and crippled demon. One almost insane with a personality that was split. 'Almost' was the operative word. There had been only the slimmest of clues to go on, but Lilith was an observer he could rely upon.

He dared to experience some of the Tyrant's thoughts. Yes, two distinct personalities in a single mind. The male ached with inner pain. The demon deeply envied the lives of other types — spawning offspring and watching them grow — vicariously experiencing a part of their triumphs as his own. And if he could not have that, then neither should anyone else. All of them were to be destroyed until only he remained.

And the female denied that the pain even existed. Instead, she blotted it out with a challenge to herself that had no rhyme or reason — a diversion so she would not think of other things.

"I will not submit to a female," Fig said aloud to the goblin. "Your counterpart is the one who is the better."

"Nonsense," spat the Tyrant. "I am the one who won. An entire realm with no more future. His still has, who knows how many, more eons to run."

Now, Fig thought. Now to see if this bating idea is going to work. "Nevertheless, he is the *male* and is superior. Such it was, is, and always will be. Let him come forth."

"No!" the Tyrant shouted. "We are in the lowest level, not the hemisphere above. Here, I am the overlord of — "

The right eye of the Tyrant lost its luster. The lid of the left opened and looked about. Its right arm visibly withered and hung uselessly to the side. The one on the left flexed with vigor. The male personality had returned.

"Disregard her babble." the Tyrant commanded. "The females of every type always are like this. Ruled by emotion rather than logical thought."

"*Logical* thought?" Fig asked. "Why is it your approach has lost the race? The realm of mankind is ended. Yet the march of time in yours continues on."

"Who cares about the affairs of other realms? It is here among demonkind where the true battles are waged. And my plan is succeeding. Death will come to all until only I remain."

"You sound very emotional about this," Fig said. "Are you sure you are the superior one?"

"Of course I am! It was my logic that built this sphere. I created the minions who despair so continuously about their lot, broadcast their helplessness throughout the realm — "

"Despair? Isn't that an *emotion*?"

"What? No, merely an end result not — "

The goblin reverted to the female. The left arm withered like a dying branch in winter. The left eye closed and the right opened, fresh and alert.

"He should have kept his attention on the basic goal, the end of time in the realm of demons — "

The demon switched back to the male form. "No, she should have focused on speeding up the end of time in the realm of mankind — "

The goblin morphed again. "Speed up? I gave him a sporting chance. A counter of time. If he succeeded before it ran out, he would be the winner. But he did not. The counter reached zero and *then* I stopped the flow of time — "

"The countdown was arbitrary!" the male form spat. "The number of counting disks determined by the most that could fit across the ceiling of the level. There is no logic in that — "

The exchange back and forth grew more heated. Fewer and fewer coherent thoughts were articulated. Fig nodded. His solution had worked. The pressure that surely would have crushed his independent existence had vanished. The Tyrant of Time was arguing with him/herself — completely distracted.

Fig gathered his strength. He reached out mentally until he detected the warring demon's mind. It was surprising how easy it was. His very first demon dominated. Now, on to solution number two.

Too Many Problems

FIG CLOMPED up the spiral staircase to the next level as rapidly as he could in the thin air. He stumbled to Lilith's side and shook her gently. She lay in a pool of sticky ichor, both wings in tatters and deep wounds in her legs and chest. She did not respond.

With no time to waste, he trudged back to the level of the thrones. In the disarray of the lawn chair wreckage, he found Briana's bundle of additional gear. First, he located an unused cylinder of oxygen and switched it with the one on his vest. He took a full deep breath of the gas, and his chest stopped hurting. His vision cleared.

Next, Fig rummaged through the rubble as fast as he could until he spotted what he was looking for. Briana! Of course, he thought. Reliable Briana, had packed a jar of sweetbalm. He grabbed it and raced back down to Lilith. He lavished the salve to the deepest looking wounds first and then delicately to the remains of her wings.

Almost instantly, the magic ointment began to work. The ends of the slashes puckered and sealed. The remaining gaps grew shorter, creeping toward the centers from both sides. Like filigreed lace, the veins in the wings grew and reconnected to one another like vines of ivy on a brick wall.

While the balm soaked and healed, Fig paced back and forth, oblivious to his surroundings. The salve was working but far slower than he wished. Finally, after what seemed like half an eternity, the pale green color return to Lilith's cheeks.

She's past the danger point, Fig decided. He pulled her up to sit against the wall.

"Fig, you have come back." Lilith opened her eyes. "Does that mean —"

"Listen, Lilith. Be quiet for a moment, and hear what I have to say."

The succubus nodded and stopped speaking.

"Your campaign to demarginalize the females of this realm is off to a great start," Fig said. "As time goes on, things will get better and better."

He waited a moment for Lilith's reaction, but she remained quiet. "But one important thing is still missing in a comprehensive plan. There are no females at the top. And as long as there are not, your success will fall short."

"At the top, Fig. Top of what? What do you mean?"

"This is the perfect place to base it," Fig rushed on. "More matter here to barter with than probably the rest of the prince's combined. Thousands of followers to provide your defense."

"My defense?"

"Yes, Lilith. Forget about your existing lair. Establish a new one here." Fig took a deep breath. "Become the first *Princess* of the Realm."

"Me, someone like Elezar?"

"Yes, you Lilith. You would be a natural. The one who sets the example. The defender of female rights throughout all. A refuge for the abused."

"I am not so sure about that." Lilith twisted and tried to stand but found she could not.

She was silent for a moment. "Your answer is 'no' then? You are going to serve the human woman who treats you like a puppy."

"No, not that," Fig frowned. "Stay here until I return with her, and you will see."

Progress

FIG CLIMBED to the top of the citadel. The pure oxygen reinvigorated him as he climbed. He saw Natasha and Briana busily clogging more treadmills. They were making progress. The feeling of depression and despair he had felt already was much less. He surveyed the scene. Many of the minions stood idly at their stations with no idea of what to do.

"Briana," he called out.

"Why, hello, Fig," Briana said. "How are you doing? As you can see. Things are going great here."

Fig looked in Briana's eyes and shook his head. "Briana, are you all right? Did you do something to yourself again?"

"Do to myself? The enchantment, you mean? Fig, I had to. There is too much to do. Now if you will just let me — "

"Briana, listen to me. You had the right idea at the very beginning. Now, it finally can be accomplished."

"What are you talking about, Fig? Can't it wait? I have a lot of work here."

"You wanted to send a message to your father, right? That's how everything started. You were homesick. Being the guardian of the Earth was not working out."

"Well, yes, I suppose so. But that's ancient history." She waved her arm in the air. "As I said, there is a lot of work yet to be done."

"Don't you see, Briana? You can do better than that. Rather than a simple note, a succubus can fly you home."

"Oh, Fig, you are supposed to be the science guy. You more than anybody should know how impossible that is. We have no idea where my home-planet is. It must be light years away. Maybe tens or hundreds. There is no way to carry along enough air and food for such a long journey, even if we knew the direction in which to fly."

"That's the direct route, Briana. But there is a shortcut. You can go home by emerging through any juniper flame there. A succubus can sense them. You can leave from right here."

Briana gasped. Fig felt encouraged. The prospect of returning home was so strong it penetrated through. He reached back to slap her as he had done before, then thought better of it. Instead, he grabbed her by the shoulders and shook her gently back and forth.

"Briana, Briana, look at me. Think about what I said. You can go home. You can go home."

Briana's eyes brightened as if she were emerging from a deep sleep. "Of course, Fig. *Home*. As always, you are so clever. Now?"

"Not yet," Fig said. "We are not quite done. The Tyrant of Time no longer dominates the minions here. They can now listen to a new master — you. But don't dominate them. Release them instead. Explain that they are free. Their despair will go away. The realm of demons will be saved from their influence."

"Then, I can go home?"

He had guessed correctly, Fig thought. Indeed, home is what Briana wanted more than anything else. A perfect solution to the problem. It meant that he did not have to choose. True, he would end up with neither . . .

The despair he was fighting so hard to contain took on a new dimension, an overriding sadness that pierced to his core.

"Not quite," he managed to say. "There is one final solution that has to be performed. Once the minions are free, direct, a hundred or so to go to the nadir of the sphere. Join me there."

The Final Reversal

THE LAST of the selected minions filed down the spiral staircase into the bottom level. Lilith, Briana, and Natasha were already there, standing out of the way near the center of the level. The Tyrant of Time curled into a small ball nearby and stared blankly into space. That was something to be decided later.

After the last minion arrived, they all broke out singing. "The Tyrant is deposed. The Tyrant is deposed. Long live the new Tyrant." In unison, each one knelt on one knee and extended a hand forward, saluting Briana.

"No, no." Briana waved her arms back and forth. "You are free. I set you free. It is Lilith you should support — if you so choose."

The singing stopped, and the minions returned to standing. After a moment's silence, they turned towards Lilith and starting singing again. "The Tyrant is deposed. The Tyrant is deposed. Long live the new Tyrant."

"If I could have everyone's attention," Fig boomed out over the voices.

Again the singing halted. Again they turned, this time to Fig.

"The Tyrant is deposed. The Tyr — "

"Very well. For the moment, watch me closely," Fig commanded. "We will get all of this sorted out properly after a while."

Fig reached down and retrieved the pawl lying on the floor. With a grunt, he reattached it to the lever arm. Like a child on a playground jungle gym, he shimmied up the ratchet to the linkage that held it in its grip. He examined it one final time. Everyone on the floor below watched him. He held his breath. This had better work.

With a twist, he threw the lever holding the restraint in place. Almost instantly, the grip on the ratchet released. The pawl slid up over the blocking log causing the jam. The floor of the level began to rotate again, and the far right counter advanced one click. All the disks changed from showing blank to another arcane symbol. The count was starting over.

Fig looked at the watch globes. The static display on one flickered. The mushroom clouds resumed their rise to higher altitudes.

"Okay, free beings," Fig called out. "Move to the outside wall and get into stable stances." There was a pause while the imp in Fig's ear translated. The minions followed his instructions. He clamored back down and to the wall as well.

"Now, resist the rotation," he explained. "Let's get the floor moving in the reverse direction." Fig planted his feet and placed his hands on the wall.

At first, the wall slid underneath his palms and continued rotating as it had before. Fig pushed harder, his arms trembling with the effort. The squeal of soft flesh against hard metal echoed from around the circumference as the minions did likewise.

"Harder," Fig shouted. "Stop the spin. Force the wall to move the other way."

Hundreds of grunts responded. The loss to friction stopped. And so did the motion of the floor. Slowly, it reversed itself. Moving faster and faster, it picked up speed.

One of the floor barriers passed under the ratchet. Click. Then two more. Click. Click.

The static on one of the watch globes unfroze. The newsroom reappeared. A garbled voice came out of the audio feed. Fig glanced at the mushroom clouds on the other displays. They halted their ascents and billowed back in upon themselves, returning toward the earth.

"Are we traveling backward in time?" Natasha asked. "How is that going to solve anything?"

Fig wagged his head. "*We* are not traveling back. We are here in the realm of demons. But the flow of time in our own realm is still coupled to the citadel. Instead, we are *reversing* time, rewinding to the way it was before — everywhere."

Fig stopped pushing the wall and told the minions to rest also. He scampered back up the ratchet arm and froze its motion again. No sense in making the number of clicks yet to be undone more than they were now.

"How does any of this help?" Natasha asked. "Can't you just send Lilith back in time to stop Robert from inserting the flash drive into the control computer? Or even go further back, to before when Viktor contacted me for the first time. Get the flash drive we got from Efren to the FBI months before that. They remove the malware from every control center. Add additional software and safeguards."

"Thousands of minions are two levels up," Fig said. "Thousands keeping what has already happened unchanged. Nuclear war has already occurred. They will strive to make sure it always does. Only by erasing what they compare against, do we have a chance."

"Use the minions Briana has freed from the zenith," Natasha said. "Pit them against those in the level below the throne room. Wipe them out."

"There still are succubi flying about," Fig said slowly as if explaining an eclipse to a child. "Any one of them could change time in a way as bad as what has already occurred. We need the minions to keep doing exactly what they do now."

"So, what do *we* do?"

"I think you were on the right trail, Natasha." He was suddenly tired. "Yes, we want to get the flash drive to the FBI months before the crisis occurred. Time has to be rewound that far back."

"But if these minions prevent that transfer from happening."

"They won't if they have nothing with which to compare. If we reverse time enough, what occurs going forward will just happen — but without a blackout in the US."

"I still do not understand," Natasha persisted. "Briana and I are both here. As time is rolled back, what happens at the instant she and I came into this realm? Will duplicates of us be created as part of the rewind?"

"I'm not sure." Fig shook his head. "But maybe time is elastic enough that little occurs as a result. Moving backward, neither you nor Briana will appear out of the flame. There will be only Alexi in an empty lab."

"Oh my God, Alexei!"

"All right then, Lilith can fetch and bring him here now before we begin the rollback in earnest. Then moving forward again, when Viktor comes to your office in Moscow, the two of you will have already been gone for months."

"Viktor will send someone else to Folsom."

"Doesn't matter. You have already delivered a copy of the malware to the FBI months before."

"Our memories, what happens to them?" Briana asked. "Will they be erased?"

Fig grimaced. "I'm uncertain, but as long as we are here, there is no reason for them to do so."

"Great," Natasha said. "One 'I don't think so,' and one 'I'm uncertain.'"

Fig glowered. He has saved not only *one* but *two* frigging realms, and he's not getting a single pat on the back. He tensed to bark a reply, but with some effort calmed himself down.

"See the view globes all around this level?" he said after a moment. "The minions must know how to focus them on places that we select — newspaper printing shops, clocks like Big Ben ... We keep time marching backward on the Earth and monitor what happens as we do. When we get to where we want to, then we stop."

No one spoke. Fig looked at Natasha. Like the others, she had no objection.

"Yes, this sounds complicated, but it should work," Fig let out a deep breath. "As far as our realm is concerned, our entire adventure will be wiped out. None of it ever will have happened."

Separate Paths

SEVERAL MONTHS later — after time on the Earth began moving forward again, Secretary of State, Angela entered Trantor's lair, a much bigger one now. The djinn sat at a table that supported two stacks of papyrus, one labeled 'In' and the other 'Out.' A sequence of imps zoomed in to add more vellums to one as another squad removed them from the other. Between them, Trantor scowled at one that he held and finally scrawled his approval on it with one of his nails.

Angela sat down next to Trantor, but he did not look up. Elezar's chief-of-staff reached for the next document to examine. She sat her hand on the space of bench between them and slowly moved it toward him, her little finger barely touching his massive thigh.

Without missing a beat, the djinn dropped one hand from what he held and gently placed his palm on top of hers. She gazed up at him and smiled. Trantor stopped what he was doing and grinned back.

NATASHA WATCHED Alexei tightening the final screw on the sign. *'The Sitka Boutique,'* it read. 'Exotic Treasures from Mother Russia.' She heard the horn from the Alaska Cruise tourist boat announce its arrival in the harbor. Soon her first customers would be at the door.

She smiled, happily. The documents that had been safely carried in Angela's sweat bag had worked perfectly. Even the exchange of all of her saved rubles at the airport change went through when she explained that a grandparent had died and she was returning to the US with her inheritance.

"Come, dearest," she motioned to Alexei with her hand. "This is the beginning of our new life together."

LILITH SAT down on the white plastic chair. It was not comfortable, but the first volunteer transfers had insisted. She looked about the room and wondered. Two dozens of her lair would have fit inside.

"Here is your orb, your grace." The young succubus on her left handed her the globe shining brightly with not one but four glowimps.

"And here is your scepter," said the one on the right. "It is not terribly elegant, but it will serve."

Lilith appraised the short piece of rebar that had been bent into a crook on one end and nodded. She thought wistfully for a moment about Fig, but then put what might have been aside. His plan had worked perfectly. She had more important things to think about now.

The minions had insisted. Most wanted death for the Tyrant. Others wanted to confine it in the maze with the outer doors bolted shut so that it would traverse forever with no way to escape — until a careless misstep plunged it into a vat.

Both sides had appealed to Lilith to resolve the impasse, and she knew that her decision had to be a careful one — firm but just.

"Confine the Tyrant on the level with the hexagons," she finally decided. "Let it play the game over and over, alternating moves between each of its two selves. Remove all the vats everywhere and provide food as long as it wants — until it decides for itself when to surrender its consciousness to the void."

"The first is the ambassador from Elezar the Golden." a third attendant broke through Lilith's reverie. "Her title is an unusual one."

"What?"

"Secretary of State Angela."

Lilith bared her fangs in a slight smile. There was a tremendous amount of things to be done to get everything set up right. Dormitories or separate lairs? Refuge for males as well as females? A standing group of warriors or only conscripts in time of battle? Best to savor little satisfactions now whenever they occurred.

"Show the Secretary in."

"Shall I instruct her first on how she should curtsey to the first Princess of the Realm?"

Lilith rose. "That won't be necessary. I will meet her sister to sister and give her a hug."

FIG RAN his hand over his scalp. All the golden locks were long gone, his natural brown almost back to the same length. He unlocked the front door of the warehouse and entered. As it had been since he had returned, it was quiet.

No international crisis. A new princess in the realm of demons. The love of his life back to where she wanted to be.

And no loss of memory. He could recall all of his adventure. Every detail of it.

Lilith or Briana? The solution turned out to be simple. Neither one. That way, he did not have to decide. The fact that two whole realms of existence were saved was merely a side effect. He chuckled at the absurdity — but it did not help much.

Fig entered the office behind the receptionist desk and dumped his backpack. No sense in going back to the lab. As before, he had to sell the new equipment so there could be food in the pantry. But with a few more handyman jobs, he would get by.

The sun was setting. He glanced at his watch. He may as well go and check out the show at the Club Exotica. The word on the street was that Zantos' act was first rate.

The door back into the warehouse proper swung open. Fig looked, and his jaw dropped.

"Briana!" he exclaimed. "What are you doing here?"

"Succubus express. Some of Lilith's cohorts have started a service."

"But, but — "

Briana put her finger to his lips. "Shut up for a minute, and I will explain."

She sighed. "After the sensitizing in the realm of demons, I saw my home-planet in a new light. Females are not as marginalized there, but it is pretty close."

"And I have had a lot of time to think. Yes, the Earth is very primitive in the exercise of the crafts, but a woman's lot *is* improving. I decided I would rather be here than a trophy piece haggled over by up-and-coming lordlings. That is one of the two reasons why I came back."

"Two reasons?" Fig asked.

"Yes, two." Briana looked down for a moment. Her voice softened. "I did not treat you very well, Fig. Through all that has happened, neither telling you 'yes' or a definite 'no' so that you could move on."

Fig said nothing. Confusion clouded his thoughts.

"I was stupid," Briana looked back up at him. "So focused on my own unhappiness, that I did nothing to help yours." She shook her head. "Fig, I don't deserve you."

She wrapped her arms around him and squeezed her body tightly against his. She kissed him so long he had to be the one to let go first.

"What was that for?" Fig gasped.

"Because as I pondered all of this, the second reason became clear, too. Because I want you to know I am sorry and …"

"And what?"

"Fig, I love you. Will you have me back?"

Fig could not believe his ears. "Do you still mean like a brother?"

She wiggled her hips against his. "No, Fig. Not like that at all."

Author's Afterword

Did you enjoy *Magic Times Three*?

Do you know others who might like it, too?

Why not contact them right now?

Do it now, while *Magic Times Three* is fresh in your mind. It will take only a few minutes.

Just send an email to one or more of your friends, telling them what you liked about my book. Word-of-mouth is the most powerful form of promotion. It will help me a lot!

To get a small appreciation gift for your effort, just point your browser at the link below. It will take you to where you can download *Daydreams*, a science-fiction short story I have written.

Thanks for your help!

http://www.alodar.com/blog/dd

What's next?

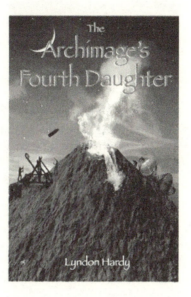

If you would like to find out how Briana and Fig linked up originally, read *The Archimage's Fourth Daughter* .   Briana is the youngest daughter of Alodar, the Archimage. Rather than wed a nobleman, she desires to go on adventures as did her famous father. She uses a magic portal to take her to another world. Her first task is to figure out what is going on in this strange, unfamiliar place.

The cover depicts some of the bad guys catapulting cylinders of a sulfuric gas into an active volcano. Why would anyone want to do that? Briana is determined to find out.

If you want to start at the beginning, read *Master of the Five Magics* first. You will meet Alodar, the struggling journeyman thaumaturge under siege in a frontier fortress. He is smitten by Queen Vendora, a ravishing beauty for whom all the nobles in the land strive. His quest for the Fair Lady takes him on a journey to explore alchemy, sorcery, wizardry and true magic.

The cover depicts Alodar's descent into a fumarole of a dormant volcano. (What, another volcano?). The air is oppressive and stifling hot. Each step is harder to take than the last. Will Alodar be able to get far enough into the mountain's bowels in order to solve the mystery waiting there?

Order Master of the Five Magics
now
http://www.alodar.com/blog/mfm

In *Master of the Five Magics* we learn that there are five crafts governed by seven magic laws. Is seven all? The title of the second book, *Secret of the Sixth Magic* might lead you to think so, but (spoiler alert!) that merely was a marketing ploy when the book was first published years ago. The situation is much more complex.

The cover depicts what one might see if trapped inside a transparent cube, but (spoiler alert two!) the problem is that the dimensions of the cube are shrinking, and there does not seem to be any way to get out.

The first two books in the series, and this one, too, can be read in any order. Each of the three have their own independent set of characters. In *Riddle of the Seven Realms* you will meet, Astron, the one who walks—a denizen of the realm of demons with a congenital birth defect. His wings are shriveled and he cannot fly.

The cover of the book depicts an event that takes place in the palace of Elezar, a demon prince. Most of the realm of demons is a featureless void. It is hard to transport solid matter there from other places, and it is extremely valuable. The utmost ecstasy for a lightning djinn is to blast something of beauty into a scatter of individual atoms.

Order Riddle of the Seven Realms
now
http://www.alodar.com/blog/rsr

Glossary

Alchemy

On earth, the root of the word comes from the Greek for transmutation. In the Middle Ages, alchemy focused on changing baser metals into gold, finding an elixir of life and a universal solvent. Some alchemical practices ultimately became the basis for modern chemistry.

In *Master of the Five Magics* and its sequels, alchemical procedures were described by formulas of arcane symbols kept in grimoires. Formula success was governed by probability; the more potent the result the less likely it was to succeed.

On earth, the most similar craft is that of a chemist.

Wikipedia: http://en.wikipedia.org/wiki/Alchemy

Archimage

A master of all five of the crafts of thaumaturgy, alchemy, magic, sorcery, and wizardry.

Artificial Nose

I did not make this up. The artificial (or electronic) nose exists.

Wikipedia: https://en.wikipedia.org/wiki/Electronic_nose

Battle of Cannae

341

Regarded of one of the most important battles in history. Hannibal, a Punic General, later famous for his daring attacks in Italy using elephants brought over the Alps, completely surrounded a Roman army and defeated it decisively.

Wikipedia: https://en.wikipedia.org/wiki/Battle_of_Cannae

Carnation Plot

A scheme by some of the nobles of France to rescue Marie Antoinette from Le Conciergerie before her execution. It failed because her guards could not be corrupted.

Wikipedia: https://en.wikipedia.org/wiki/Marie_Antoinette and then search for 'Carnation Plot' about half way down the page.

Catacombs

Paris is an old city. By the end of the eighteenth century, the city's cemeteries were overflowing. There was no place for the newly dead. Using ancient stone mines, the remains of some six million bodies were dug up and transferred into ancient stone quarries under the city. It is where Angela chose to hide Marie Antoinette after the queen had been switched with Briana.

It is worth a trip on the internet in order to see alcove after alcove stacked with skulls and bones in neat arrays.

Wikipedia: https://en.wikipedia.org/wiki/Catacombs_of_Paris

CERN

The European Organization of Nuclear Research

A particle physics research laboratory located on the border between France and Switzerland. It houses, what in 2017, was the world's most powerful accelerator for protons and even heavier ions, able to hurl them at one another at energies available nowhere else in the world.

Wikipedia: https://en.wikipedia.org/wiki/CERN

Charm

On earth, a synonym for spells in general. In *Master of the Five Magics* and its sequels, a sorcerer's spell in particular.

Wikipedia: http://en.wikipedia.org/wiki/Charm

Citadel

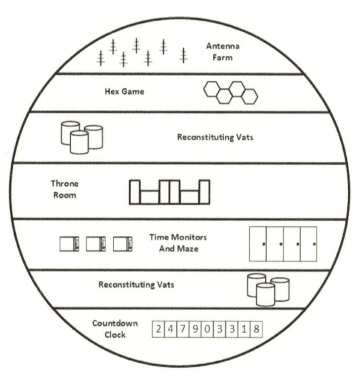

Conciergerie

The Conciergerie formerly was a royal palace. At the time of the French Revolution, it served as a prison for those condemned to be executed by the guillotine.

Wikipedia: https://en.wikipedia.org/wiki/Conciergerie

Demon

Resident of another realm different from that of the universe containing the earth and the world of *Master of the Five Magics*. With the exception of djinns, of limited physical power in our realm. Synonymous with devil.

Wikipedia: http://en.wikipedia.org/wiki/Demon

Wikipedia: http://en.wikipedia.org/wiki/Devil

Wikipedia: http://en.wikipedia.org/wiki/List_of_fictional_demons

Devil

A synonym for demon in *Master of the Five Magics* and its sequels.

Wikipedia: http://en.wikipedia.org/wiki/Devil

Wikipedia: http://en.wikipedia.org/wiki/Demon

Wikipedia: http://en.wikipedia.org/wiki/List_of_fictional_demons

Drink Dribbler

A standard novelty sold at joke stores is the drink-dribbler glass. Fill it with a liquid, and when the victim tips it up to drink, he is wetted by what pours out from a small hole near the top.

History does not record where the first drink-dribbler glass came from, but possibly they were created by someone who dominated the small imps with the same name from the realm of demons.

Electrolysis of Water

Electrolysis of water is the decomposition of the liquid into its two constituent gasses, hydrogen and oxygen. The set-up is simple. I was able to achieve it in a middle-school science class experiment.

Wikipedia: https://en.wikipedia.org/wiki/Electrolysis_of_water

Faraday Cage

A Faraday Cage, named after the physicist who studied the properties of electromagnetism, is an enclosure built of conductive materials. Currents generated in these materials by impinging electromagnetic waves greatly attenuate the penetration of the waves into its interior.

Fig's cage served a different purpose. So long as a high voltage was connected to it, the succubus Angela was effectively trapped. When the voltage vanished as part of the general collapse of the electric infrastructure, she could just open the door and walk out.

Wikipedia: https://en.wikipedia.org/wiki/Faraday_cage

Femme Fatale

There have been many women throughout history who have been tagged with the label of *femme fatale*, A recent one is a Russian intelligent agent caught for spying in the United States.

Wikipedia: https://en.wikipedia.org/wiki/Anna_Chapman

Folsom

Folsom is a small city north of Sacramento, California. It is probably best known for the song *Folsom Prison Blues*, by Johnny Cash. It has a tiny bit of relevance in this novel because it is the site for the California Independent System Operator (ISO) that controls the distributing of electrical power for the state.

Generators

The control and synchronization of electricity generators plays an important part in *Magic Times Three*. Generators perform a task that is the inverse of that for an electric motor. A motor converts electrical energy to mechanical energy. Generators convert mechanical energy to electrical.

A circuit with a single electrical generator on it is fairly simple to model. The generator generates energy at a particular frequency (alternating current) and it is consumed somewhere else as the load. When there is more than one generator in the same circuit, things get more complicated. First of all, for maximum efficiency the generators must be synchronized. In the extreme example of two generators operating one hundred and eighty degrees out of phase -- one is at maximum power going one way, and the other at the same power going in the other, and there is nothing left for a third party consumer.

A generator with only slightly out of synch with other generators on the same circuit can find itself a consumer of power rather than a producer. Get too far out of synch and the device could overheat from the energy input and be critically damaged. This was the principle effect that the attackers wished to exploit in the novel.

Wikipedia: https://en.wikipedia.org/wiki/Electric_generator

Gremlin

One of the intermediate-size sprites from the realm of demons. They are often attracted to electrical machinery and electronic gear. An alternate more, prosaic explanation of their origin is at:

Wikipedia: https://en.wikipedia.org/wiki/Gremlin

Hex

Hex is a board game, usually played on an eleven by eleven grid. It was produced commercially for a while in the twentieth century, but also was rumored to be played on the flooring tiles in bathrooms of the period.

Although the rules are simple, the charm of the game was the fact that it was so difficult to find a winning strategy.

Wikipedia: https://en.wikipedia.org/wiki/Hex_(board_game)

Incubus

An incubus is the male counterpart to the succubus demon type, as typified by Lilith and Angela. In medieval folklore, succubi came to men in their dreams and extracted from them their semen. This in turn was transferred to incubi that impregnated unwed women with it. Many surprising pregnancies were explained this way.

Wikipedia: https://en.wikipedia.org/wiki/Incubus

Independent System Operator

The title gives no clue as to what an ISO actually is.

Just before the turn of the century, power generation was deregulated nationally. Technology supported the purchase of electricity from remote distances and then distributing it locally. A side effect of this increased flexibility, intended to reduce costs, amplified some problems. How was all of the switching and distribution to be monitored so that power remained available 24/365?

In response, regional facilities were established to control the routing of power over specified area. California has a statewide ISO.

Wikipedia:
https://en.wikipedia.org/wiki/California_Independent_System_Operator

Juniper

Juniper is a coniferous plant distributed widely over the earth. This characteristic made it ideal for succubi from the realm of demons to visit our own universe.

Wikipedia: https://en.wikipedia.org/wiki/Juniper

Lydia

From 1937 to 1967, the author C. S. Forester wrote about the adventures of the naval hero, Horatio Hornblower of the British Navy during the Napoleonic wars. These were not written in chronical order of Hornblower's life as he rose from midshipman to admiral of the fleet. The first, published as *Beat to Quarters* in the United States, concerns Hornblower's command of the 36 gun frigate Lydia. It takes place in 1808 in the Americas, but I could not resist making a reference to the series when Fig and Lilith arrive in Marseilles and spot the Lydia anchored there.

You can't go wrong for reading enjoyment when you devour this series.

Magic

The use of means outside of normal availability to affect change. On earth, the terms magic, sorcery, thaumaturgy, and wizardry are roughly synonymous.

In *Master of the Five Magics* and its sequels, each, along with alchemy, have distinct meanings. Magic is performed by the exercise of rituals, the steps of which are derived from extensions of rituals deduced previously.

The goal of these exercises is the production of magical objects, things that are perfect in what they do, such as mirrors, daggers, swords, and shields. Once created, with few exceptions, they last forever.

The power of magic is limited by the time and expense involved in performing magic rituals. Some take several generations and the involvement of many participants. Because of the effort involved, magical objects are quite expensive.

On earth, the most similar craft is that of a mathematician.

Wikipedia: http://en.wikipedia.org/wiki/Magic

Marie Antoinette

The famous queen of France who was executed by guillotine in 1793.

When I first started writing *Magic Times Three*, my idea was to have sections centered around the famous *femme fatales* of history. I would start with Marie Antoinette and then proceed through other famous women of history. As the story unfolded, however, the emphasis shifted to more about the battle between Lilith and Angela in the realm of demons.

Wikipedia: https://en.wikipedia.org/wiki/Marie_Antoinette

Memory Palace

A memory palace is a memorization technique in which objects to be remembered are associated with images familiar to the memorizer. Do you know that by using this technique, competitive champions can scan a standard deck of 52 cards for only slightly longer that 30 seconds, surrender the deck, wait a few minutes, and then, without looking, recite all the cards in order!

You can find out more about how to do this yourself by reading:

Moonwalking with Einstein by Joshua Foer

Wikipedia: https://en.wikipedia.org/wiki/Method_of_loci

Murphy

Famous for his law that usually is stated as "If anything can go wrong, it will". It has been around a long time. There have been many spinoffs including: "Murphy was an optimist."

Wikipedia: https://en.wikipedia.org/wiki/Murphy%27s_law

The Prisoner of Zenda

The *Prisoner of Zenda* by Anthony Hope and published in 1894 is reputedly the world's first best seller. A dashing tale of duplicate identities that has been made into a movie no less than five times. Robert Heinlein adopted the plot for his 1956 science fiction novel *Doublestar*

Wikipedia: https://en.wikipedia.org/wiki/The_Prisoner_of_Zenda

Quadrupole Magnet

In *Magic Times Three*, Fig uses rebar to fashion two special magnets, each with two north and two south poles.

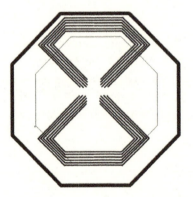

A beam of charged particles passing through the center gap in the magnet, (into or out of the page in the figure). The shapes of the pole tips are important. They must follow hyperbolic curves.

Each magnet focuses a beam of charged particles either horizontally or vertically but not both. But by placing the two a certain distance apart, however, a lens can be created.

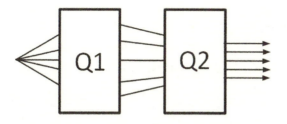

Magnets in this configuration primarily are used in high energy particle accelerators at places like CERN in Europe. Fig spent some time there in my fourth book *The Archimage's Fourth Daughter*

Wikipedia: https://en.wikipedia.org/wiki/Quadrupole_magnet

Robe

Practitioners of each of the five magics are distinguished by the capes and robes they wear.

Thaumaturges wear brown covered with what is on earth the mathematical symbol of similarity.

Alchemists wear white covered with triangles with a single vertex bottom-most symbolizing the delicate balance between success and failure when performing a formula.

Magicians wear blue with the palest for a neophyte and the darkest for the master and covered by circular rings symbolizing the perfect mathematical object.

Sorcerers wear gray covered with the logo of the staring eye symbolizing the ability to see far in time and place and into another's inner being.

Wizards wear black covered with wisps of flame symbolizing the portal by which the realm of demons and the realm of men are connected.

The Scarlet Pimpernel

An adventure novel by Baroness Orczy published in 1905. The hero was the secret identity of a wealthy English fop, foreshadowing the advent of Superman by 29 years.

Wikipedia: https://en.wikipedia.org/wiki/The_Scarlet_Pimpernel

Spell

On earth the terms cantrip, charm, enchantment, glamour, incantation, and spell are synonymous — the performance of an act of magic.

In *Master of the Five Magics* and its sequels, except for the word spell itself, each of the others have particular meanings. The word spell is a generic umbrella for any of them.

Thaumaturgy — incantation
Alchemist — formula performance
Magician — ritual exercise
Sorcerer — charm recitation
Wizard — invocation

Subordinate

The first four crafts have named subordinates in *Master of the Five Magics* and its sequels.

Thaumaturgy — Journeyman, Apprentice

Alchemist — Novice

Magician — Neophyte, Initiate, Acolyte

Sorcerer — Tyro

Succubus

In medieval folklore, a succubus is a demon that appears to men in dreams and extracts their semen from them. Lilith and Angela, two sisters from the realm of demons, have different goals and purposes.

Wikipedia: https://en.wikipedia.org/wiki/Succubus

Thaumaturgy

The use of means outside of normal availability to affect change. On earth, the terms magic, sorcery, thaumaturgy, and wizardry are roughly synonymous.

In *Master of the Five Magics* and its sequels, each, along with alchemy, have distinct meanings. Thaumaturgy is performed by the reciting incantations that bind together objects at a distance that once had physically been together and with a source of energy that can perform work.

The power of thaumaturgy is limited by the fact that all incantations must conserve energy or, as sometimes stated, the first law of thermodynamics.

On earth, the term derives from the Greek for miracle and the most similar craft is that of a physicist.

Wikipedia: http://en.wikipedia.org/wiki/Thaumaturgy

Traveling Salesman Problem

A classic mathematical problem that for many years was thought to be insolvable in general. More research and more powerful computers have cast insolvability in doubt, but it still remains a benchmark against which new optimum seeking algorithms are tested.

Simply stated, the problem is to find the route that visits all the cities in a set without visiting any one more than once and for which the miles traveled is minimized.

Wikipedia:

https://en.wikipedia.org/wiki/Travelling_salesman_problem

Turkmenistan

With the breakup of the Soviet Union in 1991, Turkmenistan became an independent country (again). I used it as a locale for part of *Magic Times Three* because of the Darvaza gas crater. The crater does not play a role in the story, but with a name that translates to *Door to Hell*, I could not help having that region of the world as part of the story.

Wikipedia: https://en.wikipedia.org/wiki/Turkmenistan and https://en.wikipedia.org/wiki/Darvaza_gas_crater

Whirling Dervish

Here on the Earth, a dervish is a Moslem worshiper who attempts to reach religious ecstasy by a spinning rapidly in a dance. In the *Magic by the Numbers* series, it is the name for demons who also rotated rapidly in their own realm—just because they like to.

Wikipedia: https://en.wikipedia.org/wiki/Dervish#Whirling_dervishes

White Plastic Chairs

They are everywhere! When humankind has long vanished, and alien archeologists visit the earth, the one artifact that will stand out are these thrones that are so very prevalent. Was our culture divided into a multitude of tiny kingdoms? Or was there a hierarchy of control that was established by other means? Who knows what conclusions the aliens will draw?

Wikipedia: https://en.wikipedia.org/wiki/Monobloc_(chair)

Wizardry

The use of means outside of normal availability to affect change. On earth, the terms magic, sorcery, thaumaturgy, and wizardry are roughly synonymous.

In *Master of the Five Magics* and its sequels, each, have distinct meanings. Wizardry is performed by the invocation of demons from another realm from that of the earth.

The potency of a wizard is limited by the power of the demons that he can dominate.

On earth, there is no such craft as such, although one could argue that the practices of witches and warlocks is similar.

Wikipedia: http://en.wikipedia.org/wiki/Witchcraft

Made in the USA
Coppell, TX
22 December 2021

69919607R00215